The Future of Our Past

The Remembrance Trilogy—Book 1

by

Kahlen Aymes

Much love from

Ryan & Julia!

Kahlen Aymes xo -

TELEMACHUS PRESS

Cover art
Copyright © ThinkStock Photo/86534108/Couple Holding Hands
Outdoors/JupiterImages/Getty Images
Copyright © ThinkStock Photo/104876724/Shinny Bright Diamond/iStock Photo

Published by Telemachus Press, LLC
http://www.telemachuspress.com

Visit the author blog site:
http://www.kahlen-amyes.blogspot.com

ISBN# 978-1-937698-96-6 (eBook)
ISBN#978-1-937698-97-3 (paperback)

Version 2012.04.16

Printed in the United States of America

10 9 8 7 6 5 4 3 2 1

Sincere and deep thanks to all who took a chance and read my work before I even realized I was a writer. Your love, support and loyalty has meant more than I can ever articulate. Your reviews and love of the trilogy has left me breathless! You overwhelm my heart.

To Kathryn, Ali, Liz and Sally, thank you so much for your time, love and patience in the meticulous task of getting the trilogy ready for print.

Jena and Samantha, who volunteered to help with my blogs and banners at the very start of this journey, I couldn't have made it this far without you.

Ana, Janice, Tanya, Marie, Bunny, Erin, Maureen, Kelly, Wendy, Sophia, Stephanie, Sydney, Carol, Dani, Danielle, Renata, Jennifer, Ally, Debra, Sylvain, Irene, Marcelo & Phoebe; you have become such good friends over the past two years, and I will keep you close always.

To my little Kacy…You have always been a great joy. I'm so proud of you.

To my parents & the rest of my family, thank you for your faith and love. Your support means so much.

XOXOX~ *I treasure you all for different reasons.* ~XOXOX

To the team at Telemachus Press; your professionalism is truly appreciated. Thank you.

Special thanks to Tony Bartello for lending his voice to the review video, and to all of you who believed enough to launch the dream on kickstarter.com.

And finally…

For my daughter, Olivia,
who lent me her name at the beginning of this.
You are so like me, yet so different…
And the greatest gift of my life.
I love you,
~Kahlen~

The Future of Our Past

The Remembrance Trilogy—Book 1

~1~

Ryan ~

HARVARD MEDICAL SCHOOL.

I'd dreamed about it since I was twelve, my parents had dreamed about it since I was born, and now the reality of it was staring me in the face. The acceptance letter fell from my shaking hands as I sank down on the sofa in the apartment I shared with my best friend, Aaron.

He and I had been best friends since we were kids. He moved in with us after his mom and dad were killed in a car accident and, a few years later, my parents legally adopted him.

Now, Julia was my best friend. She was...*everything.*

I spent most of my college career convincing myself otherwise, but the prospect of leaving her to go to Boston, was sucking the air from my lungs. I literally couldn't breathe; my chest constricted and heat infused beneath my skin in a flush. My heart was pounding so fast I thought it would fly from my body.

What was I going to do? This was what I wanted, wasn't it?

Aaron walked in and I didn't even hear him; I had my hands fisted in my hair and my elbows closed over my face as I sat there motionless, except for the heaving of my chest.

"Dude...what the hell is wrong with you?" Aaron's deep voice finally intruded on my thoughts.

"Uh...Sorry. When did you get back?"

"Ryan, I've been talking to you for *five* minutes! I got my acceptance letter. Did you?" His tone was excited and he was smiling from ear to ear.

I bent to scoop up the letter from the floor where it had fallen and went to stare out the window. Fall had left the trees barren of their lush leaves, reminding me of what my life would become if I went to Boston; a blank page, without the colors that Julia painted on my life. It seemed so bleak, a wasteland.

We met in a freshman psychology class my second semester at Stanford. I was instantly mesmerized by her flowing dark hair and translucent skin. She had a soft blush on her cheeks and I was drawn to her stunning face; lips that were full and luscious and sparkling dark green eyes. I'd never seen anything more beautiful. She made some sarcastic remark about the lameness of the class and how unnecessary it was for a degree in advertising and marketing. I found myself bursting to speak to her.

"*Or most anything...for that matter,*" I agreed. *Her bright eyes met mine and I was done.*

We'd been getting closer as time went on, completely relying on each other for anything and everything...practically inseparable and that was how I liked it.

Three years later, she wasn't sure where she wanted to live after graduation, and had been applying for jobs at various magazines on both coasts and Chicago. Everything was up in the air, except that she and Ellie planned to move somewhere together. There were only a couple of months until graduation when life would take us in different directions.

We'd talked about it a little, both of us feeling the weight of real life about to intrude on the little Ryan and Julia bubble we'd created, and the discussion had never gotten serious. I sighed loudly as I struggled to expel the emotions threatening to choke me.

"Ryan...what the fuck is your problem? Did you get rejected?"

"No. I, uh, got accepted, too. Congratulations, man," I muttered as my mind raced.

"You sound like your dog just died. Dude, we just got accepted into the most prestigious medical school in the country! Together! Are you on drugs?" He shoved me in the shoulder.

I tried to smile at him. This was a huge moment for him as well; one that we'd dreamed of sharing since we were boys. A dream that we'd worked our asses off to attain.

"You know I don't do that shit."

The door opened and several voices followed. Aaron's girlfriend, Jenna, Julia and her best girlfriend, Ellie, strode into the living room. They were all laughing and bantering with each other. My eyes flew to Julia. Her face was pink from the cold, her eyes were sparkling and laughter was falling from her lips. She was so gorgeous, she took my breath away.

Aaron scooped Jen up in a big bear hug. "I made it into Harvard Med!"

She screamed with excitement as Aaron twirled her around.

Julia put down her backpack as she searched my face intently. "Ryan?" she questioned and took my big hand in her little one.

She'd poured over the application with me, helped me organize my recommendation letters and bought me the books to study for the MCATs. She spent hours and hours quizzing me over the course of the past year, and kept me fed while I studied. Knowing what this meant to me, she'd done her best to help me get it.

"Do something about your boy, Jules." Aaron shouted from across the room as he fell on the sofa with Jenna on his lap. "He's catatonic."

"I'm very happy for you, baby," Jen planted a sound kiss on Aaron's mouth. Jenna was a nursing student and although Aaron hadn't proposed, they were tight and I had no doubt she would follow him to Boston.

Ellie glanced between us while Julia continued to look up at me, her face finally splitting into a big smile. "Ryan, you, too. Right?"

I nodded miserably before her arms slid around my waist. Against my will, I leaned my face against the top of her head.

"I'm so proud of you," Julia whispered against my shirt and her hot breath washed over me through the material.

I felt ill, suddenly sick to my stomach at the thought of not seeing her every day.

She lifted her tear-filled eyes to mine, the luminous green pools drowning me in their depths. "I knew you could do it."

Her fingers splayed out on the back of my white button down and I wanted to beg her to come with me.

"Thanks to you. You pushed me hard enough." The coconut aroma from her shampoo surrounded me and her soft hair was like silk against my face.

"What are best friends for?" she murmured as she rubbed my back. I looked down into her face, her features soft and searching. My brow furrowed and my mouth tightened involuntarily.

Yeah, so what the fuck am I going to do without you, then?

"Hey. What's your deal? You should be over the moon," she said hesitantly, leaning casually against the counter, concern haunting her features.

I made a half-assed attempt to smile. "I'm a little overwhelmed, that's all. I'll be fine once the shock wears off."

Julia's right brow rose skeptically. "After the hundred or so all-nighters I pulled with you studying for this crap, I expect you to go in there and kick ass."

Aaron bounded into the kitchen. "Ellie wants to go to Antonio's for dinner and then to hear some band. She's got the hots for that guitar player."

"His name is Harris." Julia smiled and turned to Aaron with open arms. "Congratulations!"

Aaron scooped Julia up off of the floor and spun around in circles until she was squealing in delight.

"Uh, Aaron! That's enough, man. You're gonna make her sick." I watched from a few feet away.

"Nah, Jules is tough. She's put up with you for three years, hasn't she?" he said as he set her down.

"Yeah," she nudged me with her shoulder, as she'd done a million times before. It was one of the easy gestures that had become a habit over the years. "Are you gonna get happy or am I going to have to pull out the big guns?"

"And what would that be?" I finally smiled at the goofy look on her face.

"Oh, I don't know...Black Forest cake or cheesecake?" They were my favorites.

The first time she'd made them for me was when her father had been prosecuting a big murder case and I didn't want Julia sitting around that big house alone, so I took her to Chicago for Christmas our sophomore year.

"If I mope around enough, will you make both?" I teased her gently.

My heart stopped as her fingers fluttered along my jaw. "That's better. Yes, if it will make you happy."

"Yeah, I'm going to starve in Boston." My throat tightened again. I tried to push the emotion down, hoping she wouldn't understand my double meaning.

Ellie came in and began hauling Julia away from me. "Come on. We've got to go get ready. The boys are taking us out. Right, Ryan?"

Julia rolled her eyes at me and shrugged. I couldn't help but smile back, she was so damn cute.

"Bye, you guys," Julia said as she disappeared into the other room. "Okay Ellie, enough. I'll come willingly, you don't have to drag me, girl." The exasperation in her voice was clearly forced. "Jen, if I have to suffer this humiliation, so do you. Come on!"

Jen giggled. "Pick us up at Julia and Ellie's in two hours. Don't be late, Aaron Matthews, or I'll make you pay later!" she called from the other room and then the door shut loudly.

I downed the beer in my hand, Aaron's face sobered suddenly and I bristled.

"Ryan, aren't you happy? This is the beginning of the rest of our lives, brother."

"Yeah, I know." I shrugged and left the room. He followed, shaking his head.

"Are you gonna tell Julia you're in love with her? That's what this is about, so don't bullshit me," he said quietly.

I stopped and ran my hand through my hair. "Uh…look, I have to take a shower, so…"

"Ryan! Figure this shit out. You'll blow Harvard if you don't have your head in the game and we've worked too hard to get there."

"Yes, I'm going to miss her. It just hit me that I wouldn't see her every day, but I'll deal." I hoped he was more convinced by my words than I was.

"You'll deal." His eyes never left mine as he spoke and I could see the incredulity behind them, "And how in the fuck do you propose to do that?"

I took a deep breath and rubbed the stubble along my jaw in an effort to take my mind off of my aching heart. "Well, I'm just going to have to convince her to come with me," I tried to make it sound like I was joking.

"To be what? Your study partner?" Aaron's words were harsh and right on target; asking her to follow me was selfish, but I wouldn't be able to stop myself.

"That isn't how it is. She's my best friend. I'd…"

He interrupted me. "You'd what? Tell her that suddenly you've had an epiphany? Do you even know how you really feel about her? She's *more* than your best friend and you know it. Don't fuck with her head, Ryan. She deserves better than that!"

I was speechless as I stood there motionless, struggling to find the answers he sought. Leave it to Aaron to be brutally honest.

"I…Uh, I'm…"

"Look, don't rush into a conversation until you really know what you want," Aaron went to get a beer and then returned to hear my reply.

"If I wait, she may have a job lined up and there will be no chance she'll come to Boston."

"Let's be honest. The type of companies she's applying to aren't in Boston, Ryan."

I didn't want to hear his words, but I couldn't deny their truth either. Julia deserved to follow her dreams as much as I did. I'd have to let her go even if it trashed me; and it *would* trash me.

I slowly sank into the couch, elbows on my knees, my hands clasped in front of me.

Aaron put his hand on my shoulder. "Julia will always be a part of your life, no matter the distance. But…you should tell her how you feel, for both your sakes."

I shook my head. "I can't tell her that I'm in love with her, just to leave her. That's not fair, Aaron. Besides, I can't take hearing her tell me she only sees me as a friend. That could ruin the relationship we *do have* and I won't risk losing her from my life."

"You'd rather be her friend and see her marry some other guy…yeah, right," he said sardonically.

My chest tightened as Aaron continued. "I've seen the way you look at her, how you can barely contain yourself from beating the shit out of the guys she dates. Stop lying to yourself!" Aaron's words, while trying to comfort me, were like acid eating away at my insides and I put both hands through my hair. I couldn't listen to more of this right now.

"Aaron, *enough*."

"She won't say you're just her friend, Ryan. *Wake up*, dude. It's like you're married to the girl, only without the sex. Which is a fucking waste, by the way! She's hot."

He laughed and then went to his room to get ready, leaving me to struggle with my thoughts. A rush of heat still burned my skin.

Yes, Julia was sexy and beautiful, which drove me mad with desire, but sex would complicate everything and make it more likely I'd lose her if something did go wrong.

As much as I'd wanted to touch her, kiss her, taste her, I'd never let it happen. During the many times when we'd been alone in one another's rooms, I struggled with not letting her see how deeply she affected me physically. I wanted her; but I wanted to make love to her, not just screw in some weak moment. I needed her love more than I needed her body. As my friend, she was the most important person in my world, and I wasn't about to screw that up.

Julia ~

Ellie danced around in front of the mirror admiring her short black skirt and bright yellow and black top, clearly too bare for the cool weather. The cute little ankle booties over her black hose were the only sensible choice she made for the evening; though I had to admit, she looked great.

I didn't get all wrapped up in how I looked or spend hours getting ready. I had better things to do with my time than primp and re-apply my makeup every ten minutes.

Jenna was gorgeous. Her long hair flowed over her shoulders and her red sweater and tight black pants accentuated every perfect curve. She was every man's dream girl; blonde, perfect hourglass figure, tight ass and big boobs. I smirked as I watched her painstakingly check her appearance.

"Taking Aaron down tonight, hmmm?" I teased as she spritzed perfume onto her wrists and applied bright red lipstick on her full lips.

"Uh, yeah, like *you* should do to *Ryan*." My eyes widened at her sarcasm. "You want him so take him. He won't say no."

"Ryan and I are friends. God, Jen!" I shook my head and tried to brush her off, but Ellie shot her a look through the reflection in the mirror.

"Yeah, and I'm Mother Theresa. You two are hotter than hell for each other, so do something about it already. I don't know how you made it this long! He's gorgeous."

My heart sped up. It wasn't as if I'd never thought about what it would feel like to make love with him, but I knew if I let myself be with him that way, I'd just end up with a broken heart.

I loved him, but to give myself like that, surrender my heart, soul and body, would be my undoing. If it didn't work out, I would never recover.

Ellie squeezed my shoulders lightly. "Look, Julia, you didn't dress up like this for the bartenders, right? Don't waste the time you have left with him, and don't lie to us. We know you're in love with him."

I tried to laugh it off. "Oh, really?"

"You hardly date and when you do, Ryan hates them and you drop the poor guys like hot potatoes. He hardly dates either. If you ask me that is a serious waste of a man. He should be getting it every night, he's so delicious!" Jenna insisted.

"I'll tell Aaron you said that, Jen." I felt annoyed, the heat in my face burned. "I guess we just haven't found the right *person.*"

Jen rolled her eyes and Ellie laughed as she fluffed my hair and sprayed it with a mist of hairspray.

"Uh, *okay*, Julia! Or, maybe the right *one* is right in front of you." Ellie hugged me as she said it, but my eyes welled with tears.

"I can't do this now, you guys. I'll miss him so much it's ridiculous. I can't confuse the issue by trying to make it into more than it is. He's my best friend."

"We know that, honey. But there's more to it," Ellie murmured quietly.

I dabbed my eyes, trying to pull it together before I ruined the makeup I'd spent more time on because I wanted Ryan to remember me like this. I'd chosen a short black dress with a fitted black suede blazer, stockings, knee-high boots and silver hoop earrings. I definitely looked like a woman.

Yes, there was more. I loved him so much I couldn't breathe. I dreamed of him touching and making love to me. I felt like he was *mine*. Over the years when he'd gone out with other girls; I'd felt sick, crying myself to sleep on countless occasions, never letting him know I wanted anything more from him than friendship. I wouldn't be one of those girls he dated a couple of times, slept with and then left abandoned.

You couldn't even call them girlfriends. They passed through his life like rain, but I remained constant. He sought me out…the one he spent time with. I had the best part of him, the real part. I *knew* him and he confided in me about everything. I didn't want to trade that in for a fling.

"Can we just have fun tonight? I can't think about this now, okay? I want to find someone to dance with me."

Jen raised her eyebrows and pursed her lips. "You mean some poor sap that will have his ass handed to him when Ryan gets jealous? You're evil, Julia," Jenna said as she went to open the door for the boys.

"And you're delusional, Jen," I said quietly right before Aaron's voice filled the hall as we walked out of the bedroom.

"Oh, no honey, you've got that backwards."

Aaron looked handsome in jeans and a long sleeve white t-shirt, but he was alone.

I paused, "Where's Ryan?"

"He drove himself tonight. He's sort of out of it, Jules. You two should talk," he said before he kissed Jen on the cheek and helped us all on with our coats. "I'm one lucky bastard! Three beautiful women on my arm tonight; I must have died and gone to heaven."

"Keep it up and you'll wake up and find yourself in Hell," Jenna teased. Aaron laughed out loud.

*****

Ryan's black CRV was already parked when we arrived and he was waiting in the foyer. His eyes ran over me like a caress, making me uneasy, yet excited.

"Hey, did you have to wait long?"

His fingers closed around mine, the heat from his hands searing my skin. "It was worth it. You look amazing."

"Thanks, you do too." He wore all black, jeans, t-shirt and blazer. His golden brown hair was wild and messy, like someone had just run their hands through it a million times. As if on cue, his hand swiped through the side of it and I smiled.

"What? Why are you smiling?"

"Because, it's better than crying." I stopped, realizing too late, as he raised his brows in question. "Uh…I mean, I think it's amazing how you constantly play with your hair and it still looks incredible. It's not fair."

Dinner progressed uneventfully and I didn't have a chance to talk to Ryan alone. It would be difficult at the club, too, due to the din of the crowd and music. We found a table near the dance floor and Ryan and I slid into the two chairs nearest the wall. Aaron and Jen were across from us, and Ellie rushed away to find Harris.

The band was just setting up so there was only background music playing. Ryan was leaning into me as he often did, our shoulders touching. The musky smell of his cologne enveloped me and the candles on the tables flickering across his features made my breath stop. I had to remind myself to breathe.

He was so incredibly beautiful. Over the last three years, I'd often wondered how any man could be that breathtaking; so intelligent, caring and talented and still be single. He had women dropping their panties at every opportunity, but he'd never had a steady girlfriend in all the time I'd known him.

"Julia…" He turned to me. My eyes dropped to his perfect mouth and I was mesmerized.

I shook my head a little to bring myself back. "Uh…We should do some shots. Let's get the party started." I flagged the waitress as she passed our table.

"Hi, can we get ten lemon drops, please?" I smiled at the woman who was looking Ryan over, very obvious in her attempts to get him to notice her. "Hmmph!" I let my air out in a rush of disgust. For all she knew, Ryan was my boyfriend and she was blatantly flirting with him in front of me. "Uh, the drinks?" I raised my eyebrows pointedly, until she nodded and moved off toward the bar.

Ryan was looking at me with a strange expression, smiling slightly and studying.

"What are you looking at? Do I have something between my teeth?" I smiled and raised a hand to my mouth.

He grinned, shaking his head. "Julia, you're acting funny. What is it?" He brushed a stray piece of hair back from my face.

I looked down, my hands fiddling with a napkin on the table. "I'm sorry, I don't mean to," I said softly so that only he could hear.

"I think we might need to talk, hmmm?" his velvet voice rumbled around me and vibrated on my skin. He was leaning close and his hot breath washed over my face. I swallowed hard.

"We always talk, Ryan. About everything, don't we?" I shot a glance up at his eyes, but couldn't hold his gaze.

"*Do* we?" He leaned in further still and stared into my face.

I used the band as an excuse to divert my attention. The music had started and I was thankful that it was harder to talk, so I nodded. Ryan leaned back against the wall as he continued to watch me intently.

When the shots arrived, I called Ellie over to the table. Ryan reached for his wallet and I stopped him. "No, you aren't paying tonight. This party is for you and Aaron. We're celebrating!" I opened my purse and took out two twenty-dollar bills to give to the waitress.

I set two shots in front of each of us and picked one up.

"A toast. To my two favorite men in the world! I know you'll set the world of medicine on its ass. I love you both." I felt tears welling as I looked into Ryan's blue eyes. He wasn't smiling and looked like he was struggling for words.

"Hear, hear!" Jen said, as our glasses clinked together.

Ellie choked on her drink and made a funny face. "Ewww," she murmured before setting the glass down and going back to the stage.

I turned to Ryan and touched my glass to his. "I really am very proud of you." His eyes never left mine as we downed the shots. The tension between us was palpable. Aaron and Jen shifted in their seats uneasily, turning their backs to give us some privacy.

I set down my glass and reached for another one, but Ryan's hand closed over mine.

"Don't go so fast, Julia. I don't want to get drunk tonight."

"Well, maybe *I* do."

"No. Not tonight. We need to talk."

I sat back down. "Come on, Ryan, I already told you I'd make both those damn desserts!"

"Julia," he said seriously, ignoring my attempted diversion. Our eyes locked.

"I don't think I'm ready. Not yet." I prayed he didn't hear the trembling in my voice.

His hand moved up and down my back as understanding dawned in his face. The music got slower and his hand slid to mine.

"Okay. Then will you dance with me?"

I gasped softly. In all the time we'd known each other, we'd never danced. At least, not slow dancing. I didn't know what to say. There was something in his eyes that I couldn't place; they were darker, his gaze more intense. I was unsure if I could handle being in his arms and not show him how I really felt.

Ryan didn't wait for me to answer and simply pulled me up with him. His strong arm moved around the back of my waist as he turned me toward the dance floor. He folded me into his arms and mine slid up his chest around his neck. Ryan let his breath out as he pulled me closer. My knees went weak and I leaned into him as my heart began to race. I'd dreamed of being next to him like this, so many times, but the warmth and closeness felt better than I'd ever imagined.

"Oh, Julia..." he breathed against my hair and I twined my fingers through the soft strands at his nape as our bodies swayed together perfectly, like we'd been dancing together for years. His nose was nuzzling against me and I felt his lips at my temple. I couldn't help it. I closed my eyes and sucked in my breath.

"Ryan...I'm..."

He stopped me, "Shhh...just dance with me. Don't talk. Not right now."

He held me closer, one hand settled on the small of my back while the other moved up between my shoulder blades. His hand fisted in the material of my dress underneath my jacket and he pressed his soft lips to the skin below my ear.

It was extremely intimate and felt like heaven, but left me confused. What was happening between us? Were things changing and did I want them to? Should I let myself melt into him as I ached to do?

Ryan would leave in a few months. That was a fact and I didn't know where I'd be going. I didn't want to end up in bed with him only to never see him again and left with a broken heart.

"I don't want to go, Julia. I don't know if I can do this…" he whispered against my neck. My heart dropped as his words echoed my thoughts. Jen and Aaron were on the dance floor by now and she winked at me. I attempted a weak smile in return, but the emotions welling within me made it impossible.

Ryan's hand on my upper back slid up underneath the curtain of my hair to hold my head, as his mouth barely brushed across mine. Electricity shot through my entire body and all I wanted was to deepen the kiss, to open my mouth to his and taste him. "I can't leave…" he whispered again.

I rested my forehead against his cheek and tried to steady my breathing before I pushed back a little so I could look into his face. I couldn't let him throw away his dream.

"What?! You *can* and you *will*, Ryan!" I could see the conflict flash across his features before he quickly tried to hide it from me, his jaw setting as he looked down at me.

I took his hand and pulled him behind me back to the table, slamming my other drink before holding his up to him. Obediently, he downed it before reclaiming my hand.

I grabbed my purse and led him from the club.

"Where's your car?" I asked impatiently as I began to shiver, my coat left behind in my rush to get Ryan alone.

Roles reversed suddenly, as he was the one pulling me with him toward the other end of the lot. When we got to his car, he shrugged out of his jacket and wrapped it around my shoulders before opening the passenger door and ushering me inside.

He went around the front of the vehicle as I watched, then got in and started the engine, turning the heater on full blast. He was breathing heavier as he turned toward me and took my hand.

I shook my head as I searched his features. "What's this about?"

He sighed. "Didn't you say that you didn't want to talk?" his brow dropped and I could see his struggle as different emotions flooded his features.

"You obviously need to and I wouldn't be a very good friend if I weren't willing to listen. We've always been able to talk about anything, so this should be no different, right?"

He brought his eyes back to mine. "Yeah," he said softly. I sat back and waited for him to continue. "I guess...I'm having second thoughts about going to Boston."

"But...*why*? I know how badly you've wanted this, Ryan. Now you *have* it." I squeezed his hand. "You shouldn't let anything distract you from this." When he shrugged, I pressed him to tell me the truth. "This is *me. Julia.* Tell me. Whatever it is, just fucking *say it*, Ryan."

"It's...well, it's you. It's...*us.*" I felt like the air had been sucked from my lungs and I needed a minute to digest his words. "Julia, I don't know if I can be so far away from you. I'll...miss you. You're so important to me."

I felt tears start in my eyes and I struggled to blink them back as I looked straight ahead out the front window. Finally, I turned toward him, trying to swallow the rising lump in my throat.

"I feel the same way. You're the best friend I've ever had, but that isn't going to change. I'm still here if you need me. We'll talk and see each other on breaks and holidays. Hell, I don't even know where I'll be yet. Ellie and I have applied all over."

He leaned forward onto the steering wheel as he gazed out the window. "I know," he said so softly I barely heard him.

"I'm going to miss you, too, but you *have* to do this. It's the thing you've wanted most, isn't it?" I was silently dying inside because I wanted him near me so badly but I had to convince him to go to Boston.

"I thought so, but when I got the letter, all I could think about was leaving you. Not...seeing you every day."

"Oh, Ryan," I laid a hand on his back and rested my forehead on his shoulder. We sat like that for a few minutes before he took a deep breath and continued.

"I'm feeling more for you...and I want..." he began.

I moved back and put up a hand to stop him. "No, don't! We can't change our relationship right before you leave, Ryan. Don't you see that?" I felt a tear escape and tried to brush it away before he noticed. "It's uncertainty that's making you feel this way, and I'm not willing..."

He stiffened and pulled away. I could feel him closing down.

"Please let me finish," I pleaded. The hurt behind his eyes made my heart ache. "I'm not willing to risk losing you in my life because we're both confused by the situation. You mean too much to me."

"Do you think I'm feeling these things because I'm fucking *leaving*? I've *been* feeling them, Julia! Holding you in there, it's what I've been wanting and it felt so right, didn't it? Was I dreaming?"

"No." I was shaking, and I wrapped my arms around my body. "I've...felt things for you too, but now isn't the time to change things between us. We've both got so many changes happening right now; we need the constant of each other. God, if something went wrong, being so far apart, we'd never be the same. I can't risk that, Ryan, I *can't*. And...it will be difficult enough, without...complicating everything. I *need* you." Tears dripped from my traitorous eyes.

He leaned back in his seat and reached out to touch my cheek. "Yeah, I need you, too. I had this same conversation with Aaron earlier. I told him that I couldn't risk losing my best friend."

"Then let's *not*. You are the one person I can't do without, Ryan. These other feelings will probably pass. You'll be caught up in your classes and I'll be trying to start a new career, but we'll still be in touch every day, I promise. I won't let you waste this opportunity."

"And if the feelings don't pass?" he asked softly as his thumb rubbed across the top of my hand.

"Then we'll do what we always do. We'll deal. *Together*." I snuffled and wiped at my tears. "Gross, huh?" I laughed.

He shook his head and swallowed me up in his big arms, holding me so tight it felt like he'd never let me go. "No. *Beautiful*."

~2~

Ryan ~

"Ryan!" my mother called from the kitchen. She and my dad were visiting from Chicago to help Aaron and I pack up. I was putting clothes in boxes and sorting out the ones I wanted to give to charity.

Aaron and I had flown to Boston a month earlier to find an apartment, but it was a small two bedroom with very little closet space. It would be cramped, but my dad argued that all we needed were two beds, two desks and lots of dedication.

He would know. He'd gone there 30 years before and now he was the top neurosurgeon in Chicago. After he graduated, he chose to go back to his hometown to be with his friends, family and, of course, my mother, Elyse.

I threw down the shirt I was folding into an open cardboard box before I went to see what she needed.

"What is it, Mom?" I asked. She had numerous boxes all around and the smell of black magic marker hit me square in the face as she wrote *kitchen* and *fragile* on one of them.

"Well, what are all these things? Should I throw them out?" She looked at me with a ridiculous grin on her face as she held up an assortment of koozies Aaron and I had collected over the past four years at concerts and frat parties.

"Those are to keep beer, uh...*pop* cold, Mom." I smiled at her when she raised her eyebrow at me. "We don't need them, but Aaron might argue the point since they're mostly his anyway."

"Yeah...sure they are, honey," she said knowingly as she threw them all in the trash bin. I picked up a box to take to the U-Haul truck we'd rented for the week. "Where's Julia? I expected to see her every minute of these last few days, but she hasn't been here at all."

I set the box back down and resigned myself to the answer. I'd been doing my best to keep from thinking about Julia, but her absence was conspicuous.

"Um, she's going to San Francisco to visit Paul for a few days and then flying to Kansas City to see Marin. Then she and Ellie are going to move to Los Angeles, I guess," I said derisively.

"That still doesn't explain why she hasn't been here. What's going on, baby? You two are inseparable." Mom's face was calm but concerned as she pried into my personal life. She didn't realize what a touchy subject this had become; I couldn't really blame her. Julia was always everywhere I was, and vice versa, so it was only natural that she'd wonder where she was.

"Well...I should really help Dad and Aaron load up, Mom," I said, trying to squirm out of the conversation.

"Ryan Mitchell Matthews, you will sit down and talk to your mother. *Now*."

I knew better than to argue with her when she was sporting that tone. I'd never win anyway.

The past couple of months hadn't been easy. It seemed like the time spent with Julia became less and less frequent. Not because I wanted it that way, but she always seemed busy with other things or other people. Even when all of us went out as a group, more and more she made excuses not to join in, and then I didn't want to go either.

"We just haven't been spending as much time together lately," I murmured as I folded my arms around the back of the chair I was straddling. "She's been working at the newspaper and doesn't have much free time. She works a lot of nights."

She continued to wrap glasses in old newspaper and pack the remaining glasses in the open box in front of her.

"But you're leaving tomorrow, Ryan, surely…"

I cut her off impatiently. "Look, Mom, the truth is that we're struggling with the separation and thought it would be better to create a little distance so we could deal. After I got my acceptance letter, I almost changed my mind and she basically kicked me in the ass, as is her usual habit."

My mother nodded. "Julia is wise beyond her years. I know how close you've been, and I'm sure you'll keep in touch."

"Yeah, but it won't be the same."

"Things change, baby. This is the beginning of both of your lives. What are Julia's plans?" She put down the glasses and moved to pull out the chair next to me. After she sat down, she reached for my hand and squeezed it.

"She has interviews with several magazines. She wants to work in editing and creative design. Ellie wants to design clothes and is looking for a job working as a junior designer at one of the big design firms. The only thing certain is that they hope to get jobs in the same city. Julia's portfolio is impressive so I know it won't be long. The question *is where?*"

My voice was low and introspective, almost like I was talking to myself.

"Where are they looking?"

"Ellie's boyfriend has a band in Los Angeles, but I was hoping they'd end up in New York. At least that's only two hundred miles from Boston." My mother reached out to touch my face. "Is that selfish?" I asked quietly.

She shook her head sadly. "It's normal, Ryan. I know how much Julia means to you."

"Do you?" The words were out before I could stop them.

"Yes. It will work out, you'll see," she said softly as she patted my cheek, her eyes full of understanding.

Aaron walked into the kitchen and scoffed at me. "Pfft! What the hell? I'm sweating my ass off hauling boxes and you're sitting on yours…chatting the day away?" His voice was stern but he was smiling. "Get these boxes outside so we can eat. I'm starving! Jen is on her way over with pizza and Jules is bringing dessert!"

I smiled at the prospect of seeing Julia for the first time in a week. "Wonder what she's making me," I said as I got up, picked up one box and stacked it with another.

"Oh, it's for *you*, is it?" Aaron called after me.

"Oh, yeah. It's for me and you know it." My heart dropped a little, even though I had a smile in my voice. This would be the last time in a long while that Julia would be baking something just for me and I felt a sadness I couldn't shake.

Even though we'd seen each other less than normal, we still texted and called each other daily. Julia insisted that would continue after I was in Boston and this was getting us used to the coming change. I missed her, but realized tomorrow would have been devastating if we continued to spend all of our time together.

I carried the boxes into the truck and stacked them on top of the others. The girls were pulling up just as I jumped down from the back and I went to help bring in the food.

"Ellie and Harris are on their way. We'll get this done fast if we all chip in!" Jen winked at me as she loaded my arms with pizza. "Then we have to take the truck to my place to get my boxes before we start loading furniture, right?" She smiled and flipped her hair as she turned toward the entrance to our building.

"Yeah, that's cool." I answered, watching Julia get out of the car. She smiled and went to open the back door of Aaron's Jeep. The shirt she was wearing was one of my favorites, a fitted button down in dark blue that brought out the pink tones in her porcelain skin and the warm breeze pushed her dark hair off of her face.

I wondered if she wore that intentionally.

Julia was getting the delectable dessert out of the back of the car. "Is it cheesecake or Black Forest?" I asked her with a smirk.

"You think you're so smart, don't you, Matthews?" she laughed as she pulled out the cheesecake and showed it to me. I nudged her shoulder as we walked in together, both of us laden with the food.

"Only where you're concerned, Abbott."

"Julia!" My dad came around the truck to greet her. "I want to hug you, but Ryan would kill me if I ruin this great looking cheesecake!" He leaned over and kissed her cheek.

"It's great to see you, Gabe. Is Elyse here, too?" The excitement in her emerald eyes did funny things to my insides. I loved how she and my parents adored each other.

My mother came running out and removed the cheesecake from Julia's hands, handing it to my dad before folding her into a tight embrace.

"I'm so happy to see you, honey! You look great! I want to hear all about your plans."

Julia hugged her back and my dad and I continued into the apartment to set the food on the counter.

"That girl is beautiful, Ryan...*and* she cooks. I think I'd have to marry her, if I wasn't already so happy with your mother," Dad said and patted me on the shoulder.

I took a deep breath. *Yeah.*

I glanced outside, watching the two women go back to the car side by side. Julia reached in and emerged with the Black Forest cake I adored. Smiling, I rushed outside to take it from her.

"Ah, Julia. I love you," I said before I could stop myself. Her face flushed a bright red as I tried to cover. "Thank you, for this," I said as my mother looked from Julia's face to mine.

"A promise is a promise, Ryan, remember?"

Yeah, I remember. I remember every damn word you've ever said to me.

Harris and Ellie arrived, honking the horn of Harris's old conversion van as they pulled up and then we all went inside to eat. I wanted to skip the damn pizza and head straight for dessert, but Julia took the knife out of my hand as I started to cut into the cheesecake.

"What do you think you're doing?" She tried to sound annoyed, but I knew it caused her great pleasure that I loved her cooking so much that I couldn't wait to get into it.

"What's it look like I'm doing? *Eating*," I grinned at her as I took back the knife. "This," I said as I pointed to the cake, "and not *that*." I nodded toward the pizza.

"No." She said sternly, trying to keep a straight face. "Can't you wait until the others are ready?"

"Um...*no*. I can't. What's your point?" She laughed and shook her head as I dug into the creamy dessert I'd just placed on my plate. I took a big bite and the sweet creaminess melted on my tongue. "God...Julia. This is incredible."

She smiled, taking the knife from my hand, and turned toward the beautiful cake decorated with cherries, whipped cream and chocolate shavings.

I shook my head at her as I realized her intentions. "No. That's mine." I teased her. "First and last piece, at least."

The corners of her mouth lifted in a smile that challenged me as she cut a slice from the cake and loaded it onto a plate.

"You mean, *this* first piece?" she goaded me.

"Yeah. *That* first piece." I put down my half-eaten cheese-cake, reaching for her plate.

She pulled it back and raised her eyebrows, digging a fork into it and raised it to her mouth. "Mmmm...damn! I amaze even myself sometimes!" She giggled, her face alight with laughter.

The others settled in the living room with their pizza while we bantered in the kitchen.

"Julia. I'm warning you. Not one more bite, I mean it," I growled at her, but with laughter in my voice.

"Oh... you *want* some?" Laughing as she licked the fork clean. "Why didn't you say so?" She set her fork down and dug her fingers into her cake and then smashed some of it into my face with a smirk.

I opened my mouth to try to take most of it in, but she smeared a little on my face and then licked her fingers. I laughed with her as her eyes widened. "Good, yes?"

I used my thumb to wipe some of the cake off my face and licked it off. More fell off my face onto the floor.

"Um...very. Delicious, thank you," My mouth was full and I had a big-ass grin on my face.

She picked up her fork and proceeded to calmly resume eating the cake on her plate as I watched; acting as if nothing was out of sorts, while I stood in front of her with my face a complete mess. Her eyes were daring me, teasing and sparkling as she pulled the fork upside down from her mouth.

Turnabout was fair play. Most of my cheesecake was gone, so I set my fork aside, picked up the remainder of it and smashed it in her face. "You really have to try this, too, Julia! Yummy...!"

She pushed me away. We struggled and giggled with each other, until both of us burst out laughing.

Mom's voice called from the other room. "What on earth is going on in there?" she said with a laugh.

"Oh...they're just being...*them*." Aaron shot out.

"It's good to hear Ryan laugh like that." Dad said. "He's been struggling. This is the first time I've heard him happy in months."

I turned to the sink after I got control of the laughing and began cleaning up my face with a damp paper towel. Julia had sobered too, watching me and standing still, her eyes burning into mine as I wiped the remnants of the cheesecake from the smooth skin of her cheeks and chin and then her lower lip. The tension between us was palpable.

I wanted to lick the delicious stuff off of her face, mostly as an excuse to kiss her, but I knew that I shouldn't. Ever since the *almost* kiss in the club, it was all I could think about.

"Will you go for a ride with me?" I asked as I took her hand. The time had come. We had to talk before I left.

"Um...what about helping?"

"They'll survive without us for an hour or so. I want to talk to you. Just us." She dropped her gaze and I rubbed my thumb over the top of her hand. "Come on, Julia. I know we've avoided it, but we need this, okay?"

She raised her eyes to mine and her face softened and she nodded. "Yeah."

I turned with her hand in mine and walked to the door.

"Save me at least one more piece of each of these cakes, Aaron Matthews, or I'll have your ass on a platter." I threw over my shoulder as I pulled Julia behind me out the door. The six people in the other room watched us leave without saying a word.

We drove silently until we reached the coffee shop where Julia and I spent every Sunday morning together. It was our thing to have breakfast, read the paper and talk without any of the others around. Even these past two months, we still spent Sunday morning together without fail.

I walked around and opened her door and as it closed behind her, I took her hand again. It felt like she was my girl-friend; the electricity at the briefest of touches setting me on edge.

I ordered our usual. "Double shot soy cappuccino, and iced coffee with sugar-free vanilla syrup and a splash of cream. Both large please." I paid for the drinks and brought them back to the table, and sat down opposite Julia so I could look at her unabashed.

She fiddled with her coffee, adding a packet of Splenda, and stirring it with her spoon. She was my Julia, no matter if she was dressed to kill or in cut-off jean shorts and that damned blue blouse.

She bit her lip and looked at me finally. I touched her hand across the table, my fingers tracing over hers.

"I know we've been trying to put some distance between us, but I'm going to miss you, Jules."

"I'll miss you, too. I didn't want distance necessarily, I just wanted to make it easier and it did help, didn't it?" she asked quietly.

"I won't know the answer until I get to Boston and I can't see you."

She swallowed and took a shaky breath, her green eyes liquid as she stared into my face. "You'll be an amazing doctor, Ryan; and you'll change so many lives."

"That's just great, Julia. I mean, I appreciate your support, but can you be a little less fucking philosophical, please?" I let go of her hand as I sat back in my chair angrily running a hand through my hair in frustration. "I understand your motives for pushing me away, but frankly it pisses me off!"

"What do you want me to say?" she asked quietly. "You've worked so hard, we both have, and I..."

"I want you to tell me that you'll be as miserable as I will! That you're pissed at both of us for wasting so much time these past months when we could have been together...and..."

Her eyes widened as she waited for me to continue. "And...*what*, Ryan?" she finally said, impatiently.

"That you'll come *with* me," I said in a rush, not really meaning to say it out loud.

Julia looked at me for a moment. "I suppose I could. I have the time off because I was going to go to San Francisco. I'll have to tell my dad, but I don't have any interviews lined up for a week."

She thought I was asking her to drive out to Boston with me until I got settled in, and that was all.

"No. I mean, sure, I'd love to have you make the drive with me..." I leaned forward to take her hand in mine again, "but I mean *move* to Boston with me."

I'd finally said what I'd been fighting so hard against since the day I'd gotten my acceptance letter. All the voices in my head, telling me that it was unfair to ask this of her, could go straight to hell.

She gasped and the shock showed on her face.

"But...I'm applying at places like Glamour and Vogue magazines, Ryan. Ellie is trying to get a major fashion house and those are in New York and Los Angeles. Harris's band is moving to L.A." She stopped and sighed. "We talked about this so many times, why are you bringing this up now?"

I took a deep breath and looked away, my jaw setting in protest.

"Hell! I don't know, Julia! I was trying not to be selfish, I guess."

"Ryan, Ellie is counting on me being with her and she wants L.A. so bad."

Anger welled inside of me and heat rushed under the surface of the skin on my face.

"So you will move anywhere *Ellie* wants, but you won't even consider being near me, is that it? Who the hell is your *best friend*, anyway?" My voice rose in volume and people at the next table looked at me. I wasn't fighting fair, but I felt like I was fighting for my fucking life.

"That isn't how it is and you know it, you big ass! You know the damn answer to that! I'm going to move where I get the best job offer, regardless of who's around, and you know it! Boston is *not* a city where I can land a gig at a major magazine." She was seething, her breathing getting faster as she glared at me.

My eyes met hers unflinchingly as I considered my next words carefully, my hand pulling on my lower lip.

"I know, okay?" I said finally.

"So what? If I were as selfish as you, I would've let you give up Harvard, but you mean more to me than that!"

I sighed; my chest expanding until I thought it would burst. I wanted to kiss her and yell at her all at the same time. She infuriated the shit out of me, but I loved her so damn much.

"So, can you at least say that you'll be in New York instead of fucking L.A.?"

Her eyes welled up with tears. "You're asking a lot, Ryan. Ellie will be disappointed if I don't try to get to L.A."

I put both fists over my eyes and rubbed them both furiously, before lifting my head and looking at her.

"And I'll be devastated to be 3000 miles away from you, so just...do what you have to do, then," I said, defeated. She brushed a tear furiously from her cheek as her face crumpled. I instantly regretted putting her in this position. "Look, I'm sorry. Just forget it."

"No, it's too late, Ryan," her voice trembled and she took a long drink of her coffee. "You're asking me to completely throw away all the resumes that I've sent out and start over, move to the largest city in the world alone, just so we can see each other *maybe* once a month on the weekend?!"

"Yes." I confirmed without flinching.

"*Who* does that?" she shook her head and shrugged.

I leaned toward her. "*We* do. We do, Julia."

She stared at me for a good two minutes as she struggled to control her emotions. Finally, she nodded.

"Okay, but I'm not hauling dessert on the train between New York and Boston all the damn time."

I jumped up from my chair and pulled her up and into my arms, crushing her to my chest. The familiar scent of her perfume flooded my senses and it felt so good to hold her little body next to mine.

"So...are you still driving to Boston with me tomorrow, or what?" I said into her neck and her arms tightened around my waist. We both burst out laughing and my heart soared.

"Yeah. Just try to stop me."

I closed my eyes as I breathed her in.

Thank you, God.

Julia ~

After we loaded everything into the truck, filled Aaron's jeep to capacity and stuffed the back of Ryan's CRV as full as possible, I hugged Gabriel and Elyse goodbye. They were going to fly to Chicago and everyone else was taking off for Boston early the next morning.

I needed to talk with Ellie about my decision about New York. I was scared for more reasons than one, but my heart told me it was the right thing for me. The smile on Ryan's beautiful face had been worth the price of the decision.

My heart beat wildly in my chest and a huge weight had been lifted from my shoulders. The sadness at being so far away from him disappeared. I still couldn't be certain where I'd end up, but just the decision to try to get closer had settled me.

Ellie might be upset and I didn't look forward to that conversation, but L.A. had been more her goal than mine. She was aware of my feelings for Ryan, so hopefully she'd understand.

I hugged everyone goodbye and then Ryan ran me back to my apartment. Jenna was staying with the guys at their apartment in sleeping bags in their living room. Ellie and Harris had already left and would probably be at my apartment.

I took out my phone and dialed my dad.

"Hullo," my dad's gruff voice answered at the other end of the line.

"Hey, Dad."

"Jules! What have you been up to today?"

"I've been over at Ryan's and Aaron's helping them get packed up. They're leaving for Boston tomorrow."

"Yeah, that's great. Tell them both that I wish them the best at Harvard. You okay with Ryan leaving?"

I smiled, "Yeah. Dad, about that. I thought I'd drive to Boston with him and then he'll fly me back next week. I know it's last minute but I'd really like to."

"Oh. Well, what about next week?" I could hear his TV in the background.

"I can't. I have an interview in Los Angeles with Condé Nast. Maybe after that, but it's all up in the air. I may need to cancel my trip to Kansas City if I have interviews."

"What's Condé Nast?" he asked, but I wondered if he was really listening.

"A publishing house," I answered and I saw Ryan tense and glance my way. The wheels were turning in his over-intelligent frontal lobe.

"Listen, Julia, I have court tomorrow and need to prepare. Just let me know where you are a few times while you're on the road and when you get to Boston. Will Ellie be able to pick you up at the airport when you get back?"

"Yes, Dad. No worries. I'll call. Thanks for understanding. Love you."

I hung up and turned to face Ryan.

"Okay, what's that look on your face?" I asked as my finger pointed at him.

"It's nothing!" I knew him so he wasn't getting by with this.

"Ryan, stop trying to bullshit me. I know you're pissed about my L.A. interview, but I already had it set up. I can't cancel."

He shrugged. "Ok, but what if..." I reached out and laid a hand on his arm.

"Hey, there are no promises here. I told you I'd try to concentrate on New York and I will, but I'm not going to blow off this commitment or ignore opportunities. It would be stupid anyway. Condé Nast has 20 or more different magazines and some of them are based in New York, okay?"

His mouth set. "Okay," he mumbled.

"Stop being such a moody ass and trust me."

He smiled and ran his hand through his gorgeous hair. "You love my moody ass."

"Yes, but that doesn't mean I'm enjoying it." I rolled my eyes as we pulled up to my apartment.

He reached out and touched my arm and I trembled, hoping he didn't sense my reaction. I had to remind myself that he was my best friend and not the man I was in love with.

Yeah, right.

"Julia, thank you. I know there are no guarantees, but I'm glad you're willing to try to be closer. I'll pick you up at 5 AM, okay?"

I'm already close to you. So close. That wasn't how he meant it, but I was closer to him than I'd ever been to anyone else in my life.

My head fell back as I groaned. "Ugh! 5 AM? You're gonna kill me." I opened the door to get out, followed by Ryan's velvet laughter. "Get that silly grin off of your face, and bring me a coffee in the morning." I smiled over my shoulder.

"Suddenly, I'm looking forward to this trip. I was dreading it, but now...it's different." Ryan was still chuckling as I closed the door of the car behind me. "Good luck with Ellie," he said through the open window before I turned to go inside.

Ellie was sitting on Harris's lap on the couch when I walked in.

"Hi, Julia. Are you okay?" she asked quietly, expecting that I'd be a mess, having just said goodbye to Ryan for the last time.

"Yeah. Hey, Harris." I said to Ellie's hot boyfriend. He was gorgeous; blonde wavy hair and light blue eyes. Our boys were all so incredibly handsome…Ryan the most beautiful of the three.

But I'm biased, right? I thought, but dismissed it just as quickly. He *was* the most beautiful.

I smiled as I kicked off my shoes and shoved them in the closet next to the door.

"Julia, don't take this wrong, but I thought you'd be crying. You're smiling…so what's up?" Ellie asked incredulously.

"Can I talk to you?"

"Is this serious?" She got up off of Harris's lap and came toward me to take both of my hands.

"It might be. Ryan has asked me to go to Boston."

Her face lit up. "That's great, Julia! You should spend some time with him. I mean, you guys love each other, right?"

I nodded. "Uh huh." I glanced at Harris.

"Oh, hey, do you need me to leave?" he asked.

"Um…" I began.

"It's okay to talk in front of Harris." Ellie returned to the couch next to him and I took a chair across from them.

"Ellie, you know how important you are to me, but Ryan is, too."

She flashed a beautiful smile and her face softened. "I know, sweetie. You and Ryan belong together."

My throat tightened, but I tried to swallow it and continue speaking.

"He asked me to concentrate my job search in New York. I am not ruling out L.A. completely but he…*we* need to be closer. Please don't be angry."

She was silent for a moment but she didn't appear upset. "Of course, I understand. You should have decided this a long time ago, but New York is still not Boston."

"But it's a lot closer. I'll be able see him more often and I need him, Ellie. I'm…scared to let him go completely. I'm just not ready for that."

She got up to hug me. "Julia, you'll *never* be ready to let go of Ryan. Does this mean you guys are finally a couple?" Ellie asked expectantly.

"Um…we're still friends. I'm not really sure what this means."

"It means he loves you and doesn't want to be without you. It will all work out, I promise."

"Yes." I said as my stomach fluttered at her words. "You'll be a famous designer soon and rich enough to fly to New York at least once a week for drinks." I hugged her again. "I really appreciate your understanding, Ellie. I love you."

Ryan ~

The week had flown by and Julia was flying back to California tomorrow. Aaron and I had new student orientation in the morning, so I'd be forced to put Julia in a cab to take her to Logan International. I hated it, but I had no choice.

The three day trip to Boston left us exhausted and the next two days were spent unpacking and setting up the apartment. Aaron and Jenna moved into the larger of the two bedrooms and I was left with the smaller one. By the time I got my bed, desk and keyboard set up, it left only 5 square feet of open floor. It felt more like a closet.

Jenna groaned at the lack of closet space and Aaron told her that he liked her better without clothes anyway. Julia and I laughed and Jen blushed. "Shut the fuck up, Aaron, or you'll be missing what you like best about me."

Julia kept us all fed, whipping up amazing meals in the tiny kitchen. She grunted at how small the freezer was. "So much for my plan to stock your freezer. Shit, this is small."

My heart thumped in my chest. She was still trying to take care of me and it made it even more obvious why I loved her so much. I was finally able to face it, even if I couldn't act on it.

Our time on the road and since we'd arrived in Boston had been bittersweet; a mixture of happiness and sadness as the minutes and days ticked by.

The trip had been a blast, but we couldn't keep up the constant driving and were forced to spend one night in a hotel near Cleveland. I wanted to let my instincts take over and my instincts told me to make love to her. In fact, they were screaming in the darkness, keeping me awake into the wee hours of the morning. My body throbbed painfully at her nearness.

Julia tossed and turned, too...until she finally fell into an exhausted sleep. I listened to her breathing and could feel the heat from her body calling to me as I watched her sleep. I ached to reach out and brush her hair back or touch the soft skin on her arm. She was so beautiful and soft, so warm and vulnerable.

Needless to say, I lived on coffee and Diet Coke. Julia slept in the car and I teased her at the unfairness of it.

"Suck it up, Matthews. I can't help your hormones," she rolled her eyes at me and then grinned as she looked out the window. She knew exactly how she affected me.

In the apartment, Julia slept on the couch and, even though she wasn't in the same bed, she was only a few feet away. I longed to go to her as I lay awake in my bed going over the events of the past week...most of all, the last couple of days as the end of our time together ebbed closer.

I turned on my side and punched my pillow, trying to find a position that would help me fall asleep.

Julia had agreed to look for a job in New York, but that didn't mean it would happen. There was still a good chance that she'd end up far away and the possibility was eating away at me.

We took time off from unpacking, taking the train from Boston down to New York City and ran around Manhattan sightseeing and looking in all types of interesting stores. We found a small coffee shop on the East Side where we stopped before spending most of the day in Central Park. If Julia was able to get a job here, this would be the part of town where her office would most likely be located so I wanted to get her acclimated and see how she liked it. Truthfully, the thought of her in New York, alone, worried me.

As we strolled leisurely around the city, we talked about Harvard and my class schedule, Julia's dream job and what companies she'd be applying to in New York. We talked about our parents, and spent a lot of time reliving some of our special times together at Stanford. She asked me what type of specialty I wanted to go into and pushed me to think about it in depth. I wasn't positive yet, but knew I wanted to go into surgery or trauma medicine.

The one topic we avoided was our feelings for each other. It hung over us like an unspoken storm, but I was enjoying the day and didn't want to ruin it by forcing the topic, even though I ached to tell her I was in love with her.

Our time together made it clear that I could not contemplate the future without her in it. The most immediate future consisted of her getting on a plane and flying away from me.

I gave up trying to sleep and pushed out of bed. I went into the hallway and stopped to listen for signs of Julia sleeping.

I heard her soft voice calling out. "Ryan? Is that you?"

I walked the short distance into the living room. I stopped in front of where she sat and took in her shorts and t-shirt, her wild bed hair and the sparkling eyes looking up at me.

"Yeah. I can't sleep."

She smiled. "Well at least it's not your hormones this time."

"Isn't it?" I asked softly as I touched a finger to her chin.

"Maybe it wasn't such a good idea for me to come here."

"Yes, it was..." I said quietly, took her hand and pulled her up from the couch and down the hall, back to my room.

"Ryan...I." she whispered as I took her in my room and shut the door behind us. I could feel her tremble beside me.

Still holding her hand, the mattress gave beneath my weight and I pulled her down next to me. She sat, cross legged facing me and I took both of her hands in one of mine, cupping her cheek with the other. She felt so soft...

"Julia...these last four years..." I began to speak but she pulled one hand from mine and pressed two fingers to my lips.

"Don't say something you'll regret, Ryan. I'm...scared. So scared of losing your friendship."

I sucked in my breath. "I'm scared of losing more than your friendship, Julia."

"I don't understand..."

"Will you listen without stopping me? Take the risk of hearing what I have to say." I whispered impatiently and rubbed my hand up and down her arm.

"Okay," she said quietly.

"I'm scared of not having what we're supposed to have if we don't take the risk. These last four years have meant so much. Knowing you and having you near me has literally changed the course of my life. You're my very best friend but...I feel so much closer to you than that. This thing with us... I can't shake it."

She nodded, almost imperceptibly and looked down at her lap. "I know. Me, too."

I felt a little ray of hope surge within my chest and my heart sped up. *This is Julia*, I reminded myself. She knew me better than anyone else so I should just say what I needed to say.

"Since the day we met, I've been fascinated by you, honey. It's getting harder and harder to be around you and try to deny my feelings."

"Are you trying to say you're attracted to me, Ryan? Because...I'm attracted to you, too. On many levels." She dropped her eyes to our hands again.

"In the club, the night I got my acceptance letter, I wanted to kiss you. Holding you drove me crazy, but, it was like we talked about then. I'm not willing to lose your friendship."

"If we cross that line, then what? Will we feel weird with each other or lose...*this*? Will it make being apart even worse?"

"Can it *get* any worse?" I asked quietly as my fingers threaded through hers.

"I don't have that answer, but it's something I've asked myself," she whispered.

"What I *do* know, is that I'm not capable of fighting it anymore, and that no matter what happens, I will *always* want you in my life." I searched her face as uncertainty flashed across her beautiful features.

"Ryan, do you promise? *Promise me*," she begged as she leaned her forehead on mine. Her breath rushed over my face and I could literally taste how sweet she would be in her scent.

"I promise." I lowered my mouth and ghosted it over hers. My heart was thumping in my chest so fast I thought it would explode. This was the moment I'd waited for, for over three and a half years.

Her tongue came out to lick my upper lip and my breath left me in a rush, my body tightening in response.

I held her head with gentle hands as my mouth finally settled over hers. Our open mouths were soft and searching. It felt new and exciting, but also so right. Our lips knew exactly how to mirror each other and move in perfect unison. She sucked on my upper lip and then I sucked on her lower one. I thought I'd died and gone to heaven.

"Julia, my God," I groaned against her mouth as I gathered her close to me and lay her down on the bed. I moved over her and kissed her again and again. The nearness of her, what I'd been dreaming of for so long was finally within reach, but I wanted to take it slow, to savor every touch. "Kissing you is every bit as incredible as I've imagined it would be."

Her hands moved around my shoulders and into my hair as she pulled me closer. Knowing she wanted me, made me insane. I could feel the urgency in her body, as she surged against me, and I parted her legs with one of mine. This was a fantasy that I'd had a million times, and it was finally being fulfilled.

She felt so good, her body molding perfectly to mine. I ground my hardness against her and she moaned against my mouth. "Ryan, uhh..."

"Uhhh, say it again," I begged against her mouth.

"Ryan..." she gasped before my mouth devoured hers again and again, and the friction of our bodies making us both breathless. I cupped her breast and my body swelled even more as I teased the peak until it strained in my hand. I had to taste her, and urgently pushed her shirt up to expose her bare breasts. She was perfect. Round and firm with erect pink nipples.

"You're so beautiful. I can't tell you how long I've wanted this." I groaned as I dragged my open mouth from hers, down over her neck and chest until it finally closed over one of her luscious nipples. Her back arched toward me and her hands wound in my hair as I pulled it into my mouth, suckling and flicking it with my tongue. I thrust against her hip, seeking the contact that I so desperately needed.

I had her writhing beneath me and desire for her drove me insane.

I moaned softly as her nipple popped from between my lips and I brushed her hair back off of her face. "Do you want me to stop? I don't want to do anything you don't want, baby."

She searched my face and reached up to flutter her finger tips across my jaw. "Ryan, I...I want you, but I'm scared of what will happen to us...later."

I kissed her nose and then her eyelids and cheeks before moving back to her mouth to tease it back into another deep kiss. I loved how she responded to me. It felt like she couldn't help herself and it was the sexiest thing I'd ever experienced.

Hearing her say she wanted me turned me on beyond comprehension.

"I know; me too...but you feel so good, we fit so perfectly...I can feel your heart beating against mine. I can tell how amazing we'll be together."

Her hands moved up my chest and one of mine moved down between her legs never taking my eyes from her face. Her mouth fell open and her eyes closed as my hand rubbed her over her clothes. "God, Julia, you're so hot, you drive me crazy." Her body arched against my hand and my dick literally ached as it twitched against her hip. "I've wanted you, to touch you like this since the day we met."

"Why didn't you, then?" she moaned before she raised her head toward mine, clearly seeking my kiss. I was only too willing to oblige her as my mouth took hers again in a series of hot, wet kisses, our tongues laving and playing with each other.

Yes, why the fuck didn't I?

Her hand moved down to grasp around me and I was lost.

"Julia...baby..."

There was a loud knocking on the door. "Ryan..." Aaron opened my door and came inside, the light in the hall flooding the room and blinding me. Julia tried to move away from me, but I held her where she was, shielding her so Aaron wouldn't see her behind my body. Her breathing was as heavy as mine as she looked up into my eyes.

"What is it, Aaron?" I struggled to keep my voice even.

"Um, Jen is sick and I can't find the box with all of the medicine in it. Where is it?"

"I don't think I brought it in yet. It's in my car."

"She's puking in the bathroom, and I'm not dressed, so can you get the Pepto Bismol?"

Ugh! Of all nights for this to happen...shit! "Yeah. I'll be out in a minute."

"Thanks," Aaron mumbled and closed the door.

I gathered Julia close and kissed her forehead. "I'm so sorry, honey. I'll be right back." I pushed off the bed and hurried down the hall, grabbed my keys from the table by the door and ran outside. It was dark and I couldn't see what I was doing. It took a few minutes to find the box of supplies and I ended up hitting my head on the hatchback.

"Holy hell!"

It hurt like a son-of-a-bitch and I put my hand to my head to find the warm ooze on my temple.

"It looks like Jen isn't the only one who needs medical attention," I muttered to myself as I tried to avoid the rocks beneath my bare feet. "Shit."

Back inside, I set the box on the kitchen table and turned on the small light over the sink. Digging through it I found the stomach medicine and padded down the hall to Aaron and Jenna's room. I knocked and handed it to him when he opened the door.

"Thanks, man. I hope we didn't wake up Julia," he said.

"Uh, I don't know. I'll check on her. I hope Jen feels better." I said as I turned toward my room and wiped at the blood on my head. The wound was beginning to drip, but I wanted to let Julia know I'd be a few minutes more while I tended to the gash on my head.

"Julia…?" I whispered as I pushed open my bedroom door. I moved to the bed, but she wasn't there.

I walked back to the living room and found her laying back on the couch, covered up to her chin, so I went to kneel beside her. "I'm sorry it took me a while to find it…"

She looked at me and gasped. "Oh my God, Ryan! What happened?"

"I bashed my head on the hatchback."

Her hand came up to my forehead and she frowned. "It looks bad. Let's go into the kitchen so I can clean it up. You may need stitches." The concern in her voice was clear. "Come on." She got up and I followed her.

Julia motioned for me to sit down on a chair and then turned on the light over the sink. Julia arranged the kitchen when we unpacked so knew her way around. She took a towel out of the drawer and wet it before dabbing at the cut.

I winced at the pain. "Sorry, sweetie."

She worked to clean the wound, but all I could do was stare at her breasts rising and falling in an even rhythm with her breathing. Her breasts that not fifteen minutes before had been bare and underneath my tongue.

I felt my body spring back to life as I let my thoughts wander.

"It doesn't look like you'll need stitches, but you should have a butterfly bandage. Do you have any?" she asked.

"I think in this box." I shoved it toward her. "I thought I was the doctor here, but you're doing a damn good job." I smiled up at her as she placed the bandage on my forehead and placed a kiss next to it. Her lips felt so soft and warm against my skin.

My hands moved up to her hips and I drew her closer to me, tilting my head up to nuzzle her chin with my nose as she stood in front of me. "Hey…" I said softly

"Ryan…we should sleep. You have an important day tomorrow, and you're injured." She leaned her head on mine and it felt like the most natural thing in the world to have her here, in my arms, in my life…in my heart. Her hand fluttered along my jaw.

My head was starting to throb. As if she read my mind, she reached in the box behind me on the table, found some Tylenol and handed it to me. She pulled away from me to get a glass of water.

I put two pills in my mouth and swallowed. "You always take such good care of me, baby." Setting the glass down, I pulled her to stand between my legs and wrapped her in my arms.

"Listen, Julia…the interruption just now was the biggest case of bad timing in my life, but I need you to trust me. What's happening here is really us, okay? I don't want the light of day seeing you pull away from this."

She nodded silently and kissed me softly. When she moved away, my hands drew her back closer and I took her mouth harder, my tongue sliding into the warm recesses of her mouth as she opened to me. We kissed again until finally she pulled away.

"You need sleep, Ryan, okay?" I sighed and dropped my forehead to her shoulder.

"Will you sleep with me if I promise to be good?" I smiled up at her, but felt the sadness in my heart as I looked at the clock on the stove. It was 2:37 and she would need to leave by 7:30. My throat tightened as I held her close. I felt a huge loss at not being able to make love to her as I wanted, but more, the loss of her coming departure with all this uncertainty between us left a hole in my chest.

"Yeah, ok. I'm really going to miss you."

I pulled her close again and rubbed my hands up and down her back as her arms wrapped around my shoulders in a tight hug. It felt so great to hold her like this and know she wouldn't pull away. That she *allowed* me to touch her as a lover and not just a friend.

"Missing you is…I can't even talk about it. There are no words for how much it hurts."

I took her hand and shut off the light. She followed me down the hall to my room and we crawled into bed together. I reached for her under the covers and pulled her close. She snuggled into my shoulder and her arm slid around my waist.

I sighed and pressed a kiss to her temple. I felt content as I let myself fall asleep.

*****

In what seemed like 5 minutes, the alarm was beeping and Julia was sitting up and running her hands through her hair before getting out of bed. Again, loss and panic rose in my chest. She wouldn't look at me as she hovered at the foot of the bed.

"Can you come here for a minute, please?" I asked uneasily. I didn't really know what was going on, but I needed to make sure we were okay.

She sat next to me and I reached for her.

"Are you upset about what happened between us last night?" I was terrified of her answer, but I had to ask.

She shrugged. "Not upset, exactly...I just worry..."

I squeezed her hand. "Stop. I thought it was incredible and something I've wanted for a very long time. I wanted to finally make love to you, Julia. Please don't regret one of the most beautiful moments of my life. Please."

"I don't," she said softly as she gave me one of our nudges. "It felt amazing, but I'm scared...of the distance, scared of missing you more than I already will," her voice broke on the last word and she lifted her liquid green eyes to mine. "I'm afraid I'll make the wrong choices, turn down jobs I should take or any range of other stupid things. Maybe distract you from medical school when you need to focus."

"Don't worry about me. I'll do what I need to do, and *nothing* could make me miss you more than I already will. So can we just be us, and roll with this please?"

She nodded and I pulled her close to me. My eyes closed as love flooded through me. I wondered if I should tell her how I felt but didn't know if she was ready to hear the words. Last night was a huge step, even if we hadn't made love.

"Just don't forget to remember me while we're apart. We'll work it out, Okay?"

"I could never forget you, Ryan," she said softly as she hugged me back and turned her head to kiss me. "You're burned into me forever."

~3~

Ryan ~

Gross.

A truer statement had never been made. Two months in and I still gagged every time I walked into my Gross Anatomy lab. The smell was more than any normal person could stand. Our professor had passed out little jars of Vicks ointment on the first day of class, telling us that this would become our very best friend. He laughed at the looks on our faces when he instructed us that we were to put it just inside our nostrils before we ever walked into the room.

I'd laughed at the time, thinking to myself that it couldn't be *that* bad. It fucking *was*. It was *worse*.

First semester med students were no doubt weeded out if they couldn't make it through that damn class. If you were one of the lucky ones who didn't run home screaming with your tail between your legs, you got a reward. And what could possibly be better than dissecting a human cadaver over the course of three and a half months?

Oh, right. *A study in recycling.* We'd continue to dissect the same fucking one for the second half of the year. I was *so* looking forward to that.

Aaron, on the other hand, made a joke out of it, naming his cadaver Marcy and referring to her as his baby.

Ugh!

I felt bad for the poor bastards that we chopped up, but I guess it was all in the name of science. The cadaver in my group was male and we called him *Joe.* In the beginning, Aaron taunted me about getting his dick to stand up so he and *Marcy* could get it on, touting that he didn't need Viagra anymore since now he had rigor mortis.

The sick bastard. I shook my head as laughter vibrated through my chest. *Funny*, but sick.

During the first few weeks, I couldn't get the smell out of my clothes and ended up burning them on a regular basis. Sure, we wore scrubs, but doing so didn't leave the clothes underneath unscathed.

It became an expensive problem until one Sunday morning, the genius voice on the other end of my cell phone found the solution.

"Why don't you just wear the same clothes and shoes every day and get a locker in the gym to store them in? Go change before and after class. Gyms are stinky anyway."

"And never wash them Julia?" I'd mocked her.

"Gah! Of course, *wash* them, but they're ruined anyway, right? So bleach the shit out of them. That should help with the smell."

I smiled as I laid the clean, snow-white scrubs on the locker room bench. I changed into my lab clothes, which consisted of a plain white t-shirt and now bleached out jean shorts. After donning the scrubs, I shoved my street clothes in a plastic bag, sealing it to keep the stench out before I threw it back in the locker. Even so far away, she was still taking care of me.

It had been two months and I missed her. Sometimes so much, I couldn't even breathe.

She was still in L.A. with Ellie, who had gotten a job as an apprentice with a prominent stylist.

Julia got the position with Condé Nast publishing and was working as a junior content and style editor for Glamour Magazine.

Of course, she got the first damn job she applied for. She's brilliant and gorgeous with an insane work ethic that kept her from trekking to Boston for a visit. To be fair, I hadn't been able to get to L.A. either. The situation sucked.

I sighed on my way toward the Health Sciences building for my Human Body class. That was the more politically correct name for it, but Gross Anatomy was so much more apropos. I took the stairs to the 5th floor two at a time.

Julia. She was all I could think about.

After that night in my room, we hadn't really defined our relationship as anything different than best friends. I was terrified that it was somehow a dream and was left wondering if it really happened. We both had a lot going on and I'd been very disappointed when she didn't come to New York. We seemed to avoid the topic when we did talk and it left me uneasy and confused.

When she took the L.A job, I picked a fight instead of doing what I should have done by offering my congratulations and support. But damn it, I was upset!

After almost making love to her and telling myself that we would *finally* be together as a couple, I didn't handle it well.

She'd hung up on me with a trite, *"Thanks for the support, asshole."*

We made up after two weeks of my pouting and then another of her ignoring my calls. After that we avoided the subject of *us.* And now, two months later, it seemed like years.

I buried myself in school and she was working to establish herself as *indispensable.* My heart constricted. The better she did her job, the less likely she'd be able to leave it. And Julia never did anything half-assed. Then, where would I be? "Hmmph." I let my breath out. *Missing her desperately, more and more as the time passed.*

I took out my trusty vial of Vicks before walking into the lab. The other five members of my group were already waiting for me. I wasn't late, but I wasn't so damn eager either.

The group was quite diverse. Min Sing, a little Korean girl who barely spoke, except to answer the professor's questions, had a sad homesick look about her all the time. I tried to engage her in conversation, but she was so introverted it was practically impossible, so after the first couple of weeks, I'd given up.

Tanner Cromwell was friendly and jovial. His personality was a lot like Aaron's, always poking fun at the dead guy on the table. Sometimes the professor had to ride his ass, but he made the class bearable.

James Davis was a conundrum. He looked like a biker, with long hair and tattoos, but was smarter than hell. Claire Morris was sort of pretty, but was always bitching about something and emotionally very immature. Two traits bad enough on their own, but combined, it made her completely unlikable.

Then there was Liza Nash. I inwardly cringed when I walked up to the table and she put her hand on my arm. I'd take Claire's bitchy ways over Liza's constant flirting any day.

"Hi, Ryan." My eyes made brief contact with hers at the greeting before quickly looking away. I guess you could say she was beautiful in a conventional sort of way, but she seemed so artificial. Hard, cold and unapproachable; which was weird considering she was constantly pursuing me. She batted her eyelashes as I withdrew my arm from her hand.

Long, dirty blonde hair, blue eyes, big tits and a good figure. I wasn't blind, but I just wasn't interested. I was civil to get through the class, but her obvious attempts had gotten old and monotonous. Constantly brushing her off had not deterred her one bit.

"Hey, you guys." I said as I pulled on the latex gloves and stood in my spot at the side of the table.

Tanner met my eyes and wagged his eyebrows at me. He was well aware of Liza's efforts; always ready to throw it in my face. He thought I should just take what she so flagrantly offered and not think about it too much.

Not likely. I mean, it wasn't like I wasn't a normal guy with physical needs. I was. There were ways to deal with that when necessary, but the last thing I needed was to complicate my life with something meaningless. Liza could've been a Greek goddess and it wouldn't have mattered. Even though the situation with Julia was a little shaky, I wouldn't risk it by screwing around with some twit.

All I could think about was Julia and, despite the precarious state of our relationship, I loved her beyond reason. I only hoped that she loved me as much.

Stupid ass. Why didn't you just tell her?

After class, when Liza ran up behind us, Tanner laughed when I muttered under my breath, "Walk faster."

"Ryan! Wait!" She panted. She finally caught up and it was rude, but we kept walking.

"Oh, hi." I said, hoping my obvious lack of enthusiasm would have the desired effect.

"Do you want to get some coffee? I have some questions about microbiology."

So much for her getting a fucking clue.

We didn't have any other classes together, but still had some of the same cores. She'd gotten my entire schedule out of me through small talk in HB lab before I realized she had an ulterior motive.

"Uh…I'm sort of swamped, Liza. I promised to do something with my roommate and I only get coffee on Sunday morning."

Me and my big mouth.

She smiled. "Sunday morning? Okay, I can meet you Sunday morning," she said hopefully. Tanner looked between the two of us with a knowing smirk.

"Well…it's sort of something I do by myself." I moaned inwardly.

"Ryan, Claire told me that you were brilliant in micro. I'm almost failing! *Please* help me."

Am I really going to fall for this bullshit?

I looked at her sappy face and gave in. I didn't want her failing on my conscience.

"Okay, look, Liza. I'll meet you in the lower level of the library at 11 am on Sunday then."

"No coffee? Wouldn't we be able to talk better at Java Joe's than at the library?"

Java Joe's is my place to call Julia.

"Nope. I need to go to the library later in the day so that works better for me. I'll see you there."

I turned and motioned with my head for Tanner to continue walking, leaving her there on the sidewalk with her mouth hanging open.

"Bye, Liza," he murmured.

After we got a few feet further across the commons, Tanner finally spoke up.

"That girl wants your ass bad, Ryan. Damn!"

I shrugged. "She's…not my type," I said sardonically but I couldn't help grinning. Sure it was flattering to be wanted, but she didn't have chestnut hair and liquid green eyes.

"Um…she's *every* guy's type. She's a *willing* piece of ass. I've never seen a woman so willing to be violated. It doesn't have to mean anything."

I cringed at his crudeness and shrugged.

"It would complicate my life and I guarantee that it *would* mean something to *Liza*. The way she looks at me creeps me out. She'd turn into a stalker or something."

He laughed. "I'll take that kind of stalker. She's hot."

It all depends on your perspective.

"Have at it, man." We walked across the parking lot to my CRV. He lived a few blocks from me and it had become my habit to drop him off on my way.

"What's the real reason, Ryan?" he probed.

I paused before turning on the ignition.

"I'm here to work, not chase tail."

He leaned back in the seat in exasperation. "Hell, Ryan. You're either gay or seriously in love to not take advantage of that opportunity. I know you're not gay or you'd be chasing my fine ass." Tanner laughed out loud, clearly amused with himself.

I smiled as I pulled up to his apartment complex. *Like being gay and in love were mutually exclusive?*

"Well, I'm not gay." I smirked at him and waited for his inquisition.

"Who is she then? Do I know her?"

I shook my head. "It's…well, it's complicated and you'll just make fun of my ass."

"Dude…I won't."

My phone jingled in my pocket. Julia. *Right on cue.*

I pulled it out and read the message.

Day from hell. Had a story miss deadline, so holding presses and chasing down photos. Still at the office so can't talk tonight. I'm sorry. Missing u.

I sighed. Even our phone time was getting less frequent, sometimes as long as two or three days between conversations. My disappointment was written all over my face as I shoved the phone back into my pocket.

"I bet that was the complication," he guessed wisely.

I smiled. "Yeah. You have no idea how complicated, Tanner."

He raised his hands. "Well?"

"I don't really know what to tell you. She's been my best friend for years, but I'm in love."

"And?" Tanner prompted. "How does she feel about you?"

"She's admitted that I'm the most important person in her life." He looked at me and whistled.

"What? We'd only begun to explore our feelings and now she's got this huge-ass job in Los Angeles and I'm here."

He brought a hand down on my shoulder. "Well...that's a long way from here. You could still play around a little, man. She'd never know."

"*I'd* know. And...I told you before. I'm not interested in anybody else. I've waited four damn years for Julia to see me as more than a friend. I'm not about to fuck it up. For *any* reason; certainly not Liza Nash."

I smiled at the truth in those words. The thought of sex with anyone else left me cold and I didn't care if Tanner thought I was a pussy for admitting it.

"You're right. It *is* complicated."

I nodded and ran a hand through my hair. "Maybe you'll meet her. Then you'll get it."

He opened the door and the chilly air rushed in. Tanner laughed at me as he closed the door.

Whatever, man. You'd never understand having a real connection with a woman. Dickhead.

*****

I sat at the table with my soy cappuccino and waited for Julia's call. She'd texted earlier and said she was going for a run and would call when she got to her Starbucks. I glanced at my watch. *10:15. Shit.*

I went over my microbiology and immunology notes so that I'd be prepared for Liza's questions. My plan was to get in, help as quickly as possible and get out. I felt the bile rise up in my throat at the thought of sitting alone with that ditz for an hour. I vowed I wouldn't allow it to be any longer than that.

"Ah...finally." I breathed into the phone, picturing her face, flushed and wind-burned, her hair wild and eyes sparkling. "There's my girl."

Julia's musical laughter rewarded me. "Ya think?"

"Mmmmm...I *know*."

"So are you sitting at the table by the window?" her voice was a little out of breath.

We'd even taken some photos on our phones and shared them, making it easier to imagine what the other was doing that way. It was comforting to picture her in her surroundings.

"Yes. How was your run?" I asked, closing my eyes and wishing she were sitting in front of me.

"Eh...You know I hate running." I could hear the scraping of the wooden chair against the floor as she pulled it out.

"Then why do it?" I asked quietly.

"Ryan...would you have my ass explode? My work schedule keeps me from going to the gym enough, so I have to squeeze in whatever I can."

"Yeah, I know the feeling." I was talking about her squeezing me into her schedule like she did exercise, but she'd think I meant I had a hectic schedule, too. "You'd never explode." Thinking of her body made a warm flush seep under my skin. She sensed the change in my voice and changed the subject.

"What are you doing today?"

"Oh, studying for a while and then Aaron and I are organizing a game of football in the park."

"Mmmm…that sounds fun. Wish I could watch." Her voice was warm but it sounded distant, like she was preoccupied.

"I do, too. Aaron brings Jenna, but she's more like the heckling squad than a cheerleader, and she never brings treats."

Julia's laughter tinkled on the other end. "Hmm…funny you should say that, cause I sent you something, moody boy."

Pleasure enveloped me and I grinned. "Really? When?"

"You were disappointed Friday when we couldn't talk on the phone, so I stayed up and baked. I mailed them Saturday. Probably get it tomorrow."

"You're amazing. I don't deserve you." My voice was low and throaty. I longed for her, ached for her in ways I never dreamed were possible. My fingers fiddling around my coffee cup blurred before my eyes.

"That's for sure," Julia teased. "I have to go into the office later. Sound fun?"

"They work you too hard, Julia. I don't like it."

"One of the photographers lost a digital card and we have to redo an entire shoot. It's putting the January issue behind because I had to secure the models and locations all over again. The money we're losing is astronomical, so we had to increase the page count by 16 to pay for it. The Sales Department is scrambling to sell more ads. I can only fill fifty percent of the space with editorial or we'd still be in the red. An eight page fill is a lot to come up with at the last minute," she groaned.

"You sound like a full-fledged editor. Why does this fall on you?" I asked, exasperated. She sounded so tired and they were literally working the hell out of her.

"Ah. Well...no, the junior editor gets the *shit detail,* i.e. nights and weekends. It's just part of it. I'm working on getting a promotion, you know. Some gorgeous man I know wants me in NYC." The smile behind her words made my heart pound.

"Couldn't happen soon enough for me, babe, but I still hate how hard you have to work." I ran a hand through my hair as the familiar ache settled in my chest, "I miss you."

"For some reason, I'm really missing you, too..." I smiled as the ache eased a little at those beautiful words. I hoped the reason was because she was as in love with me as I was with her.

"Ryan!" I started in my chair at the annoying sound of Liza's nasally voice. I glanced around. She was coming toward me before I could warn Julia.

I held up my hand to hold her off, but Liza pulled out the chair and unloaded her backpack on the table with a thud.

"So...*this* is Sunday coffee!"

Damn it! Couldn't she see I was on the phone?

Julia was hesitant on the other end and I could feel her pulling back, becoming distant.

"Well...I guess I should get going."

"Julia, wait. Please."

Liza looked at me expectantly and I could feel my mouth settle into a tight angry line at her intrusion.

"Um...it, uh...sounds like you're busy and I've got to get to the office. Mike is waiting for me anyway."

The sound of his name grated on my nerves like nails down a chalk board. I didn't know anything about this guy other than he was a photographer that worked with Julia *a lot.*

"What should I order?" Liza interrupted again.

"Can I call you later?" I said softly into the phone.

Julia's voice was stiff when she answered after a brief hesitation. What *the hell* was she thinking?

"Um...I'll be busy the rest of the day, Ryan. Seems like you are, too. Let's just...talk when we talk. Bye."

"Julia..." the phone went dead in my hand.

I sat staring angrily at Liza as she opened her backpack and took out her notebook. "So? What's good here?" She completely ignored my irritated expression and prattled on.

"Liza, I thought we were meeting at the library, in what? 20 minutes?" I was annoyed and didn't care if it showed.

"Oh, we were, but I thought this would be more fun." It was apparent in the way she was dressed, her facial expression and how she looked at me that she was hoping to turn this into a date, one that ran beyond morning coffee or tutoring.

I had my notes out already, so I flipped a couple of pages back and waited.

She got up and ordered a beverage and then looked at me. I hastily got up and paid for her coffee. I felt irritated at being forced into this situation but my mother would kill me if I didn't act properly.

"So Ryan, where are you from? Claire told me that you were from Illinois, but what part?" Her cheeks flushed as she watched me stare at her. My eyes were hard but I sighed.

"Chicago. Look, Liza, let's just get to the books, ok? Do you have questions?" I asked sardonically.

She pouted as she looked at me. "I just want to know you better, is that so bad? I saw that movie, *Chicago*."

Seriously? I inwardly cringed. The movie was set in the 1920's and didn't show any of the city as it was now.

"Anyway, it looked sort of pretty, but so much crime, right? Ick."

Not any more than any other major city, dipshit. "Make sure never to move there, then," I said flatly. The fine rein I held on my annoyance was slipping fast. "Liza, it's important that I remain focused on school during my time in Boston. You should, too, judging by the trouble you're having in microbiology. I'm really, uh, not looking..."

Her lower lip trembled, her feelings clearly hurt. Instantly I felt contrite, but I was also worried about the repercussions with Julia.

"Look...I'm sorry. I'm just preoccupied. I've got a lot on my mind."

"My micro teacher hates me. When I ask for help, he just tells me to read the book. I *hate* reading!"

I wondered how in the hell she ever got into Harvard at this rate. Fuck, she made my head ache.

"Who was on the phone?" she asked coyly, trying to gauge my expression. I stopped digging in my backpack for a pen and glanced up at her quickly before resuming what I was doing.

"That isn't important. We're here for microbiology, so..."

"Ryan!"

I pulled the pen out and opened the book to the chapter on viruses and how they attached to human cells. "Yeah?"

She reached across the table to put a cold hand on mine. "Can't we be friends? We're forced in that damn lab together, and I just thought we might make the best of it. What's wrong with that?"

Nothing, if that was what she wanted.

I pulled my hand back and picked up the coffee as I leaned back in my chair; as if getting farther away from her physically would make her back off. Her perfume was making me gag anyway. It was sweet and flowery and made my nose burn.

"Look, Harvard has always been my dream and friends are just…not a priority for me. It's nothing personal."

"All work and no play make Ryan a dull boy. And besides, whoever was on the phone was a *friend*, so…" she began but I cut her off shortly.

"No. She was not a friend. More like a lifetime commitment."

For a brief moment I saw disappointment and hurt flash across her features before it changed into a calculating stare.

"But she's not here…in Boston?"

I bit my lip and waited. "Are we studying or not? You have ten seconds to decide or I need to leave."

"Ok, we'll study, Mr. Cranky Pants. But Ryan, I *am* in Boston," she said suggestively and scooted her chair closer around the table. "Don't forget that."

Just focus on the pages, Ryan. And get away from this bitch as fast as you possibly can.

Julia ~

I was exhausted after a full day of working with Mike on location. The apartment was dark, so Ellie was either out with Harris or in bed. I turned the small lamp on in the entryway and threw the mail on the side table.

I loved my job, but hated the long hours and never seeing Ryan. I longed for the days when I'd call him and within minutes he was plopping down next to me. Lately, we weren't even talking much.

Like today. I missed him so much it was practically unbearable.

My heart thumped inside my chest at the sound of that woman in the background. Things were getting weird, which I should expect, with the distance and lack of communication between us.

This was the longest we'd ever gone without seeing each other and there was so much we didn't know. For instance, what were we to each other and who was that woman? Was he dating someone? What was he doing with his time and who was he doing it with? Was he lonely? Did he miss me?

Maybe I didn't want to know. It was my own damn fault. I should have taken the opportunity to have him that last night in Boston. Then maybe I wouldn't be feeling sorry for myself and he'd have no doubt that I wanted him.

I kicked the shoes off my aching feet and wandered into my bedroom, unbuttoning my blouse and going into my closet to hang up the jacket to my plum colored suit. The closet was full of similar outfits. Thank God Ellie had connections in the fashion industry. She set me up with everything I could possibly need. I had two dozen suits from the hottest designers and just as many pairs of the latest shoes and bags lined the shelves.

I shed the rest of my clothes and padded into the bathroom and turned on the water in the tub. I took a towel off the rack and, wrapping it around me, went to get a glass of wine. The bright numbers on the microwave clock glared at me. *11 PM.* I silently groaned, letting my head fall back on my way back to the bathroom.

So much for Ryan calling *later*. It was 2 AM in Boston.

I lit the candle and sank down into the hot, scented water. With the wine balancing in my right hand, I closed my eyes and tried to clear my mind of work, of Mike's blatant flirting, and of missing Ryan.

Missing Ryan.

I sighed and brought my free hand to my temple. My head ached and my fingers pushed to offset the pressure. Was I was trying to erase the pain or the sound of that irritating voice behind Ryan's on the telephone? I struggled to picture the face and body that went with it.

Ugh. I was back in college again, alone and longing for him while he was with some other woman. *If being on opposite coasts didn't change that shit, what would?*

I drew a shaky breath. Ryan and I needed to talk. This wasn't working and it was driving me crazy; this helpless feeling that made me sick to my stomach. Since I wasn't moving to New York anytime soon, the only way to avoid it was to create even more distance from him, and know even less of what was going on in his life. But, was knowing less even possible? Considering how we are at the polar opposite of where we were two months ago, I didn't think so. *That amazing night in Boston...*being so close to him, thinking we were finally going to be more, had completely messed up our best friend dynamic.

Now this woman; what I didn't know, wouldn't hurt me.

Yeah, right.

What did I expect? I took this job and was devoting every waking hour to it. *I did this* knowing he'd wanted me in New York.

He was beautiful and intelligent, with everything to offer. Women must be throwing themselves at him, and one thing was certain, he was all man. I couldn't expect that he'd be celibate, especially when we hadn't even talked about the state of our relationship.

I'd placed my Blackberry on the small table beneath the window next to the bathtub within reach, just in case. Pathetic.

I sat there for a while and added more hot water to the tub, sipping my wine until my eyes started to droop, when the phone vibrated on the table.

I reached out and grabbed it quickly, my heart praying it was Ryan. Water splashed out of the tub and onto the tile floor, saturating my towel.

Crap.

"Hello?"

"Hey." Ryan's voice was tired, but still velvet and soothing.

"It's late, Ryan. Why are you still up?"

"Well…I'm happy to talk to you, too!" he snapped.

I sighed. Shit this wasn't where I wanted to begin this conversation.

"I am happy to talk to you, but I don't want you to be tired."

He was irritated. "Fuck, Julia. I'm a big boy. I go to med school and *everything*."

My lips flat lined and I frowned. "Did you call just to be a dick?"

"No." He sighed deeply. "I thought we needed to talk and I can't reach you any other time of day." His frustration poured through the phone.

"I'm sorry, but um…you've been pretty unavailable, too. It's just how things are right now. It isn't the way I want it."

"How *do* you want it then?" He was impatient and pissy.

"Do we have to have this fight again? I'm doing everything I can to get a damn promotion but I haven't been here long enough, Ryan!"

Silence. I could hear him breathing hard on the other end of the phone.

When he didn't answer, I continued softly, "Besides, it sounded like I'd just be in the way anyway."

"Don't start that shit!" he answered sharply. "You know I want you here. That girl was just someone I was helping with coursework."

"How convenient it was in the middle of our phone call," I said bitterly. "Why didn't you tell me?" I felt my throat thicken and tears prick the back of my eyes. My voice was trembling and I wasn't sure if it was my emotions or the water getting cold around me that was making me shiver.

"She followed me! We were supposed to meet at the library!" I could picture him running his hands through his hair.

"It doesn't matter, Ryan. It's none of my business."

"I can't take this shit, Julia. Of course it's your business!" he said angrily.

I didn't answer; instead rising from the water and finding a towel in the hall closet, since the other one now lay in a saturated heap.

"You were in the bathtub?" He heard the water slosh.

My teeth chattered as I answered. "Y…y…yeah."

He groaned on the other end of the phone, "Oh, God."

I wrapped the towel around me and went into my room. The sheets were soft and welcoming as I pulled the covers up to my chin.

"I'm freezing. Sorry for the chattering."

He took a deep breath.

"So now you're in the bed, *naked*? You're killing me."

I felt my body react to his voice and his words. My skin practically vibrated with it.

"Ryan…I realize that this distance thing is a problem and we should have talked before. I get how unfair it is. I mean…I don't even know what the hell is going on with you."

"What I know is that I miss the shit out of you," he said softly, but with defeat in his tone.

My eyes burned like fire. "I miss you, too…but what do you miss? I mean…are you missing your friend?"

"Yes." My heart sank and a tear slipped silently from beneath my lashes and fell onto my pillowcase. "But I also miss what we should have between us. I feel cheated. I mean we were finally…" he began tentatively.

"I know. I don't know what's going to happen now, but the fact is…I'm here and you're there. I…well, it doesn't look like I'll be able to transfer until I've been at Glamour for at least a year. It seems like forever and…you're a man—"

"What exactly are you *saying?*" his voice was sharper again, sardonic and pissed.

"I'm saying that I understand if you just want to be friends…for now."

"Julia, why are you pushing me away? Is there someone that *you're* seeing? That photographer?"

"What? No! Ryan…but it doesn't seem fair that you…" My voice was betraying me, emotion making my words stilted. I tried to swallow the lump in my throat as more tears fell. I snuffled.

"Julia. Please stop this. I can't do this on the phone."

What am I supposed to do? I felt like I was falling apart.

"This is what I've been afraid of; that trying to have some sort of romantic relationship would make things weird between us, and I really don't want that. I…just…"

"I can't…don't cry. I'm sorry. I'm just so nuts when we argue, especially when I can't get to you to fix it. Are you going to San Francisco for Thanksgiving?" His voice was tired and I ached to put my arms around him.

"Maybe, I don't know for sure. Dad might have to work anyway and who knows what emergency will come up here. If I have to work the Friday after, I won't have time to go home. Are you going to Chicago?"

"No. I'm coming to you. That's…if you want me. We need to figure this shit out and not on the damned phone."

I rolled onto my side and curled into a ball, drawing my knees to my chest. "Of course, I want you." The double meaning of the words throbbed through me. Did he understand?

"I miss you, sweetheart; so much." Hearing the endearment made it more like he was my boyfriend, like maybe this was real. I ached to tell him I loved him, but didn't want the first time to be on the phone.

His voice was throbbing with emotion. "That girl really was just some airhead from my Gross Anatomy group. She's nothing but a pain in my ass. Really, Julia."

"Okay."

"What is Ellie doing for Thanksgiving?" The velvet voice became even more velvet.

"Going to Harris' parents, I think."

"For the whole weekend?" His words were slow and I could picture him in my mind; sitting on the floor in front of his bed, plucking at his eyebrow or lower lip.

"I think so. Why?"

"Can you tell Paul that you can't make it and I'll tell my parents that I have to stay at school? I'll come to Los Angeles. We're going to finish what we started that night in Boston, okay?"

My heart thrummed in my chest and heat and moisture pooled in my lower body. He was so sexy; his voice was making love to me.

"Jules?"

"Yes. I'm scared, Ryan."

"Of me?"

"Of losing you. As much as it kills me to think of you with someone else, I can't bear losing you. What if…"

"Julia, you can never lose me. Don't you know that yet?"

I nodded even though he couldn't see and took a shaky breath that he must have heard. "Mmm huh."

"So, I'll fly in the Wednesday before Thanksgiving."

"Mmmmm, hmm."

"Are you okay? I worry about you all the time." I closed my eyes and love swelled through my chest to the point of not being able to breathe.

"Yes, now that I can finally hear your voice," I said breathlessly.

"Oh, baby." I heard the blankets rustle and the throp when he punched his pillow. "We'll make this work because I can't live with any other option. I miss you, honey, but I'm going to let you go to bed. Get some clothes on your sexy ass or I won't be able to sleep just thinking about it," he teased lightly.

I smiled through my tears.

"And Julia? Don't forget to remember me…okay?" He said the words he'd said before I left him in Boston.

"That's impossible," I said achingly. "I hope you enjoy the package. You should get it tomorrow."

"You're an angel. I can't wait. I'll call you."

"Yes. Goodnight, Ryan."

"Night, babe."

I rolled over and closed my damp eyes as the call ended. Three and a half weeks and I'd be in his arms. My heart and body ached in anticipation. I'd never want that weekend to end.

~4~

Julia ~

I put the story boards for the February issue in my office and locked the door behind me, rushing madly to get out of the office and on my way to the airport. Smiling from ear to ear, I ran down the hall to the elevator. I was so excited about seeing Ryan after so long that I wasn't paying enough attention to where I was walking and a split-second later, felt myself slipping on the smooth marble of the corridor, falling backwards and struggling to avoid landing flat on my ass. My hand flew out to brace myself on the wall. By some miracle, I managed to stay upright but my purse went flying and the contents scattered in several directions.

"Shit," I muttered. I glanced at the time as I shoved my phone back into the bag. 6:16. Ryan's plane was landing at 7:30. and if I didn't hurry I'd never make it to the airport in time. Traffic this time of the evening was the worst.

Andrea, my boss' personal assistant, ran over to help me pick up my things.

"Julia! Are you okay?" Andrea was a beautiful girl with a rosy complexion, sparkling blue eyes and mops of red tresses that hung to the middle of her back. She started at Glamour a few months before me. I coordinated a lot of the photo shoots, production schedules and talent through her, which required us to work closely together. We had become good friends.

Andrea handed me my wallet and a lipstick that had fallen out of my purse with my phone. "Big plans, huh?" she asked.

"Uh, yeah. My…" I hesitated. *What was Ryan, exactly?* "My best friend is visiting. I haven't seen him since August." I couldn't stop myself from smiling and I quickly stood up. We resumed the trek to the elevators.

"Him?" She smirked at me. "Is he gorg? What does he do?" Andrea was inquisitive by nature, but especially when it had something to do with the opposite sex. She was a big flirt, but didn't have a steady boyfriend. I hadn't mentioned Ryan before. I was keeping him a secret until I knew exactly what the hell was going on between us.

The floors dinged past as I fiddled with my car keys. "Yes. He's very handsome." I closed my eyes and tried to steady my voice. "He's a med student at Harvard." I couldn't help bragging Ryan up a little bit. I was so proud of him.

"Wow, a would-be doctor, and *Harvard*." Her eyes widened. "Even more impressive."

"Yeah, that pretty much sums him up, all right." The elevators opened and I headed to my car. "Happy Thanksgiving, Andrea!" I said as I hurried off.

"Hey, he sounds amazing, Julia. Maybe you can hook me up?" Her laughter echoed off the concrete walls of the garage.

"Nope! He's all mine!" I said happily as I opened the door to my car and threw my purse in the passenger seat.

As I drove through Los Angeles on my way to LAX, I almost chewed off my lower lip.

Why was I so damn nervous?

Yes, I was so excited that I was jumping out of my freaking skin, but I was uncharacteristically nervous, as well. This was *Ryan*, and things would be as easy between us as they'd always been.

We'd spent almost every waking, and a lot of sleeping, hours together for the last four years, and knew each other inside and out. He gave me comfort, made me laugh and feel safe. But…this was also the Ryan who made my panties damp and my heart beat faster. I loved him more than anyone else in my life. More than I'd *ever* love anyone for the rest of my life. I knew it as sure as I was breathing. He could take me to heaven or drop me in hell and that fact scared me to death.

I took a deep breath, trying to steady my nerves. Tonight would change everything between us. Whether we made love or not, I planned on telling him that I loved him. The words had been aching inside of me for so long, especially since the night in the car after we'd found out he'd gotten into Harvard, and then the last night we'd been together in Boston.

My heart thumped hard within my chest as I pulled into the terminal parking garage and I found a spot close to the elevator.

I wondered if Ryan would think it weird to see me in my Dior pencil skirt and Jimmy Choo heels when he was used to me in jeans and Converse. I glanced in the rear-view mirror as I ran a hand through my hair and dotted some light pink gloss on my lips. I looked different but hoped he'd like the changes.

Here goes nothing…

As I walked into the terminal, my stomach was a mass of butterflies but I couldn't stop smiling. People were smiling back at me as I went. A few men were very obvious in their appraisals of my legs or looking me up and down. Normally, I might be annoyed by the blatant ogling, but nothing could ruin my happy mood.

My phone dinged in my purse and I struggled to pull it out and keep walking toward the security check point and wandered around looking for a good place to wait. I found a Starbucks and took a seat before reading Ryan's message.

I'm on the ground. Hope you're already here. I can't wait to see you!

My body was shaking and my heart racing as my eyes searched the stream of people pouring out of the United terminal. I watched for a wild head of sexy golden hair to move through the throng, but the minutes ticked by and hundreds of people passed without any sign of him. The clicking of my shoe on the floor drew attention so I got up to pace back and forth in front of the window, glancing back through the crowds as I went.

Get a grip, Julia!

I shoved my hands in the pocket of my skirt and stopped dead. Ryan was coming up the long ramp carrying his black leather duffle bag and blue parka. Wearing a Stanford University baseball hat, a white button down with the sleeves rolled up to his elbows and jeans, he made my breath stop. I was frozen to the spot as I watched him move toward me.

When he came into the terminal he stopped and looked around... My hungry eyes devoured him as the seconds ticked by. He was so beautiful and I hadn't seen him in so long, I allowed myself this one small indulgence.

He searched in a circle until finally his eyes fell upon mine. He paused to look at me, taking in the differences, and his head moved to one side slightly and his eyes narrowed. A huge grin split his face as he began moving quickly toward me.

I willed my frozen legs to move and ran to him. Immediately, he dropped his bag at our feet and gathered me close, his arms tight around my waist under my suit jacket and his face buried in my hair. I wound my arms around his neck and turned my face into him, resting my forehead just below his ear. He smelled delicious and his hot breath on my skin felt like gold. Like Ryan.

"Julia," he breathed. "I missed you so fucking much."

Emotion surged through me and I felt the familiar stinging behind my eyes and the tightness in my chest as I held on to him for dear life. *If I let go, he'll disappear.*

He kissed the side of my face and my temple until finally I raised my damp eyes to his beautiful blue ones. "Ryan, I..." he stopped me when his mouth swooped down and took mine in a hungry kiss. He kissed me like it was the end of the world and I let him, the tears falling softly on my face at the same time as my mouth moved frantically with his. Our tongues laved each other and the kisses became slower, deeper but just as intense. My body started to react and I was losing myself.

All that existed for me was this man.

Someone walking by whistled and brought us out of our little bubble. Ryan dragged his mouth from mine, and his hand brushed my hair back from my face as he stared into my eyes.

"What?" I asked breathlessly.

"You're gorgeous. I can't take my eyes off of you." He smiled softly and rested his head on mine. My mouth ached to reach for his again but I remembered where we were.

"You don't have to for the next 4 days." I smiled happily. The stubble on his chin tickled my fingers. I kissed him briefly on the mouth before stepping back and taking his hand in mine.

"Promise?" he said softly. I nodded and nudged his shoulder gently with my own, the gesture so familiar.

"Come on." I tugged on his hand.

He smiled, picked up his bag and coat and we walked through the airport to the garage.

Ryan loaded his bag into the backseat of my new Mazda and I threw him the keys.

"Are you sure? This is your baby." His eyes sparkled as he came around to open the passenger side door for me. I couldn't resist touching him and I brought my hand to the front of his shirt above his belt. The flat of my hand moved up over the taut muscles of his abdomen to rest over his heart. I could feel it beating beneath my fingers.

"Yeah. Of course. You always drive, don't you?" I said as I slid into the black leather seat. The sound of the shutting door echoed through the garage. Smiling, Ryan went around and got into the driver's side.

"Ugh," he said as he banged his head on the ceiling and then reached down to slide the seat back to accommodate his height. "Some things never change, eh? Except with those heels, I'd expect you to have the seat further back."

I rolled my eyes. "My toes are still the same distance away no matter how high the heels are. Duh."

The warmth in his eyes made me flush as he started the car and put it in reverse.

"So, um…you noticed the shoes then?" I smiled at him.

He stopped at the booth to pay for the parking and gave the attendant some money. "Uh…I noticed everything, Julia." He looked at me. "You're really…beautiful."

"I was afraid you wouldn't like me all *'officed' up*…that you'd prefer me in jeans and a t-shirt." I leaned back in my seat but turned toward him so I could study his profile.

"Do you really want me to answer that now?" His hand reached for mine. "Later." The word sounded like a promise.

Heat infused underneath the skin on my neck and face, and I bit my lip, trying to hide the smile that I couldn't contain. It felt good to be with him like this, knowing that finally we were both willing and wanting to take the relationship further. It felt…perfect.

His thumb ran circles over the top of my hand, his fingers threaded with mine. There was a live current of electricity that raced over my skin with each little movement he made. My mouth went dry and my body reacted. He had me teeming with desire with only the briefest of touches.

I can't believe how much I love him.

I gave him directions that took us past downtown L.A. and east of Beverly Hills. Ellie and I shared an apartment in Glendale. It was close enough to downtown for me and even closer so that Ellie could get to her ritzy job in Hollywood. The apartment was modest, but very nice and we kept it clean.

The sun had set two hours earlier and I sat in the dark, watching the passing lights reflect off the planes of Ryan's perfect features. He seemed content to hold my hand and drive, listening to the soft strains of the satellite radio. He looked deep in thought, like he was concentrating on something.

"What are you thinking about?" I asked softly, not wanting to disturb him, but desperately needing to know. He smiled; his white teeth bright in the darkness. The lights from the dashboard softly illuminated the space inside the car.

"Oh, you know...*you*," he paused and rubbed my hand again with his thumb, "It's incredible to *finally* be with you like this, baby. I'm just taking it all in."

I knew what he meant. We were a couple and it was evident in the way he touched me, how he looked at me and the tenor in his voice. My heart sped up and I sighed. He looked at me and then at the road. "What?" he asked.

"Nothing...just...Ryan, I've missed you. Too much." I swallowed as emotion welled again. "I was so afraid I'd lose my best friend, but I'm not going to. You're still with me, but it's..."

"So much more."

"Yes."

"I've been a complete idiot. I should have done something about this years ago. We wasted so much damn time, Julia."

"I like to think that things happen for a reason, Ryan. I still had you in my life, and really, I wouldn't change a moment of the time we spent together." I hoped he didn't hear the catch in my voice but the look on his face told me differently.

His lips were warm and reverent as they softly brushed across my knuckles, then Ryan rested our entwined hands on his thigh. "Julia." He smiled and shook his head.

"Yeah?" I smiled.

Ryan laughed and shook his head. "Nothing...just, *Julia*."

"Well, Matthews, I need to stop at the grocery store if I'm making a big spread tomorrow. I don't suppose you'd be satisfied with cold cereal and toast?" The corners of my mouth quirked in the start of a grin as I anticipated his reply.

"Pfft. Hell, *no*! I want it all! Turkey, dressing, potatoes, fresh bread and lots and lots of dessert!" Ryan said happily.

I wasn't prepared for how elated it made me to hear him talk like that and to know that I could make him so happy. I pointed to a grocery store off to the right that was only three blocks from my apartment. He parked near the door and turned the car off.

"Of course, you leave out salad or vegetables. Fucking *typical*," I added mockingly and he burst out laughing.

"Oh, okay. Salad and *vegetables*," he said reluctantly. "If you're gonna *make me*."

"*Can* I make you?" I laughed.

"I'm thinking you can make me do any damn thing you want right about now."

"Hmmm...now that sounds *really* good." My mind raced at all the things I'd like to make him do. He meant that he'd give me anything that I wanted.

"Yes. It does," he agreed devilishly and leaned over to kiss me, greedily sucking my lower lip into his mouth before pulling away. "Mmmm...so delicious."

I smiled and I couldn't resist one more little taunt. "You know what they say... Whatever makes *me* happy, will set *you* free." I bit my lip as my eyes lifted to his.

"I'm sure of it. Let's get these damn groceries, so I can start getting my orders, shall we?"

I giggled as we both got out of the car. Ryan threw his arm around my shoulders and kissed my temple on the way into the store.

Ryan ~

I was staring, but I couldn't help it. I could tell she noticed by the little glances she threw at me and the smile that danced around those gorgeous lips.

She was so incredibly beautiful. Her legs went on forever in those damn spiky heels and I wanted to ask her to take off her jacket so I could see the way her blouse clung to her body. This was Julia, but so sophisticated and sexy. She had a new confidence about her that I found extremely irresistible. She was everything I could want.

"You're sure you want turkey tomorrow?" She looked quizzically at me as she gathered some fresh herbs from the produce department.

I grinned. "With *all* the trimmings, please." I was pushing the cart, which suited me because it gave me an unobstructed view of her. I took my jacket off and threw it in the basket. "Um, aren't you *hot*, Julia?" I teased. "Maybe you should take off your jacket."

She shook her head and rolled her eyes. She knew exactly what I was up to and laughed softly.

"Ryan. You're acting like you've never seen me before," she said as we headed to the meat department and began looking over the birds. She picked out a small one that wasn't frozen after she'd rummaged through the bin.

"Well, you are different, honey. But it's *all* good." I laughed and grabbed her arm as she placed the bird in the basket. I pulled her to me and wrapped my arm around her waist.

"Stop," she said breathlessly, but I placed my mouth on the skin of her neck below her ear. I couldn't help myself. The scent of her skin, mixed with the muskiness of her perfume was enough to make me want to ravish her right there. Her hand came up to my chest and pushed against me a little.

"Mmmm…you smell so good," I whispered as I nuzzled her neck with my nose.

"I think we should finish shopping before we get arrested for indecent exposure." She was flirting and I loved it. We'd always been so careful of our feelings to keep our relationship from going anywhere romantic, and I found this new playfulness a huge turn-on.

"I don't care. I'm only kissing you a little." I let my hand slide lower to her hip and pressed her closer to my side. "I thought I was allowed now." I smiled, nuzzling a little more and my breath rushed out over her skin.

She pulled back slightly. "You're allowed…but let's get this done so we can get out of here, hmmm?"

I laughed at the tone in her voice. She wanted to be alone with me as much as I wanted to be alone with her. I wasn't about to let go of her completely, so my hand slid across her back and out to take her hand. I sighed. "Okay…more shopping," I said reluctantly.

I watched in amazement as Julia gathered everything she needed. She didn't have a list, just asked me if I wanted this dish or that and then picked out the ingredients. I would never get used to how perfect she was.

Beyond the Thanksgiving meal, we bought things to make some of my favorites, lemon muffins, Eggs Benedict, blueberry pancakes, cheesecake and Pad Thai. Things she made back in college. My heart clenched at how much my life in Boston lacked her presence. I missed her beyond reason and I'd come to depend on her more than I'd realized.

I nodded when she held up a bottle of Pinot Grigio, a Pies Porter and a Merlot. "That should hold us for the weekend, huh?"

"I'm hoping we'll get to your apartment and never leave, so get everything you need." I lowered my head and ran my hand through my hair, but my eyes never left hers.

"Um...Ellie invited us out on Friday night." She smiled when I grimaced at the prospect. "Harris' band has a gig and she wanted to see you. I'm trying not to be selfish. How about we stay in all the rest of the time?" Her green eyes sparkled.

"I guess *I'm* being selfish. I haven't been thinking much about Ellie. Soooo sorry," I teased as I squeezed her hand. My heart soared at the sympathetic look on her face as her little fingers curled around mine. "But, okay."

Julia laughed. "Mmm...thank you. Only one night," she said reassuringly.

I paid for the groceries and loaded them into the trunk of her car. The temperature had turned cooler and it was starting to mist. Los Angeles never got as cold as Boston and I found myself missing the holiday weather.

"Do you miss the cooler weather in Northern California?" I asked as I settled in behind the wheel. I thought back to the many times we used to go for walks with the snow falling and how she loved to go skiing and sledding. We had so many fun times making snowmen or having snowball fights. My favorite part was when she would start to shiver and I'd take her in my arms to warm her up.

"Yes. I miss a lot of things. But, the thing I miss the absolute most is sitting right next to me. So, I'm good," she said softly.

My heart swelled to the point of bursting as I brushed the silky skin of her chin with my fingers.

"Come here," I commanded. She leaned in and I touched my mouth to hers. "Julia," I whispered against her mouth. "I can't believe how much I've missed you."

"I can," she whispered, her lips ghosting over mine. "It's like an ache that won't go away."

My eyes closed. *God, I love this woman.*

Her fingers lightly brushed against my chin as I deepened the kiss and then her hand slid behind my head to twine in my hair. It was so sexy, having her tug on my hair and pull my mouth tighter into hers. My body reacted and my jeans suddenly got uncomfortably tight, but I couldn't stop kissing her. She was like the sweetest nectar I'd ever tasted.

Both of us panting, I rested my head against hers as we struggled to get control. I finally sat back in my seat and looked at her flushed face. Her skin was pale and translucent but for the rosy glow in her cheeks. We smiled at each other softly.

"It's like we're in high school, making out and steaming everything up! If it were colder, I'd be writing '*I heart Ryan*' on the window."

Thump. My heart stopped and the amusement left my face.

"Julia," I began but she put two trembling fingers to my mouth.

"Just...let's go home, Ryan. Please?"

"Is that an *order*?" My body protested; my mouth wanted hers.

She leaned toward me and placed a hand at the back of my head to play with the hair at the nape. Her touch made my body quake with anticipation of what was to come. My breath caught as she nodded without hesitation. "Yes. It's an order."

Julia ~

The sexual tension between Ryan and me was palpable. My skin literally vibrated whenever he looked at me. His brilliant eyes roaming over me was almost like a physical caress. Four years of waiting and wanting...*finally*, it was going to happen. Just thinking about it had me throbbing in all the right places.

Ryan brought the last of the groceries to the marble countertop while I continued to put things away.

He threw his jacket over one of the upholstered chairs in the living room before coming back into the kitchen to lean his hip near the sink. I felt nervous, my skin on fire as his gaze burned into me. I fluttered here and there between the counter, the refrigerator and pantry.

Ryan watched for a few minutes in silent contemplation, until I couldn't stand it anymore.

"Um...so how are Jenna and Aaron? You haven't mentioned them the last couple of times that we've talked."

He removed the bottle of wine I was unpacking from my hands and set it on the counter, then slid his hand down my arm and gathered my hand in his. His clear blue eyes were intent on my face.

Tugging on my hand, he brought me closer until our bodies were only a few inches apart and his other hand rested on my waist. He smelled so good and the heat radiating off his skin scorched me alive.

"They're good. Jen's working a lot of nights so she's tired and cranky, which makes Aaron cranky too." His mouth quirked at one side. It was evident that his expression wasn't about the conversation. I opened my mouth, but no words came out.

"Why the abbreviated version?" I asked finally, trying to control the tremble in my voice.

"Julia. Are you...*nervous?*" His head cocked to one side. "It's me. It's just *me*," he whispered as his hand came up to brush my hair back. "Nothing is going to happen that you don't want to happen...I promise."

I smiled a little and searched for the words I needed. "I'll talk to you about everything that's going through my head, but first, do you need anything? A shower, a drink, some food?"

The crooked grin that I loved and adored split across his face. "Yeah, there is something that I need, but it can wait...awhile," he teased and brushed his fingers down the side of my neck. Shocks ran through me, beginning where his fingers touched me and running along the nerves in my entire body.

"Hmmph." I let out my breath and then moved away from him slightly.

I kicked off my heels and sank down to my original height, allowing Ryan to tower over me. He was still 3 or 4 inches taller than me in heels, but without them, I barely reached his chin.

"I need a drink, even if you don't," I said as I went to the refrigerator and pulled out a bottle of Chardonnay that Ellie and I had opened the night before. I pulled the cork and grabbed two wine glasses from the cupboard.

With the wine and glasses in my hand, I went to the living room, flipped on the gas fireplace and poured a glass for Ryan. He reached for the glass and took a long pull on it, his eyes never leaving mine. I began to fill mine but never had the chance to finish. Ryan removed the bottle and my half filled glass and set it next to his on the coffee table.

"You're not going to let me have that...?" I began as I reached for it and took a drink. He took it from me again and returned it to its former place on the table.

Before I knew what was happening, Ryan grabbed me and pulled me down on the couch. I squealed as I landed on top of him and we both laughed briefly. He quickly situated us so we were lying on our sides facing each other, our legs twining together. His expression became serious and he pulled my hand to his mouth.

I gasped in surprise, but his face was so serious, I stopped completely and met his gaze, the prospect of the wine, forgotten.

Ryan's voice was velvet and soft. "Do you want to go first or should I?" Warmth seeped between us as his thumb traced the line of my brow and moved to my cheekbone and back again. So magnetic, I could feel the live electricity racing across my skin. I never wanted him to stop touching me. I was drowning in the deep blue depths of his eyes, completely mesmerized.

"You can...I...if you want."

"Okay." He swallowed and bit his lower lip, leaving me breathless in anticipation before he finally continued.

"I've missed you. So much."

"I've missed you, too."

He smiled at my interruption. "I thought I was going first..." His index finger came up to touch my nose softly and then my lower lip. I couldn't breathe, but my mouth turned up slightly.

His demeanor was slightly teasing, yet so serious, intent and with purpose. "I'm completely...and utterly in love with you." My eyes widened and my heart raced so fast I felt like I would die. "Night and day, you're all I think about. I miss my best friend, but I want so much more with you. From the moment we met, you've had me...captivated. It feels amazing to finally be able to say the words."

Tears welled in my eyes and my throat began to ache. His eyes searched mine as I struggled to speak.

This is it.

There was no going back. I closed my eyes and swallowed the emotion that threatened to overflow.

"Why didn't you tell me?"

"We'd become so close...I didn't want to rock the boat, but I always hoped it would turn into more." I closed my eyes as his fingers brushed the tears from my cheeks. "So, are you going to put me out of my misery or what?" he whispered, his mouth mere centimeters from my own.

I opened my eyes to find his still on my face. "I love you, too, Ryan. So much. For what feels like forever."

His hand trembled as he paused in his movements over the skin on my face. "I've needed those words for so long." He groaned as he gathered me close and let his mouth take mine hungrily. My arms slid up around his neck as I opened to his need and greedily sucked his tongue inside my mouth.

Ryan rolled over on top of me and my legs parted automatically as he sank into the cradle of my body. It felt so good to be in his arms like I'd wanted to be for so long. He was clearly as aroused as I was and his hardness pressed into me as our hips surged together, his heart beating above mine.

"Oh my God," I breathed against his mouth, unwilling to let his lips leave mine. Feeling him with me like this, and hearing him finally say that he loved me, sent my emotions into overdrive. First one then another tear squeezed from behind my closed lids.

Ryan dragged his mouth from mine to kiss the side of my jaw and up my cheek to my temple. When he tasted my tears on his tongue, he pulled back to look into my face. I closed my eyes as more tears fell. He rose up on his elbows above me and tenderly brushed my hair back as he kissed my cheek and temple again. His lips so gentle, worshiping me with each touch.

"Julia, Julia...don't cry, my love. Never cry. Did I hurt you?" The sound of my name coming off his velvet voice was like beautiful music, so reverent that it made me cry even harder and my shoulders began to shake.

"Honey...what is it? Tell me, please," he pleaded gently.

I nuzzled his nose with mine and wrapped my arms around his waist before finally bringing my eyes back up to his. "It's just...that it's a little overwhelming. I've loved you for s...so long, and I'd pretty much convinced myself that you'd only ever see me as your friend. I didn't think this would ever happen."

He smiled softly and placed one small kiss on my mouth. His mouth was open, soft and sucking ever so slightly on mine and when the kiss ended, he smiled against my lips. The flames in the fireplace cast a warm glow which flickered across the strong planes of his face. His eyes looked darker, almost black, his skin glowed golden, and his hair reflected many shades of dark and light.

He was the most beautiful thing I'd ever seen.

"Even after that last night in Boston?"

"I was afraid to hope for what I wanted with you, Ryan. We were going to be so far apart and I thought..."

"I can assure you that I have *always* seen you as a woman, Julia. Yes, you are my best friend, but I love you so much, it consumes me. I was afraid you'd shoot me down and laugh if I told you how I really felt." He paused when I shook my head.

"You know me...you feel me, don't you?"

"I was as worried as you've been, baby. And as incredible as this feels to finally be holding you like this," he pushed his hips into mine and kissed my mouth gently, "nothing is worth losing you. Nothing."

"Uhhh..." I sighed as his hips gyrated into mine. "So many times when you'd touch me or say things...I felt that maybe you loved me, but I kept telling myself that I was dreaming. I wasn't willing to lose you either...not even for a dream."

He let out a deep sigh, his chest pressing into mine. My body came alive as he touched my body, over my hips, then up again, making me tremble and crave him even more.

"I can't believe you're in my arms like this after all the wanting. But, if you'd feel more comfortable taking things slow, I'm willing to do whatever you need." His voice was seducing me even in contradiction to the words themselves.

"Really?" My blood was thundering so loudly in my excitement, that I could barely hear my own voice.

There was no way in hell that we weren't going to make love tonight, but it was fun to play with him a little. I could see the disappointment flash briefly across his perfect features before he nodded.

"Really. You give me everything just by letting me touch you like this. To be able to finally kiss you is...God, it's amazing." He rolled back and pulled me onto my side, removing the contact of our bodies directly in the spots that were driving me wild. I silently cursed at my stupidity. Ryan nodded and moved his arm around my lower back.

"I want this to work. So yes, whatever you need from me. Even if you don't want to make love until we're geographically closer. I'll understand." His fingers wound in my hair as his hand cupped the back of my head and neck. I shivered in his arms.

Our conversation of a few weeks ago came rushing back. "I only said that because I can't expect you to be celibate when we're so far apart." I knew my voice was trembling, aching as I said the words.

"Julia. Stop. I can and I will. Even if I can't be with you, I don't want anyone else. I'll give you any part of me that you want." He shrugged. "I don't...have choices where you're concerned."

My chest constricted and I gasped quietly. His words were so beautiful, the way he touched me so tender and the look in his eyes so loving, that there was no way I could doubt him.

"What if I *do* want you?" I whispered.

His eyes were as deep as the ocean when they snapped back to mine. "I'm yours. I can deny you nothing."

Did that mean he'd be okay with taking my virginity?

My heart skipped a beat. Since the day I met him, I could think of no other man touching me like that. I dated a few guys in college, mostly because I was trying to get over the love and lust I felt for Ryan, but they all paled in comparison and left me aching for him even more. My quest to distract myself from the fact that he was dating and bedding other women had failed miserably.

Should I tell him? Will it stop him from making love to me?
I didn't want to think about it, I just wanted to *feel* him.

I slid my hand down over his chest and up again, beginning to undo two of the buttons and slid my hand inside. He gasped at my touch. His skin was warm and my fingers tangled in the soft hair I found there. When I flattened the palm against him, his hand came up and pressed mine into his body. I could feel his heartbeat and his chest rise and fall with each breath.

"I've dreamed of your hands on my body, fantasized about making love to you a million times," he whispered against my mouth. I let my tongue dart out to lick his upper lip and that was all the invitation he needed to press his mouth to mine.

"Ryan...I've wanted you, to feel you pressing into me like this...wondered what it would be like to kiss you, to taste you..." I took a deep breath and said the words he needed to hear. "I've wanted to feel you inside of me."

"God, Julia. I just told you I'd wait, but I'm going to die if you keep talking like that when I can't...have you." He raised his eyes to mine and I felt my body react at his words and his hands on me, a flood of wetness spreading and the throbbing becoming unbearable.

"You *can* have me."

He was very still as his eyes searched mine, but his heart under my hand was racing, his chest heaving with the effort of his breathing.

"Are you sure? There is nothing I want more, but I want you to be sure."

My face tilted up to his and I silently begged for his mouth to return to mine. "So sure..."

He kissed me over and over, both of us clamoring to get closer to each other. Our faces tilted so our mouths fit perfectly over one another's and our tongues moved over and around, deep in each other's mouths.

He was so incredible, tasted so amazing in my mouth, his muscles playing beneath my hands as he moved to pull me closer. The kisses were deep and less frantic as Ryan struggled to gain some control and his lips tugged and teased mine, coming back for more kisses each time I thought he would stop.

"Baby...I love you so much, I'm dying," he whispered against my mouth. "I know we'll be amazing together." He was so incredibly sexy, I almost came at his voice, telling me he wanted me in that low, oozing tone was more than I could take.

"Uhhh…" I sighed. "Let's go into my room," I said softly and he nodded moving off of me and taking my hand to pull me up with him. He lifted me, sweeping me up in his arms as if I weighed nothing and strode down the hall toward the bedrooms.

"Which is yours?"

"On the left, just past the bathroom."

I snuggled into his chest and tried to calm my nerves. I was almost 23 years old and a virgin. Would his view of me change? We'd shared everything; but our sex lives with others was carefully avoided. I could see now that Ryan hadn't wanted to know the details of my dates any more than I had wanted to know the details of his.

He laid me gently on the bed and placed a soft, wet kiss on my mouth before turning to close the bedroom door. His shirt was almost all the way unbuttoned from my play in the living room but he finished the job and threw it off his shoulders on his way back to the bed.

I gasped at how beautiful he was.

The muscles of his broad shoulders and strong arms, his chest and abs, all left me breathless. The small amount of hair on his smooth skin grew thicker in a line that disappeared into the low waist of his jeans. I sat up on my knees so I could touch him, my fingers sliding up from his stomach and over his chest. His arms slid around my waist, his hands fisting in the back of my dress as he drew me close and buried his open mouth in the curve of my neck and shoulder.

He groaned against my skin as his mouth sucked on the sensitive skin, sending shivers through my entire body. "Oh, Ryan…God."

He drew back to look into my eyes, one hand coming around to cup my face, and his thumb rubbing my lower lip until my mouth parted and my breath left in a rush. "Jesus, you're so beautiful. You're beautiful to everyone, but to me there is nothing more exquisite than seeing the love...the *want*...in your eyes when you look at me. It's a miracle."

My hands moved into the hair at the back of his head and pulled his mouth to mine as my body throbbed and ached for his to fill me. "Make love to me," I begged.

I trembled as his fingers unzipped the back of my dress and slid it down, his touch igniting every inch of my skin. I had dressed carefully that morning in anticipation of this moment. I wanted to please him, to give him everything. I gasped against his mouth as his hands followed the dress down around my knees where I kneeled on the bed.

Ryan's eyes darkened as he looked upon the black lace bra and my chest heaved in anxious anticipation. His hands moved over me, discovering the matching thong panties and he shuddered. "Oh, God. Look at you," he whispered as his other hand ghosted over the swell of my breasts visible above the top of the lace, before he bent to place his open mouth where his hands had been.

"I want to taste every inch of your skin. It's all I've thought about. Julia..."

His fingers curled around one of my bra straps and dragged it down as his hot mouth followed the path it took across my skin. He had me gasping for breath, my head lolling to one side as I clung to him helplessly.

I reached behind me and unhooked my bra, letting it fall away from my body. Ryan's hands came up to cup the outsides of my breasts, both of his thumbs grazed over the nipples. I was already on fire, but they tightened even more under his delicate touch.

Suddenly, Ryan's arms enfolded me and lowered me to the bed, his mouth hungry on my own. He kissed me deeply before dragging his mouth down my neck and across my chest as he loomed over me. His mouth sucked one nipple in as his tongue played and licked. He moaned against me and I almost died. His mouth was scorching and the ache in my lower body intensified.

"Ryan...I want...will you come to me?" I turned my head and kissed his forearm that was supporting his weight.

He stood up and pulled the dress from around my feet, tossing it aside before lifting one leg and then the other to remove the thigh high stockings and letting them drift to the floor. "Oh, babe, you're so sexy. I'm...undone."

He unbuttoned his jeans and slid the zipper down before completely shedding them along with his boxer briefs. He was so beautiful and his erection rock hard and ready. I stared as he lay down beside me and rested his head on one hand so he could look down upon me.

His hand softly brushed over my skin, sending goose bumps cascading everywhere he touched. I was hesitant, but I reached out to touch him as his hand flattened on my stomach, between my navel and the top of my thong.

Ryan's head fell back and he gasped as my fingers closed around his length. "Is it ok to touch you like this?" I whispered.

"It's...incredible. Uh...Oh, Jesus."

My heart swelled in my chest. "I want to give you pleasure, Ryan." I squeezed as I pulled my hand up from the base over the head, my thumb catching the clear drop of fluid there to rub it around the skin. It felt like steel encased in silk.

"I'm wound so tight, you have to let me touch you first...I need to taste you, my love."

He bent to kiss and suckle the skin along the top of my panties as his thumb hooked under the edge and began to drag them down. I kept touching him and his hips surged in my hand. He moved down on the bed to a place where I couldn't reach and placed his forehead on my hipbone. He inhaled deeply and I blushed, knowing what he wanted.

I felt him shudder as his hand moved from the flat of my stomach down to the secret place that ached for his touch.

He kissed my stomach and the top of my thighs as his hand nudged my legs apart and parted the tender flesh he was seeking. He groaned against my skin. "Julia...Finally. Mmmm, you're so wet..."

"It's you, Ryan. Because of you."

I felt him insert two fingers inside me and I gasped. "Dear God, you're so tight. Open for me, Julia. Please." The tone in his voice was dripping sex, low and urgent. I couldn't deny him and my legs fell open to him.

He bent his head and kissed me, running his tongue up my center as his pushed his fingers inside again. "Uh..." My back arched of its own volition and I surged toward his mouth. It was like nothing I'd ever felt and pleasure shot through my entire body.

"Mmmm," he groaned and the vibrations against the sensitive skin made me writhe and clench beneath him. I must surely be dreaming another of my intimate, amazing dreams where Ryan made me completely his. His tongue and mouth continued the sweet torture and his fingers inside of me pressed upward to rub back and forth. I lost track of time and didn't know if it had been seconds or hours, but the sensations were more than I could bear and I felt myself start to lose control. My body began to clench and spasm around his fingers and against his mouth. Wave after wave, he brought me through it.

"You are so incredible, so beautiful." He kissed me one last time and then moved up my body, his mouth running across my stomach and breasts until I couldn't stand it anymore. "You don't know how many times I've wanted to do that, Julia. There were so many times in the dorms or our rooms as we studied that I wanted to throw you down and have you. So many damn times that I could barely contain myself," he whispered against my mouth, "I've literally ached with it. The way you smell and taste is more than I could have dreamed of."

My heart was pounding in my chest and I wanted him more than I'd ever wanted anything in my life. I wanted to feel him inside my body, be around him, and to consume him.

"Kiss me, Ryan…Oh God, have me." The muscles on his body were solid and defined, and my arms pulled him down and he settled between my legs. I could feel his erection, hard and huge against my thigh and I turned slightly to bring it into direct contact with my center.

Ryan was staring at my mouth and then his eyes closed as I moved against him. "You're so hot," his voice thickened as his hips rocked into mine, grinding and rubbing our most sensitive parts together. My fingers raked down his back and grasped the muscles of his butt. "Are you sure you're ready? Are you protected? Should I get a condom?"

He lowered his arms to rest on both sides of my head and brushed the hair back and I nodded. I licked my lip and pulled his mouth to mine. "No, I mean, I'm on the pill and I trust you. Please."

His beautiful blue eyes stared down into mine as I felt him seeking and finding my entrance. I tensed, knowing what was coming, but he moved against me sliding back and forth against my clitoris and the sensations began to swell all over again. Wetness surged between my legs and the tip of him slipped inside. He watched my face and moved in a little more. When he felt the barrier of my hymen he stopped dead, starting to pull out, but my hands on his butt held him in place.

"No. Don't stop."

"Julia…are you a virgin?" The expression on his face went from wonder to confusion and trepidation.

"I wanted you to be the first Ryan, okay? I love you so much." I felt the tears well up. "Please don't stop." I surged against him and he sank a little deeper into me, but yet he resisted.

"I don't want to hurt you, baby. Uhhhh, Julia," he gasped against my mouth as I moved against him. "I don't think I *can* stop now even if I wanted to."

"Then don't. Please. Just kiss me, Ryan. I'm yours."

He licked my upper lip and sucked my lower one into his mouth as he pushed in further. I felt the stinging and burning begin, but I wanted him. I was throbbing with need that went beyond any pain, and the love I felt for this man consumed my very soul.

His mouth parted my lips in a hard kiss, his tongue laving mine as his body surged fully into mine. Pain shot through me and he stopped at my gasp, holding perfectly still inside me and waiting for my body to adjust to his. He kissed me without moving and then raised his head.

"Are you okay, honey?"

I waited for the burning to subside a little before I answered.

"I'm perfect. Move in me, baby. I need to feel all of you."

"I love you, Julia." He began to thrust into me slowly at first until my hips began to echo his rhythm. His kisses and movements were so tender it brought tears to my eyes. He rocked against me and my body reacted to the pressure, the building beginning and the pain completely subsiding. Emotion flooded through me even as my body began to tremble and come around his.

Kiss after kiss, he was so passionate and giving. I felt him pour all of his love into me and finally he tensed and shuddered as he came. "Julia…" he groaned and kissed my neck as he spilled into me.

"Oh, Ryan. I love you." I tightened my arms and legs around him and turned to kiss the side of his face and then his shoulder. "I love you more than anything."

When he finally raised his head and looked down into my face, his eyes were glassy and his cheeks were wet. "Julia." His fingers moved the damp hair back off of my face, his body still embedded in mine. "Oh babe, why didn't you tell me?"

"I thought you might not want to be the first," I said softly as the tears fell from the corners of my eyes. Ryan's thumbs wiped them away.

"Nothing could make me not want you. It was a gift, Julia. My heart is so full of you right now that it physically hurts. It was beautiful. I can't tell you what it means to me…to know that no one else has…" His eyes closed and his words dropped off before resting his forehead against mine. "My God." His mouth brushed soft kisses on my eyelids and cheeks before settling once again for a slow passionate kiss on my mouth.

Ryan raised himself up and out of me gently, trying to be careful. "Does it still hurt, babe? Are you okay?"

He lay on his side, his hand supporting his head. His eyes searched mine and I could see the questions behind them. The worry.

I shook my head. "No, I'm fine. It was incredible. I knew you'd be amazing."

He smiled. "Considering I'm the only one," he said as his fingers brushed against my chin. His expression sobered. "Julia…I mean, I had no idea…all this time…?"

I turned toward him and brushed the hair off of his face. I wanted to touch him like he was touching me. "What would you have had me say? Ryan, I'm so in love with you that I can't stand anyone else touching me?" My throat tightened, making it hard to get the words out. I tried to joke about it, but his eyes darkened and he got the little crinkle between his brows as he studied me.

"Yeah, that would have worked." His mouth quirked and then his expression became thoughtful. "You dated. I thought…"

"I dated, yeah. To try to get you out of my system." I lay back on the pillows and brought a hand to my eyes. "You can't know what I went through, trying to have sex with someone else so that I could try to fall out of love with you." The memory of those times was still painful enough to bring new tears to my eyes and my throat was aching.

"Jules," Ryan said softly and reached for my hand. "Please don't pull away from me. I do know what it was like, because that's what I did too. I couldn't shake you, no matter what I did."

"Don't you mean *who* you did?" I asked. I knew it was unfair of me, bitter even, and that wasn't how I wanted the evening to be. I regretted my words the instant they were out. He sighed heavily and pulled back from me but I reached for him and drew him closer. "I'm sorry, that was unfair of me."

"I…wanted you from the minute we met. I ached for you but I basically resigned myself to the fact that you only wanted to be my friend. I tried to get you out of my head because it was killing me. And physically, I was on edge all the time. I was so turned on, my body was constantly in agony…but I couldn't stay away from you either. I was totally fucked. So yes, I tried to get you out of my head and my heart. And I failed every time."

"I cried myself to sleep every one of those nights you went out. I was in hell, praying for daylight when you'd be with me and not them." Finally, he knew everything and admitting it to him was like letting the water out of a dam and I couldn't stop the tears. He gathered me close to his chest and put a hand on the back of my head. He kissed me on the forehead and breathed me in.

"Oh, honey. I'm sorry, my love. I was an idiot."

"You couldn't have known, and you always came back to me. They never lasted very long."

"Because they *weren't you*." His voice vibrated over my skin and my arm tightened around his waist.

I drew in a deep, shaky breath. "That's why I was scared to let this happen…to let myself love you, to make love with you. I was afraid that I'd become one of your flings and I would rather be your friend than your lover for a week or two. I couldn't risk that shit."

"Julia, it's all us now. I will never touch another woman again. And after this…I cannot have any other man touching you. *Ever*."

"If it was impossible before, how in the hell do you think it's possible now? You've ruined me for anyone else."

His finger slid beneath my chin to tilt my head up so he could kiss me softly, sucking on my lips with his. "One thing I know, Julia. You have got to get to the East Coast, love. Either that or I need to find a med school out here. I am not going to survive this separation now."

I snuggled into the love of my life. He was right. I loved my job, but Ryan was where I needed to be. "You're not screwing with Harvard, Matthews. You got me?"

He chuckled softly and rubbed my back gently. "Yes. I've got you."

~5~

Julia ~

Ryan got up after we made love and went into the bathroom, washing off and then bringing in a warm washcloth to tenderly wash the blood from my lower body and legs. His features were soft, his eyes burning with emotion.

"Julia, I'm…overwhelmed," he whispered as he gathered me close to him after he'd returned to bed. I felt extremely safe as I snuggled into him, resting on his shoulder and wrapping an arm around him. It felt so perfect. "There are no words to describe how much I love you. Thank you for trusting me, and—" his words dropped off as he nuzzled into my hair at the side of my neck, "for loving me enough to wait for me." His arms tightened around me. "I won't survive losing you now."

I sighed against him and kissed his chest. "You know that isn't possible. As long as you want me, I'm yours."

His voice caught on emotions and his hand rubbed up and down my arm. "Promise me that nothing will come between us."

"I promise. Forever," I whispered. He finally drifted off to sleep but my mind was working overtime, my heart too full to sleep. I lay there for a long time just listening to him breathe, but I was restless and didn't want to wake him up.

I lifted his arm carefully so I wouldn't rouse him, yearning to kiss his mouth, but settled for brushing the hair from his forehead and touching his jaw with my fingertips. The stubble had started to grow which only served to make him even sexier, if that were possible.

"Julia..." he sighed and flopped over on his stomach. My heart fluttered at my name on his lips. He'd said it many times as we made love and the emotion in his voice made my heart explode into a million pieces. It was amazing and somewhat surreal. I was afraid I'd wake up and find that it had just been another of my fantasies.

The soreness between my legs reminded me that it was indeed real as I padded into the bathroom and turned on the hot water in the shower. I looked at myself in the mirror, trying to find some difference from the person I was 5 hours earlier. My hair was wild from his love play, my lips slightly swollen and there was a pink flush to my skin. Nothing major, but definitely changed forever.

I shivered and ran my hand through my hair. He had been amazing, tender and so unbelievably loving that he took my breath away. The physical pain of his entry into my body paled in comparison to the way my chest clenched when he said he didn't think he'd be able to stop. After four years of waiting and wanting, there was no way in hell either of us could stop. The emotion between us was undeniable and beautiful.

I lifted my face into the hot water and let it cascade over me, quickly washed my hair and rinsed it before turning off the faucet. I donned a white terrycloth robe that Ellie had given me for my birthday and wrapped my wet hair in a towel. I didn't want to be gone from Ryan too long, but I wasn't feeling tired. The light from the bathroom cast a soft glow across the bedroom, illuminating Ryan's beautiful form. Still on his stomach with his arms curled underneath a pillow beneath his head, the sheet had fallen low on his hips leaving the glorious muscles on his back and the beginning curve of his ass laid bare to my view. I stopped in place as my breath caught in my throat. He was so perfect; I sometimes thought he was a figment of my imagination.

We had everything now. Everything we could possibly want between us. *And about 3000 miles that we didn't want.* My heart ached slightly at the thought of him leaving Sunday to return to Boston. Suddenly, my life in Los Angeles wasn't so great. I'd missed him terribly, but now...it would be completely unbearable. Our admissions would make being apart more difficult, which had been one concern of letting our relationship progress back in college.

I sighed as I knelt down beside the bed so I could look into his face and hear him breathing. He smelled so familiar to me; the same Ryan that had been by my side, my best friend who made me laugh and teased, who comforted and pushed. He'd been the most significant person in my world since the moment I'd met him. I inhaled so deeply that the expansion of my lungs actually hurt. My eyes welled with tears as my hand brushed his hair back from his perfect features again.

"Julia." He stirred softly, the words a breathy whisper. "I love you so much."

I put my hand over my mouth so I wouldn't make a sound. Finally hearing those words, and in the unconscious state of sleep, brought home just how incredibly true they were. I leaned in and kissed his temple as my heart squeezed to the point of pain.

I love you, too, Ryan. More than I ever thought I could love anyone.

I loved him before, but now, after we'd been so intimate, connected in body and soul, I knew I couldn't live this far away from him. I needed him, and I wanted to be everything to him.

To give him everything he could ever need. My heart pounded wildly as I moved to the upholstered chair near the window and leaned over to turn on the small lamp on the table beside it.

I didn't have much free time. The new job with *Glamour* was so demanding and the hours so long I hadn't taken the time to draw at all. In the past four years I'd drawn several pictures of Ryan, some of them done on the nights that he'd gone out on dates, when I was heartbroken. It had given me some sort of twisted comfort as I kept reminding myself that I was the only constant woman in his life.

Looking back, it was ridiculous to suffer and not take the risk of telling him the truth about the love I felt. I'd been so scared, but, in hindsight, I should have been honest. My true feelings and my virginity had been the only secrets I'd kept from him in all the time we'd known each other.

I scoffed at myself and at him. We'd both been so stupid. I told Ryan not to think of it as wasted time and here I was, letting my silly ass do that very thing. I shook my head.

My portfolio was filled with sketches of him doing various activities; studying, playing the piano, daydreaming, running his hands through his sexy hair, or talking with Aaron or his parents. Most I'd done from memory, but now I had the chance to do one unobserved. I didn't have any of him sleeping and couldn't resist taking the opportunity this moment presented. He was so beautiful in the dim light, boyish and angelic, his gorgeous face relaxed and content.

I went quietly into the other room where I had an art table set up in the bay window. Lately, both Ellie and I were so busy that we weren't using it much. I turned on the light to search around until I found sketchpad, a soft lead pencil, and my kneadable eraser.

Settling back into the chair by the bed, I curled my knees under me and began to draw the general outline of his face. Taking note of the direction of light, I put the pencil to the paper.

His face had very prominent angles, his jaw and brow very strong, the nose straight and perfect and his lips soft and full. Mmmm...I loved those lips. I smiled to myself as I drew their arcs before moving up to the sweep of his dusky lashes that rested so peacefully on his cheeks. He had a slight rosy glow, no doubt left over from our lovemaking, but this would be a black and white, so I would need to rely on how the light fell on the planes of his face to add depth.

I worked late into the night, being careful with every detail, and once in a while Ryan would stir slightly. I finished his face and moved on to the pillow and his arms, his glorious hair. I glanced up as I worked the shading on his bicep and his blue eyes were open, glowing at me, a slight smile curving the full lips.

My hand stopped on the page as I gazed at him, completely speechless at the sight he made.

"Are you stealing my soul like Dorian Gray?" he asked, chuckling softly.

I laughed softly as he reminded me of the literature class we'd taken our sophomore year at Stanford. We had to do an essay on a famous author and a major piece of work, and I'd chosen Oscar Wilde and his only novel, about a man who retained his youthful beauty while his portrait aged in his place.

"Mmm...could I?" I leaned over and set the pencil on the table and flipped the cover on the pad closed, quirking an eyebrow in his direction.

"You already have, my love," he whispered.

"Hmmm...but, it wasn't his soul, silly. It was his *youth*."

"Well, it is my soul that's been stolen…and my heart," Ryan said thoughtfully and mine raced. "Do I get to see it?"

"No. It's not finished yet." The truth was that I had many that I'd never shown him. He had no idea how much I had obsessed and I had always felt embarrassed at the possibility he would know that I loved him and wanted him in that way.

"I'm lonely over here," he suggested seductively and rolled onto his side, propping his head on a bent arm. "I miss you, sweet. I need my beautiful girl." The sheet fell even lower on his hips at the move, letting me glimpse the delicious trail of hair that led down his stomach and got thicker toward his man parts. I laughed softly at the thought.

He smiled and raised his brows in question. "What?"

I got up and moved to the bed to sit on the edge. Ryan reached out to take my hand and kiss the inside of my wrist. Electricity shot through me where his lips grazed softly across my skin, his eyes never leaving mine. "Hmmm?" he prodded and brushed his lips across my skin again.

"I just never thought that I'd be in a position to see you like this. It's…" I paused for a second when he took one of my fingers and sucked it into his mouth. I gasped. "Uh, Ryan, that's not fair."

He laughed softly and pulled on the tie of my robe allowing it to fall open. His eyes grew dark as he looked at me and pulled me further onto the bed and into his arms. His hand came up to brush my hair back and then cup the side of my face. His thumb moved across my cheek and his fingers closed around the back of my head to pull me closer.

My face reached toward his as his lips hovered above mine. I wanted him to kiss me, to feel his lips and tongue devour me.

"All's fair in love and war. You know that, Julia." His tongue came out to lightly trace my upper lip and then he sucked the lower one and nibbled a little with his teeth. My head fell back and my arms slid up his bare chest and around his neck.

"Is this love or war?" I whispered as he took my mouth in a deep, very slow and passionate kiss. My body responded to his touch and his mouth on mine, my nipples hardened and the moisture began to pool. I felt my body begin to open.

"Uhhh..." I moaned against his mouth as he shifted my body underneath his. I moaned again as I felt the evidence of his desire pressing into my core. God, I wanted him.

"I think I should tell you," he said as his mouth played with mine, teasing and leaving me wanting more, "that if this is war, you're going to lose and lose *huge*." Ryan smiled against my lips before his mouth resumed the deep, sucking kisses. His tongue slid into my mouth and I opened to him as his arms tightened around me. The bare skin of our chests against each other felt glorious. There was something delicious about the skin on skin, both of us moaning as we rubbed against each other, his lower body surging against mine.

"God, Ryan. I love you so much. I can't believe this is happening." His answer was to kiss me again and again as his hands moved over my body and deftly removed the robe completely. At last, we were naked and rolling around with each other on the bed, writhing and panting, kissing deeply, like we'd never get enough.

"Oh, Julia. *Finally*. This is magnificent. It's madness," he groaned against my breast just before he pulled the nipple into his mouth. He suckled first one, then the other, his hand stroking down my thigh and back again to rest on my hip. He pulled me closer and pressed his hardness into me again. "See how much I want you? I've always wanted you like this, babe."

I arched by breasts toward his mouth as I bit the skin on the top of his shoulder lightly. "Yes, Ryan...please," I begged.

His kisses became softer until finally he drew back to look into my eyes. "You'll be sore right now, honey," he whispered against the curve of my neck, his tongue coming out to lick the skin before he blew softly on the wetness left behind. I shivered and his hand traced up my arm. "We can still play a little, but no penetration, okay?"

"Okay, playing is good," I breathed against his mouth as my hand traced down his chest and stomach to grasp around his hardness and began to slowly move up and down. He groaned against my shoulder. We needed no more words as we both touched and kissed each other until we both exploded in ecstasy beneath the other's hands. The sun was coming up before we fell into an exhausted sleep, satisfied, content and completely wrapped around each other.

Ryan ~

My phone was ringing in the distant recesses of my mind, but I fought waking up. Moaning in protest, I rolled over, glancing at the clock on the bedside table in Julia's bedroom. A huge grin split across my face.

Julia's bedroom.

I was in her bed and we had shared the most incredible, intoxicating night of my life. She was incredibly responsive to each and every touch. It felt like we were made only for each other. No other woman in my life had ever made me feel so fulfilled, so possessive or so ready to burst. My heart swelled as I climbed out of bed and rushed to my pants to grab my phone.

Aaron.

"What?!" I practically snapped.

"Whoa. Happy fucking Thanksgiving to you, too!"

I sighed and sat back down on the edge of the bed. "I'm sorry, Aaron. I was sleeping."

"Sleeping? It's three PM!"

"Not here it isn't, moron," I teased. "Happy Thanksgiving."

"You better ask that boy if he finally grew a pair and took what that girl has been dying to give him!" Jen called happily from the background.

"Uh, yeah. We want to know if you finally tapped that fine ass," Aaron laughed.

Neither of them minced words, that's for sure. "Uh...that *fine ass* is not up for discussion." I smiled as I reached for my pants and slid them on, standing to finish the job.

"Ryan. It's *me, Aaron.* You *have* to tell me, for crying out loud! We've been watching the two of you do the dance for years. So spill already!"

"Okay. *Yes.*" I laughed happily; amazed at how pleased I was to tell him that Julia and I were finally a couple.

"*That's* what I'm talking about! Congratulations, man!" Jenna shrieked in the background. "Jenna is doing the happy dance around the kitchen right now," he laughed. "How was it?"

I paused, wondering where Julia was. I didn't want her to be upset that I was telling Aaron about our lovemaking. I smelled something delicious coming from the kitchen and assumed she was already working on the meal for later in the day.

"It was...*incredible.* Like nothing I've ever experienced."

"It's about damn time. You both deserve this. Jules is a great girl," he said seriously.

"Thank you. I know I sound like a sappy shit, but I love her so fucking much I can't even breathe, Aaron," I said softly.

"You always have, Ryan. Newsflash! She has too."

I padded into the kitchen to see my girl at the stove stirring something that was sautéing in a skillet and then bending to take a cookie sheet filled with bread from the oven.

"Yeah. Amazing, isn't it?" Julia turned when she heard me laugh and smiled widely. "She's already making *the feast*, Aaron. She's...*perfect*." She was wearing my shirt and some cut off sweats and her hair was piled in a knot on top of her head. It made my heart skip a beat at the sight. This was *my Julia.*

"Really? Jen! Get your ass in the kitchen and start making dinner. Julia is three hours behind you and she's already started!"

I laughed out loud again when I heard Jenna's response in the background. "You get *your ass* dressed. The turkey will be served at McFarland's. Corner of 15th and Nichols. Bring your wallet, asshole."

"Ugh! See how lucky you are?" Aaron groaned.

"Yeah. I'm well aware of how good I've got it," I said softly, watching Julia begin to break up the bread into a large bowl.

"Let me talk to Julia."

"Ok...have a great day and tell Jen I love her."

"You too, Ryan. And I am really happy for you."

"Thanks." I handed the phone to my girl. "Aaron wants to say *hello*."

She wiped her hands on a towel and reached for the phone, but I grabbed her hand and pulled her to me. "Good morning," I whispered against her mouth before giving her a soft kiss.

I heard Aaron screaming on the phone. "Ryan, keep it in your pants! Let me talk to Jules!" We both laughed out loud as I released her.

"Hello, Aaron. How are you guys?"

I tried to figure out the conversation by listening to Julia's responses, but there were bound to be holes.

"I'm…wonderful. Thank you for asking." A beautiful smile split on her face and she glanced at me.

"I doubt that will be necessary." She laughed. "He's been perfect."

"I know pathetic, right? Yes. I do. Tell Jenna Happy Thanksgiving for me. What? Well, I'll have plenty if you want to hop a flight. Dinner's at seven."

"Ok. Love you. Bye."

Julia was smiling from ear to ear when she handed me back the phone. I pulled her to me again and lifted her chin so I could kiss her sweet lips.

"What was that all about? Please don't tell me you invited them to invade this weekend," I whispered against her mouth, licking and sucking playfully.

She kissed my mouth, then my chin before finally pulling out of my arms. "Ryan…I need to get back to the dressing. The sausage will burn if I don't keep my wits about me." She went back to the stove and took the skillet off of the heat. "Are you hungry?"

"Of course I'm hungry, but you didn't answer, honey." I lifted my eyebrows and reached into the skillet to take out a chunk of the crumbled sausage and pop it in my mouth.

She giggled at the look on my face. "Nothing. Just being a good *big brother*. Very sweet."

I leaned my hip against the counter and took in all of the ingredients scattered around. Herbs, vermouth, hazelnuts, celery and onions, apples and pears, lined the counters. Shit, I didn't even remember my mother going to this extreme. "Yes, but *what* did he say?" I persisted.

She giggled again. "You know this is fun. I could tease you all day with this, sweetie."

My heart thumped at her use of the endearment. "You can tease me, sure, but not with Aaron's call, okay?" I added suggestively and then gave her my pouty face, sticking out my lower lip. She wouldn't be able to resist for long.

Julia sighed as she dumped the sausage into the same bowl that held the dried bread. She cocked her head to one side and then shook it slightly but smiled. I knew I had her then.

"Just that he'd beat your ass if you didn't take good care of me. He was playing with me. It was cute."

"He's a good man. Jen was giving me a ration of shit, too. Do you need any help, my love?"

"You can help me after you've had breakfast." Turning, she pulled out some fresh lemon muffins from the oven and removed them to a plate. My favorite.

In college she used to make them for brunch, usually accompanied by some fruit, Eggs Benedict and fresh orange juice. Aaron used to complain that she didn't make blueberry enough since they were what he liked best. When she did, she always made the lemon, too. I smiled at the memory. How did I miss how much she loved me back then? She spoiled me rotten.

On cue she went to the fridge and pulled out a bowl of freshly chopped fruit and set it in front of me along with a plate holding two of the warm muffins.

"Juice and coffee?" Her soft green eyes rose to meet mine and I brushed her hair back from her face.

"Yes, please. Why are you so perfect?"

She smiled and shrugged. "I'm not, Ryan."

"Of course you are. I've known you all this time and I haven't found anything I don't love about you."

"I piss you off a *lot* when I don't give you your way," she teased. "Sometimes we fight like cats and dogs."

"Technicality. Nothing more," I scoffed and then lathered butter all over one of the muffins before popping half of it in my mouth. "I only get two of these?" I smiled with my mouth full.

"Pfft! What do you think?" She went back to chopping up the onions and some celery stalks before putting them in the skillet and then returning it to the stove.

"Well, I think...that you're going to give me my way in *everything* this weekend." I wagged my eyebrows at her. "At least...I'm hoping."

"Your way is mine, too. It works out well, doesn't it?" Her soft laughter was like music to my ears.

"Extremely well. I love you, you know."

She glanced over her shoulder as she stirred the contents of the skillet, the delicious scent filling the air as she did so.

"Yeah, I know." She shrugged offhandedly and then laughed. "I love you, too."

I pushed my plate away and pulled up a stool next to the counter bar where she worked.

"Julia." I watched her face as she finally emptied the rest of the vegetables into the bowl and began chopping up fresh sage, rosemary and thyme.

"Hmmm?" she said absently as she worked, so focused on what she was doing, like she'd done it a million times before.

I wanted to talk about last night. "Julia, last night was...a miracle. I'll never forget it," I said softly. "It was the best night of my life."

She stopped what she was doing and set the knife down. "It meant the world to me, too. Thank you for being so gentle. It couldn't have been better, Ryan. Truly. You made me feel so special."

"Come here," I begged and took her in my arms. "You *are* special. That's why I didn't make moves on you before. I didn't see you the same way I saw other women. You were so much more." Her arms wound around my waist and I pulled her tight against my chest and kissed the top of her head. "I love you so fucking much."

She breathed in and nodded against me. "I know, and it's okay. Looking back, I'm sorry I didn't tell you how I felt, but at least we were together."

"My best friend, Julia." I sighed against her temple then placed a series of soft kisses on the side of her face and the corner of her mouth. "So beautiful, irresistible and amazing that no other woman could hold a candle to you. Not even close."

"Not that irresistible. You resisted almost four years," she reminded me.

"I was dying with it, though. And the other guys," I huffed, "I wanted to kill every one of them; sure you'd figure me out. I tried to get over it but couldn't stand thinking of them touching you and kissing you. When I discovered that you dumped them after I let you know I hated them, I used it." I smiled. "I was a selfish prick."

"I just thought you were being overprotective."

"More like territorial. You were mine...in my head, at least." I turned her face toward mine and let my mouth take hers in a deep kiss.

God, she melts me.

"Not just in your head. It's like I said last night, Ryan. It hurt me too, but there wasn't a damn thing I could do about it. I tried to change how I felt, but nothing worked."

"Why didn't you tell me you were a virgin before? I thought we shared everything," I asked softly as I brushed her hair back and stared into her face.

Her eyes filled with tears. "I didn't want you to think I was a loser or worse- that I was in love with you. I didn't want you to figure out I couldn't let anyone else touch me. I mean…It would have been humiliating."

I sighed and pulled her tight against me again. "Oh, baby, no it wouldn't. It would've gotten my head out of my ass that much sooner. I'm sorry you were hurt by those girls, my love. So sorry. They meant nothing. You're the only one I've ever loved. It's always been *just you*."

She breathed in and her shoulders shook in a sob. "I know. It's over. I'm just glad we're together."

"Don't cry, sweet. I can't bear to see your tears. It's all going to be perfect now, Julia. I promise."

She raised her teary eyes to mine and finally answered. "As perfect as we can make it from so far away. I wouldn't trade it, though. I'll take you from 3000 miles over any other man in the same room with me."

I smiled at her words as my heart expanded to the point of pain. "Enough tears. We've got all weekend to talk about it and as long as it takes to figure that shit out. Okay?"

"Okay." She wiped her tears and moved back, resuming her task of chopping the herbs on the cutting board. "Ryan, will you put those hazelnuts on that cookie sheet and set the timer for 15 minutes?"

I smiled as I moved to do her bidding.

This is my life. This is going to be my life. My life with Julia.

If I had to drop out of Harvard and move to the West Coast, I'd do what needed to be done to be with her.

"Stop thinking about leaving Harvard," Julia said shortly. I paused at her perception.

How did she know what I was thinking?

"I can tell by that serious look on your face that you're trying to figure out a way to get out here. Forget it, Ryan. I mean it. I'll move there. Maybe not Boston, but at least New York."

"Julia, I—" I began but she interrupted me.

"Was I wrong or was that what you were thinking about?" she asked, her brow knitted as she paused to look up at me.

"No. You're right, but I can—"

"No. We both worked our asses off for you to get into Harvard and I won't let you give it up. We've got forever, isn't that what you said?" She said sternly, all the while continuing to put the dressing together without missing a beat.

"Yes, but I *need* to be with you. *We need*—"

"I know. But I need you to finish what you started out there. It's your dream."

"My perspective has changed. You're my priority, now." I felt my voice grow in volume.

"Why are you getting upset? We have the same priorities. But it will happen on the East Coast." Julia loaded the herbs into the bowl and began chopping up an apple and a pear.

I didn't know what to say. She was amazing. Once again, she was giving me what I wanted above all else. Letting me have Harvard *and* have her near me. She would make the sacrifice necessary to make it happen, and do it without even flinching.

Finally I found my voice. "Julia, you don't have to give up your dreams for me. That isn't fair."

"Who said I'm giving them up? I'm moving them to the other side of the country or, worst case scenario, putting them off for a couple of years. What's three or four years?"

I was stunned. "You're amazing. I don't deserve you." I walked around to stand beside her and ran my hand down her back and began to rub soft circles over my shirt.

"You deserve any damn thing I want to give you, got it?" She nudged me with her shoulder. Our nudge. I nudged her back. I wasn't going to win this argument and I gave in willingly.

"Yes. Love you."

"Yeah, well you better! I'm moving to fucking New York, for God's sake!" The laughter in her voice was a beautiful thing. "I must love you, too."

I took the knife from her hand and enfolded her in my arms, lifting her so that her mouth was level with mine. We kissed again deeply, her hands fisting in my hair and pulling my mouth tighter against hers. When we were both breathless, she finally dragged her mouth from mine. "Unless you want raw turkey, you need to let me get this thing in the oven," she breathed against my jaw and then kissed it.

"If I must. Right now, raw sounds okay, though."

Julia ~

The day sped by. We worked in the kitchen together until the turkey was in the oven, the yams were candied and the bread was raising on top of the stove, letting the warmth of the oven assist in the job.

We curled up on the couch and he turned on a football game while I leaned up against Ryan's chest, content to do nothing but lie there folded in his arms. I snuggled in and he pulled me even tighter, sighing against the side of my head that rested against his shoulder.

I closed my eyes, letting myself savor the moment. This was where I needed to be for the rest of my life and it didn't matter if it was in New York, Boston, L.A. or Timbuktu. He was home to me and nothing was more important than being with him.

Dinner was glorious and it was fun watching Ryan help make the gravy. He loved watching me and was amazed at the amount of Vermouth I had him add.

"Dump?" he asked incredulously. "Don't you measure it, Julia? I don't want to mess it up."

"Just dump. I'll tell you when," I laughed. "The same thing with the cream. Keep stirring the whole time with that wire whisk, unless you want lumps."

"This has been such a great day. Thank you."

I put my hand to his cheek. "Don't thank me, babe. I'm very happy you're here with me."

He reached down to kiss me and then I handed over the fork and carving knife. "Would you mind?" I asked and he smiled.

"Of course not. This feels like—" Ryan stopped abruptly and glanced at me after he'd started carving the bird.

"Yeah. It feels damn good," I said softly.

His blue eyes sparkled as he nodded.

"So good, Jules. I've really missed you."

"Hey," I said, feeling a lump rise in my throat, "no missing me tonight. I'm right here in front of you."

"Okay. You're right."

I quickly had the potatoes whipped and the bread on the table with everything else we'd made together. "Are we ready?" he looked at me expectantly. He looked like a kid at Christmas and I laughed.

"Yeah. I'll get the wine and meet you at the table."

Ryan lit the candles and then turned off the overhead light as I poured the wine. He pulled me into his arms and held me, sighing deeply and kissing first my cheekbone and then my temple.

I raised my mouth and placed several kisses along his jaw. "I love you. I know I say it too much, but now that I can, I can't stop." His velvet voice melted my heart.

I nodded. "I'll never get tired of hearing it. I love you, too…so much."

He held out my chair for me and we looked at each other until he reached for my hand.

"Jules, you know I'm not all that religious, but I do believe in God and I believe that you and I are meant to be." I felt the familiar sting at the back of my eyes and willed myself not to cry at his beautiful words. "If there is anything I am thankful for on any day…it's you."

I blinked a few times at the stinging in my eyes. "Ryan… Nothing will ever be more important to me than you. To finally be able to be open about how I feel, it's…a *miracle*. Thank you for being in my life."

His eyes filled with tears and he squeezed my hand. "Will you look at us?" he laughed through his tears.

I was overwhelmed and the first tears slipped from my eyes as I struggled to contain the emotion building up in every cell of my body.

"Yes. It's beautiful. I never want to look at anything but your face for…" I stopped before I finished, afraid of the implications of what I wanted to say, but Ryan finished my thought.

"For the rest of my life. I feel the same, okay?"

I brushed the tears from my face and tried to smile. "Sounds good."

"It will be. I promise."

Ryan ~

I watched Julia laughing with Ellie and could tell by the way they were looking at me and giggling that Ellie was asking some very personal questions. What could I expect? Everyone knows that women talk more about sex than guys. Guys just *do it* and women like to talk about it. Well, to be honest, I don't mind talking about it, but I'd be damned if it would be with anyone other than Julia.

She was so beautiful and I couldn't take my eyes off of her. She was wearing tight black jeans, a dressy white t-shirt and a short leather jacket, topped off by high-heeled boots and wild hair. She looked good enough to eat.

The weekend, so far, had been beyond my wildest dreams. I ached with the knowledge that 48 short hours from now, even less, I'd be on my way back to Boston. *Alone.*

I tried to bottle up the sadness. Each moment was precious and Julia was struggling, too. I tried to focus on the amazing nights we spent together and the fun we'd had today shopping and fighting the crowds. Julia was getting more gorgeous with each passing moment and every time she touched me, I fell more and more in love with her. I didn't think it was possible to love her more, but it filled me up until I felt I would explode.

Ellie went to talk to Harris, who was onstage with his band, so Julia came back to me. I pulled her down on my lap and nuzzled her neck.

"Mmmm…you smell so good."

Her arm went around my shoulders and she turned her face toward me, inviting me to capture her mouth with mine. Now that we'd crossed the line, we couldn't get enough. The flood-gates were open and I wanted to lose myself and savor every touch that I still had left to me.

"Stop or you'll make all the women here want to kill me," she laughed softly and brushed her nose against mine.

"It's the men I'm concerned about. You feel insane, babe. Let's leave," I begged against the curve of her neck and she shivered in my arms.

She sighed and leaned her head against me. "We can't yet, Ryan. Ellie would be so disappointed. You haven't even had a chance to talk to her. This will be fun, won't it? We can dance and maybe even make out a little bit...hmm?"

I rolled my eyes. The last thing I was concerned with was the others, but I had to admit the rest sounded good. "Okay," I said begrudgingly. "What was Ellie grilling you about?"

"What do you think?" She laughed and took a sip of her wine.

"Mmm...I figured. What did you tell her?"

"The truth."

My eyes widened and I brushed my knuckles across her cheek. "Oh, really. What exactly would that be?"

"That we are very happy." She kissed me softly. "That I love you." Her mouth dropped another kiss. "That...we're together, and you are...*incredible* in bed," she whispered against my mouth and then kissed me again, but this time I slipped my tongue into her mouth and slid my hand behind her head to pull her closer. I forgot about the crowd around us as my body sprung to life beneath her and my hand slid down her arm to her leg and hip.

Julia gasped and pulled her mouth from mine. "Ryan..." she said breathlessly. "God, don't do this to me here. It's not fair."

"Remember I told you," I said against her mouth, "love and war, and I want you."

"Ugh...later." Julia rested her head on mine and threaded her fingers in my hair. "You know I want you too."

Fuck. That wasn't helping the new problem rising in my pants.

"Hi, Ryan!" Ellie's cheery voice broke into the bubble that we'd disappeared into.

My arm tightened around Julia, letting her know I wanted her to stay put on my lap so I could hide my uncomfortable circumstance and, anyway, I didn't want to let go of her.

"Hey, Ellie. It's nice to see you. I've got a little problem right now, so I'll hug you in a few minutes, if that's okay," I said dryly.

Ellie's eyes danced as she laughed. Julia gasped and shoved me in the shoulder. I laughed out loud and they both joined me.

"I understand, honey. How is Boston?" Ellie asked.

"It's okay. School is good. A lot of work, but it makes the time go faster. How are you and Harris doing? When's the wedding?" I teased. Ellie flushed and looked pointedly at Julia.

"Hey, I didn't put that in his head, El. He's pretty sharp on his own, you know," Julia said loudly over the din of the crowd and band, saving Ellie by changing the subject. "Is Harris going to get a break so we can talk to him?"

"In about an hour. They take 10 minutes at the top of each hour." I groaned inwardly but realized I was being selfish by wanting to steal Julia away.

"They sound great, Ellie. Really good," I said as I felt for the bare skin of Julia's back beneath her shirt and jacket. I rubbed little circles and she leaned into me further. It felt wonderful just holding her close.

A couple of assholes at the bar were eyeing Julia when she went to talk to Ellie. I glanced in their direction. They were staring and talking between themselves. I glared at them before nuzzling into her neck again. Julia didn't notice the men as she rubbed my back and chatted with Ellie and another girl.

Yes, that's right. She's mine. Don't even fucking think about it.

I was having a serious case of déjà vu.

So many times in college I'd seen a similar scene go down when we'd all go out to clubs, but back then I didn't have the right or the ammunition to openly squash it. Never overly obvious; I had to rely on quietly walking up to guys and warning them off of Julia without her knowing it even happened.

I'd been such a bastard. I realized how unfair that was, but damn it, I couldn't stand seeing them pawing all over her, or even looking at her with lust. I was always very possessive and protective of her. Not that she needed me every time. She'd been more than capable of telling unwanted admirers to fuck off, and she had done so many times. Only a few times had she needed me to intercede, allowing me to get in their faces openly. Aaron had given me so much crap over it, telling me to shit or get off the pot.

Immersed in her conversation with Ellie, Julia was unaware of the exchange or the men watching her, but my eyes narrowed on them as they continued to ogle her. They were either intoxicated, had very little class, or were just fucking stupid.

"Ryan."

Julia stood and pulled on my hand to have me join her. "Will you dance with me or are you too busy flirting with those guys at the bar?" Amusement danced in her eyes as she looked up at me.

A smile lifted my lips as I reached down to wrap my arms around her, lifting her up to carry her toward the dance floor, her feet dangling. She wrapped her arms around my shoulders and laughed softly.

"You caught me. Just letting them know that you're mine, sweets."

Harris's band was finally playing a slow song and it was a perfect excuse to hold her. I lowered Julia to the floor, but didn't relinquish my tight hold on her. My hands roamed up and down her back as she settled her head onto the curve of my neck, her high heels giving her the perfect height to allow easy access to her luscious mouth. I resisted the temptation as long as possible.

She fit against me perfectly as we swayed together. I closed my eyes, letting her scent envelope me.

"You feel so great." She raised her head until her mouth was under my ear and her hot breath rushed over me. My arms tightened around her.

I dropped my forehead to her shoulder and turned my face to kiss her neck, letting my mouth open and my tongue graze her skin and then sucked a little before raising my head.

"You're so delicious…I'm just starving, my love."

She moaned against me and it was all I could do not to ravish her mouth on the spot. "I can't take much more of this. It's wonderful but I want to get you alone and make slow love to you. Do you want that?"

She brought her hand to my face and her fingers danced along my jaw while she looked at me with those big doe eyes. "Always have. But now, knowing what I've been missing, it's insane."

My heart quickened at her words. "Julia…" I felt my dick swell and I pulled her hips against mine so she could feel the effect she had on me. "God…as amazing as last night was, I want more."

"I love when you touch me, when you taste me…having you inside me," she moaned against my neck and my body started shaking.

"God, this is torture. Please, say we can go," I groaned and looked down into her face, my body on fire. Her skin was so perfectly smooth and her mouth, full and beckoning, cried out for my kisses.

"I want to, but look at poor Ellie, Ryan. We have to stay for a little bit. I'm sorry I teased you, I just can't seem to stop the words." She looked up at me apologetically as the song ended. "Will you dance with her just one time? She loves you and it will give her a chance to drill you too." She flashed a beautiful smile that I couldn't refuse and I bent to place a soft sucking kiss on her lips.

"Like I can deny you. Will you miss me?" I teased.

"Every second. I'll wait for you at the table. Should I order you anything?"

"Crown and Coke." I kissed her hand as she turned from me and I went over to Ellie, smiling the whole way.

"Hey short stuff. Will you honor me with this dance?" I mock bowed in front of her.

Ellie's face lit up. She was a pretty girl and had been a good friend to both of us. "I didn't think Julia would want to share you once she'd sunk her teeth in you," she joked, and had a huge smile on her face, as we walked back onto the dance floor. "She *does* have her teeth in you, doesn't she?"

"To the bone." I nodded and laughed.

"Yeah. I told her years ago you were in love with her but she wouldn't listen! She's loved you for a long time, Ryan. I'm very happy for you both."

I hugged her tightly. "Thanks, Ellie. Your support means a lot. How are things with you and Harris, really?"

Another slow song started and she put her hand on my shoulder and I took the other in mine.

"Hasn't Julia told you?" she said, resuming the conversation after we started to dance.

"Only that you guys are close. Harris is a good dude. You could do a lot worse, and for sure he could." I smiled at her.

"I think things are going to work out for all of us. It seems to be heating up on all fronts, huh?"

"Yeah. In case you're in any doubt, I love Julia with all my heart."

Her grey eyes smiled at me. "I know. Everyone did, except Julia, I guess. I expect her to move out East, yes?"

"We're talking about it. We don't want to be apart. If that happens, will you move in with Harris? Julia worries about you being alone."

Before she could respond, I looked over Ellie's head toward the table and didn't like what I saw. The waitress was delivering the drinks and one of the men who had been eyeing Julia earlier was speaking to her. She looked up at him and shook her head as she tried to pay for the drinks, but the man handed a bill to the waitress and waved her away.

I felt the blood begin to pump around my body and my skin lit on fire.

He knew she was not here alone and she didn't want his attention, yet he was hitting on her with no regard for any of it.

"Ellie, I need to go take care of Jules. I'm sorry," I said softly. "Excuse me."

Her gaze followed mine to the table. Julia's annoyance when the man sat next to her was obvious. Her scowl increased when he scooted closer, her exasperation evident by the hand she ran through her hair. When I approached, a look of relief flooded her delicate features.

"Come on, little lady, loosen up. Maybe you need a real man." He didn't sound drunk but my palms began to sweat as I clenched my fists at my sides.

Julia stood up when I reached her and I wrapped my arm around her in time to hear her response.

"As you can see, I have one. But, thanks for the drink." She tried to brush him off without needing my help, but I seriously wanted to punch him in the face. I smirked as his expression changed from eagerness to anger when her hand came up to rest on my stomach. He reached for her arm, trying to pry her from me.

Oh Fuck, no! He did not just touch her.

"I recommend that you remove your hands from her. *Immediately.*" My face tightened and my voice lowered so as not to make a scene, but it was more like a growl. I was more furious than I could ever remember feeling in my life.

Julia pushed him away and he stumbled back a little but soon regained his balance and came back toward her.

"Look, asshole," she said, "I don't want you to die, so listen to me very carefully. You don't have one damn thing that I'm interested in. Ryan is being very calm right now but I suggest you leave us alone before you piss him off."

"Ryan? Are you her fucking husband?" He looked at me pointedly. He was shorter than me, heavier and out of shape. I'd be able to lay him out without much effort if needed.

"Yes," I answered without hesitation. Julia's arm tightened around the back of my waist.

"Well, you've got great taste, man." I relaxed a little when it seemed like he was going to back off. It was too much to hope for. "Too bad that she ain't," he continued and took a hold of her arm again. "Come for a dance, baby,"

Julia recoiled back from him again as I held her and the rage boiled up inside my chest. I'd had enough.

I growled fiercely and reached for the hand on her arm twisting his fingers backward until he winced.

"Listen, you sorry fuck. Take your hands off of her *now* or I swear to *God*, I'll break every one of your fucking fingers. Now, I strongly suggest you move along if you *ever* plan on jerking off again. Got me?"

I waited for him to nod and then let go of his hand, flinging it away from me. He moved away clutching his hand and I wrapped both arms around Julia, glaring at him over her head. She giggled into my chest. I smiled with her when I saw him finally slink back to the bar.

"Dickhead! I swear, I can't take you anywhere," I laughed against the top of Julia's head and rubbed her back with both hands.

"Oh, my God! That was hilarious...but sorta hot, too. I think I like this side of you." She nuzzled my neck.

We sat back at the table and I lifted the drink Julia had ordered in salute to the asshole at the bar, before I downed it. "Thanks for the drink," I said and hoped to hell he could read my lips. Julia was laughing so hard she had tears in her eyes.

"Holy shit," she gasped for breath between fits of laughter.

I reached for Julia's chair and scooted her closer so I could hold her hand and rest my arm across her lap under the table. Whenever she was near, I had to be touching her in some way.

Ellie was shaking her head and laughing with us. "Wow, Ryan! I think that guy just pissed his pants."

The band was on a break, so Harris came over, shook my hand and leaned down to kiss Julia on the cheek.

Casually slinging an arm around Ellie's waist, he spoke. "Remind me never to make you mad, Ryan. That was classic."

"I had to save that poor schmuck from Julia. She was ready to kick his ass." I smirked and she elbowed me in the ribs. "Hey," I protested.

"Yeah. She's badass, for sure," Harris teased and Julia rolled her eyes.

"Have you figured out a way to accelerate your years at Harvard yet, Ryan? I figure if anyone can do it, it's you." His eyes followed my movements holding Julia and he raised an eyebrow at me.

Now that Julia and I were together, it would be even more important to me to finish as quickly as possible.

"Yeah, a little. I considered asking my dad to bribe the dean," I joked, "but you can't rush med school. It is what it is."

"Have you decided yet what you want to specialize in?" Ellie interjected.

Julia was resting her head on my shoulder and held my hand under the table, reminding me how badly I wanted to get her home. It felt so natural being with her, like we'd always been together. No one ever belonged together as much as we did. It settled over me like warm honey. She belonged with me and I was wrecked for the rest of my life. *Gone.*

Julia nudged me and brought me out of my reverie. "Ellie asked you a question, hon."

"Um, either some sort of surgery or trauma."

"Trauma? Ewww," Ellie retorted. "Wouldn't that be gross, Ryan? You mean people from accidents, right?"

"Anything that is an emergency, really, Ellie. Someone has to do it, right? Plus, I'd have a regular shift at a hospital and I wouldn't be on-call all of the time, which might come in handy at some point." I let my middle finger scratch the inside of Julia's palm under the table and she squeezed my hand in response. "I don't know for sure yet, though. I'm going to talk to my dad and try to get some time in ER before I make a decision."

"What about Aaron? Has he decided, babe?" Julia questioned. "Seems to me that he'd pick something like that, too."

"He's more interested in Internal Medicine and wants a regular practice. I think he's planning on popping the question soon." Julia's eyes widened. "Don't say anything to Jen, you guys. Aaron will have my ass if she finds out before he gets around to it."

I leaned into Harris so I could speak in a low tone. "Thanks for letting Ellie stay with you, man. I really appreciate the time alone with Julia."

Harris looked at me knowingly and nodded slyly. "Yeah. Did you finally seal that deal, dude? Seeing the two of you, I'd say that you two are definitely on another level now."

"Yes, and it feels great. It's been a long time coming."

"Congratulations." He patted me on the back before the girls' chattering together interrupted us.

We chatted with them until Harris' break ended. Julia spoke to Ellie while I finished my drink and waited impatiently for a sign that I could take her home as soon as possible.

I watched my girl approach and my hands settled on her hips as she stopped between my legs. Her arms slid around my neck and I pulled her in tight.

"Take me to bed," she whispered suggestively in my ear before her mouth trailed along my cheek to my mouth and we kissed passionately. I sucked her lower lip into my mouth and tasted her like she was the sweetest ambrosia. *Wine and sweetness. So, so good.*

I lifted my mouth from hers reluctantly, but was anxious to be behind closed doors with her.

"Jesus, you taste amazing. Let's get out of here."

Julia nodded. "Yeah."

I wrapped my arm around her waist and led her toward the coat check to get our coats before we could leave. We passed the man who'd accosted her and he turned his back to us. *Thank God.* I just wanted to get out of there and avoid another confrontation with the loser.

We didn't speak on the walk through the parking lot or on the drive back to her apartment. With my hand in hers and her head on my shoulder, the air was charged with anticipation and silent communication that we were both anxious to be alone together, to have our mouths and bodies meshing for hours on end.

The minute we pushed through the door of her apartment, I threw the keys on the entryway table, pulled her to me and latched on to her mouth, pushing her clothing aside in heated fury.

We were frantic. The closeness of the evening, the sexiness of holding and touching her for hours, all the while wanting to take her down and have her had driven me to the breaking point. The sexual tension was finally more than I could bear.

I lifted her up and her legs wrapped around my waist as I pressed her back against the closed door. My pelvis pushed into hers and her heat made my breath hitch. My erection throbbed, aching for friction, my need for her vibrated through my entire body. Feeling her desire, made my blood sing. The little mewling sounds she made in her throat excited me even more, my dick so full and hard it was almost painful.

I'll never get enough of this woman.

My heart was pounding, all the while kissing her over and over again, devouring, and sucking her tongue into my mouth. Her hands clasped in my hair as one of mine clasped around her breast and I kneaded the perfect mound, feeling her hardened nipple press into my palm through the thin fabric of her shirt. I wanted it off, no barriers between us, her skin on mine. She was moaning in need of her own and it drove me to distraction.

"Julia, God... You're so hot. The sounds you make drive me insane. You're mine. Always mine."

Her hands groped at the front of my shirt, but our mouths kept returning to each other again and again, distracting her from the task.

"Uhhhhh...Ryan...I want to feel you."

"Fucking rip it off of me if you want. I don't care." I pressed into her, establishing the rhythm that we both needed as I held her against the door. She moaned into my mouth before the buttons on my white shirt went flying, the fabric giving way as she pulled the shirt open over my chest and her warm hands splayed out on my skin.

I lifted her off the door and carried her toward the bedroom, one of my hands twisting in her hair and pulling her head to one side so I could bury my mouth in the curve of her neck as my tongue traced a trail up her neck to her ear. "How did I live without touching you like this? I must have been insane."

"Ryan...I want you...now..." It was music to my ears, reinforced by the pounding of her pulse beneath my lips, and how she writhed against me. The smell of her skin and perfume was intoxicating, making conscious thought almost impossible.

I lowered her to the bed and followed her down, my hands finally free to lift the white shirt from her body. I slid my hands underneath and pushed it upwards over her ribs. She sat up slightly and raised her arms, allowing me to remove it completely before leaning back, watching me as I slowly worked the snap and zipper of her jeans before sliding them down her shapely legs.

How many times had I dreamed of doing this very thing after a night out with her?

My chest constricted at the look in her eyes. They were darker, to the point of being black, and her hair was in disarray against the pillows. The site before me was my undoing. Julia lay still as I gazed upon her perfect form, clad now only in white lace bra and matching string bikini panties. Her skin was so creamy and translucent, her hips and breasts softly swelling in perfect proportion, her legs long, her gorgeous face full of longing. I struggled to breathe and my heart pounded so fast I felt it would fly from me.

"You're gorgeous. I could spend hours just looking at you."

"You're the beautiful one…" she breathed and reached for me. "But I need more than just looking, Ryan. Touch me." Her arms ran up my chest as I leaned over her and she pushed my shirt off of my shoulders, kneading my flesh and scratching her nails down my arms. I felt my body start shaking and I quickly stood up to shed the rest of my clothes. I couldn't take my eyes off of her face as she watched me, her eyes falling to my erection, so rigid and ready for her. The want in her eyes was the sexiest thing I'd ever seen.

I moved to sit on the bed and pulled her into a sitting position, pushing the straps of her bra down, kissing the flesh on her shoulders, finishing the job by unhooking the back and throwing the beautiful lingerie aside.

I cupped her cheek and kissed her mouth lightly, pressing a series of kisses all over her face and she moaned, her tongue coming out to graze mine, pulling me in. I gave in to both of us and kissed her deeply, pressing her back on the bed and following her down. Her hands skimmed down my body and closed around my length, making me gasp.

"Julia…" I breathed against her mouth. "I've never wanted anyone so much in my life."

"I'm yours, Ryan." She closed her eyes and kissed me passionately as her hands excited me beyond imagination. It was all I could do not to push her down and plunge into her. My hands traced down her body and she shivered, arching her back and causing her mouth to pull slightly from mine. "All yours," she whispered again.

My hands pushed the delicate lace panties down her legs before sliding back up to touch her in her most private place. Her moist heat welcomed my fingers. I wanted her so damn much it caused my mouth to go dry, but sex was still new to her and I didn't want to move too fast.

"Your body tells me that you're ready for me, my love, but I don't want to hurt you, honey. I want you to take control, okay?"

Her mouth parted as her breath left her body in a rush and her lids lifted to look at me. I moved up into a sitting position against the headboard, pulling her up and guiding her to straddle my lap as I looked into her beautiful face. Her eyes were heavy, her lips swollen.

"God, you're beautiful." I felt my heart swell with emotion and my throat tightened. I groaned as I pushed her hair back with one hand and moved the head of my dick against her, rubbing it back and forth in the slick wetness.

Her head fell back and her mouth opened wantonly.

"Ryan…mmmmm." I found her entrance and slid the hand at her face down her body, touching until I found her clitoris, rubbing little circles with my thumb. So responsive, she instinctively started to arch into me and lower her body onto mine.

"Baby, go slow. I don't want to hurt you. Only do what feels good, Julia."

Her head snapped up and her eyes opened as she looked into my eyes. She lowered herself, completely sheathing me. I gasped at the heat and the look in her eyes.

"This is what feels good. You inside me. All the way, Ryan." Her hips rocked against me and I continued to stimulate her with one hand and the other grasped her hip to help guide her movements. Her arms wrapped around my shoulders and her fingers tangled into my hair as we began to kiss deeply.

The kisses were incredible, so intimate, as we sucked on each other and moved together. I'd never felt closer to another human being in my life. We went slowly, feeling every touch, every inch of every thrust and every nuance of each and every kiss until she was finally panting and trembling around me. I felt myself losing control of everything I had. Body and soul, she owned me.

"Uhhh...Ryan."

"Say it, baby. I need to hear you say it," I moaned against her breast as my arm wound around her waist and pulled her harder onto my body, increasing the pressure and the pace.

"You're making me come, Ryan. Oh God...I love you."

"I can't live without you. I need you like air."

Our hips moved together and I exploded inside her as she cried my name into my shoulder, both of us shuddering and quaking together for endless seconds. We held each other and kissed the sides of each other's faces as I raked my hand down her back.

"Oh, babe. *Julia*," I breathed as her body jerked one final time.

I was still shaking as I moved, holding her to me, still buried inside her body, lifting her with me to lay her down on her back on the bed. I propped myself on my elbows and looked down at her. She raised her tear filled eyes to mine and I brushed the tears from her face.

"Shhh…love, are you okay?" Julia nodded and touched my face with gentle fingers as she gazed into my eyes.

"Perfect. I just…" she closed her eyes, "I can't believe how much I love you, Ryan. It takes my breath away. It's like…*not possible* that this much love even exists."

"I know. You're my whole life." I ran my nose up one side of hers and down the other before kissing her mouth, tracing her top lip with mine. She sucked my lower lip into her mouth until I deepened the kiss as she demanded. I couldn't help myself and felt myself growing hard within her again and her hips surged against me.

"More," she whispered against my mouth as we began to make love again and I knew that we'd be sleeping late tomorrow. Tonight I had other plans.

~6~

Ryan ~

The weekend flew by and I was sitting across from Julia for the last time in what would be God knew how long, as we both picked at our breakfast. It was a shame because it was perfect Eggs Benedict. I begged Julia to stay in bed with me, but she insisted she make breakfast. Unfortunately, it was tasteless in my mouth and I struggled with every bite, my heavy heart overshadowed everything else. Julia was pushing the food around her plate, barely eating in the same lackluster manner as I was; her eyes downcast and preoccupied, a small crinkle between her perfectly arched brows.

"Hey," I said softly, longing to see her beautiful dark green eyes rise to meet mine, but afraid of the sadness I'd find there.

She glanced up and tried to smile, the corner of her mouth barely rising. "Hey, handsome."

I stared for a long moment, unable to tear my eyes away. She was tousled from our night of passionate play, her hair messed by my hands; my t-shirt was falling off of one bare shoulder, the neckline too big for her slight frame. She turned her face to the side, presenting me with her profile as she tried to blink back the tears and swallowing hard in the process. My stomach dropped as I watched her struggle with her emotions.

She was the most beautiful thing in my life and my mind had settled long ago that she always would be. I loved her so much I could barely wrap my mind around it. It was like the sun being the center of the universe, the planets all held captive around it, unable to break free of the pull and unable to sustain without its magnificence. She was my sun, the absolute *center* of my universe.

"Come here," I murmured and set my fork down before pushing my plate away. My arms were aching to hold her, my whole body screaming to be near her, and my eyes beseeched her to come enfold herself in my arms.

She stood up suddenly and took her plate to the sink, tossing it in carelessly, the glass clanking against the side of the ceramic. She leaned against the counter and dropped her head as her shoulders visibly slumped. She was on the verge of breaking down and didn't want to show it, thinking it would make me even more miserable leaving her.

"Julia. Please. I need to touch you," I begged, my voice low and aching.

She turned around and looked at me, stretching her hands out on the counter on both sides as she leaned against it, her eyes filled with tears on the brink of spilling over, her chin trembling.

"I don't want to do this, Ryan. I *never* wanted to do this," she said brokenly.

Oh, God.

Her voice was shaking as she covered her eyes with her right hand. "This is why I resisted loving you. I knew it would kill me to be away from you. I just…I don't know if I can do it after…" She broke off as the silent tears slipped from her eyes and she angrily wiped them from her cheeks.

I got up from where I was sitting at the kitchen bar and gathered her close to my chest. I turned my face into her hair, but she refused to hold me in return and my heart broke. Her resistance was not something I expected after the beautiful weekend we'd shared.

"Baby, are you mad at me? Why aren't you holding me back? I need to feel you, Julia. I want to touch you every second we have left to us."

I felt her body go limp against me as she gave in to the silent sobs that started to shake her shoulders, and her arms finally enfolded my waist to pull me closer as she cried. "I don't want you to go," she whispered as if her heart was breaking. "I don't want to ache for you when you can't *be with me!*"

My heart exploded in my chest, a mixture of elation and misery. My arms tightened around her and I kissed the side of her tear-soaked face. "I love you so much." I held her as if my life depended on it and stroked her hair with one hand until her sobs quieted a little.

Finally, she found her voice. "I-I'm s-sorry," she whispered brokenly.

"Sorry for what? For loving me so much? The last thing you should be is sorry." I tried to soothe her by rubbing small circles on her back but, in truth, my heart was shattering like glass, the shards falling to slice me open. I kissed her face again using my hand at the side of her jaw to raise her mouth to mine. "Please don't be, Julia. I'm sure as hell not sorry," I whispered against her mouth. "Nothing means more to me than you, you *have* to know that." I placed a series of soft kisses on her lips and dragged my mouth along her jaw. My hand slid behind her head and I fisted in her hair while I pressed my open mouth to the pulsing vein in her neck, sucking on the warm skin.

"I know it…but it doesn't make this any easier, Ryan."

She moaned and I expelled my breath as her hands ran through my hair to tug my mouth back to hers. She was angry at the situation, maybe even at me, but she wanted me and I was lost. My mouth opened to devour her. Our lips moved in unison, tasting and sucking on each other, our tongues dancing together in intimate play; perfect mirrors, each one knowing when to give and when to take.

These long, sensual, deep kisses were ours. Just ours. I'd never felt so connected over a kiss with anyone in my entire life. I caught her lower lip between my teeth and pulled it with my mouth as I raised my head. "God, babe. I don't ever want to stop kissing you…it's so good. You taste so damn good."

I pressed my hand on her chest over her heart and rested my head against hers, struggling for breath. I closed my eyes as her chest heaved under my hand, her heart thudding beneath my fingers. The whole time my body was swelling to the point of pain, my heart was aching and pounding so fast it felt like I was dying.

How is it possible to ache so much in so many places, and be so damn hungry, desperate and heartbroken at the same time?

"God, Julia, I'm going to miss you." My hands were frantic in their search for more of her skin, as they found both of her breasts under the material of the shirt. The tender flesh was so soft and supple in my palms, my thumbs brushing across both nipples at the same time and she moaned.

She pulled my lower lip into her mouth and then slid her tongue along my upper one; doing things to me I couldn't explain or understand. A low groan tore from my chest almost against my will.

"Ryan…" she breathed my name, her voice throbbing with want and love. I could hear it dripping off of her words like honey and knew I had to have her one last time or I wouldn't survive. "Ryan, please," she begged against my mouth.

"No…*Julia, please*…I need you." The desperation was overwhelming us both as my arms tightened and I lifted her so her mouth was level with mine.

"Yes…yes," she breathed, her hot breath fanning over my face.

I wrapped my arms around her body and continued kissing her over and over until finally she lifted one leg to wrap it around my hip. I pulled it higher and could feel her heat and I wanted more. "How do you want me, babe? Anything you want and it's yours," I moaned against the skin of her cheek and jaw as I dragged my mouth from hers.

Julia was breathing hard and took hold of my jaw while her hot little tongue came out to flick lightly and oh, so softly, on my upper lip. "Take me to the couch, Ryan," she whispered and I moved to do her bidding.

I lowered her down, returning my mouth to hers as my knee sank into the cushion at her hip. I wanted to taste every inch of her, feel every smooth surface of her skin, and hear the delicious little sounds she made as my body took hers. Mostly, my heart ached to be closer, to imprint upon her that she belonged to me, body and soul. I wanted to be the only man she wanted, the only one to ever kiss her or touch her for the rest of her life.

"My God, Julia. I'm...so in love with you." Her knees came up on either side of my body and I surged into her, pressing my hardness into her hot softness and she moaned, her hips rising to increase the pressure even more. "You're so beautiful." I continued to move on her, rubbing against her through the thin material of her panties and my silk pajama bottoms.

I rose up on my elbows so I could look into her face. "Please look at me," I whispered as I brushed her tangled hair back from her face with both hands. "Open your eyes, baby."

Her hips moved with mine while her mouth dropped open and her breath rushed out. I nuzzled her nose with mine until she finally opened her eyes. They were darker green, almost black and full of fire. "Can you come like this?" I asked as I moved my hips with hers. "I want to make you come more than once. I'm the one who does this to you, Julia. Just me."

"Uhhnnn, Ryan. I love you. You're the only one who will touch me like this. *Ever...and yes.*" Her hands were clawing at my back, moving down to urge my hips forward, increasing the delicious friction. "Yes, you can make me come like this...but I want *you with me.*"

I dropped my head to hers and closed my eyes, my body throbbing and twitching against her. Her voice was so sensual and she moved her body against mine while she said those delicious words. The combination of her voice, her breathy moans and her body beneath me were almost my undoing.

"I will...but not yet." I moved on her with more deliberation, watching her face and listening to her gasps and sounds as I tried to determine just which of my movements felt the best for her. It was only a few seconds until I had it and then I could let my mouth go back for more of the kisses that I craved. She moaned into my mouth and I knew she was getting close. Already, I could play her like a finely tuned instrument made just for me.

I let my hand caress her breast, pulling and tugging on the taut little nipple as I moved the head of my dick against her clit again and again, our clothes soaking with her wetness; I wanted to rip them from between us.

Every one of my senses was assaulted. The feel of her skin beneath my hands, how she tasted on my tongue, hearing her sounds, the scent of her perfume and arousal, the passion in her features...it was almost more than I could bear. I was gasping for breath against her mouth and wondering if I'd be able to stop myself from coming right along with her. I felt my balls tighten and my stomach clench when finally she arched against me. Julia cried out my name in a soft moan, raking her hands down my back. It hurt, but I wanted more because it meant I could give her pleasure like she'd never experienced. My heart was ready to burst when she breathed my name again.

I stilled against her so I could get control of my body just in time to stop my release, but continued to kiss her. "Mmmm…I love seeing you like this. It's stunning. I've fantasized about it so, *so* much, but nothing compares to being with you," I breathed against her forehead and moved to kiss her temple. She lifted her head off the pillow, reaching toward my face so that she could run a series of feather kisses along my jaw.

"I love you," she sighed against my skin. Something as simple as her breath rushing over me meant so much; that she was close, that I had satisfied the woman I loved more than life, and that she was content in my arms.

"Are you okay?" I asked softly. She was quiet and I was worried that she was sad or anxious again, but she nodded.

"I'm perfect. You're incredible. When you touch me, I melt. I'm out of control…completely. I knew it would be amazing with you, but it's even more than that."

My heart swelled and I tightened my arms around her. I felt overwhelming love and pride that this incredible woman would love me like that. "Baby…" I breathed into her hair and kissed her mouth lightly. "I want to give you everything, Julia. Every-thing."

She raised her eyes to mine and smiled slightly, lightly brushing back the hair that was hanging down on my forehead as I loomed over her. "All I want is *you*," she said simply and shrugged as her fingers stilled on my cheek. Looking at her face, the seriousness and the serenity in her features, calm spread through me at the obvious truth of her words.

"I'm so lucky." I bent my head and took her mouth again and again, my body springing to life in renewed desire as I lay on top of her, her gorgeous curves molding perfectly to me, so warm and responsive beneath me.

She pushed on my chest and ripped her mouth from mine. We were both breathing hard and I was afraid I was crushing her and I instantly lifted myself up off of her. "Did I hurt you, honey?"

"Uh uh. I just want to take care of you now. Can I taste you?" She ran her tongue from the base of my neck toward my ear and sucked the lobe into her mouth. Her words were so sexy; my cock turned to granite and throbbed in response. Her teeth nibbled a little before her mouth moved up and she whispered in my ear, her breath causing shivers to run through me. "Do you want my mouth on you, Ryan?"

My head fell back and I closed my eyes. *She did not just say that, did she?*

"More than anything."

She smiled seductively at me and bit her lip as she peeled my silk pajama bottoms over my hips and down my legs.

"Okay. Then...let me." She pushed me back further until I was sitting on the couch and she was kneeling between my legs, her hands moving up my chest and back down again, across my naked hips and down my thighs. Her touch left a blazing trail of fire on my skin and it was all I could do not to pull her up on my lap and thrust into her body. Only the anticipation of what she was promising to do held me still and waiting. I was barely breathing as her eyes bore into mine.

"You know how much I love you, right?" I asked her seriously. She bent to kiss the top of my thigh, her hair tumbling around her face and raining like silk on my lap.

"Mmm, huh. I know, Ryan," she whispered against me as her mouth moved up across my hipbone and on to the muscles of my stomach, which contracted involuntarily in response. Her breath was hot and I couldn't help how my body throbbed and twitched toward her mouth. Her mouth opened and she sucked on the skin below my navel, her chin grazing my length.

"God, babe," I breathed. "You're going to kill me. It's such delicious torture."

Her fingers splayed out on my chest dragging down my body and she pressed her forehead where her mouth had just been and her hands finally raked down my thighs. Shudders went through my entire body as her tongue ran around the head of my cock and she kissed it, sucking on the tip slightly. My breath left me in a rush as I felt the pre-come seep out the tip. I wondered if she could taste it.

"Uhgnnn, Julia. Oh, Christ," I groaned at the delicious feeling of her hot little mouth on me.

I'd had a lot of head in my life, probably more than I should be proud of, but this was *Julia*. *My* Julia. The one woman who I held in reverence and she was taking me into her mouth. I wanted to see the magic she was giving me, so I gathered her hair up in my hands and lifted it away from her face so that I could watch. It was the most erotic sight I'd ever seen.

Her hands grasped me around the base of my cock and the sight of her pink lips around me, along with the sensations of her licking and sucking, were more than I could take. I felt the pressure building too quickly and I wanted this to last. For being inexperienced, she was incredibly adept and had me trembling and writhing in minutes. It was all I could do not to thrust deeper into her mouth.

As if she read my mind, she moaned as her hand and her mouth worked together, bobbing up and down on me as she found her rhythm and taking me in as deep as she could. When I felt the back of her throat on the head, I almost came instantly. I sucked in my breath and put my hand on her shoulder to still her.

"Julia, stop. I can't take it, honey. Stop or I'm going to come and I don't want to yet." The words ripped from my chest in a guttural groan. "Uhhnnn, God. *Stop!*"

Her head popped up and she looked at me, but her hands were still on me, pulling gently.

"Honey, please, stop. I want to make love with you, to be inside your body, so *stop*." It was all I could do not to spill into her hands, and I reached down, my hands finally closed around her wrists to stop her movements and pull her forward and up to me. I let go of her hands and slid mine around her body, under her legs and lifted her so that she was straddling my lap. Her perfect breasts bounced at eye level as she settled over me, her eyes languid and her hair was in wild disarray from my play in it.

"I love it when you beg," she teased breathlessly, a wicked smile dancing on her beautiful mouth.

"You're so gorgeous," I murmured as I pushed her hair back off of her face and curled my hand around the back of her head, while my thumb caressed her jaw. Her eyes were full of desire, the lids half closed and her glistening mouth had fallen open. I itched to touch every inch of her so I let my other hand slide underneath the t-shirt she was wearing, over her hip and up the side of her ribs, to the side curve of her breast. My thumb brushed across her nipple and although it was already a hard little button, it grew even more beneath my touch. She gasped and a low moan escaped. Never had I imagined that she would be so openly abandoned to my lovemaking and so wanton.

I've never seen anything more beautiful in my life.

The hand around her neck gently pulled her head down toward me as I lifted my face to ghost her mouth with mine. "Ryan..." she whispered and it was my undoing.

"Say it again, my love."

She leaned into me to kiss me harder, grinding her hips against mine, the delicious heat where we touched, burning us both alive. "Uh...Ryan," she moaned into my mouth.

I couldn't take anymore...I wanted to see her body, to feel her skin on mine. My hands slid down to her hips again, pulling her forcefully to me. I needed her to feel how hard I was, how much she was affecting me and I showed her with my hands how I wanted her to move against me. She ground into me over and over, her hips moving in small circles as both of my hands slid up her body, underneath the shirt.

I lifted her arms so I could slide it from her, wadded it up in a ball and threw it aside. I wrapped one arm around her waist and cupped her left breast in the other, dropping my head so I could lave the nipple and finally suck it into my mouth, flicking it over and over with my tongue, her sounds of pleasure urging me on. Her skin was hot and delicious beneath my mouth and I was starving for more. She kept moving on my body and I could tell by her reactions she wanted me as much as I wanted her. The heat pooling between her legs was so much that I felt the wetness through her panties.

Her movements excited us both and I had to be inside her or die.

I lifted her and hooked the edge of the lace with my thumb and pulled them down, placing open mouth kisses below her navel as I panted against her skin. She lifted her hips to help me and then my fingers found the secret place I wanted to touch. "Honey, you're so...I want you so much."

I slid a knee between her thighs, my weight sinking into the cushions of the couch. Julia willingly spread them wide for me as I surged against her, easily sliding against her until I slipped inside, filling her to the hilt. Her tight heat surrounding me felt amazing, the sensation shaking me to the core. I dropped my forehead to hers as I started to move inside her, my strokes slow, long and deep. I wanted her mouth on mine...I wanted to make love to her with everything I had and have her shuddering beneath me and around me. I wanted her to feel every inch of me as my body staked its claim on hers, the desire to imprint my possession of her stronger than I'd ever felt in my life. I wanted to take this moment with me back to Boston.

I needed her to want me, to love me; needed to hear my name on her lips. I needed Julia with me forever and the emotions welling up inside me were so consuming, I thought I'd completely lose it.

"Julia," I gasped against her mouth as her breathing increased and she started to make those little mewling sounds that drove me to distraction. I'd grown to need hearing them.

"You are mine." I kissed her mouth, and she opened to me, pulling my head down and slanting her mouth with mine so our tongues could go deep inside. We were devouring each other until we were both gasping for breath, my body taking her like she was taking me. I was drowning in her, but with no desire to save myself.

She started to spasm around me and she ripped her mouth from mine to bite into my shoulder. It sent me over the edge and I came hard inside her body. I continued to thrust hard against her as my body poured out into hers. "Only mine," I ground out while I bent to take her mouth again in frantic need to be closer and closer to her. I wanted to possess her body and soul, to own her like she owned me, and I kissed her like I'd never kiss her again, worshiping her mouth with my own. My heart was breaking at the prospect of leaving her and I tried to push the pain down, even as the shudders from my orgasm still racked through me.

She was still lifting her hips to mine, her muscles squeezing around me, milking every drop and every shuddering sensation out of me. Even after I stilled, she was still working around me and it was too incredible for words.

"Uhhh," she sighed as I looked down upon her flushed face, her chest and cheeks rosy and glowing. Her eyes were closed, but she slowly opened them as I nuzzled her nose and brushed some kisses along the side of her face. "Ryan, you've completely wrecked me." Her voice cracked as she spoke and my heart stopped. "If I wasn't before, I am now. I didn't believe it was possible to love you more than I already did...but I do."

"Julia..." her name felt like a prayer. I closed my eyes against the pain. I wasn't sure if it hurt because I was leaving her or because of how much I loved her. "You *own* me. I can *never* be with anyone else, I never *want* anyone else...I *only* want you for the rest of my life..." My throat tightened and ached as I struggled to contain the emotions that threatened to break from my chest.

First one, than another tear fell from her lashes, slipping out of the corners of her eyes onto the pillow beneath her head. I bent and pulled her top lip between both of mine and kissed her softly.

I love you so much I can't even-fucking-breathe.

I closed my eyes against the pain I felt and knew that I would see it mirrored in hers. "Babe, don't cry, my love. Are you okay?"

Her arms tightened around my shoulders and she locked her legs around my waist. "I'm incredible...but I'm not okay," she said brokenly. "I'm...too much in love and I'm scared."

I rolled onto my side and pulled her to me, rubbing little circles on her lower back with one hand. "I'm in love, too. So much, Julia." She turned her face into my neck and wrapped an arm around my waist. "So why are you afraid?"

"It's just...this is going to hurt."

My chest filled with air before I spoke. "But it hurts so good, my love. *So* good," I tried to make her smile.

She nodded against my chest and I kissed the top of her head. "I missed you so much before but now...it's going to be so much worse."

I sighed against her forehead. "It's going to be hell...but let's just concentrate on how we can get you to New York, okay?"

"Okay."

"How are we going to do this? I mean...what do you want?"

"Just to be with you. That's all I've ever wanted, Ryan," she said so softly that I barely heard her.

She is so perfect. I brought my hand up and brushed my knuckles softly against her cheekbone and she raised her eyes to mine.

"So what do we need to do to make it happen?" I asked hesitantly. I still felt guilty at the fact that she was going to sacrifice everything and move to the East Coast, but I wanted it so bad I was beyond considering any option that didn't put us closer together.

I felt her shrug against me. "You go back and be brilliant and I'll talk to my boss tomorrow. It might take a little time, but I'll work it out."

"What if they say *no?*" I asked with trepidation.

She shrugged against me. "If they won't help me transfer out there, I'll just have to quit."

I struggled to find the right words. I wanted to say *"Yes, quit." Move to Boston and live with me,* but my brain knew that wasn't fair to Julia and I had no right to ask that of her. "I already feel like an ass for wanting to be near you without making you sacrifice your job for me."

"Pfft!" She rolled her eyes and I grinned. "Since when did you ever feel bad about getting me to do what you wanted, huh?" She nudged me and laughed softly. Leave it to her to put it all in perspective. Yes, I wanted her near and yes, I would let her move to accomplish that. If I had my way, I'd have a lifetime to make it up to her.

"I'm sorry, sweetheart. I know it isn't fair, but you're right. I want you with me. I want it so bad I can't stand it," I said urgently. I felt desperate; like, if I didn't have her with me, part of me would be suffocated or lost. As much as I had loved her all these years, the intensity of my feelings now was more than I had ever dreamed possible.

Julia sensed my trepidation and leaned in to nuzzle against my neck and then kissed the side of my face. I held her close as her hand played with the hair on my chest and stomach.

"It's gonna happen, Ryan. We'll make it happen because we *have* to."

*****

Julia ~

This was the end of our weekend and I was doing my best to put on a brave face and remind myself of all that I had to be thankful for. And there he was, right in front of me, all six foot, one inch of him, his wild dark gold locks, scruffy, unshaven chin and bright blue eyes. So beautiful, but so sad, his brow crinkled and his face tense. I drew in a deep breath as I watched him put his things in his suitcase and duffle. He glanced up from what he was doing and his features softened as he looked at me.

I got up and walked across the room, sitting on the bed beside his suitcase, beginning to rub his back. His muscles were tense as they flexed under my hands when he moved. We had both showered and his hair was still damp. I longed to run my hand through it and tug on the ends. He loved it when I did that and it would comfort him in some small way.

I grabbed his arm and pulled him to sit next to me, curling around his back and holding him close. Ryan reached up, grabbed my hand and brought it slowly to his mouth, brushing his lips over my knuckles lightly, his lips ghosting back and forth over the skin before finally kissing it.

I kissed his back and closed my eyes, trying to steady the trembling in my voice before I spoke. "I'm so happy you came to see me. This weekend has meant the world to me, Ryan," I almost whispered against his black button down shirt that was stretched taut across his shoulders.

His thumb brushed over the skin on my wrist as he held my hand. "Me, too." He turned to me and looked into my eyes, a small smile lifting the corners of his mouth as one hand reached out to cup my left cheek. "Can I see the drawing before we go to the airport?"

"The drawings are so personal."

"*Drawings?*" he asked, raising an eyebrow. "How many are there?"

I smirked back at him and shrugged. "Matthews, you didn't really think this was the first one, did you?"

"Sometimes I'd catch you drawing when I was studying, but I felt like I'd be prying if I asked what you were doing. Your face was always so intense."

"Like I said…It's very personal to me." As intimate as we had been, I suddenly felt shy. "I poured all of my love into my sketches. I was afraid if you saw them, you'd know. Um…I was afraid you'd freak out and I didn't want to lose you."

Ryan laughed softly. "Julia, I was so in love with you the entire time. Watching you, so intently working, I longed to be the thing you were thinking about that caused that look on your face. We were so stupid."

"Something like that, yeah."

"Okay, so show me already!" His eyes were excited and I scratched my fingers across his shoulders one last time before I went to retrieve the sketch pad resting between the two pieces of furniture on the floor. I went back to the bed and handed it to Ryan, slightly nervous over what his reaction might be.

"Be nice," I begged. Ryan just looked at me for a long moment.

"I've seen your work. You're incredibly talented, so what are you fidgeting about?" His voice was lighter, full of amusement and my heart leapt. It was better than the sadness that was there just minutes before.

"I'm silly, I guess. You're right. You've seen my work, so…" I let my voice drop off, not really sure what I wanted to say.

Ryan's hands quickly moved to flip open the cover of the book and he instantly froze, looking at the still unfinished drawing, his hand hovering over the image on the page.

"Obviously, I'm not finished with it," I began.

Ryan stared at it for a few minutes before he looked up at me. "Julia…if this is how you *see* me…I'm…speechless."

My throat began to ache as I tried to blink away the tears, willing myself to speak. "Uhgghh…" I tried to clear the emotion out of my voice. "Um…I see you as *perfect*. The most beautiful thing I've ever laid eyes on," I said honestly as I sat slowly on the edge of the bed near him.

"If I searched a hundred years, I couldn't find the words to tell you how you make me feel...or how much I love you. Do you *know* that?" he asked earnestly, his eyes burning into mine preventing me from looking away. His face blurred before my eyes until first one, and then another tear slipped down my cheeks. Ryan set the drawing to the side and put both hands to my face, wiping at the tears with his thumbs, his touch soft and so very gentle.

"My baby. You make me so happy. Please don't cry, honey." His voice was like velvet as it washed over me and he placed a soft kiss on my mouth before leaning his forehead against mine. "Can I have it?"

I looked down at my hands and immediately both of his reached out to take one of mine between them. "It's not finished yet."

"It's a masterpiece just like it is. I want it, Julia. Please?"

I nodded because I couldn't get any words out. Ryan gathered me close and held the back of my head, turning his face into my hair. As he breathed me in, the hardness of his chest pressed into the softness of my breasts and he felt amazing. We needed to leave for the airport or he'd miss his plane, but I never wanted to let him go.

"Julia, this is going to hurt *like a bitch*! I never want to leave you," he moaned into the curve of my neck and my hands slid up his chest to fist in the back of his hair, holding on for dear life and kissing the side of his jaw. "But...I'm so glad we're *us* now. I love you." He stood up and pulled me with him, still in his arms, pressing my hips to his and then wrapping his arms tightly around my waist and back.

"So much. I'll miss you every single second." I willed my voice not to betray me, the words breaking free in a throbbing ache as I struggled not to full out sob. My heart hurt, but my brain clung to the hope that I'd be able to move to the East Coast very soon. I raised my face to look at him and Ryan took my mouth in a brief but deep kiss before reluctantly letting me go. He picked up his suitcases to carry them into the other room to the door. My heart was thumping in my chest in protest and I felt like I was losing my best friend. I tried to talk myself out of my sad mood, telling myself silently that this was the start of our life together. Certainly, this was not something to be sad about.

Then why the fuck do I feel like my insides just fell out and piled at my feet?

The silent war continued to wage inside me. Ryan felt it, too, because his hands rubbed up and down my arms after he helped me on with my jacket. He kissed the back of my head and for a long moment just rested his head against mine. He reluctantly moved away and once again picked up the bags. The loss was already a tangible thing.

"Ready?" I said sadly, grabbing my purse and car keys. I turned back to him to see him shaking his head his eyes glistening.

"No. I'll never be ready to leave you."

I put a trembling hand to his face. My fingers clutched around his jaw as I kissed his mouth, breathing in his sweet scent and letting my lips move with his. His hands were full of the luggage so he couldn't take me in his arms, but I felt his urgency in his mouth and tongue as he kissed me. "It's going to be okay," I whispered against his lips.

"I know." He tried to smile as I opened the door and held it for him. "We'll be fine, Julia. But it's better when you're near me. That's what I want for Christmas, okay?"

I smiled in return while we walked to the car and I opened the trunk. Ryan put his stuff in the back and once again I tossed him the keys. "Okay. Christmas," I nodded. "I'll do my best to give you what you want."

"You always do," he said as he opened my door and I slid inside.

The drive to the airport was mostly spent in soft touches and contemplation. I watched his features as he drove, never taking my eyes from his face. He seemed lost in thought, save the times when he'd glance at me lovingly or bring the hand he held constantly, to his mouth.

My heart was constricted and I finally had to face forward and look out the window or risk breaking into tears. His thumb rubbed over the inside of my wrist and I knew he understood what I was going through. He knew me better than I knew myself.

"Hey, weren't you the one who said this would be okay?" he reminded me. He was hurting too but was stronger than I was. I was feeling so fragile, like I would crumble and blow away into nothingness, but I made myself answer in a stronger voice.

"Yeah. I know it will, babe."

"Jules, you probably want to come in with me, but I'm just going to get my boarding pass and wait. It won't be that long before I'll have to go through the security checkpoint and you won't be able to join me, so why don't you just drop me off at the terminal?" His eyes flicked to my face and then quickly away, like there was something he wasn't saying, but was trying to hide from me.

We entered the airport property as a plane landed loudly overhead. I was thankful for the time it gave me to organize my thoughts and get control over the trembling in my voice.

"But...Ryan, I was hoping..."

His hand tightened on mine. "This will be so hard, I just...think it's best if we just say goodbye at the curb, babe."

His voice broke slightly on the words. "I feel like such a fucking pussy!"

I started slightly at his expletive, but I drew a shaky breath and nodded. "Okay."

"Julia..." he began, his voice tortured as he pulled up to the American Airlines terminal and put the car in park. He turned his tortured blue eyes to mine. "Remember my Christmas present, okay?" He touched my chin with his fingers as I nodded sadly. "It's gotta happen, so I guess this is it. Will you hug me good-bye?" Ryan asked softly as he stared into my eyes.

"Of course, you idiot." My chin was trembling and I put a shaky hand over my eyes as Ryan opened his door and popped open the trunk of my Mazda.

I reluctantly grabbed the handle and pushed the passenger door open and walked to the back of the car as he was setting his bag on the curb. Instantly, I was in his arms and he was kissing the side of my face and then my mouth in a wild, deep kiss. His tongue slid into my mouth and I opened to him as if I was starving and he was the last nourishment on earth.

His mouth lifted and his lips played and nipped at mine lightly. "I love you so much, baby. I have to go."

I nodded but pressed my mouth to his once more. He didn't deny me and his arms tightened.

"Thanks for coming. I'll miss you."

He touched my face and kissed my cheek one last time before he stepped on the curb and started walking into the airport. I watched him for a few seconds before I called after him. "Ryan!" This was the only time he left me that he hadn't said the words, and I needed them. He turned and looked back at me, stopping as he did so. "Don't forget to remember me, right?"

He smiled sadly and shook his head. "Never." He looked at the ground for a second, the muscle in his jaw flexing. He finally raised his eyes back to mine and I could see the tears shining there. "I love you."

"Love *you!*" And with that he disappeared behind the doors, and I was left trembling and aching, the tears making it almost impossible to find my way back into the car. Other people going into the airport and the men checking bags were probably staring at my pathetic display. I didn't care. I couldn't help it even if I wanted to.

My hands gripped the steering wheel and I lowered my forehead to rest on them as tears began raining down uninhibited. *God, it hurts!* Finally my hand reached to put the car into gear and I brushed the tears off of my face in an attempt to get control.

Just breathe, Julia. Breathe; and, first thing tomorrow morning go talk to Meredith. That's all you can do.

I tried to reason with myself and it helped to a degree. Being away from Ryan should be easier since I'd been doing it for 5 months, but now that we were lovers and had admitted our feelings for each other, I felt like my heart was ripped from my chest and was on its way to Boston.

I scoffed at myself as I moved away from the terminal and merged into the moving traffic.

He IS my heart...so duh.

My phone had fallen out of my purse onto the passenger seat where it vibrated. I grabbed it with one hand, and quickly glanced down at the text on the screen.

You are my heart. The most beautiful and precious thing in my world. Don't forget that.

I was still feeling fragile and so my eyes welled again and I longed to send him a message in return, but traffic was too bad to risk it.

He is so damn perfect.

~7~

Julia ~

Landed in boston. Thanks for finally being mine. I love you with everything I am.

I smiled, glad that he was home safe but aching with loneliness for him already. I quickly typed out the obvious response.

Always was. You're just aware of it now. :-)

It wasn't long before he responded, and I quickly opened the message.

I'll be dreaming of you tonight, love. As always.

Hmmm…what to say? I contemplated for a minute and then rolled onto my back and began pressing the keys.

Real Yummy—Adorably Naughty. Awake or asleep…you're what my dreams are made of.

I sighed and stared at the ceiling as I lay on the couch in silence; the same couch where Ryan made such passionate love to me only hours earlier. I closed my eyes and put a hand up to my temple trying to push back the tears that threatened to overpower me.

I should be so damn happy. I have everything I've dreamed of now. I had Ryan and he loved me, so what was my problem?

I rolled onto my side and tried to swallow the rising lump in my throat. He was beautiful, brilliant, talented, and mine. *Mine*; something I thought would never happen. It was eight o'clock in the evening and pitch black outside. The lights were off in the apartment and I lay there with only the eerie silver-blue glow of the moon to cast dim shadows around the room.

Ellie's arrival was heralded by the rattling of her key in the lock. She flipped on the entryway lights and threw her keys on the table under the mirror in the hall. Her bags made a loud thump as she dropped them on the floor.

"Julia?" she called.

I rubbed my eyes and tried to wipe away the smears of makeup that would undoubtedly be underneath them. "Yeah, Ellie. I'm here." I sat up on the couch and turned toward her. "How was your Thanksgiving?"

Ellie was in the kitchen getting out a bottle of wine and pouring a glass. "It was nice, thank you. Would you like some?" she asked.

I was still feeling shaky and very tired. Wine sounded good. "Sure. Thanks."

"Harris' mom is sweet, but she cooks one dry damn turkey, let me tell you! He said next year it's my turn to do the spread." She finished pouring two glasses of wine, bringing mine into the living room. "Shit. Can you imagine? Me cooking?" she mocked; her rosy face was glowing as she sat next to me and pressed the glass into my hand. "So? Tell me, how was your weekend with Ryan?" She looked into my face for the first time and her eyes widened as she noticed my swollen eyes. "Julia, what's wrong? You two didn't argue, did you?"

I laughed and took a swallow from my glass. The wine was smooth and soothing as I shook my head. "No. Far from it, El."

"Yeah. I could see it on Friday night. He told me that you talked about moving to the East Coast," she said softly but with a gentle smile.

I was nervous about her reaction. "Yes, we did talk about it.
I-I mean…" I struggled with how to position it to her, but she
read my mind and reached for my hand.

"Honey, you don't have to explain. I understand that you
want to be with Ryan. He loves you so much, Julia."

I nodded and looked down at our hands. The tears were
threatening again. "Shit, I'm such a damn mess! Can you believe
this? All I've done since he left is bawl my eyes out and I hate
that fucking shit! You know that, right?" I laughed mockingly,
even though tears slid down my face. "He's amazing, Ellie. I
thought I knew how incredible he was, but he's even more to me
now. I never thought I could love him more than I already
did…but I just…*do*."

Ellie set her wine down on the coffee table and curled her
legs underneath her. "Tell me. I want to know everything.
Absolutely everything!" she said with a grin. Her arm leaned
over the back of the couch and she propped her head up on her
fist, looking at me expectantly.

My heart filled as I recounted the weekend to her. "It was
beautiful. Every second like a dream. Even if we didn't do anything but lie around and talk! I want nothing more than to be
with him, Ellie. It's so…profound…it's frightening. I can't put it
into words, but I swear I'd chuck it all to be with him."

"I can see that. Friday night it was obvious how possessive
he is; but then, it's always been obvious to me." She grinned as I
leaned back against the soft cushions. "It's about time the two of
you finally admitted it! I'm sure Aaron and Jen will be happy to
see Ryan in a better mood."

"Hmmmph." I let my breath out. "I'm not sure if he'll be in
a better mood or not, considering we're both fully aware of what
we've been missing now." I wagged my eyebrows at her and she
burst out laughing. I couldn't help but join in.

"Like I said...tell me *everything*!"

Ellie listened intently as I told her about the weekend, drawing him in his sleep after his tender lovemaking, making dinner together, shopping and then the pain of our goodbye. When I got to that part, my eyes welled with fresh tears and I cursed myself.

"Am I a damn faucet or what? I feel so helpless."

She reached for my hand and squeezed it again. "Honey, why don't you fill up your glass and go take a hot bath. You'll feel better."

I nodded and pulled myself off of the couch. Ellie rose and hugged me. "I'm really happy for you. The rest of us used to make fun of you guys behind your backs. So much friggin' sexual tension that it made us all horny for God's sake!" She laughed in my ear.

I drew back and went to grab the wine bottle. "Why, Ellie Jensen! I'm surprised at you! A proper southern belle like you, using the word *horny*. Holy shit!"

"Aaron used to say just being around Ryan's unrequited lust gave *him a boner*. He was so hilarious!"

Aaron. I rolled my eyes and grinned, walking down the hall to the bathroom.

My thoughts turned to how I was going to discuss this with my boss the following day. I loved my job. More than loved it and I would be sad if I had to give it up, but I'd do what I needed to do. Since my trip to Boston, I knew he loved me, but finally hearing it and the experience of being in his arms was more than I'd ever expected. I knew now how much I needed him...like food or air or water.

I started the water in the tub and sprinkled in a generous amount of bath salts before I started stripping out of my clothes.

Ellie knocked on the door. "Julia?"

I wrapped a towel around me and she handed me my phone. "I think you have a text from someone that you want to hear from."

I smiled and raised an eyebrow at her.

"What? I can't help it that it shows on the screen who it's from. Who in the hell else would it be from anyway? Unless you're holding out on me about Mike!" She left the room with a smile and I opened the message.

Are you naked yet?

I laughed out loud. Ryan's sense of timing was incredible. I slid into the warm bubbles and shot a message right back.

Mmmm...Wouldn't you like to know?

The water felt great. In combination with the wine and the sweet messages from Ryan, the night was looking up. He made me feel better even from clear across the country. I felt sleepy and a warm calm settled around me. A connection was all I needed. We continued our electronic conversation as I lounged in the bath, letting the warmth relax me.

I do know. Take a picture and send it to me. I miss touching you.

I miss you with me, next to me, inside me. And yes...I'm naked, Ryan.

Fuck, don't do that to me. Please. What are you doing?

I laughed. He was begging for mercy and asking for more in the same text.

Can't help it. If I tell you that you do the same to me, will it help?

It only makes the suffering unbearable...but I wouldn't have it any other way. So...TELL ME what you're doing. LOL

In the bath.

Mmmmmm. Wish I were there. Don't forget about me. I'm the one who loves you.

I remember you, Matthews. Always.

You're always on my mind and in my heart. It doesn't hurt that you set my body on fire, either.

Now who's killing whom? Love you and miss you madly.

Why don't you just call me, babe?

I want to, but I know we'll be up all night and you need to be fresh tomorrow for your talk with Meredith. I love you, beautiful girl. Sleep well.

I didn't. Not at all.

*****

Ryan ~

"What the hell are you smiling at, Ryan? You look like an idiot!" Aaron boomed as he came slamming into the apartment. The neighbors would be knocking the door off the hinges in protest soon.

I was sitting on the couch, my bags still in the doorway and just finished texting Julia. My heart was aching the entire way back to Boston, but our seductive little exchange had changed my mood completely. Spelling out my name with words was only something Julia would do and my heart swelled with emotion. I was grinning from ear to ear as I shut my phone and set it on the coffee table, wincing at the time. 1:30 AM.

"Aaron! Even your sorry ass is not going to get to me tonight! No way!" I called. "Where's Jen?"

"At the hospital." He came into the room and fell into the armchair near the sofa. His huge body took up the entire space, his feet crossed on the coffee table, he took a pull on his beer. "I guess you had one thankful Thanksgiving from the looks of you." He smirked at me knowingly. "I thought you'd be home earlier. What happened? Was the flight delayed?" He raised his eyebrows at me.

"Um, something like that. I was delayed, yes." I smiled and went to pick up my bags and take them quickly down the hall to my room before going back to talk to my brother. I needed sleep, but I felt the need to talk about Julia.

"Hmmmph!! Delayed or *laid*, dude? It's written all over you. Jules is a hottie, right? I knew she would be," Aaron stated matter-of-factly. "This is the most relaxed I've seen you in months."

My brow furrowed. Aaron didn't mean anything by it, but something clenched inside at his knowing comment. "Oh?" I asked.

"Come off it, bro'. Even though she played all innocent, she smolders underneath. She's sexy as hell. As you now know *first-hand*."

"Yes." What else could I say? It was the truth. Obviously, he wanted to know more.

"Ryan, come on. Did she finally cave and tell you she loves you?"

I stopped and looked down at my hands, tenting in front of me as I leaned my elbows on my knees. I nodded, and my hair fell across my forehead. I reached up to push it away.

"So, what? Am I talking to myself?" Aaron looked at me incredulously.

"What is it you're asking, exactly? It was all I hoped for and more. Yes, she told me she loved me and has loved me just as I've loved her. While it made me incredibly happy, I was sad because we should have been together all this time. And *pissed*."

"Dude...you *were* together. *Night and day* for four years, so what was wasted exactly?"

"Hmmph." I let out my breath. "Yeah, that's exactly what Julia said. And…she didn't *play* innocent, Aaron."

His eyes widened and he leaned forward in his seat toward me, obviously expecting some detail of my time with Julia, but I wasn't going to expound. Aaron had shared many of his sexual escapades with Jenna, despite my protests, but what I had with Julia was mine and mine alone.

"What are you saying, Ryan? That she started it?"

I shook my head in response.

"She *was* innocent, Aaron. I'm not going to give details, but she *was* innocent."

His eyes widened as understanding dawned on him. "Ryan, really? 23 and still with her cherry? Are you serious?" His face lit up like a candle.

"I'm only telling you because I need to talk about it, but can you please use a little discretion? This is *Julia*. Not some random chick I banged on a one night stand," I said impatiently.

He sat back and rubbed the stubble on his chin thoughtfully. "No shit!" he said like he couldn't believe me. "Julia was a *virgin*?" he said more to himself than to me.

"She's…*special*, Aaron. She's not like other women. I never thought she was, but this weekend, I discovered a whole new side to her."

"Ryan, I love Julia. I know how much she means to you. I love Jen, but I don't think it's anything close to what you and Julia have. Did she tell you why? I mean, she's had boyfriends—" he paused. "So I thought…" his words dropped off and he shrugged.

I got up and filled a glass with water out of the refrigerator. I paused, my back to him, as I spoke.

"She said that she couldn't let anyone else touch her. Can you believe that, Aaron?" I asked incredulously. "She said she couldn't bear to be with anyone else because of how she felt about me. All the time when I was going mad with jealousy, she wasn't even going there...I can't tell you what knowing that does to my insides. I'm...stunned."

Aaron watched as I walked back to join him on the couch. "Fuck me," he said.

"I know." I ran a hand through my hair and tugged on the ends. "It just makes me love her even more."

"Yeah, right. You drove me nuts *before*. Always mooning around but never admitting it. It was frustrating living with your moody ass then, now it will be insane." He laughed; the sound coming from somewhere deep in his chest.

I smiled. "But I *do* love her more. She's amazing. Innocent, yes, but so damn passionate. It's like we're one person and we instinctively know what the other needs. The love she has for me seeps right into my skin whenever she touches me, Aaron. It's that intense. Being with her was like nothing I've ever experienced in my life." My tone was serious and reflective as I lost myself in the memory of her mouth and body moving with mine.

"Did you talk about your, um, habits, Ryan?" Aaron asked hesitantly. "Ryan?"

I looked up, snapped out of my memories of the weekend.

"You mean dating other women?" I shrugged. "Yeah, it came up, but not like you think. She wasn't grilling me." I thought of the drawing in my bag and quickly stood up. "Wait a minute."

I went and retrieved the sketch book. It was almost like I was sharing one of Julia's secrets, but I couldn't explain this any other way.

"It hurt her, yeah, but she said that she knew they wouldn't last, and she and I always remained close. She said she didn't want short-term gratification and risk losing what we had. I can't believe she hid her feelings, but, I guess I did the same thing."

"Julia is very smart, Ryan. She had your number all along."

I smiled. "She had me alright. I was a fucked up mess. I should have known it was hopeless to try to get her out of my system and nothing could make me fall out of love."

"Especially since she was your *best friend*, dickhead. How do you fall out of love with someone you can't stay away from?" he scoffed. "Jen and I used to bet on which one of you would crack first."

I chuckled softly and shook my head. Leave it to Aaron to blast me with a dose of reality whether I wanted one or not. "Who won?" I raised my eyebrow at him sardonically.

"Neither. You both caved at the same time and all it took was a little thing like Harvard Med."

He reached for the book in my hand but I pulled it back. "Julia used to sketch me on the nights I went out." The corners of my mouth lifted in a sad smile. "I wish I would have known how much it hurt her because it wasn't worth that to me. Wednesday night after we made love, I fell asleep and she drew this..." I finally handed it to him and he flipped open the cover.

"Holy shit, Ryan," Aaron exclaimed quietly after looking at the half-finished drawing. He stared down at the drawing, admiring the fine details and pencil strokes so lovingly placed on the page. "She's very talented. It's perfect, almost like a photograph." He looked up at me as I stood above him.

I moved to the couch and sat down slowly. Aaron looked at the drawing again and then shook his head with a smile on his face.

"I know how incredible it is," I said softly. "It's like she looks right through me or into my soul or something. I can't even find the words to describe how I feel."

Aaron closed the cover on the sketch pad and set it on the coffee table, leaning back in the chair. "So…what are you gonna do about it?"

"We talked about her moving to New York. She's going to ask her boss about getting a transfer."

"We've been over this. Has some seismic activity altered the state of the universe or is New York still two hundred and twenty miles from Boston? Distance is still distance."

"Yeah, well two hundred and twenty is better than three thousand. At least we can see each other more often. And we need that. Neither one of us is forgetting our goals or responsibilities, but we have to be closer to each other."

He rolled his eyes. "I'm just sayin'…I know you, Ryan. You won't be satisfied until Julia is in Boston, preferably living here."

He was right. Everything inside of me screamed for her, to have her near me, accessible whenever we needed each other. I was terrified of Julia being in Manhattan all alone and still being four hours away. What if she needed me and I couldn't get to her fast enough? My chest tightened.

I nodded. "I know that's true, but she's worth going through anything. I'll deal."

"Again with the *dealing* bullshit! Am I having déjà vu? Didn't we have this same damn conversation that night we both got our acceptance letters?" I started walking down the hall toward my bedroom.

"Screw you, Aaron!"

"Ok, fine. Whatever, Ryan. You go *deal*. Riiiiiight," he mocked after me.

I flipped him off over my shoulder and he burst out laughing.

As I closed the door to my room, stripped off my clothes and lay down in my lonely bed, I suddenly ached for Julia, wishing it was her bed. At least then I'd have her scent.

"Gah!" I groaned in my frustration, rolling over onto my stomach and grabbing the pillow. I bunched it up underneath me and rested my chin on my forearms. Sighing, my mind flooded with memories of the weekend spent in her arms. Such beautiful, love filled days and nights.

Suddenly my arms and my life felt very empty indeed. *Julia...I love you.*

I closed my eyes and tried to lose myself in the memory of her voice breathing out my name, her beautiful face lost in the passion we'd shared and the blissful contentment in the knowledge that she loved me. *She loved me.*

Julia ~

I smoothed the material of my black pencil skirt down over my hips as I walked into my office. I noticed Andrea on her way in as well and she bounded into my office, flashing a bright smile on her way. She had her red mop piled on top of her head in an attractive, but messy, up do.

"So? How was the weekend? Did your hottie friend make it into town?"

I smiled up at her because I couldn't help myself and a flush of heat crept up on my cheeks. "Yes. He did. We had a fabulous time together."

"Hmmm...I can see that by the look of you. I thought this dude was just your friend, Julia."

I flipped on my computer and waited for it to boot up. "Yes, he's my best friend. We met when I was a freshman in college."

"So? Do I have to drag it out of you?" She laughed and plopped down in the chair in front of my desk. My office was small and the desk, the two chairs and the art board took up most of the space.

"Did you get those photos back from production? The ones for the *Men's Sex Secrets* feature?" I rolled my eyes at her. Some of the articles we did amused me, but it wasn't my job to question the content, only make it look good.

"Do I have to do it now? Can't we talk first?" she practically whined.

"Get the photos and then we can talk and work at the same time. Please?" I glanced up from my computer screen and pursed my lips.

"Oh, okay! Slave driver!" She hurried from the room.

My eyes flashed to the corner of my desk and a picture of Ryan and me at a Dodger's game. Ellie had taken it one weekend when we'd all road-tripped to Los Angeles our junior year. He had his arm around me and was dumping beer into my open mouth from a cup a few inches above it. We looked so happy it made my heart lurch.

Ryan could have been the model for this shoot and though the pictures would be gorgeous, I wouldn't want to have him spread all over the pages of the magazine in his underwear. I smiled at the memory of the weekend, his naked body and how it had claimed ownership of mine. My breath left in a rush, desire and love washing over me in a wave. Finally, I could say he was mine. I smiled secretly to myself.

"What's that about, Julia? That face looks like you got laid this weekend. If that's what you wanted, I certainly could have obliged." Mike walked into my office and leaned in the door frame. He was blonde with blue eyes, a muscular build and attractive.

I glanced up at him as I waded through my inbox. "Hey. Um...thanks, but no thanks." I smiled as he put a hand over his heart.

"Julia, you wound me deeply!" he groaned. "I'm the best catch around." He *was* attractive in a slick, narcissistic sort of way, always dressing trendy with an edge, his hair always perfectly coiffed. It was more his personality that put me off. He thought he was funny, but sometimes he was just annoying.

"That's why we never dated, Mike," I scoffed and rolled my eyes but kept avoiding his gaze. "You love yourself too much!" I started typing an email to production regarding a proof on the layout for one of the fashion features for the January issue.

"We never dated, because I didn't try that hard." He sat on the edge of my desk knocking the picture over and I reached quickly to keep it from tumbling to the floor.

"Oh? Was *that* it?" I asked flatly.

"Of course," he said as he brushed back a strand of hair that had fallen out of my low ponytail. Instinctively, I pulled away and glared.

"Pfft. Whatever. If it makes you feel better to think so, have at it."

Andrea walked in carrying several boards of photos and laid them on the slant table, glancing at Mike on her way in. I had a feeling that she wouldn't mind a little of his swarthy attention. She'd said on more than one occasion he was hot and she wouldn't mind a sample.

Gross.

Andrea was still eyeing Mike but he was watching me as I walked to the table. Obviously he wanted me, he'd made no secret of it, but my love for Ryan had always held me back from anything. Even if he'd been Adonis with a personality to die for,

I wouldn't notice. Truthfully, he was a great guy and extremely easy to work with, but his tactics didn't move me in the slightest.

I stood over the photos, Mike and Andrea behind me, examining with a critical eye. The pictures were full color; the man had a tanned, muscled body and gorgeous face, in various poses with a scantily clothed glamour girl draped all over him.

"These shots are very good, Mike," Andrea gushed. My brow furrowed. They were sort of overkill. I wanted something more subtle, and could have sworn we'd talked about it during casting, but now I was stuck with this. *Shit!*

"Julia, what do you think?" he breathed in my ear. I prickled and moved away, seeking the barrier of my desk, and taking the photos with me.

"Um…well," I bit my lip. "It's not really what I wanted. The guy looks good, but the girl is sort of whorish. I didn't approve that God awful red lipstick. I wanted *hot* real people, not a hot guy with a…well, a hooker. Ehh," I wrinkled my nose in distaste.

He winced. "Sorry, Mike. It's my job. I gotta be honest. After all, it's *my* ass that's on the line for the final look."

"And what a nice ass it is," he stated, leaning back to check it out. I plopped down in my chair.

"Ugh, really? Did you just say that to me? You know sexual harassment is a serious offense, right?"

"Puh-lease," Mike sat down across from me, an expression of boredom on his attractive features. "You know you *love me*, Julia," he mocked.

"Yeah, but not like that, and you know it," I teased.

Andrea was leaning against the art table and didn't look happy. "Julia's got a boyfriend, you know," she shot out and my head popped up to look at her as my eyes widened.

"Andrea."

"What? You do! Is it a secret?" she asked, her expression completely changing when I raised my eyebrows and shot her a look that told her to zip it.

"Um..." I didn't know what to say because I'd never referred to Ryan as my boyfriend. It seemed so parochial and sure as hell didn't do him justice. A hot flush rushed over my face. "Uh...let's just get back to work. I need to get this done so that I can catch Meredith before she leaves for lunch."

"Touchy subject, eh? Well, I'm not giving up, sweetheart," Mike said, rubbing his chin and looking unflinchingly into my face.

"You might change your mind if you saw her...uh, *boyfriend*." Andrea's eyes lit up with a sparkle as she said the words. "He's way hotter than this dude here," she said, nodding at the boards and wrinkling her nose as she looked at it.

"Andrea! Enough. Work, remember?" I asked sternly, adamant that we focus, but doing my best not to smile. It was damn hard, too.

"Well, we're screwed because the female model is out of the country for some fashion show in Brazil, so what will we do? We only have a day or two until this goes to press," Mike stated matter-of-factly. "Right?"

"Hmmm...Andrea, is the guy available? If so, get to work on finding a new girl ASAP. We'll have to redo the shoot late this afternoon or this evening if we can."

Mike groaned. "Shit, Julia. Don't you have a life?"

I'm about to, I hope.

"Well, why didn't you call me when you saw the model? Surely you knew this wasn't what we discussed and it would have been a hell of a lot easier to send her back to wardrobe and make-up than to shoot it and deal with this mess," I admonished.

"If we can't redo the shoot, then we'll have to Photoshop the shit out of one of these, I suppose."

I took two of the boards, one in each hand and contemplated which would have the most potential. I was leaning toward one where the woman was standing behind the guy and he was the main focus of the shot. "Either way, this is another budget problem. I'm tired of this type of crap."

We finished brainstorming about how to change the photo and then I shooed them both out of my office. It would be possible to change her lipstick color, soften her harsh hair style and maybe even make the bed shrug she was wearing longer to look more like a robe.

"Don't forget, you've got to spill. Later girl," Andrea reminded me as she walked out.

I glanced up and smiled. "Okay, maybe lunch?"

Her face lit up. "Yeah, great!"

After she left, Mike lingered in the doorway. "*You* could always do it, you know."

"What?"

"You're a beautiful woman, Julia. I'd love to photograph you half dressed."

"*Goodbye*, Mike."

"I'm just saying…you're bitching about the budget, so think about it."

I raised my eyebrows. "I'm no model." I smiled and shook my head, hoping he'd drop it.

"You *could* be."

"Hmmph," I scoffed. "I'm way too short. I'm only five six."

"So get some Jimmy Choos, then. That shit is hot. So are you, Julia."

I laughed out loud, the thought so ridiculous. He was funny even though he was shameless in his pursuit of me. Since I started at Glamour, we'd bantered and goofed around. While he was serious in his flirting, he was great to work with and a generally nice guy. He chased and I blew him off. End of story.

"Stop, for God's sake. Get out of here. I want to get some work done." I shoved him out the door and closed it loudly. My eyes rolled as I glanced at the clock and noticed it was 9:30. I had an email from Meredith in response to the one I sent earlier.

Sure, honey. Pop in around 11.

My stomach dropped. I really loved my job and the people I worked with and I'd be a little sad to be leaving. But life is a series of choices and no matter what decisions came up throughout my life, if Ryan was one of the options, he would always win out.

At the magazine less than a year, I was nervous about this conversation with my boss, but hoped she could understand my predicament. She was aware of Ryan from the photo on my desk and the drawings in my portfolio. I'd told her that he was my best friend when she'd asked who he was. I suspected she knew I was in love with him by her response.

"He is drop-dead gorgeous Julia, and your drawings are just insane. Are you sure he's only your friend?"

I'd bitten my lip and nodded.

"Well, what a waste! I don't know how you can resist. Mmm, mmmm, mmm." She'd smiled big as I put the drawings away and blushed. "Girl, if I were you, I'd get on that immediately."

I pulled out my phone. When Ryan answered, his voice was low and breathy. "There's my gorgeous girl!"

"Hi! I miss you."

He sighed on the other end of the phone. "Oh, honey, I'm pretty sure I miss you more. Did Ellie give you the third degree? Aaron bounced me the minute he walked through the door," he said and I could literally hear the smile in his voice and knew his blue eyes would be sparkling.

"What do you think? Of course! Probably not as bad as Aaron's interrogation, though." I laughed. "Did they have a good Thanksgiving?"

"As far as I know. We didn't really get to that. So, uh…"

I sat down and turned my chair toward the window. "Yes?" I knew what he was going to ask.

"Um, what's the verdict?" Ryan asked softly.

"I haven't had a chance to talk to her yet. I've had issues with some photos that need to be redone. I'm meeting with Meredith at eleven." I hoped the nervousness I felt wasn't coming through on the phone.

"Are you nervous?"

Shit! So much for that.

"I'm about to go ask my boss of a few months to transfer me to another magazine and out of state. I'm…*freaking out!*" I ran a hand through my hair and then picked at some lint on my skirt.

"Baby, you don't have to do this if you don't want to."

"Oh, well…okay, then," I said, trying to keep my voice even and heard his sharp intake of breath on the other end of the line. I smiled and tried to keep from laughing out loud.

"Really?" he asked hesitantly.

"Um, yeah." I was feeling mischievous and it was fun to play with him. I realized that Ryan didn't think it was funny when he didn't respond.

"Babe, I'm kidding!" I added quickly. "Of course I have to do this, okay? I want to."

Still he was silent. "Are you sure? You sound like you might be reconsidering."

"Matthews, I was *kidding*." I waited. "Ryan?"

"I just...I'm feeling guilty about asking you to move out here. It isn't fair, Julia," he said and I could hear his reluctance as the words dropped from his mouth.

"Hey. I love you, so it's done. I'm doing this for me, too. I can't be this far away from you. It was hard enough before, but now...forget it."

"Yes, I'm struggling more now, too, and it's only been twenty-four hours." He chuckled softly.

"We're pathetic, but I like it."

"Oh, babe...I keep thinking about last weekend. I'll never forget it."

"Mmmm. Me, too. Ryan, I'm..." I began softly as memories from the lovemaking started to stir my body to life. Here in my office, three thousand miles from him, he could make me tremble and quake.

"You're...?" he prodded softly, his velvet voice rolling through me like an electric current.

I'd always been honest with him but this was so revealing. "I'm...*aching.*"

He sucked in his breath. "I am too. It was beyond anything I expected. Just remembering how you felt and your voice, makes me rock hard. I want you so bad."

I felt the throbbing warmth and wetness in my core increase but couldn't let this continue if I was going to function properly at work. "Ugh, Ryan. You have to stop," I whispered. "It's torture."

"If this is torture, you can kill me right now, Julia. I love you so much. Remember that when you're talking to Meredith."

"I love you too. I'm coming out there, one way or another, so just *know* that."

"You make me very happy. I don't deserve you."

"We've had this conversation before. You deserve whatever I want to give you, remember?" I laughed softly.

"I don't know how I got so lucky, but I won't argue with you." Ryan's low laugh was smooth as silk.

"You're so damn sexy, Matthews. Quit it," I smiled into the phone.

"As long as you think so, that's all that matters. I hate to go, but I have class baby. I have to run."

"Okay. I'll call you tonight."

"You better. Good luck with Meredith."

"Who needs luck? I have you. Bye, sweetie."

"Bye, honey."

I continued to work through the morning, slightly stressed when Andrea had trouble lining up another model on short notice. The agencies we normally worked with were scrambling, but I had a budget and a time constraint that we were finding it difficult to work around. I called the head of the art department and gave instructions on how the photo may need to be altered. Just in case.

Finally, it was time for my meeting with Meredith. I took a deep breath as I rode up the seven floors to her office. I was fidgeting and willed myself to stop.

Get a grip.

The executive offices were posh with hardwood cherry floors and large glass doors that separated the offices from the elevator foyer. The receptionist looked up from the paperwork she was working on.

"Just go on in." She smiled warmly and indicated with her hand in the direction of Meredith's office.

I clasped my hands in front of me and walked toward Meredith's open door. She was on the phone, but looked up when she saw me hovering and motioned me in.

"Yeah, you could be right. She's here now, in fact. Um...I'll get back to you. It's a great idea. Thanks."

Meredith raised her eyebrows, pointing to one of the blue leather chairs in front of her large desk. There were pictures from all over the world adorning the walls of the office. Meredith and her husband had no children, choosing instead to be well-traveled and carefree. She was a strong woman who knew what she wanted out of life and how to go after it. Hopefully, that characteristic would help her understand my predicament.

"Okay, okay. Later." She hung up the phone and leaned back in her chair smiling widely.

"Julia, you look gorgeous. I love that color on you," she said, admiring the chartreuse silk of my blouse under the black suit jacket. I sat back and crossed my legs, my foot bobbing nervously.

"That Mike Turner! He's a trip, isn't he?"

I wondered if the conversation that they'd just finished had anything to do with the botched photo shoot.

"Um, yes, you could say that. Did he tell you about the pictures? I just didn't think the look was right. He should have called when the model didn't match the story boards."

"Yes, he told me, Julia. He, um...well, he had an idea that we should use you as the model since we can't seem to line any-one else up."

My mouth fell open and I started in the chair. "Uh, I don't think so," I said quickly.

"Why not? You're a beautiful girl. It would save us $10,000 and solve the time problem too. Andrea can clear your schedule this afternoon and we'll get the whole thing done right away. She's already got the male scheduled."

Heat rushed up my neck and over my cheeks. It was intense and my face had to be bright red. "Meredith, come on.

This...isn't part of my job description, and I have no experience," I tried to protest.

"Julia. Let's just try it, shall we?" She looked at me pointedly and I shut my mouth. I recognized that tone. Her mind was made up.

Damn Mike, anyway.

She glanced at her watch and then back at me. "Was the botch-up what you wanted to talk to me about? If so, problem solved! Voilà!"

Meredith patted her elegant chignon and then leaned forward, looking at me expectantly. She had olive skin, dark hair and striking features. The epitome of what a creative director in fashion should look like, her make-up and clothing were always impeccable and of excellent taste.

"No. I thought I'd handle that without bothering you. Too bad Mike didn't think along those same lines."

She smiled. I wasn't getting out of the photo shoot. "Okay, then...what?"

"Meredith, do you think I do a good job?"

"Oh for God's sake! Of course, Julia. Don't be absurd! You're one of the best creative assistants I've ever had. I see a huge future for you with this company."

I took a calming breath. The fact that she valued me would prove invaluable in the next few minutes.

"Thank you. That means a lot. I really do try to do my very best for you."

She looked at me quizzically. "Julia, what's this about? Are you asking for a raise?" She smiled and raised her eyebrows.

"No. It's kind of personal and if it's alright, I'm just going to say it." I took a deep breath and plunged in. "I need to move to the East Coast and I'm hoping I can get a transfer to one of our magazines in New York." I let my breath out in a whoosh and waited for her to respond.

"What? This is very sudden, isn't it? Is there some emergency?" she asked, the concern evident in her features.

"No, it's nothing like that. Remember my portfolio..." I began but she cut me off, her eyes widening at the same time.

"Oh, yes. Mr. Gorgeous Harvard Best Friend, hmmm?"

I blushed at her quickness. She was a brilliant woman who could read people easily.

I nodded. "Yes. Ryan. He's been my best friend, but honestly Meredith, I've loved him for years. This past weekend we admitted that we're in love with each other. I just...I need to be closer to him while he's in medical school." I glanced up from my hands and into her face and she was smiling softly. "I know it's asking a lot, considering that I haven't been with the company all that long, and it might take a while to make it happen, but I wanted to see what the possibilities are."

Meredith considered it for a moment. "I'll hate to lose you, Julia, but I do understand. I'll have to make some calls to see what's available out there. Are you willing to stay here until I can find a suitable fit and to help find your replacement?"

Relief washed over me. I nodded quickly and ran my hand through my hair. "Of course. Anything. I want to make it as easy on you as possible, Mere." I felt like laughing out loud. "I can't thank you enough for even considering this!"

"You don't have to, Julia. That man is mouthwatering. I can see why you want to be near him," she said and smirked. "But right now, get your ass down to wardrobe and make-up. Mike is waiting for you in studio four."

Ugh! She was serious.

"That's blackmail and you know it," I said rising from the chair and walking toward the door to her office.

"Well, learn from the master, honey. You do what you have to do to get it done," she said as she picked up the phone and started to dial out.

I smiled on my way to the elevator. Lunch with Andrea would have to wait. I pulled out my phone and dialed Ryan's number since he'd be out of his last class and was probably chomping at the bit for my call.

He answered on the first ring. "Hey, babe. How'd it go?"

"Oh, just great!" I mocked. "No problem."

Ryan laughed and amusement laced his voice, "Really? Don't play with me or I'll have to spank you."

A throaty laugh escaped my chest. "Oh sure, get in line, babe. Meredith will help me get a job out there but isn't sure how long it will take. I also have to help hire my replacement, and as you know, I'm irreplaceable," I laughed.

"That's it? It was that easy, sweetheart?" I could hear the elation in his voice.

"Well, that and I have to pose in my underwear for next month's issue." I was nervous as hell but it was funny and I giggled softly. Ryan sucked in his breath, apparently not as amused.

"What the hell is that supposed to mean?"

"Well, you want me out there don't you?" I teased.

"What are you talking about, Julia?" The happiness turned to trepidation, his voice getting more strained with each word.

"Relax. We had some photos tank and now there isn't time to get a new model. We're doing a reshoot and I was elected to stand in," I said as I walked into my office past a giggling Andrea, who had obviously already heard.

Good news travels fast.

"No! I don't want you doing that Julia," he said adamantly.

"Why? You like me in my underwear, and out of them, right?"

"Julia, this isn't funny. Are you really doing this?"

I laughed softly. "I'm sure the pics will be horrible and then we'll go to plan B, which is to Photoshop the originals. Don't worry, Ryan. I'm in charge of all of the creative so I won't let it be too revealing. You know...you might even *like* it," I added suggestively, making my voice as seductive as I could.

There was silence on the other end for a moment until he finally answered. "I would if it were for my eyes only, then yeah, but not the whole damn world. Who's taking the pictures? Turner?" There was a hard edge to his voice.

Ryan hadn't met Mike yet, but I'd told him generalities and how he'd asked me out on numerous occasions.

"Isn't it always Mike's jobs when something gets so fucked up?"

He sighed loudly on the other end, clearly very upset. Teasing hadn't helped so I softened my voice and got serious.

"Ryan, this is no big deal, okay? I'm on a deadline and my options are limited. Besides, I'm no model. They probably won't even turn out."

"Julia, you don't see yourself clearly. You're stunning; of course the pictures will be amazing. That's what I'm afraid of."

I smiled and my heart couldn't help expanding. He was jealous. "Have you forgotten I'm moving to New York? It's a go, so don't let this shit overshadow that. Be happy! I am, okay?"

I sank down in my chair trying to soften my voice another level. My heart raced at the thought of Ryan seeing the photos and my motivation changed. Suddenly, I wanted them to turn out. Maybe I'd ask Mike to take a few shots of me alone so I could give them to Ryan for Christmas. When he remained silent, I tried again.

"Hey. Are you still there?"

"Yeah. Just don't let him touch you and make sure you're covered up."

I wanted to laugh but it would just piss him off. It was a bedroom scene so there would be some skin, but I'd deal with that later. I was more nervous for Ryan's reaction than anything else.

"This is not a big deal, I promise. I like that you're jealous, though. It means you really do love me," I whispered into the phone.

"You know I do and I fucking hate being jealous! I don't like how it feels."

"I have to go get ready. I love you, Ryan."

"I know. I'm sorry I'm being a baby," he sighed. My mind's eye could see his face and that little smirk trying to play on his full lips. I wanted to kiss those lips.

"It's okay." I changed the subject to take the focus off of the shoot, all the while admonishing myself for even telling him. I should have guessed what his reaction would be. "Will you be able to help me move?"

"Julia, I'll try. It depends on when and what's going on with classes. I want to."

"We'll figure it out. Love you."

"Love you more. Tell Turner I'll rip his head off if he even thinks about you in the wrong way," Ryan teased and I could tell he was more relaxed.

I laughed. "He thinks about everyone in the wrong way. He's twisted like that. I'll call you tonight."

"Don't forget about me when you're half naked."

"It's impossible, no matter what state of dress or undress I happen to be in. You know that."

He laughed. "Leave it to you to soothe the savage beast. Okay, honey."

"I love you, baby. Bye."

"Goodbye, my love."

Happiness flooded through me. I put away my phone and motioned to Andrea to join me as I rushed down to the studio floor. I glanced at her and then it hit me. I knew how to make my move happen even faster and the transition for the company even easier.

"Andrea, I'm going to New York to be near Ryan. How would you like to have my job?" I asked as her mouth dropped.

~8~

Julia ~

Is that me? Holy shit!

I leaned forward and tried to find myself in the mirror. The make-up was more pronounced, the lips brighter, the eyeliner thicker and the skin bronzed and glowing. They'd covered my body with a layer of airbrushed tan, my usually pale skin now golden brown. The green shadow on my eyes made my eyes seem larger in combination with the heavy layer of mascara.

My hair was wild and big. Teased to look like I'd just been made mad love to and someone had run their hands through it over and over again. I puckered my lips and raised my eyebrows at my reflection. My lips weren't overly bright, they were darker, and not the blood red of the last model.

I'd discussed the layout with Mike and Andrea earlier and we'd agreed that the male model would be the focus and I'd be in the background, preferably in profile or a back shot. I didn't want my face plastered all over the magazine. Not that anyone would recognize me anyway, but Ryan would be less agitated if it wasn't obviously me.

The most effective shot would be to have Nick in his boxer briefs, all muscled abs and arms, standing in front of the bed with a smoldering stare into the camera, while I would be on the bed in the background, wrapped in a sheet. I was nervous about the sheet because even though wardrobe had put me in nude boy shorts, I couldn't wear anything on top so the sheet could drop low on my back. At least I'd be a blur in the photo, but the illusion had to be there.

Andrea patted me on the shoulder.

"Is it so obvious?" I cringed.

"Of course, Julia," she soothed. "You look amazing though!" She smiled at my reflection in the mirror and I pulled the white robe closer around me.

The make-up artist that had slaved over me for the past two hours groaned. "Julia, don't. You shouldn't even be wearing that damn thing. You'll rub off the tan!"

"Oh, crap. Sorry, I'm just…I'm not used to this."

"Just be more careful." She was clearly not sympathetic to my plight. She had a sort of punk rock style going on, with jet black hair, and numerous piercings in her ruddy face. I grimaced as I noticed the tongue ring and the one through her left eyebrow. *That shit had to hurt.*

She had a dark demeanor and she didn't talk at all during the entire time she worked on me. I'd tried to start up a conversation several times, but finally gave it up as a lost cause. I was damn glad to be getting out of her chair.

Andrea hustled me down the hall and into the studio. I wobbled slightly on the platform shoes. They were black suede Louboutin pumps and the heels were at least 5 inches high. I loved them and wondered why I needed shoes considering my feet wouldn't show in the shot if it turned out like I wanted.

A low whistle filled the empty space as I walked on set. Mike was checking the lighting and had stopped. "Can it, Mike. I'm not interested in your pseudo admiration," I said shortly.

He stood there staring and I stopped ten feet in front of him. "Oh, it's the real deal, baby. You look ah-ma-zing, Julia. I mean it." He smirked at me and went back to adjust the camera on the tripod. "The camera is going to love you."

"Yeah, well, we talked about this. Background, background, background! Got it?"

He laughed as Andrea moved over to chat with Nick, the male model. "Spoilsport," he pouted. "You ruin all my fun."

"Can we just get on with it? I have a real job to get back to."

"Take off your clothes and get on the bed, Julia." Mike was looking through the camera lens as his throaty laugh followed me when I walked toward it. Andrea was right behind me, holding the sheet that I would wrap around me when I dropped the robe. Mike cleared his throat. "I've been dreaming of saying that to you since we first met."

"Fuck off, Mike. I mean it," I said sardonically. "I don't need your bullshit."

"I love it when you talk dirty." I turned sharply and shot him a hard look. Nick looked bored, except for a sardonic smile playing around his lips as he listened to my exchange with Mike.

"Mike!"

"Oh, okay. Hell, lighten up, Julia. I'm a professional. Even if you *are* drop-dead gorgeous." He winked at me. I sighed and looked at Andrea who held the sheet up to hide me from the men while I dropped the robe.

"Arms up," she said and I resisted because they were instinctively covering my bare breasts. I looked over my shoulder at her. "Julia, I can't wrap this around you unless you raise your arms." I nodded and complied.

With the sheet firmly around me, she moved out of the shot. I started to ask Mike how he wanted to position me but heard the camera click in fast succession and the assistants with the reflectors moved into position around me. I was standing behind the bed that Nick was lounging on.

"Nick, stand in the foreground, and Julia, sit on the edge of the bed with your back to him like we talked about. I need you to drop the sheet low and then look over your shoulder at Nick. Hold the sheet in front of you with one hand but let the other arm straighten and take your weight with your hand on the mattress," Mike instructed.

I loosened my hold on the sheet, my heart racing. The bed creaked slightly when I lowered to it. Andrea came over, pulled my hair back to smooth it down my back and adjusted the sheet to expose the top curve of my ass. I raised my eyes to her and she laughed. "It's only your ass dimples, Julia. No butt crack, I promise!"

"Ugh!" I breathed in disgust. Ryan was going to lose it when he saw this.

Mike talked me through several more shots, and after a few minutes, I felt more at ease. All of the important stuff was completely covered, so my apprehension was eased slightly.

He took a whole card full of shots and then swapped it out. "Julia, I want to try one thing we didn't talk about, okay?"

"Uh…" I hesitated.

"Just roll with me on this, okay? It will be a great shot. Nick, I want you to stay facing the camera but lie on the bed and reach out and grab Julia's sheet and sort of drag her to you. Look into her face and make it intense. Julia, you look into the camera this time and put one bare leg on the bed to take your weight, but resist Nick slightly. I need you to look sexy. Think of something that gets you hot. I want to see desire on your face, honey."

My mouth set into a tight line and I huffed. "Mike," I started to protest.

"Think of Ryan, Julia. Think of all the stuff you haven't been able to tell me about yet!" Andrea shot off from across the set. My heart raced at the mention of his name. "When you look at the camera, imagine you are looking into his eyes. Are you in love with him, Julia? What about him? Does he want you? All you gotta do is let that show."

A soft smile twitched at the corners of my mouth as I glanced down. Nick grabbed the sheet and I grasped it more tightly to hold it closed over my chest and placed my knee on the bed as I was told. I closed my eyes and thought of Ryan's hands and mouth on my body while I tried to tune out everything else. The air rushed from my lungs and my mouth dropped open.

I raised my head and looked into the camera and five minutes later it was over and I blushed at my shamelessness. I felt vulnerable, exposed, like I'd just let these people see a very private part of myself, that I shared only with Ryan.

"Okay, that's it," Mike said. "Julia…that was…well, you're a natural." He smiled and shook his head.

"Uh…thanks, Mike," I said as Nick moved off of the bed.

He smiled at me and winked. "Great job. Better than Natalie did, for sure," he said as he walked away.

"Thanks, you too."

I glanced at Mike, debating whether to ask him to take a few shots of me alone. "Um…Mike, can we take a few of me alone?"

"Why?" he asked, curiosity crossing his face, but his lips curved in a wide smile.

"Um, I'd like to have a couple for a Christmas gift. Maybe?" I bit my lip and waited for him to start giving me shit. It didn't come. He just smirked as he processed my request.

Andrea was still watching silently, her eyes full of laughter until she interjected, "Julia, that's a terrific idea!"

Mike raised his eyebrows. "Ah…" Mike shrugged. "Sure, why not?"

"Thank you. So…can you tell me how to pose? But keep it clean," I hesitated.

"Yeah. What is your goal with these pictures, Julia? I need to know what I'm after."

"Uh…I guess…um," I stumbled around the words, struggling to figure out what I wanted to say. "I want them to look like…well, like they're being taken for one person and one person alone. Like I'm looking only at him…kinda." I felt embarrassed and pensive as I bit my lip and waited for Mike's reply. When he didn't, I continued, "I want him to know how much I love him."

Mike rubbed a hand over his jaw as he considered my answer. "And…and want him *bad*, right?"

I licked my lips and clutched the sheet closer before breaking his gaze. I nodded. "Yeah. Exactly."

"Okay. So…will you trust me to get the best shots, Julia? Can you let go of the control freak inside of yourself that we all know and love? Let me do my job?"

I laughed nervously. He was right, I did like to be in control of everything but if I wanted the best pictures, then I needed to let him do his thing. "Okay." I nodded.

"I really have to meet this guy. He's one lucky son-of-a-bitch." My eyes shot to his and he shook his head and went to switch out the lenses.

The girls took some instructions from Mike and positioned the reflectors around me and the bed.

I tried to relax and give myself over to Mike's directions. To be fair, he was respectful and succinct, a consummate professional as he went about taking the pictures and moving me around. I filled my mind with images of Ryan and the memories of our lovemaking, imagining looking into his handsome face instead of the camera. In no time at all, we were finished.

Mike had me in various poses, some sitting up or kneeling and others lying down with the camera above me, but in all of them the sheet was pulled and placed around me so that a lot of skin showed, even one where the curve of my breast was visible under my arm as I looked back over my shoulder.

I examined the digital images afterward and had to admit that they would make Ryan's heart race. Especially the one where I was lying on the bed and the sheet barely covered me. I was looking straight into the camera, my head to one side and the index finger of my right hand at my open mouth, my eyes half-lidded. It gave the illusion that I was completely naked under the sheet with only those damn heels and some large necklaces that Andrea had brought in at the last minute. I had to admit, her instincts had been right on.

My breath rushed from my lungs as I looked at it and I knew that was the *one*.

"Great job, Julia. We'll have some beautiful shots. I think they'll have the desired effect on the lucky recipient. I promise." He winked at me again. Andrea repeated the process with the sheet wall, while I threw the robe back on. Soon we were walking out of the studio and back to wardrobe where I could get back into my own clothes.

My instinct told me that Ryan would adore getting something so personal from me, something so vulnerable that opened me up so fully. The only hesitation came because I was a little worried about Mike's involvement. Ryan knew he flirted with me outrageously. I'd just tell him how professional Mike had been and hope that the actual photos would completely obliterate any other thoughts from his mind.

I smiled to myself and Andrea saw it. "Feeling devilish, Julia?"

I laughed out loud, surprised at myself and my intentions, knowing the reaction the photos were likely to get out of Ryan.

"I hope you plan on getting very thoroughly fucked, because that, my dear, is what is going to happen when he sees these pictures," she teased.

"Oh, I can dream, Andrea. I can dream." We both were giggling when I disappeared into the dressing room.

Ryan ~

The words blurred on the page. I'd spent the last four hours in this study carrel, at the library, working on research for my molecular biology class. Struggling to keep my focus, my thoughts were a hot mess over the passionate weekend with Jules and knowing she was in a photo studio half-naked with that cocksucker, Mike Turner. From what she said, the dude was a lecherous bastard who did nothing but chase her skirts. Though I'd never met him, I couldn't help hating him. I leaned back in my chair and ran both hands through my hair.

"I gotta get out of here," I muttered under my breath. I glanced at my phone. It was 10:30 and it would be too early in L.A. for Julia to be finished working. She was frustrated and fed up with fixing Mike's mistakes, but she would do what was needed to get the job done right. I was beginning to wonder if maybe he didn't mess up on purpose so that he could spend more time with Julia. The fixes seemed to happen in the evenings since they were constantly pushing those damn deadlines.

I longed for the times at Stanford when Julia would be studying right next to me. I would get stuck on something or frustrated and she always had a way of distracting me or calming me down so I could get my focus back. We'd taken many walks in the middle of the night, talking about anything and everything and I missed having her near. I'd been missing her all of these months, but after the past weekend, I was miserable.

I pulled my backpack off the floor and slammed my book shut before stuffing it and the notebooks into the bag. I wasn't anywhere close to being finished with the assignment, but it was apparent that I wasn't going to get shit done tonight.

I quickly dialed Aaron. "Hey, bro'. What's up?" he said a little out of breath.

"Aaron, I need to go do something. Go to a bar, play pool...anything. I can't focus on studying. Are you up for it?" I asked impatiently as I quickly threw on my black leather jacket, picked up my pack and flung it over my shoulder. Julia had given me the jacket for my birthday two years ago and it was my favorite piece of clothing. My parents had gotten me a new down coat last Christmas, but it hung in my closet untouched. I had many memories of Julia wearing it when I'd draped it around her or she'd forgotten her own and we had made midnight grocery runs. It smelled like her for days afterward.

"Uh, Jen is here, and we're sort of, um...busy."

Jealousy surged through me. I was happy for Aaron that he was able to be with Jen on a regular basis, but it only emphasized how empty I felt without Julia. Aaron was planning on asking Jenna to marry him over Christmas or New Year's while Julia and I were on opposite ends of the continent. Her move to New York would help, but it couldn't happen soon enough, and, as Aaron had pointed out, there would still be distance to deal with.

"Oh, I'm sorry. Okay. Well, I'm going to Kelly's if you change your mind. I just need a distraction for a while."

"There won't be much going on since it's Monday night, Ryan, but I'll see if she wants to. Just give us an hour or so, okay?"

"Yeah, later."

I walked out of the library and across campus to my car. I unlocked it and threw my book bag in the back before sliding in behind the wheel and digging the window scraper out of the glove compartment. I turned on the defroster before quickly scraping the windows, shivering by the time I got back into the car.

That's what I get for not remembering to wear gloves.

I pulled my phone out again. It would be too early for Julia to be free to talk, but I couldn't help myself. It immediately went to voicemail which meant her phone was turned off.

Hi, this is Julia. I'm sorry I'm not able to take your call right now, but please leave your deets and I'll get right back to you. Um...if this is Ryan, I'm thinking of you this very minute and I love you.

I laughed out loud as a huge grin split my face. She knew I'd be anxious tonight and she was doing her damnedest to make me feel better. She was so friggin' amazing. After the beep I left a message.

"Hey, baby girl. Knew you wouldn't be finished yet but needed to hear your voice. Thanks for knowing I'd call and the sweet message. I love you, too...and miss you." I sighed heavily into the phone. "I...just, I *really* miss you. So much, I can't even study. Call me later if you can. I'm going out with Aaron and Jen so I should be up. If not, I'll call you tomorrow. Bye, honey."

Kelly's pub was one of those hole-in-the-wall places where everyone liked to hang out. Despite it being Monday, there was a decent amount of people milling around. Some of them were regulars that I recognized, but I pulled up a stool at the bar, not feeling like socializing.

"Hey Becky," I said as I shrugged out of my jacket and hung it over the back of my chair.

The bartender was a pretty woman in her late thirties, with blonde hair and blue eyes. Aaron, Jen and I came here on occasion to play pool and just hang out, so we knew her pretty well. "How was your Thanksgiving, Ryan?" She smiled.

I smiled back. "Really good. You?"

"David sat on his ass and watched football all day while I slaved in the kitchen," she laughed. "Pretty much par for the course. Did you and Aaron go to Chicago?"

"Nope. I went to Los Angeles, and Aaron stayed here with Jen," I said, leaning back and throwing my wallet on the bar.

I ordered a Molson and glanced around. The bar was dark and had a rustic feel with lots of dark wood, leather and brass fixtures. The antique bar was a huge carved monstrosity that had been salvaged from a century ago with a huge gilded mirror. There were a myriad of shelves filled with bottles of liquor and a variety of glasses on either side of the mirror.

Setting the bottle in front of me, she picked up a five from the money I laid out for her. "What's in L.A.?"

I took a sip of the beer and then poured the rest into a glass. "Um…My best friend from college."

"Yeah? What part of L.A. does he live in? My brother lives out there now," Becky said as she laid the change down.

"Keep it." I motioned for her to pocket the change. "*Julia* lives just north of Hollywood," I smirked.

"Oohhhh, *Julia,* is it? Are you sure she's just your best friend, Ryan? That's a hike to visit your best bud," she said, knowingly.

"She's more than that…but she *is* my very best friend in the world," I said reflectively, staring into my glass, concentrating on the bubbles rising to the top of the beer.

"Is that why I haven't seen you with any women in the past six months? You had me worried. I was beginning to think you were gay!"

"Pfftt. Hardly. You wound me!! You're already taken, so what is a guy to do?" I teased. It was harmless since she was a friend and also so much older.

"Yeah. Whatever," Becky laughed as she went off down the bar to help another customer, and I looked around trying to forget the lonely ache I was feeling. I could be surrounded by a hundred people and I'd still be alone. As long as Julia wasn't with me...I was alone.

Pathetic. I rolled my eyes as I chastised myself.

"Hey, Becks!" I heard Aaron's big voice behind me and was glad to have him join me. I turned to see him and Jenna walk up next to me. Jen put her arms around me in a tight hug.

"Hey you," she said as I hugged her back. "Did you have fun with Julia?" She looked at me and smiled as I released her. Aaron must have told her what I'd said by the look in her eyes.

"Yes. It was wonderful. Thanks for asking."

Aaron pulled up a chair and grabbed Jenna by the waist.

"I didn't expect to see you guys here so soon," I said lightly.

"Oh, you know, we took pity on you. Jen and I can do the humpty dance any old time."

Jenna brought the flat of her hand up against the back of Aaron's head.

"Hey!" he complained.

"Nice! You're such a dickhead," she admonished. "You'll be resorting to ma thumb and her four daughters after that stupid-ass remark."

I burst out laughing. *Hilarious.*

"Ryan, give this idiot some lessons on how to treat a lady, would ya?" She pushed out of Aaron's arms and took the stool on the other side of me.

"What?" Aaron said with a confounded expression on his face. "I was kidding! You know I adore you, baby!"

Jen smiled and leaned in toward me, completely ignoring him. "Tell me about your weekend with Julia. How's she doing?"

"Great. She loves her job and she's doing very well at it."

"And?" she prodded her eyes wide as she watched for my reaction. I smiled.

"And…we're great too, if that's what you're asking."

"I'm very happy for you, Ryan. It's about time that girl got her head out of her ass. Ellie and I have been telling her for years that she should have told you the truth."

My heart swelled at the thought of Julia talking about me to her friends. "Did she tell you how she felt? Before?"

"She didn't come right out and say it, but we knew, Ryan. It was in everything she did. The way she talked about you and how you both gravitated toward each other, and how she'd blow off us off if you called. It was pretty obvious. And she always moped around whenever you were out with your latest bimbo. Every time."

Regret surged through me. I ran a hand through my hair, my face sobering.

"Hey, all's well that ends well." Jenna smiled.

"Yeah, but I hate that I hurt her like that. I didn't realize."

"Really, Ryan? I mean, *you* loved *her* didn't you? How could you think it was any different for her?"

"I guess I never analyzed it. I didn't think I was worthy, but yes, I've been in love with her for…ever."

"Right. We knew that, too."

Aaron sat a glass of white wine in front of her as my phone vibrated in my pocket. I sighed in relief as I opened Julia's message.

"Excuse me for a minute, Jen."

Finally finished and exhausted. Going home. Love you.

I texted back immediately as Aaron tried to sweet talk his way back into Jenna's good graces.

Will you use the photo for the magazine then?

Yes. It's much better and easier than reworking the old one.

Oh. How provocative is it?

I waited for her response but the text didn't come in. Instead my phone started to ring.

"You guys, I need to take this outside. It's too damn loud in here. Back in a bit," I said as I grabbed my coat and answered the phone.

"Hey baby," I said as I headed to the door.

"I love that you're worried about the pictures and are protective of me, but you need to trust me. I won't be naked in the magazine, I promise."

"Only *almost* naked?" I asked because I couldn't help myself. I was sulking and she could hear it in my voice.

She sighed. "Ryan."

"Okay. I'm sorry." I shoved one arm in the jacket and then switched my phone to the opposite hand so that I could repeat the process on the other side without breaking the conversation. "I just...that shit is *mine*, Julia. I don't want to share and I don't give a damn if I'm selfish. I'm not going to apologize for it."

"You aren't *sharing* anything. You can't even see my face clearly in the shot we're using. I'm blurred in the background. Relax." I could hear her breathing softly over the phone and I remembered how her breath felt as it rushed over my skin as we made love. My body reacted involuntarily.

"Okay."

"And, I love that you're possessive. It makes me feel all warm and gushy inside," she breathed softly.

"I love you so much, Julia. I wish I could touch you. I can't wait until you're closer."

"Me, too." I could actually hear the longing in her voice. "I'm working on it. I think Andrea will take my job and all I have to do is find someone to replace her. Well that, and wait for Meredith to find a position for me in New York."

"Thank you for moving, love. It means a lot."

"You don't need to thank me. I'm dying, I miss you so much. You know that, right?"

"Yes, but it's nice to hear."

She yawned. She was dead tired. "I'm sorry, it's been a long day and I didn't sleep great last night. Aren't you tired?" she asked. "It's so late there."

"Not really. Jenna and Aaron just met me at Kelly's, so I'll be up for a while. Are you going to bed?"

"Pretty soon. Tell them I said hello."

"I will. Julia?"

"Yeah?"

"Mike didn't..." I began but she cut me off.

"No! Not at all. He was totally professional. Stop worrying. Please?"

I took a deep breath, expelling some anxiety with it. "How sexy are these photos?" I cringed at myself because I even asked the damn question, but I wanted to know. I hated the jealousy that surged inside of my chest at the thought of another man, seeing her like that, but there wasn't anything I could do to push it away.

She chuckled softly. "They're *sexy*, Ryan. We did this to go with an article about sexual secrets. That's the *whole* point."

"Yeah," I said, knowing I couldn't keep the apprehension out of my tone.

"Do you keep secrets from me?" she said seductively and instantly my mood shifted from anxiousness to desire.

"Well...I'm sure there are some things we don't know about each other yet, honey, since that part is so new for us, but I don't intend to keep anything from you. What about you?"

"Mmmm, you know I can't keep secrets from you," she almost whispered. And I did know that, so it was completely ridiculous for me to worry or be jealous.

"Hmmm, yes." Warmth spread over me at her words, and my blood pressure increased, giving me an instant hard-on. I tried to adjust my pants as it became uncomfortable. "Just this little bit of sexy talk on the phone and I've got a raging erection. I don't mean to be so caveman. I'm sorry if I got a little pissy over Mike seeing my girl half dressed, but I can't help it, Julia."

"It's okay. Do you think I'd be with anyone else now when I wasn't capable of it when we were just friends? I was thinking about you the entire time, so when you see the photos, don't forget that. I love *you*."

I smiled at her words, a swell of love and pride filling me up. I could hear how tired she was, so I needed to end the call. "I won't. I'll let you get to bed, my love. Call you tomorrow?"

"Uh huh. Goodnight, Ryan."

"I love you, Julia. Sleep well."

I walked back into the bar and found Aaron still sitting there, but with Jen on his lap.

"I guess ma thumb's out of business tonight after all, eh?" I laughed and resumed my seat.

Aaron joined the laughter. "Yeah. How's Julia?"

"She's good, man. Tired. She just got off of work." I picked up my previously abandoned beer and took a drink after I pulled off my jacket.

"What the hell is she doing at the office at eight o'clock?" he grunted.

"Yeah, I thought I was the only one lucky enough to work all damn night," Jen interjected.

"Apparently there was a problem with some photos and they had to reshoot them. The model wasn't available so…Julia did it." I smirked at Aaron's stunned expression.

"Wow. So she's a model now? That's totally hot," he said, nodding his head with a smug look on his face.

"Uh…well…" I began.

"What type of photo was it, Ryan? Was it for an article or a feature?" Jenna was showing genuine interest and she pushed off of Aaron's lap to sit next to me again.

"Something about the secrets men keep from their women. I don't know." I shrugged and ran my hand through my hair.

"So what? She's doing a bedroom scene, bro'?" Aaron's hormones were already raging; I could see that along with the unabashed amusement in his face.

I shifted uncomfortably on my barstool and leaned my elbows on the bar. "Something like that," I answered quietly.

"Doesn't that get your dick hard, Ryan? Your *girlfriend's* an underwear model! Shit! It even get's my dick hard!"

Jenna shoved him in the shoulder. "Ugh! Aaron! You're so insensitive."

She was watching me while he downed his beer and saw that I wasn't exactly happy with the situation. She reached out and put her hand on my shoulder, squeezing gently as she spoke. "I'm sure it was completely tasteful, Ryan. Julia has too much class for anything less."

I nodded. "I know. That isn't it. The photographer is after her and it seems like his photos are always the one's that get fucked up. It's just a little too convenient. She's said he's come on to her many times, so I just get a little uneasy having him take those types of photos of her. I'm sure it will be fine." The corners of my mouth twitched.

"It will. Julia can handle herself. Now, my situation, on the other hand is terminal. I'm stuck with this big asshole." She nodded toward Aaron. "What do you think about that?" She laughed.

I raised my eyebrows as a grin split my face and I turned toward her. "Well, I think that you both are damn lucky that you're in the same city. I'm so jealous; I can't even put it into words. Enjoy each other as much as you can and be thankful. Even if he *is* a big asshole, his heart's in the right place. He loves you a lot."

"You know what? You're right." She looked straight in to my face, her long blonde hair falling over her shoulder. "Julia will be in New York soon, won't she? Aaron said she's getting a transfer."

"Hopefully, before the start of the New Year, but we don't know for sure. As Aaron always so succinctly points out, 'it's still a good distance away,' so while the situation is better, it isn't ideal."

"Well, leave it to Aaron to find the ray of sunshine in any situation!" she said.

We both looked at him and laughed.

"What? What'd I do now?" He looked from Jenna then back to me.

I held up my hand in front of me. "Hey, don't look at me, dude! I'm innocent."

"Like hell you are. Fuck the both of you. Becky! Can we get another round please?"

Julia ~

I was meeting Ryan at Denver International and we were renting a car to take up to Estes Park for Christmas. My stomach fluttered with butterflies as I walked off the plane. Ryan's had arrived an hour earlier and he'd be waiting. It was a month since I'd seen him and I was anxious to have his arms around me.

All of my things were packed and the movers were coming to pick up the stuff on the Monday after Christmas. Dad was driving my car to New York and would fly home after he'd helped me move in. Ryan would fly with me to New York after Christmas and stay for the last week of his break before his new semester started at Harvard. Aaron was taking the train down, and with my three strapping men to help me, it would be a breeze.

Ryan, Aaron and Jenna had gone into the city a couple of weekends earlier and secured an apartment for me on the Upper West Side of Manhattan, not far from my new offices. Ryan sent digital pictures with all of the details for my approval. It was a blessing that there were so many people willing to take such good care of me.

The apartment was more than I could afford, even though I was getting a cost of living increase, but Ryan told me that he'd take care of it. I was hesitant in taking money from him, but he insisted that I be in the safest part of the city. I couldn't argue because it did make me feel better, and my dad, too. I was slightly apprehensive about being in such a huge city alone, but Dad and Ryan were in protective mode and would not allow anything less.

Ellie cried her eyes out the last week that I was in L.A., but Harris was moving in, which helped. My heart hurt at leaving Ellie, my job and all of the new friends that I had made, but being closer to Ryan would be the right thing for both of us.

My heart thudded wildly. I was still amazed at how much I loved him, and more so, that he returned it in the same measure. I couldn't ask for anything more.

It was all falling into place. Andrea was taking over my old job and Meredith secured a position for me as creative assistant at Vogue, with the condition that I keep in touch with her in case I ever wanted to go back to Los Angeles. She worked hard to keep me with Condé Nast and I was grateful for her ongoing confidence.

The best part of all was nonchalantly leaning against a pillar in the waiting area at the gate as I came through the doors of the jetway. He was wearing the black leather jacket that I'd given him, a white t-shirt and blue jeans. Broad shoulders, slim hips, muscled thighs, and the signature sex hair. I was one lucky girl.

God, he's so gorgeous. He'd look good in a paper sack.

A huge smile split my face as I hurried along, closing the distance between us. I was anxious to get my hands on him. When he saw me, Ryan pushed off the pillar with his shoulder and the crooked grin I adored spread across his face. Our parents weren't happy that we were ditching them for Christmas, but we wanted and needed this time alone.

His arms opened and gathered me tightly against his chest, as I turned my face into his neck and dropped my carry-on. He lifted me up so that our mouths were on the same level and I wound my arms tightly around his neck as his musky scent assaulted my nostrils. When his mouth descended upon mine, he kissed me long and hard, his tongue melding with mine over and over again. We were oblivious to the others milling past and around us, some of them undoubtedly staring at our blatant display, but I didn't give a damn. He smelled and tasted so good and I never wanted to let him go. I tugged on his hair to pull his mouth tighter against mine and thrilled when he moaned into my mouth.

I inhaled his breath as our kisses finally ended and he looked into my face, his blue eyes moving over my features as if he were memorizing each one separately and then together.

"Julia," he said softly and then bent to kiss me again gently. "You taste so damn good. Oh baby, it's great to have you in my arms, finally."

"I missed you," I whispered and reached for his mouth with mine once again. "Kiss me again."

He smirked and let out his breath in a huff. "Demanding little thing, aren't you?" he asked, but didn't let me down. My eyes challenged him and his mouth met mine again for another deeply passionate kiss before he set me back on my feet.

"Come on, there's a cabin and a snow bank with our names on it." I giggled as he picked up our bags and flung them over his shoulder, lacing his fingers through mine and we walked off in the direction of the rental car counters and the baggage claims.

Electricity vibrated between us and my entire body was alive with it. I stared into his face as we walked. He was smiling, white teeth flashing. I noticed how women who passed stared, but he seemed oblivious.

"What?" Ryan finally asked as we made our way through the terminal.

Embarrassed that he would catch me watching, a blush crept up beneath the skin on my neck and cheeks. His hand tightened around mine.

"I'm just so happy to see you. To be able to look at you." I shook my head and shrugged. "I took that for granted when we were together all of the time."

He nodded in understanding. "Me, too. You're so beautiful, Julia. I'll never get enough of looking at that face." His eyes roamed over me and he smiled at me. "Or that body. God, I missed you, love."

I laughed out loud and we walked for a while without speaking, content to be in the same place, holding onto each other. We got our bags and I checked my messages while Ryan took care of getting the car.

Dad called, asking that I call him when we arrived. I quickly dialed his number.

"Hey, Dad, I'm in Denver."

"Is Ryan with you? I worry about you, honey," he said gruffly.

"Getting the car. He was waiting for me when my plane landed. Between the two of you, I'm all taken care of."

"I'm happy about you and Ryan, you know. He's a good kid with a good head on his shoulders." I dropped my head and ran a hand around the back of my neck, smiling softly to myself.

"It means a lot to hear you say that, Dad. We...really love each other."

"Yes. I can tell that. He'll take good care of you. I'm still not sure about you being in New York alone, though."

"Oh you know...it's only a few years until Ryan gets finished with med school," I teased.

Ugh! Four years until he'd be with me full time. My heart sank. It wasn't like I hadn't thought about that before, but moving to New York would not guarantee that we'd see each other much more. We had good intentions, but life had a way of interfering.

"Ok, I'm going to leave in three days and I'll meet you guys in New York on Friday."

"Did you get the directions that Ryan emailed? I don't want you getting lost."

"Of course I'm going to get lost!" Dad chuckled. "That goes without saying, but yes, I got the directions. Go have fun with Ryan, Julia. I'll call you from the road."

"Take good care of my baby. I mean, don't wreck it." He grunted in exasperation and I laughed. "I'm only teasing. I love you."

Ryan finished at the car counter and came to where I waited with the bags, dangling the keys in front of me.

"Love you, too. Bye, Jules."

"Bye, Dad."

Ryan loaded up the bags, leaving me to pull only the smallest one through the garage. We were soon speeding north on I-25 out of Denver the seventy or so miles to the quaint little town of Estes Park in the front range of the Rocky Mountains.

We'd only been skiing once when Aaron, Ryan, Jenna and I had taken a trip to Lake Tahoe for Spring break our junior year in college. He was so graceful, I felt like a complete klutz in comparison. My knees ached so badly after wedging down the hills, but Ryan was very patient trying to teach me how to ski, even if he'd been laughing his ass off on the inside. He'd been very attentive, running a hot bath and massaging my legs as I sat with him on the couch in front of the fire, drinking the hot cocoa that I'd made.

Ryan's eyes were hidden by his sunglasses, but turned toward me. "What are you thinking about? You've been so quiet, babe."

"Just how horrible I was at skiing before and hoping I won't be so bad this time," I laughed softly.

"Hmmm...you were adorable. I felt so bad watching you struggle, but you were such a good sport. I thought you were going to shove those skis up my ass, but you just kept on trying. You never gave up." His hand enfolded mine and brought it to his lips.

"I was horrible. I'm surprised you put up with me." My lips lifted at the corners as I turned in my seat so that I could curl my legs up and look at him.

"I'll always put up with you, my love. Forever. You can't get rid of me."

"You promise?" I said seriously and the smile left his face.

"I promise, Julia. I love you more than anything in my life. That will never change."

I leaned over and rested my head on his shoulder and wound my free hand around his bicep.

I nodded against his shoulder. "Okay. Just checking." He turned his head and kissed my forehead.

"So, what did you get me for Christmas?" Ryan asked anxiously with a smirk.

"Mmm...you'll find out."

"When?"

I laughed, softly. "Stop. You're worse than a kid."

"When?" he persisted.

"It's Christmas Eve, so maybe tonight, maybe tomorrow morning."

"I choose tonight. It's more romantic and I'm feeling *very* romantic." His breath left his body and he brought my hand over to rest on his thigh, pressing it into his flesh.

"Whatever you want."

"Mmm...that sounds about perfect."

"Yes, doesn't it? Lucky for you, I love giving you everything you want. Lucky for me, too."

"Stop. See what you do to me?"

He moved my hand higher in his lap until it was resting over the hardness straining in his jeans and I let my fingers clasp around him and rub up and down. "Mmmm...Ryan," I breathed.

"Shit, Julia. That feels amazing, babe, but I don't want to kill us." He lifted my hand off of his body and turned it to place an open mouth kiss on my palm, letting his tongue dart out to lick me.

"Now who isn't playing fair?"

"All I do is dream about making love to you."

"Oh? Do they have a new course of study in that at Harvard?" I teased and he shook his head.

"I wish."

Estes Park was a cute little town situated between two of the smaller ski resorts, and was at the edge of Rocky Mountain National Park. Ryan and I spent a few hours on Skype looking at places to stay when we'd decided to meet over Christmas, and we decided on a resort called Glacier Lodge that had individual cabins with fireplaces and kitchens.

We didn't have anything set for our time in Colorado, except that we just wanted to go with the flow. We could ski if we wanted to, shop if we felt like it, or hole up the entire time and stay in bed if that was what we decided to do. The point was to have no pressure and just focus on each other.

The cabin was gorgeous, built in classic log-cabin style, the walls and ceilings all rounded timber, the furnishings rustic, with a Southwestern motif. The bed was huge, draped with a Southwestern patterned comforter and the furniture was plush and comfortable, upholstered in brown leather. A big fluffy rug lay out on the floor in front of the fireplace that reminded me of the piles of snow outside and the kitchen, while simple, had all that I needed. The bathroom was Italian marble with a large whirlpool tub which I looked forward to using with Ryan.

"Wow," I said as I walked around the place. Ryan was leaning up against the back of the couch with his arms crossed, just watching me. "Let's move here!" I said, feeling a bit mischievous.

Ryan smiled and slowly moved toward me. "Um…I can't commit to that unless…" his arms slid around me and under my legs and he lifted me up and threw me on the bed, "this bed is fully functional. We have to test it first!"

I squealed in delight and laughed as I landed in the middle of the mattress.

He immediately came down on top of me and the laughter between us died as our eyes met. His body settled into mine and I arched up into his, aching to feel him next to me, inside of me. His hand came up to my face to brush my hair back and he pressed me into the bed with his body, both of us moving against the other, creating the friction we both desperately craved.

"Julia…I've missed you. Please don't make me wait to make love to you. I can't stand it." He nuzzled the side of my face with his nose and I turned my mouth toward his.

"Ryan…" I breathed just before his mouth took mine.

He kissed me deeply, and I kissed him back with everything I had. I wanted him; I loved him and nothing else mattered. His hand slid up my thigh and over my hip and ribcage to cup my breast through the thin material of my black cotton shirt and lace bra. My already taut nipples hardened even more under his palm. Ryan groaned when he felt it, too. "God, Julia. You're body is so responsive, it drives me crazy."

I answered by sliding my hands beneath his shirt and pushing it up over the strong muscles of his back and shoulders.

He sat up on his knees and impatiently pulled it over his head and flung it across the room. "I wanted to go slow, but I'm just...my whole body is vibrating. I want you so much." His eyes bore into mine as his fingers flew to undo the opening of his pants and then moved to do the same to mine before he leaned down and kissed the side of my neck. His hands moved up my body under my shirt and soon it was a thing of the past.

I reached for him, pulling him down so that he was lying on top of me, in the cradle of my body again. I wanted to feel him closer, to have every inch of his skin against me and to resume the delicious kisses. We kissed urgently, but not without purpose as our mouths tasted and teased each other. "Uhhh," I breathed against his mouth as his body surged against mine, "you feel so good."

Soon the clothes separating us were strewn about the room and I gloried in the feel of his bare limbs combining with mine, his hard body thrusting into me, filling me again and again. "God, baby. I can't..." he gasped against the curve of my neck, "I can't stop."

"I don't want you to. Never stop, Ryan." He pushed the hair back off of my face, both hands holding my head and then he kissed me deeply, our mouths sucking and licking each other as we moved in perfect unison, the movements deeper and longer. God, I wanted more and raked my hands down his back to grasp around the muscles of his ass. I could feel them flexing beneath my hands in response to his thrust. It was so hot.

"Come for me, Julia. I love you, baby," he urged. His hands were moving over my body, brushing my nipples and then down lower between my legs. He pushed his hand between us so he could touch me and instantly my muscles tensed as my orgasm exploded, leaving me gasping and clutching around his hardness.

"Uhhh, God," Ryan groaned as he gave in to his own release, but then brought his mouth back to mine and kissed me, sucking my lower lip into his mouth and then deepening the kiss, laving my tongue with his, mimicking the movements of his body as he moved inside me.

His body slowed and the kisses lightened until he raised his mouth and rested his forehead on mine, both of us breathing hard, struggling to regain control. Emotion flooded through me and I wrapped my arms and legs around him. He kissed the side of my face and nuzzled my nose as a tear trickled down my cheek.

He felt it with the thumb that was brushing along my cheekbone. "Julia, don't cry, love. I'm right here with you, and you're everything to me."

I nodded, but my throat tightened, making it hard to speak. I felt ridiculous; crying when he was with me, but the love I felt for him was just so overwhelming that I couldn't contain it. My face crumpled and I turned into his neck as my shoulders began to shake in silent sobs.

"Julia, honey...Look at me," Ryan whispered urgently. "What is it? Can you tell me?" He tried to move off, but I tightened my arms around him.

"No, don't separate. Not yet," I said softly and touched his face, reaching up to kiss his jaw gently. "I just...love you more than I can even stand, Ryan. It's...overwhelming and amazing. My heart is so full of you, I can't even breathe. You...fill me up." I surged upward, emphasizing his body still buried within mine. "In more ways than one," I tried to smile through the tears.

Ryan's eyes were soft and the start of a small smile lifted one corner of his mouth. "God, I love you, so, so much. It's beyond words for me too, honey. I'm so pissed at myself for not having the balls to tell you before. To think we could have had this…the whole time."

I shook my head to silence him and reached up and ran my hand along his face, to grasp the hair at the nape of his neck.

"Don't say that. I cherish every moment I've had with you. Every single one, okay? Even when we fight. Don't wish it away. Maybe we wouldn't be *us* if things had been different. And I want this…the way it is between us now is worth all of that waiting and longing."

Ryan moved to my side and pulled me close, across his chest, and I lay in silence, listening to his heart beating. He took a deep breath, his chest rising beneath my cheek.

"What is it?" I asked and gently ran a hand down his bare chest to rest below his navel. When he didn't answer right away, I pressed him. "Ryan?"

He sighed again. "It's just…I *want* this, Julia. I want it every day, and still we're…" his words dropped off and his fingers flew threw his hair before moving back to slide down my arm and take my hand.

"I know." I swallowed the lump in my throat. "But seeing you even once a month is better than once every five or six. I'll take it, because it's *you*."

"Julia…" he breathed and we were both clinging, our arms tightening around each other. I leaned over and placed my open mouth on his chest, and the light hair tickled my skin.

"Just be with me now, Ryan, okay? We have ten days. Ten whole days. I just want to drown in you and enjoy every second. For ten days, I want to lose the constant ache."

"Where did you come from?" Ryan said; his voice husky and deep as he pulled me up until my head was resting next to his on the pillow. "You're so damn perfect you shouldn't even exist. Just…look at you." He stunned me by the sudden movement and when I looked into his eyes, they were deep blue and swimming in tears.

My eyes welled and I kissed him, his lips warm and soft against mine. I pressed my hand to his chest, over his heart. "This is where I came from. Right here."

Ryan ~

It was late. I had fallen asleep in Julia's arms after we'd made love again, but now my stomach was rumbling, stirring me from the soundest sleep I'd had in a month. A month without Julia and a month full of studying and final exams.

The cabin was dark but warm, the full moon shining in from between the blinds and casting a bluish glow across the bed, on the white sheets and Julia's still form. Her skin was smooth as porcelain, her face serene in sleep, the dark lashes and luxurious mane of hair almost black in the moonlight. I leaned in to gently kiss her shoulder and pulled in a long breath inhaling her sweet scent, a luscious mixture of floral shampoo, perfume and Julia. Another soft kiss later and she stirred softly.

"Ryan..." she breathed, still asleep and my heart thumped wildly in my chest. I picked up a lock of silken hair and worried it between my fingers. Everything about her was so damn soft, so alluring. My undoing. I knew I'd never be able to drag myself away. I longed for those gorgeous green eyes to open and look at me, but I didn't want to disturb her. The cabin was small, but to me it was paradise, because I was alone with Julia. She was all mine, if only for a short time.

My stomach rumbled again and I reluctantly pushed myself off the bed and padded out of the bedroom. Hesitating to flood the rooms with light, I lit the few candles that were scattered around and decided it was much nicer that way anyway. It was eleven o'clock on Christmas Eve and there was a small tree in the corner with multicolored lights on it. I went back into the bedroom to get the two gifts I'd brought and placed them beneath the tree and then went to find something to eat.

The refrigerator was stocked with basics, but nothing that looked particularly appetizing. I leaned on the open door when something occurred to me; Julia would have made something I loved, to bring on this trip. I smiled in satisfaction. Surely, knowing her, there was some delectable thing packed inside her bag. She wouldn't mind if I went looking for it, and I could play the pouty, starving card. She'd always given in to that. But...maybe there was a gift inside that I wasn't supposed to see?

Hmmm...I patted my grumbling stomach and decided I'd take my chances. I quietly moved back into the bedroom, careful not to wake her, but stopped at the sight before me. She'd rolled onto her back, the sheet barely clinging to her curves, her legs bare and the curve of her breast starting to swell above the edge as her arm flung out beside her head. Her hair was splayed out on the pillows in glorious disarray, screaming for my fingers to thread through it, and her mouth was slightly open. She was so gorgeous and my body stirred as I remembered the feel of her beneath me and the little mewling sounds she made as she came. I swallowed and my mouth went dry.

I tore my gaze away and glanced around the room, searching for her bags and found them against the far wall. If she brought a treat with her, it would most likely be in the carry-on. I carefully unzipped it, as quietly as possible. My hand felt around blindly and quickly found a plastic container. My face split into a grin. She was so damn good to me.

It was too dark to see exactly what was inside, but when I pulled the lid free, the delicious scent wafted out. They were some sort of cookies. I took the container into the other room and opened the refrigerator again, using the light to look inside. Mmmm...one of my favorites. Cranberry, white chocolate and macadamia nut. Delicious and soft, they were just as I remembered them. Aaron and I used to eat the entire batch before they were even cool from the oven. Julia pretended to be pissed, but enjoyed that we loved them so much.

I found a bottle of water and turned toward the living room, carrying the entire container of cookies with me, but stopped short when I saw her leaning on the doorjamb in the hall, wrapped in the sheet.

"And just what do you think you're doing with those, Matthews?" She laughed softly.

"Um..." I said with my mouth full. "Devouring them, hopefully. They're just delicious, honey. Thank you."

"Hmmm..." She walked forward and grabbed the bottle and took a drink. "I'm so thirsty."

I took her hand and pulled her down on the couch next to me. "Want one?" I asked, before diving in for another cookie.

"Uh uh, but don't let me stop you." She snuggled into my side, resting her head on my shoulder.

"It feels so good to have you with me like this, Julia."

"I agree. I miss you more than you know."

I swallowed the cookie and then set the container on the end table next to one of the flickering candles. It cast a glow over us and danced on her soft features.

"Oh, I think I do." I pulled her across my lap and kissed her on the temple, settling us both in. I wrapped my arms around her as she fit so perfectly into my body. "Are you tired, my love?"

Her little hand was drawing circles on my chest and I was rubbing her back. "Julia?" I said into the soft hair on top of her head.

"Just a little, but I'm okay. I don't want to sleep right now. Merry Christmas, Ryan."

"Oh, yes…is it time to open my present yet?" I laughed softly. I could feel her pleasure at my words. She smiled against my chest.

"What? Are you ten?" she teased.

"Yes," I insisted and she burst out laughing.

"I'm a little nervous about it."

"Why, babe?"

"It's really personal," she said hesitantly.

"Everything *about us* is personal. My gift for you is personal, too. Would you like to open it first?"

She lifted her head and looked into my face. Biting her lip, she nodded. I bent to kiss her, licking her lips softly. She moaned and our kiss deepened, her hands gripped my jaw and the back of my neck.

When I pulled my mouth from hers, I went back and kissed those luscious lips gently. "Ok. I'll get it."

She scooted off of my lap and gathered the sheet back around her while I went to the tree to retrieve the gifts.

I sat beside her on the couch, turning to face her and handed her the smallest package.

"Did you wrap this yourself? It's so beautiful." Julia's hand gently brushed over the shimmering silver bow and the brilliant red paper, which looked like shades of burgundy in the candlelight.

"Yes. Are you surprised?" I smiled and brushed her hair off of her face. She nodded slightly. "I have to tell you, Miss Abbott, you look so tempting sitting here in that sheet, like you've just been made passionate love to. You make me hungry for more, so open the presents already."

A small laugh burst from her and she smiled brilliantly. Her hand came out to thread through my hair that had fallen over my forehead. "I love you, Ryan. You're the only thing I need."

I wanted to pull her close to me and make love to her right then and there, but instead, pressed the box more fully into her hands. "Open it."

Slowly her fingers pulled the bow and set it aside, before carefully separating the corner folds on the box. I was more anxious for her to open it than she was. Finally, the small white box was revealed and she lifted the lid.

I'd gotten her a platinum and diamond bracelet, the center being the cursive letters R and J that were entwined together, the bottom of the R running into the top of the J, and a diamond in the center of where they connected. The band was set on each side with three diamonds, each one a little smaller than the last as they moved away from the letters.

"Oh, Ryan...it's just gorgeous." Her eyes were full of tears as she raised them to mine. "I'll treasure it, always. I love it. Thank you." I took it from the box and placed it on her left wrist, and pulled her hand up so I could place my lips beside the bracelet.

"I love you, Julia. I hope you don't think it's too early to get you diamonds, but I needed to get you something that would mean something and say that you belong to me."

She gasped at my words and slid her arms around my neck and hugged me tight. "Anything you give me means something, babe. I love it, truly."

The diamonds sparkled on her wrist as she got up. "I'll be right back." Julia disappeared down the hall and returned with a flat square box about 30 or so inches square. It was wrapped in beautiful gold paper and some sort of sheer fabric bow full of gold sparkles.

My face lit up as I reached for it, but she held it back from me, still clutching the sheet around her. "Ryan, I need to tell you about this first." The tone in her voice was apprehensive and her eyes were wide as she looked into my face.

I was quiet as she sat with the large box on her lap.

"I had this made for you."

"What is it, Julia?"

"It's one of the photo's from that shoot I did last month." I started to speak, but she put her fingers to my mouth. "Please, I know you're impatient, but let me finish, Ryan. I asked Mike to take some extra photos because I wanted to do this for you. I was only thinking of you the whole time. Your eyes, your voice...the way you touch me and make me feel." Her voice began to tremble. "I told him why I wanted these pictures, so he knew they were for you."

"Are there many of them?"

"I'll give them all to you, but this is the one I chose." She handed me the box and I was scared to look inside, my hand shaking, but I took a deep breath and ripped the wrapping away in one fast motion.

I glanced at her. She was biting her lip, and if she wasn't careful, she'd be bleeding.

I lifted the lid and separated the tissue paper which encased a large silver frame with a black and white photo inside it. Julia was lying on her back, wrapped in a sheet with such an amazing look on her face, much of her body exposed, so much like she had been earlier in the bedroom, but in the picture her eyes were open. A mixture of love, desire and longing like I'd never imagined softened her features and made her lids heavy. I'd never seen anything more beautiful. I was mesmerized; stunned.

The air rushed from my lungs as I stared at it. "You're so beautiful. Just...fucking gorgeous." My throat was aching and my vision blurred. "It's...perfect, love. Thank you." My hand ran down the silver frame to some engraving on the bottom.

Body, Heart and Soul...I Belong to You. Forever.

I felt a tear fall onto my cheek as I read it, an echo of the words I'd said just minutes before..._I needed to get you something that said you belong to me._

"Baby...I can't tell you how much I love you right now. My chest feels like it's going to explode, it hurts so much."

She leaned in to kiss my face where the tear trailed down and threaded her fingers in my hair. "I mean every word. You own me. You always have."

I gathered her close and kissed her, gently, tenderly. "You're everything. I can't even breathe without you." I wiped another stray tear from my face and then one from hers as I stared into her liquid green eyes. My hand at the side of her face pulled her closer and I kissed her cheek and then her temple.

"I have another present for you." I lifted the larger of my two gifts into her lap.

"The bracelet was so much, Ryan, you shouldn't have..."

"It's not that kind of present. I hope you'll like it. It's the truth, honey. Every word."

She ripped the paper open as I had done on the photo. I had written it in my own hand, in a gold pen that I'd gotten at a craft store, and then had it matted and framed in antique gold.

"Ryan...Oh my God," she breathed as she raised her eyes to search my face. I couldn't look away if my life depended on it,

as the diamond tears fell in soft cascades down her cheek. I
started to recite what I wrote,

~Julia, I love you because...
The first time our eyes met, I was lost.
You're my very best friend, and you know me better than I know myself.
Your smile lights up my life.
You complete my thoughts and my words...like we are the same person.
You know when I'm hurting and exactly how to comfort me.
Your touch melts me, like no other ever could.
Your eyes see me for who I am, and you accept everything about me.
You trust me freely and with all that I am, I feel safe in trusting you.
You give of yourself so completely.
You spoil me rotten.
You're the most intelligent, beautiful and giving person I've ever known.
Your heart sings to mine. I am the moth to your flame.
You can make me desire you with a look, or a word or a touch...
yet without any of it.
You set my body on fire like no one ever has.
The light changes when you walk into a room.
You own me, body and soul.
Because you love me so much. Unconditionally. It is evident in how you
speak to me, how you look at me and in every single touch of your hand.
Because you are the greatest gift of my life...I don't deserve you,
yet here you are with me.
You reach into my chest and squeeze my heart, and fill me so fully.
You give me peace, sanctity and safety.
You are everything I could ever want or need.
My life was not complete before you came into it...
My need for you consumes me.
The sound of your voice is the last thing I need to hear in this life.
My soul recognizes yours...and yours mine.
You make me want to be better, to be more, to deserve you.
Our love is endless; it transcends earthly bounds and
the endless peripheries of heaven.
You breathe your life into mine and are all my dreams come true.
You are only mine, forever...

Because of all of this and so much more...
I need you. I want you. I adore you. I love you...more than my own life.
~Ryan

She was shaking by the time I finished and took the frame from her hands. Julia fell into my arms, tears raining down her face. My throat ached with the emotions flooding through me.

"Don't cry my love. I'm sorry."

"God, don't be sorry for that," she sobbed into me before pulling back to look in my eyes. "I don't know what to say...it was so incredibly beautiful. So romantic and perfect. It's a perfect reflection of you."

"You don't have to say anything. Just tell me you're mine."

"Always. You're the love of my life. You know that," she whispered against my skin, right before her open mouth sucked and nipped at the corner of mine.

"Yeah, I know," I said huskily and scooped her up and carried her down the hall to the bed. "From the moment we met, I've known. Julia," I moaned into the side of her neck as I kissed and dragged my open mouth along it. "Make love with me. I want to drown inside you. I never want to be without you, again. I feel like I'd die if you ever left me. It sounds weak, but it's the truth. I love you that much."

After that, words were lost; the only sounds were our panting breaths, our kisses and moans of passion. We both gave everything and wanted to give more still. Every touch was reverent as we worshiped each other, body and soul.

~9~

Ryan ~

Something was tickling my face. I batted at it impatiently and rolled over. *Sleep.* I wanted more sleep...I was having the best dream; *Julia and I were walking in a beautiful snow shower and I loved how the flakes caught on her beautiful face. She was smiling and leaned in and kissed me full on the mouth. Mmmm...I could feel the snow falling softly on my face and hair as we kissed, her warms lips moving so gently with mine. She smelled so sweet...*

"Okay, that's it!" Julia's voice was soft but firm as she smashed a handful of snow in my face and giggled while I yelled in shock.

"Arrrgghh!" Instantly I was wide awake as I looked up at her. She was straddling my hips over the top of the covers, fully dressed in her green and black ski suit. Her eyes were alight with mischief and her cheeks were flushed pink from the cold. She'd obviously been outside already, judging from the now melting snow on my face and running down my neck. "You're gonna get it, Abbott. That was horrible of you...you little brat!" I admonished and sat up quickly to grab her, flip her on her back and attack her. She giggled and wrapped her arms and legs around me. The cold still clinging to her suit made me shiver as my mouth found hers in a hungry kiss. Her mouth opened eagerly beneath mine and my body sprang to life. "See what you do to me? Even when you're being mean..." I moaned against her mouth.

"Mmmm...I love that." She licked my upper lip, our kisses slowing and softening as she spoke against my mouth. She could drive me insane, fully clothed in a damn Eskimo suit. The desire for her never lessened, and I was glad of the torment. "And, I'm *so* mean to you..." She kissed the line of my jaw and bit my chin playfully.

"Why are you up so early...and wearing so damn many clothes?" I complained as I nuzzled the side of her neck, pulling at her turtleneck with my teeth. I groaned in frustration, rolling off of her onto my back. "Gah!!"

She burst out laughing. "Ryan, get your ass out of bed. I thought we were going skiing today. It's eleven o'clock, for God's sake. Or were you planning to laze around in bed the entire day?" She'd moved onto her side, propping her head up on one arm while the other hand slowly slid down my chest and lower, below my navel.

I turned my face toward her and crooked an eyebrow. "Don't start something you aren't prepared to finish," I teased, grabbing her hand, bringing it up to my mouth for a kiss. The sunlight reflected off the diamonds on her bracelet to send a spectrum of colors scattering around the walls. I kissed the inside of her wrist reverently. "This looks perfect. I love seeing it on you."

"Yeah, it's like a brand," she said softly, her gaze suddenly turning serious. "Is that what you intended?"

I grinned and brushed my fingers lightly along her jaw. "Something like that. Is that okay?"

"It's perfect. It's a miracle that I never thought would come true."

I leaned in, kissing her soundly on the mouth, but not letting myself give in to the passionate play I was craving. "You're stuck with me now; the good, bad and the ugly." My stomach growled loudly and Julia's eyes widened, a throaty laugh bursting from her chest. "What are you feeding me for breakfast? Some vixen totally sapped my strength last night. I doubt I can make it to the ski lift, let alone get down the mountain. My legs are still shaking and I'm *starving*."

Julia smiled as I pushed up on my forearms and then got fully off the bed. "Yeah, yeah. You're in horrible shape. I can see that. Breakfast is served, milord." She got up and bowed dramatically. "As soon as you put some clothes on that fine ass."

My heart swelled as I watched her leave the room. My face hurt, I was smiling so much, but I couldn't stop. In fact, I wanted to laugh out loud. Being with Julia was pure happiness and the only thing I really needed.

I quickly pulled on some long johns and jeans, wool socks and a navy turtleneck sweater. "Julia? Baby, did you wear long johns under your clothes? If you didn't bring any, I bought some for you," I called down the hall as I dressed.

She poked her head around the edge of the kitchen into the hall. "Wow. So we skipped the newlywed stage and went straight to our 25th anniversary?" She smirked and the dimples in her cheeks grew more pronounced. "You're buying me long underwear, now? How *sexy*. What's next? A vacuum cleaner? Thanks, Hon."

I walked down the hall toward the luscious smell of freshly brewed coffee and bacon. Julia had taken the parka off and was flipping pancakes on the stove. She had glasses of orange juice, butter and maple syrup on the table. "Mmmm…This smells delicious," I said as I sat at the table, just as she plopped three huge pancakes on the plate in front of me. My eyes shot up to hers.

"What?" she asked and raised her eyebrows. "You said you were hungry, right?"

"This is a mountain," I said, but grabbed the butter and began to spread it between the cakes and then poured a generous amount of syrup over the top until it was dripping down the sides of the stack. I grabbed a piece of bacon off of the plate in the center of the table and took a bite, watching Julia ladle more batter onto the griddle on the stove.

Contentment settled over me and filled me to bursting. The woman I loved was making me pancakes in the middle of the Rocky Mountains. And we were completely alone. It was perfect.

"I'll apologize in advance since I'll be on my butt more than my skis. You'll probably have to carry me down the mountain!"

I smiled and dug into the pancakes. "These are really delicious, honey. Thank you. You won't be on your ass," I scoffed and shook my head. "We'll start on the easier slopes until you get used to it, I promise."

"Oh? You mean like last time when you and Aaron tricked me up onto the black runs?" She was remembering the last trip. Aaron and I thought it would be fun, but it ended with Julia being taken down the side of the mountain by the ski patrol in one of those sleds. She was so pissed that she hardly spoke to me for three hours. Three whole hours. I smirked at the memory.

"Yeah, laugh it up! You weren't the one on your damn back! I looked like a complete idiot!" She was trying not to laugh. I could see it on her face and the way she was biting her lower lip, both were turning up at the corners despite her effort.

"You were adorable," I teased. "I mean, considering how mad you were. All spitting fire. I thought you were going to deck me when you got out of that damn thing." I couldn't help it; I burst out laughing. She'd stormed past me into the lodge at the bottom of the run, as fast as she could in the bulky ski boots, so furious that tears of frustration had come to her eyes. I felt a lot of regret afterward, but looking back on it, it was damn funny.

Julia was sitting across from me, pouring syrup on a pancake on her plate. Her hair was pushed back by the ear band she was wearing, making the contours of her bone structure more pronounced. She looked up and laughed. "I suppose it *was* funny, but I was upset at the time. Don't even think about pulling something like that today! I'll be denying you more than my words."

I leaned forward and took her hand in mine. "Nothing is worse than not being able to talk to you, Julia. Don't you know that?"

"Hmmm, so I can hump your brains out, but as long as I keep my mouth shut, you'll be in agony? Is that what you're asking me to believe?" she asked flatly.

The happiness inside pushed out in a deep, breathy laugh. "Yes. Exactly."

"Uh huh." She grinned, tongue in cheek, and then got up to clear the table.

As usual, I couldn't take my eyes off of her. As much as I wanted to go skiing, I wanted to stay inside and keep her all to myself even more.

"You're very beautiful today. Thank you for breakfast, my love." I walked up behind her as she rinsed the plates and wrapped my arms around her. My mouth found the sensitive skin behind her ear. I knew she found the gesture particularly arousing. "It was almost as delicious as you are. So let's get the hell out of here before I forget what I'm supposed to be doing." She arched back into me and turned her face toward mine, clearly wanting me to kiss her. I turned her in my arms and cupped her chin with my hand, tilting her mouth up to mine. "I love you," I said softly as my lips took hers. I kissed her deeply, my tongue sliding into the sweetness of her mouth and I groaned when she slid her hands up to fist in my hair. I didn't want to leave...If we never left here again, I'd be fine.

"Jules..." I breathed as I rested my forehead against hers, passion raging between us. I'd never get used to it. "Uh, you turn me on like crazy."

She didn't speak, her hands, still clutching at the nape of my neck, urged my head back down toward hers. Her nose nuzzled near the corner of my mouth and I wanted nothing more than to kiss her for hours. I kissed her gently once more and brushed my knuckles across her left cheekbone.

"Mmmm...Ryan," she whispered against my mouth. "I love you."

I kissed her on her temple and ran a hand through my hair. "Honey, we need to leave now or we never will, okay?" I swatted her on the rump and summoned the strength necessary to move away. "Come on, let's get a move on. I can't wait to see you conquer the slopes today." I flashed a bright smile and went to get our shoes from near the door.

"Don't get your hopes up. You know how I hate to disappoint you," she admonished and rolled those gorgeous eyes. I shook my head in disbelief, while the corners of my mouth lifted slightly and my brow furrowed.

"Not possible. If you spend the entire day on your ass, you're perfect just as you are. Got it?"

"You're so graceful, it makes me feel like a klutz," she moaned.

"Well, obviously, I won't be today. I don't have my own skis. Rentals won't be the same."

"Oh, *poor baby*! I feel so bad for you, Mr. I-Can-Do-Anything-And-Everything! How will you manage rented equipment?" she mocked.

I put my arm around her head and started rubbing the knuckles of my other hand on the top of it as she squealed in protest. "That's enough out of you. I think I owe you a face full of snow!"

Julia ~

Okay, so I was doing pretty well. I didn't fall too much and I was even starting to enjoy myself. My knees weren't hurting like I remembered and I was actually having fun. Honestly, I'd been dreading the skiing part of this vacation, but Ryan loved it so much, I wanted to at least try for his sake.

Colorado was beautiful. The Rocky Mountains rising majestically in all directions, glistening with fresh powder and the scent of evergreen and blue spruce hung in the air. The sky was a brilliant blue, with cottony clouds floating in its endlessness. The sun reflecting off of the snow made me thankful for my sunglasses.

Ryan was waiting at the bottom of the run as I skied the last fifty yards. He looked gorgeous, but what else was new? The sun was shining brightly and reflecting off of Ryan's hair, giving it a golden, multi-tonal cast. He flashed me a bright smile as I glided toward him. I forgot what I was doing and was having trouble stopping. I was going to plow right into him.

"Ryan! I can't stop! Move so I don't hit you!" I called, but he just threw down his poles and held his arms open, laughing the entire time.

He cupped his hands over his mouth and burst out, "Julia! Don't worry! I'll catch you!"

In my panic, I was losing my balance as I rushed toward him. It was like an old movie, everything moving in slow motion, yet there was nothing I could do to stop. He was still laughing when I finally made contact. His arms wrapped around me and our bodies collided with a thud. I think he could have stopped me, but fell backward into the snow, taking me with him. I landed on top of him, breathless.

"Ugh! I'm sorry!"

He was laughing his head off. "I'm not!"

"Hey, Julia! I'll save you!! How about a drink at the lodge?"

I rolled over and tried to figure out where the voice was coming from. Ryan's mouth set as he pulled himself up, his skis still attached. Mine had come off my boots and he grabbed the front of my parka, pulling me up after him to set me on my feet as if I weighed nothing.

Two guys on the lift above us were calling down to me.

"Hey, dickhead! Am I invisible?" Ryan admonished with a grin.

"Oh, aren't you her brother?" one of them called back, joking and playing along.

I flushed as Ryan brushed the snow off of me, paying extra attention to my ass.

"Hardly!"

"You're gorgeous, Julia! If you change your mind, 7 PM in the lodge lobby!" the other yelled down.

I started giggling and waved up at them as Ryan took me in his arms. "That's funny, is it?" He brushed some snow out of my hair with a gloved hand. I wanted to laugh, he was so adorable. I bit my lip and nodded.

"Yes. I think it's hilarious," I choked out and then burst out laughing. It warmed my heart to see his jealousy, even if it was only a little bit.

"Oh, really? Flirting with those guys is fun, huh?" He lifted me up, dumping me back in the snow and falling back on top of me.

"Ahhhhh!" I screamed in surprise.

Ryan's warm breath rushed over my face as he spoke and nuzzled the side of my face with his nose. His voice lost its laughter. "I think I let you up too soon. Kiss me," he commanded.

He shoved his goggles up and bent to take my mouth with his as he pinned me in the snow.

I cursed my gloved hand when I couldn't feel his hair under my fingers, so I slid my arms around his shoulders. I loved this man so much I couldn't put it into words. Every touch, the easy teasing between us, how he looked at me...all of it meant *everything*. I sucked his lower lip into my mouth and he licked at my top one, before his mouth devoured mine, his tongue teasing mine into passionate play. We both forgot where we were until others began hooting and whistling.

"Jesus, Julia," he groaned against my mouth, the sound of his arousal turned my insides to jelly. "I'm gonna have a problem when we get up," he whispered softly and smiled against my cheek.

I laughed gently and placed another small sucking kiss on his mouth. "Mmmm, well? What do you expect when you dry-hump me in front of a mountain full of people?"

"I expect to get a raging hard on and be frustrated as hell. Satisfied?" He was still above me and smiling the crooked grin I loved. His blue eyes sparkled like diamonds.

"No. But maybe later?" I teased.

"Ugh!!! Definitely. Many times." He rolled over and pulled me with him, using his arms to push me up onto my feet at the same time as he stood up. He threw an arm over my shoulder and pulled me close one more time. "I love you."

"Me, too. So much it's sickening!" I wrapped my arms around his waist and pressed my face into the warmth of his neck above the collar of his coat. He smelled so good and his arms around me felt amazing. There was nowhere else I'd rather be and I found myself wishing I could move to Boston instead of New York.

"Mmmmm...don't stop. Ever," Ryan said softly.

"I can't. I've tried."

"What?" He released me and bent to pick up both pairs of skis, putting them over one shoulder while I gathered up the poles and we made our way into the lodge. "*When?*" he asked in a tone that clearly stated that was impossible.

"Um...every time you went out with some bimbo and broke my heart, that's when." I nudged into him with my shoulder and then he nudged me back.

"Yeah. I was an asshole," he said seriously.

"You didn't know I loved you."

"I *should* have known. You were always so good to me. I was blinded by my love for *you*."

"Stop. It's over. I did the same thing." He placed the skis in a rack outside the lodge and as we went inside, I started unwinding the scarf from around my neck and pulling off my gloves. The lodge was gorgeous, a huge log monstrosity at the base of several mountains. There were multiple fires blazing; with a restaurant on one side, and a lounge on the other, with huge windows looking out onto the lighted slopes. The sun was beginning to set behind the trees and contours of the mountains. It was a beautiful site.

Ryan unzipped his blue parka and grabbed my now bare hand, pulling me beside him into the lounge area with a big stone fireplace with plush leather furniture surrounding it. My thighs were cold, despite my many layers and I was shivering slightly.

Ryan pushed my coat from my shoulders and then his before sitting in a large chair and pulling me onto his lap. I leaned my head on his shoulder and he rubbed his hands over my legs to create the fiction necessary to warm the surface of the skin. I brought my knees up and curled into him like a child while he wrapped his arms around me. "Mmmm..." I sighed into him. I was content and his arms tightened and he kissed my forehead.

The cold made me tired and now I was warm and my eyes were very heavy. "This feels nice. I could hold you forever," Ryan said softly against my skin.

"I wish."

"Are you tired, baby?" I nodded without speaking. "Do you want to go back to the cabin?" he asked. "Or...if you want to skip the drive, I could get a room here tonight. Would you like that?"

I ran my hand up his chest and around his neck to curl into the soft hair at the nape. He was really telling me that he didn't want to wait those couple of hours to make love. I smiled and turned my face to place an open-mouthed kiss on the strong muscles of his neck. He gasped quietly and shifted beneath me. I knew what I was doing and loved the fact that I could affect him that way. My nose brushed along his jaw before I kissed it softly. "Whatever you want," I whispered.

"Julia..." he moaned. I felt his hands grasp the back of my head to tilt it up toward his mouth and he kissed me slowly and spoke when he lifted his head.

"I mean it...It doesn't matter where we are, as long as we're together," I said so softly only he could hear. I pressed my forehead into the curve between his neck and shoulder. My body was vibrating with want. He wasn't even touching me in a sexual way, and I was dying for him to take me.

His hand moved down the back of my head, wrapping around the nape of my neck while his left slid beneath my legs as he stood up. Before I knew it, I was sitting in the chair he'd just vacated and Ryan was striding across to the concierge desk. I felt the heat rush up beneath my cheeks and I bit my lip. He felt the same urgency that I did. I gave up trying to hold in the smile and a soft chuckle broke free of my chest.

"Hey...that sounds nice. Remember me?" I glanced up as a dark-haired man sat in the chair next to mine. He had olive skin and thick, wavy hair, and was maybe of Italian or Spanish descent, quite handsome, with dark eyes and strong bone structure.

Not as beautiful as Ryan.

I glanced over at him and recognized the dark blue and red ski suit as one of the men from earlier. "Julia, right?" I nodded. "Is that your given name?"

"Yes, Julia," I said before I could think.

"Ah...Such an elegant name and you're such a beautiful woman, it suits you. I am Vincent." His foreign accent made his vowels thick and heavy.

"Hello. It's nice to meet you." He picked up my hand to kiss it and I pulled back abruptly, glancing over at the desk. Ryan was turned, his gaze burning as it settled on Vincent. "My, uh...I'm not alone. I'm waiting for someone."

"Ah yes. The gentleman on the slopes, no doubt. He was amusing. I was serious about wanting to buy you a drink. I would like to know you better. I am an excellent skier. Perhaps I can instruct you tomorrow."

A pair of blue eyes was still watching, leaving me nervous about what Ryan was thinking. "I'm sorry, Vincent. That won't be possible." I shook my head as Ryan made his way toward us.

He wasn't hurried, but the muscle in his jaw was working over-time. I grabbed the coats, stood up and walked the few feet that separated us. His arm shot out to wrap around me possessively.

"Are you ready, my love?"

"Yes. Ryan, this is Vincent. Remember, from the lift?"

Ryan extended his hand graciously, but he still had steel in his eyes. "Nice to meet you. Maybe we'll see you on the moun-tain tomorrow. Enjoy your evening." His arm tightened as he dismissed the other man.

"Goodbye, beautiful Julia." Vincent bent and kissed his fin-gers before extending them toward me in a silent kiss.

"Bye," I murmured. Ryan stiffened, still holding me close to his side as we walked to the elevators. "Hey," I placed a hand on the front of his sweater, "so, I guess we're not making the drive tonight. I don't have my pajamas." I looked up into his face and tried to get him to smile. "Soooo, it's a good thing that you don't have yours either."

"What did he want?" he asked gruffly, ignoring my gentle teasing as the elevator doors opened. "I mean, what did he say?"

"Nothing of consequence."

"Damn it, Julia! Tell me what he said!"

"He asked my name and offered to teach me to ski. I said no thank you. End of story."

He removed his arm from around me, but grabbed my hand as he led me down the hall toward our room, put the key card in the slot and pushed the door open.

We went inside and I dropped the coats on an upholstered bench near the door. Ryan moved to the end of the bed, and sat down, pulling me toward him. His hands landed on my hips and he bent his head toward my chest as I laced one hand lovingly through his thick hair. The fingers of my other hand fluttered across his jaw. He needed comfort, some ease to the jealousy that was eating at him.

His breath rushed out in a sigh, the warmth pushing through the material of my shirt. "I hate how I feel when other men come on to you."

"Ryan, there is absolutely no need for you to feel that way. I don't even look at anyone else. You're being silly."

His arms slid around my body and I hugged him close to me, my arms wrapping around his head and shoulders. "I know. I'm sorry. I just...I won't be with you and you're so beautiful. Of course men will want you."

I smiled into the top of his head. "Stop. It's no different than women coming after you. Like that chick from Gross Anatomy class, right?"

"Yeah, I guess. I can't seem to get away from her."

"*Because* she stalks you. I'm not freaking out about her, and yeah, it bugs me, but I won't let it come between us."

His hands started moving to pull my shirt up over my rib cage. "Okay, I see your point. Two hundred miles is still too far, baby. I don't think I can stand it after being with you like this."

"Just *don't forget to remember* how much I love you...I'll never let anyone else touch me like this...you know that. It's not possible."

His hands traveled up the sides of my body, under my shirt until they came in contact with my black lace bra and his thumbs brushed over the fabric. My nipples hardened instantly.

"Like this?" he whispered.

My head fell back. "Uhhhh..." The breath whooshed from my lungs when his hot breath washed over my skin as he placed several kisses over my breasts. He pushed the shirt up further, lifting my arms and pulling it all the way off.

"Julia...God, you can't know what you mean to me," he breathed into my neck. He stood up and put his arms around me, lifting me as his mouth moved up and down my neck. His touch sent a million tingles up and down my spine as he walked with me into the other room.

"I..." I struggled for the words as his mouth searched for mine. "I do, Ryan. I *feel* you even if you never touch me again."

"When you say things like that, you make me so hard." He set me down in the bathroom and grabbed my hand, bringing it down to press it into his erection. My hand closed around him and he groaned. His hands found the closing of my pants and slid the zipper down; pushing them down as far as his arms would reach, exposing the matching black lace thong. His fingers traced the edge of the lace lightly and his head dropped, his mouth seeking mine. He grew even more in my hands as his hands slid down over my butt cheeks while his tongue teased my lips apart. I kissed him back with everything I had. He tasted delicious, warm and seeking, sucking on my tongue and making me moan in pleasure.

"Uh, Ryan..." I let my arms slide up his chest and I tugged impatiently at his sweater. He pulled me closer and pressed his hardness into my stomach. The wetness pooling between my legs was making my panties damp as my body opened, preparing to feel him inside me.

"I don't know how I ever kept my hands off you...or how I'm going to survive without touching you. How did I live without this?"

My breathing was coming in short bursts as Ryan lifted me again. Turning, he set me on the counter beside the sink, up against the mirror on the wall. The light by the door shone in, sending the left side of him into shadow, and his features were even more striking, his eyes glowing darkly as he looked upon my almost naked body. I sat watching in silent hunger as he stripped off his sweater and t-shirt, his magnificent muscles playing across his chest, shoulders and stomach as he moved. Turning away, Ryan started the water in the big tub. This suite was expensive, with a whirlpool bath, a huge king-sized bed, plush furniture, fireplace and a balcony that overlooked the center of the resort. There was a basket of shampoos and bath salts on the counter next to me and he poured some into the running water. The scent of vanilla and sandalwood filled the room, mixing with the steam that began to rise and gather on the mirror. He tugged at the button on his black jeans and pulled the zipper down as he moved toward me again.

"You're so beautiful," Ryan said urgently before his hands reached out and palmed both of my breasts. His mouth started its sweet torment down my neck and onto the slope of my shoulder. He squeezed slightly and then released the front clasp of the bra, freeing the flesh he was seeking. I wrapped my legs around him, attempting to pull him closer. I wanted to feel him pressing into me, needing friction to ease the aching inside of me.

"Julia...I can smell how much you want me. Uhh...it's so...it makes me so hungry for you. I'm going to explode." His hand ghosted over the top of the wet lace between my legs and I couldn't help the mewling pants that escaped my mouth. His hand slid around the front of the panties and pulled them away and down. I kicked them off as he knelt in front of me. His hands grasped behind my rear and pulled me forward until I was sitting on the very edge of the counter in front of him. I braced myself on my hands while he parted my thighs with both hands. His intentions were clear as he gazed down at me and I flushed. This was so intimate, so exposed, but I trusted him implicitly and I loved him with everything I had.

Seeing him like that was so hot. I thought that I would come the minute his mouth touched me, but he teased with sweet torture. He began by kissing my inner thighs, moving closer to the place I needed him, breathing on my center and moving to the other leg. My legs were already shaking and he hadn't even touched me.

"Uhhhh…Ryan, please."

"Oh, babe…Can you feel how much I love you?" he asked softly before he finally brought his mouth down on me, laving in long stokes. I thought I would die, it felt so good. He alternated between that and sucking the tender flesh into his mouth and flicking it quickly with his tongue. He held me steady as I trembled under his expert ministrations. It was only a few short minutes and he had me quaking and coming hard. "Uh…uh…Oh, God," I panted. He eased the pressure but kept up the gentle sucking until I couldn't stand anymore. "Oh God, Ryan. You have to stop. I'm too sensitive." He kissed me softly one last time and then stood up to gather me close.

"Jules, you taste so good. I could do that all night."

I collapsed in his arms, satisfied and shaking. He lifted me into the tub and as I slipped down into the hot water, he stripped off the rest of his clothes and finally slid in beside me. He kissed my mouth and I could taste myself on his lips and tongue. It was so intimate and amazing; we were connected on so many levels.

He moved me in front of him and held me tight. "I'll never be able to tell you or show you how much I love you. It overwhelms me." He kissed the side of my neck softly, moving his mouth up and down on my skin. "*This* is us, Julia."

My heart was so full of him and the love I felt poured out of me in waves. "Baby…" my voice throbbed and I arched my neck and head back onto his shoulder and turned to kiss his jaw. "I love you more." My hands traced over his forearms. "So much."

"I hope I just proved that you belong to me. You're mine."

I smiled and chuckled softly. "Mmmm...is that what that was? Maybe I'll need you to prove it to me again. Just to make sure I don't forget."

His breath rushed from his body as he smiled against my temple. "Anytime. It's my pleasure."

"You're so good to me." I turned in his arms, wanting his mouth on mine and needing his body inside me. I sat on my knees in front of him and his eyes roamed over my face and down my body, lingering on my breasts and then back to my mouth. He licked his lips. I could see the want in his expression. I ached to give him the intense pleasure that he'd just given me.

His hand reached out and pushed the hair back off my face as he sat up and pulled my face toward his. As his mouth opened wetly over mine, my hands slid into his hair. Ryan groaned into my mouth. His free arm wound around my hips and pulled me up onto his body until I was straddling his hips. His cock was full and long, pressing into me and I moved so that my slickness moved over him. He grunted and dragged his mouth across my jaw, when I moved over him, gyrating my hips in little circles. It felt amazing and I watched intently for his reaction and gasped at the desire I found in his beautiful face. He closed his eyes and I moved my hand down to grasp around his length, to guide him to my opening. I rested my forehead on his as he slid deep inside me, filling me until I couldn't stretch anymore.

Ryan's breath hitched. "Mmmm...Nothing will ever feel as perfect as making love with you."

I brushed his hair back and then kissed him as I started to rock my hips into his. The water sloshed out of the tub in the dark bathroom, the sound becoming a regular rhythm with our moans and soft pants. Each and every kiss was deeper and more reverent than the last as the movements of our bodies became more urgent. He moved deeply inside me, his hands guiding my hips in slow, deep strokes…the minutes ticked by, the sensations building in both of us. My nipples rubbed against the soft hair of his chest, adding to my arousal. I felt the tightening begin again. Ryan knew my body so well, he whispered against the swell of my breast…"That's right baby, let it go. I want you to come again, Julia."

Hearing those words tumbling from his lips, his voice so velvet and filled with passion, sent me over the edge. I clawed at his shoulders as I spasmed around him, my body sucking on his until he lost himself in his own release. "Unnnnn…Julia…you feel so good."

I was wound around him and his arms slid around my waist and back to pull me tight against him. We were both kissing each other's shoulders and faces. I tugged him back so that I could kiss his mouth once more, licking at his lips. "I never want you to stop making love to me, Ryan. I never want to be away from you."

"Oh, honey," he sighed and kissed the side of my cheekbone.

The water was getting cold which told me we'd been making love for quite a while. Time didn't seem to exist. Ryan felt me shiver and lifted me with him out of the bath. He grabbed a couple of towels with his free hand and proceeded with me in his arms, into the bedroom. There was an electric fireplace and he flipped it on as he made his way to the bed, then pulled the covers back and placed me underneath. I watched him move and he wrapped a towel around his waist and then got the remote to the TV and turned it on.

"Do you want to watch TV or would you rather have music?"

"Whatever you want."

"Julia, you have to stop saying that. I'll be ravishing you all night if I have my way."

"Well...that works for me." I smiled as I watched a grin split his face. The fire was casting a reddish glow across his striking features and turned his hair to copper. "You're gorgeous. You take my breath away."

His brow dropped over his eyes and he shook his head. "Julia."

"Go ahead and scoff at me. You are. So shut up and take a compliment, Matthews." He completely ignored me. *Is he that oblivious to how beautiful he is?*

"I vote for music. Is that okay with you?"

"*Anything* you want," I said again and his mouth quirked softly at the implied meaning behind the words.

He selected a soft rock station on the Music-On-Demand channel and then crawled under the covers next to me. I threw off the towel on my head and settled into his body as he pulled me close. His chest rising and falling beneath my cheek was comforting and I closed my eyes. Words were unnecessary.

We let the firelight and the music envelop us, both of us reaching out to the other with soft feather touches. I let myself concentrate on the music, as several songs played. Ryan had chosen well. I loved acoustic guitar and the soft strains of a jazzy Latin rhythm began to fill the room in low tones, and I let myself dissolve into the words. It was sexy and sultry, but the lyrics were perfect for us. It spoke of longing and overcoming obstacles and a determination to be with the one you love...no matter what had to be overcome, certain love could last forever. It was beautifully poignant and heart wrenching; it branded us.

His arms tightened around me, letting me know that he was listening to the words as much as I was. I felt my eyes begin to burn and my throat tighten. I closed my eyes and held onto the man in my arms.

The tears slid softly from my eyes and fell onto Ryan's chest. "Julia, we *will* be together. I'd give anything if you could be with me all of the time, *now*...but it will happen, eventually."

The last strains of the song faded out. "I know. I just miss you more than I ever thought I would," I said, trying to keep the throb out of my voice.

I felt his lips in my hair. "I miss you, too. You're all I think about."

I turned into him and slid a leg between his as we continued to lie there together, the warmth of his body seeping into mine. He touched me softly, soothingly, until my eyes grew tired and I felt myself drifting into sleep, the words of the song still haunting me. "It won't be enough, Ryan," I said sleepily.

"No. *Forever* isn't long enough," he answered and pulled me up to kiss me softly on the mouth and run a finger down my cheek and over my lower lip. "You know I'm going to marry you, right? I'm not fucking around. You're *it* for me, Julia."

More tears slipped from my eyes as his fingers brushed them away. I nodded. "Yes," I gave him the answer he needed.

"Go to sleep, my love," he said as he pulled me gently across his chest and I wrapped an arm over his waist. "I'm not letting go of you until I absolutely have no choice."

Ryan ~

Where had all the time gone? We dropped Paul off at LaGuardia and Aaron left earlier to go back to Boston. He was great, helping us move Julia in, but also understood my need to be alone with her. She was sitting in the center of the backseat of the cab, her head on my shoulder, neither one of us speaking. Yes, she was closer now, but still…we wouldn't be together. Not the way we both wanted. I turned my face toward her and kissed her forehead, breathing in her sweet scent. I closed my eyes. These past ten days had been heaven and now leaving would be hell.

Her arms tightened around mine and she sighed loudly. My heart was heavy and she was very upset, despite her attempt to hide it. I tightened my grip. My arm rested across her lap and my hand closed around the knee furthest away from me.

"Thank you," she said softly. "For this time…"

"Oh, babe…there is nothing I love more than being with you, Julia," I murmured. I tried to put a smile on my face as I nudged her shoulder. "Do you want to go out tonight? I'll take you anywhere you want to go."

She shook her head. "Uh uh. Moving wore me out. Aren't you tired? You worked so hard." She nudged me back and looked up into my face, smiling, but it didn't reach her eyes. The sadness in the emerald orbs made my heart break. My thumb brushed the edge of her jaw as I bent to kiss her mouth. Her lips clung hungrily to mine and I never wanted to let her go.

"Yeah. I'm tired," I said, my lips dragging up to place a soft kiss on her cheekbone. The cab stopped at her new apartment. A one-bedroom walk-up that Jen, Aaron and I had found while Julia was still in Los Angeles. It was small, but so expensive that it was all she could afford, even with my help.

I passed the driver a twenty as Julia waited on the sidewalk. "Come here, baby." I took her hand, pulled it over my shoulder and bent to lift her leg and hitch her up onto my back. She didn't argue and curled around my body, her arms and legs wrapping tightly around me. I put my hands under her bottom and carried her piggy-back into the building and up the stairs. She bent toward me, placing an open-mouthed kiss on my neck. Her mouth was hot and wet. I felt my heart and body tighten.

"I love you, Ryan," she whispered in my ear. I wanted to be happy for her...her new job was an amazing opportunity and it did get her on the right side of the country, but our time together was so wonderful, I hated to see it end. I wanted her with me constantly.

I climbed up the stairs and at the top Julia dug the keys out of her pocket. I turned her so that she could unlock the door while she was still on my back.

"You can put me down, honey."

"Nope."

Julia laughed softly. "What?"

"I said *no*. I didn't stutter, did I?" I teased. I pushed through the door and it closed behind us.

"Hmmph," she snorted. "What's this about, Matthews?" She threw her coat off and it landed on the floor beside the door and reached up and took the baseball hat off of my head, tossing it on top of her coat.

"I just don't want to let go of you tonight. So sue me." I grinned as I sat on the couch, pinning her behind me. She pulled my coat down off of my shoulders and I took it out of her hands and threw it aside. I pulled both of her feet together in front of me and started untying her shoes, pushing them off and letting them drop with loud thumps to the floor. I leaned back into her and she squealed while I used each foot to push my own shoes off.

"Hey, you're smashing me," Julia complained with a laugh, and poked me in the ribs. I loved being with her, doing nothing more than this.

"You poor thing," I retorted sarcastically as I started to rub her feet. She relaxed behind me but I tensed when her little hands burrowed beneath my shirt to rake her nails softly down my back. I shuddered under her touch, the tingles running down my spine. "That feels good, babe."

"Yes it does." Her arms wrapped around my waist and she rested her head on my back. I pulled one of her hands up and held it between both of mine. The bracelet, sparkling on her wrist, glistened in the low light. "The time with you goes by so fast," she whispered achingly.

I paused for a few seconds, trying to shake off the sadness welling up inside my chest. I kissed the top of her hand, then turned and pulled her around me. I lay down on the couch and pulled her small form to lie on top of me; both of us wrapped our arms tightly around each other.

"Hey, none of that. You're starting a new job and there's so much to look forward to. You'll make a bunch of new friends, and you have this amazingly expensive and *tiny* apartment!" I teased. "It's like a cracker box. There isn't even enough room to put up any of those pictures you've drawn of me."

She chuckled. "Yeah. I'll manage. At least *I'm* not sharing it with Aaron and Jen."

"Sure, add insult to injury, why don't you?" My hands were running up and down her back. I loved the way she fit into my body. Trying to be lighthearted, my heart was aching at the prospect of leaving her.

"Mmm…I had a wonderful few days with you. The time in Colorado was so precious, Ryan."

I drew in a deep breath, trying to expel the tightness in my chest. "It was perfect. Every minute." Julia nodded beneath my chin and my fingers brushed against her velvet cheek. "I love you, Julia," the words fell from my lips like a prayer and I closed my eyes tightly.

"So…coffee date tomorrow before you leave?" she murmured, her voice trembling with emotion.

"What do you think? It's *Sunday*, isn't it?" We hadn't missed a Sunday coffee date since we met and I didn't plan on starting now. "It's always been my favorite part of the week even if it was only on the phone. I won't pass up a chance for one in person."

"Yeah. I love our coffee dates, talking to you, hearing what's going on...what I'm missing from your life," she turned into my neck and kissed the point where my pulse was throbbing uncontrollably. My heart hurt. She was still my best friend. My lover. My life.

"I love talking to you, too. *Remember?*" I lowered my voice, trying to keep it even.

"That's right," she sniffed and laughed through her tears. "You don't care if you touch me as long as you can talk to me, yes?"

"Uh..." I said, rolling her onto her back. I took hold of her hip and shifted her beneath me. She opened her legs so I could settle down on top of her. "Maybe I spoke too soon." I smiled as I brushed her hair off her face. Her eyes were serious as she looked up at me and our hips moved together. "God, Julia. Mmm...much, much, too soon."

~10~

Julia ~

Today was Valentine's Day. It gave me an excuse to send something to Ryan. Not that I needed one, but hopefully, this would be the last year we'd be apart.

I smirked to myself. The sheer red chemise and g-string that I sent him along with a note asking he bring it to New York left nothing to the imagination, adding just the right amount of temptation. I'd been naughty and flushed at the thought of Ryan opening my gift. Besides wearing it so it would smell like me, I'd sent it to him at the hospital instead of his apartment. He'd be working and I couldn't wait until he received it the next day. My heart raced with excitement. Three dozen red and white roses sat on the sideboard in my office; but it was the card that melted me.

~J
You are the love of my life...of my *forever*.
Words can't express what you mean to me, but I'll tell you a hundred times a day for the rest of my life. I love you.
~R

Ryan would graduate Harvard Med in June and then start his surgery and ER residency at St. Vincent's in Lower Manhattan. It was quite a jaunt from my apartment, and we discussed moving to Greenwich Village or somewhere in the middle. I argued it was more important to be near the hospital since he'd be on call at all hours of the day and night.

Ryan's academic advisor and clinical professor, Dr. Brighton, sent an excellent recommendation to the Chief of Staff after Ryan applied for his primary residency. Graduating at the top of his class assured he'd be accepted anywhere, but I was thankful he was willing to relocate to New York City. Pride threatened to split me apart.

I'd been promoted several times, and kept in touch with many of my friends from Los Angeles. Andrea was now my creative assistant, having moved to New York when I was promoted to Creative Editor ten months ago. I worked hard these past three years, in part because I loved the work, and in part to keep my mind off of missing Ryan. Soon, missing him would be a thing of the past and the constant ache would go away. I sighed. *Finally.*

Ryan had clinical all week but said he'd be able to take the train down on the weekend. I planned to surprise him with a concert at Madison Square Garden and then a late supper at my favorite Thai restaurant uptown. I smiled to myself; *and black forest* back at my apartment. I'd planned to go shopping tonight and make the cake when I got home so it would be ready tomorrow, then I could meet his train and take him directly to the concert. I was buzzing with excitement and anticipation.

My heart raced. Something told me Ryan was going to give me an engagement ring on Friday night. We'd talked about getting married many times, ever since our ski trip to Colorado before I first moved to New York. Three years later, we were still together and we still loved each other just as desperately. Nothing would make me happier than being married to him, to wake up in his arms everyday and someday, have his children.

I coughed and reached for a tissue; stupid damn sinus infection. I'd been sick all week, missing two days of work. I'd been curled up in bed, coughing my fool head off, when Ryan had insisted I go to the doctor.

"Damn it, Julia. It won't get better until you get on antibiotics. Why are you so stubborn?" he'd admonished impatiently. *"I don't want you to suffer and I'd rather have you well when I come to New York. Get to the clinic, at least."* It was an ongoing joke between us that he was my family doctor, so why would I waste time with finding another?

The years apart were difficult. We hadn't seen each other as much as we wanted, and less in the past two years once his clinical started. He was working at Mass General which had the best and busiest trauma department in the city. We were lucky to see each other every five or six weeks. The only thing that kept me sane was our coffee Sundays. They had to be rescheduled sometimes due to work, but it was still our time to talk. After all this time, I still missed him so much that sometimes it became a physical ache.

I ran my hand through my hair and picked up the story on spring fashion for the March issue. I was working on the look of the article and Andrea had just left with the wardrobe order and the list of talent I wanted hired. I was trying to work it in with a shoot for another article to save budget. I was paid bonus on margin, so the more money I saved, the more I earned. I was getting damn good at it, too. Ellie kept me in designer suits and shoes so I looked the part for my job. I was well established and my future with the company was secure.

I picked up the phone and dialed layout. "Hi, Grace. It's Julia Abbott. Our creative department will leave a thirty-seven inch copy jump on page 142. What else is going on that page?

Do you have enough editorial for it, or do I need to order creative fill? Yes, the deadline is in 8 days, so please let me know by Monday, close of business."

A shadow fell across the desk and startled me. Meredith McCormick, my first boss from Glamour, walked though my door, a big smile on her face. I gasped in surprise. She looked as professional and chic as I remembered, the years not aging her at all. We had a big Christmas party each year when she and the other executives would fly in, but this time of year, a visit was unusual.

"Uh, okay. I'll tell Andrea to get on the feature story for April. Yes. Thank you." I put down the phone and ran around my desk to hug her. "What are you doing here? Why didn't you let me know?" I asked incredulously. "I'm so happy to see you! Can I get you some coffee?"

"Sure. You look fantastic, Julia. Quite the fashion maven," Meredith said as she sank into one of the navy blue leather chairs across from my large cherry wood desk. Her eyes roamed over my Prada suit and I rolled my eyes.

"My best friend, Ellie hooks me up. She's a stylist in Los Angeles and gets deals from all of the big designers." I smiled wide and sat in my chair. "She tells me I can't be Creative Director for a major mag and look like Ugly Betty."

"Ugh! Hardly, Julia. You were always gorg." Meredith leaned back in her chair and crossed her legs.

I picked up my phone and dialed my secretary. "Susan, can you bring in two cups of coffee. The usual for me and one black," I looked to verify with Meredith and she nodded. "Thanks." I hung up the phone. "So?" I raised my eyebrows in question.

"Ah, Julia, you never did beat around the bush," she sighed. "Have you heard about plans to send a few chosen ones to Paris to work on the European editions of Vogue?"

"Sure."

"But...you didn't put in for it?"

"If you're heading it up, you obviously know that I didn't." I smirked and shook my head. Susan knocked on the door and came in with the coffee. She was young, still going to night school and very timid, and had just joined my staff. I smiled at her and she looked a little less nervous.

"Will there be anything else, Miss Abbott?"

"No, thank you, Susan. And I told you, please call me Julia."

"Yes, Miss Abbo...um, Julia."

"It's okay, Susan. You're doing a great job," I reassured as she left quietly. "So, where were we?" I asked as I picked up my coffee and took a sip.

"You were going to explain to me why you didn't put in for that job? It's one hell of an opportunity, Julia. It would give you all the experience you'd need to come back and land a Creative Director position at one of our major pubs."

I shrugged. "Yeah, I thought about it, but the timing isn't right."

"Why not?" she asked skeptically. "These types of opportunities don't grow on trees."

"Um...well, Ryan has secured a residency position at St. Vincent's after he graduates medical school in June."

"Oh, yes...that gorgeous hunk, *Dr.* Ryan. Can't say I blame you for thinking twice, but I need you to take this job."

I set my cup back on the table and sighed. I couldn't believe my ears. "Well...haven't you had any applicants? There are several talented people you could promote. I'm flattered that you asked me, though."

Meredith tented her hands in front of her and contemplated her next words carefully. "Yes, but..." she began and my eyes widened at her tone, "I *want you*. You and Ryan have lived apart for almost four years, Julia. What's one more? I'm not taking no for an answer," she said matter-of-factly.

I considered her my friend so I could tell her the truth. "What it is...is another three hundred and sixty five days without him. I miss him. We've had enough."

My heart was racing. The opportunity was more than I'd even dared hope for and here she was, offering it to me on a silver platter. "It is a wonderful opportunity, and if Ryan still had a year of school, I would seriously consider it, but he's almost done and we'll finally be together. He'd be devastated if I left now." I looked her in the eyes without flinching. "*I'd* be devastated. I can't tell you how hard being away from him has been."

"I have forty-some resumes on my desk and none of them can hold a candle to yours, Julia. This is *your* job. I'll let you name your own staff, though I have a few recommendations. You can't say *no*. Ryan wouldn't want you to. It's the opportunity of a lifetime."

I sighed and shook my head. "I know it is, Meredith, but...I don't want to be away from him. His graduation is so close."

She rolled her eyes and threw her hands up. "I'll bring you back for his graduation and at least once every three or four months."

"Ugh!" I stood up and turned my back, pacing in front of the window in the large office. "That's not enough."

"Okay, once every two or three months and for the graduation, okay?"

My heart squeezed inside my chest and my vision blurred. "I have to talk to him and see how he reacts. I can't promise at this point." I squirmed in my seat, trying to get her to let it drop, but she was like a rabid dog with a bone.

"Look, honey, I've already arranged for you to take Andrea with you, and Mike Turner is being sent as the photographer on the unit. The old gang will be together again. You can pick two artists...the writers will be from Paris, due to language barriers, of course, but you can choose your assistants, production manager, a translator and secretaries. I'm giving you carte blanche on this. You'd report directly to me."

I faced her and put my hand on my hip, smoothing the navy blue fabric of my skirt nervously. "I have to talk to Ryan before I can commit, okay?"

"Okay, honey, but this is your baby. You'd be insane not to jump on it."

"Thank you for your faith...it's incredible that you think so highly of me." I stumbled for the right words.

"Bullshit, Julia. You're the most talented person I've ever worked with, and I can count on you to do the job right. It's just a fact. This isn't a fucking favor. I *need* you for this job." She looked at me pointedly and rose out of the chair. "I have to go upstairs and speak to John. I get to tell him I'm stealing his star right out from underneath him. This should be fun." She laughed and then came around the desk to hug me. "Ryan will be proud. You've accomplished so much for one so young. If he's everything you've told me, and what I've seen of him on the few times we've met, he will support you one hundred percent."

My heart sank as I pictured the look on Ryan's face when I told him. "How long? I mean, when would I need to leave?"

"A month, maybe? Depends how long it takes you to make arrangements, get people in the right places. Replacements for whomever you choose, that is."

I was still in shock and slightly numb. If it weren't for my situation with Ryan, I would have been over the moon to be offered this position, but to leave him in the face of almost being together, it was the last thing I wanted.

"Meredith, does it have to be a year? If I agree to six months, will you let me come home after that? I mean, can we compromise? Then it will only be two months added. I want to do this, but I can't be away from him for a year." I shook my head as my brow dropped. Could she tell that I would quit before I'd leave him for a damned year?

She looked at me, taking in my pained expression. "Yes, I'll compromise."

"And, you'll bring me back to the states for a full week every two months. And for his graduation. I want your word."

"You drive a hard bargain. That's why I love you, but yes."

I nodded. "I still have to talk to him first. This is only a maybe until I can work this out with Ryan."

"If you can't?"

I shrugged. "Simple. I don't go. He's the most important thing."

"He must be amazing in bed," she teased. "And it doesn't hurt that he's beautiful," she laughed and nodded toward the framed drawing of him on my office wall.

I laughed despite myself. "No. It certainly doesn't…brilliant and wonderful and very loving. He's absolutely perfect."

"Okay, seriously? That's just sickening, but I bet he *is* amazing in bed!" I blushed as Meredith laughed. "I bet he's got a huge…" she began but I cut her off.

"Meredith!" I admonished. Ryan's anatomy was not up for discussion.

She chuckled, picked up her purse and left my office.

I fell back into my chair and wondered how in the hell I was going to tell Ryan about this. The full extent of what it meant began flooding over me.

Shit.

I picked up the phone and pressed Andrea's extension. "Please come in here."

"Are we going to Paris?" she asked excitedly through the phone.

Nice. She knew before I did?

Suddenly, the beautiful weekend I had planned with Ryan had a huge cloud hanging over it. I ran my hands through my hair and closed my eyes.

"Just come in here, please. I'm leaving early." I hung up the phone on my desk and dug my cell phone out of my purse, quickly typing out a text to Ryan.

I'm in the mood for a coffee date. Do you have time?

Andrea knocked on the door frame and then walked in, eyeing me wearily. She'd cut her hair to the top of her shoulders after she came to work here, insisting that her long locks were too wild for chic New York. "Julia...you look upset. I told Meredith that you probably wouldn't want this job," she said, disappointment dripping off of her voice. "I understand why, though" she nodded as her face fell.

"Um...it isn't that I don't want the job. It's an amazing opportunity for all of us." She was looking down at the floor but she glanced up.

"I was afraid that maybe you'd want to take another assistant."

"No, if I go, you're coming with me, don't worry...but I'm torn about this, Andrea. I'm pretty sure that Ryan is proposing this weekend. And won't that be great for him? Yes, I'll marry you, but first I have to go to Paris for several months?" My eyes welled with tears, and my voice broke.

Andrea moved forward and hugged me. "I'm sorry, Julia."

"It doesn't feel like I have much choice," I murmured, more to myself than to her, as I moved out of her arms. I was wiping at my eyes as my phone vibrated in my other hand. I opened the message, anxious for Ryan's words.

I'd love to, baby, but I'm on rotation until 7. Can't until after that. I'll call you. Are you okay?

"Andrea, I need to walk and think about everything. Can you handle things? Clear my calendar." She nodded slightly and I grabbed my coat, already heading for the door. "Okay, call if you need me," I threw my purse over my shoulder and the next thing I knew, I was walking alone in Central Park. My phone vibrated again and I realized I hadn't texted Ryan in return.

Julia, are you okay? I'm worried now. Please answer me.

I'm fine. I just miss you. I wanted to hear your voice.

I can't wait until this weekend. I won't stop telling you how much I love you...and want you.

Love you, too. So much. Go back to work. I'll talk to you when you're finished. XXOO

You forgot to say you want me. You do, right?:-)

Of course, shithead. As desperately as ever. Obviously you haven't gotten your surprise or you wouldn't need to ask. If you have...OPEN IT NOW.

He had a way of making me smile, even when my heart hurt. He was amazing. I tried to concentrate on the weekend and how much I was going to soak him in; trying to figure out when would be the best time to tell him about the job offer. My heart lurched. It wouldn't be fair to let him propose and then dump this on him. It had to be before that. I closed my eyes as my throat started to ache. At least then he'd be able to change his mind, which would be fair.

Meredith promised it would only be six months, but I knew how this shit went down. Once she had me in France, it wouldn't be so simple to get her to let me come back. If it all went as I'd hoped, Ryan would only be in New York for two months without me. I just had to do everything possible to get back as quickly as possible.

Another message came in.

God, Julia...I can smell you on this! I'm fucking ACHING...You're so mean! LOL.

I smiled despite my new dilemma, my body blooming with heat and throbbing at his written words even as my eyes welled with tears.

I'll wear it for you later. The roses are gorgeous...just like YOU. Love you, so much.

In that moment, I decided not to tell Ryan until Saturday. I wanted Friday night to be perfect and to give everything I had to him. I needed to make him see how much I loved him so that he wouldn't be as hurt when I finally told him about Paris. I needed to see him happy and fulfilled...we hadn't been together in almost eight weeks.

I hailed a cab to take me back to my apartment. I still had my car, but it was easier to take a cab to the office. The extra money for the garage was a small fortune and I had seriously considered selling it, but it did come in handy when Ryan was in the city. It was Wednesday and so there were two more days until I'd be in his strong arms. He was arriving at two on Friday and we'd have enough time to get back and drop his things off at my apartment and then get downtown for the concert.

It was starting to snow as I pushed open the door to my building. "Hello, Miss Julia! Happy Valentine's Day. Is Mr. Ryan visiting today?" Adam, the day doorman, asked brightly as I walked past him.

I smiled. "Not until Friday, Adam. Did you get your wife something nice?"

"Oh, yes ma'am. Did you get a nice gift?"

I stopped and turned back to him, "Yes, he sent me three dozen roses at my office."

"No doubt, one dozen for each of the three words, *I love you*?" He smiled and winked at me. The corners of my mouth went up slightly.

"You know, I never thought of that, but that sounds like him, though, doesn't it?"

"Oh yeah, that man's got it bad, honey," Adam winked again and I burst out laughing.

"Thank you, Adam. I hope so, since I'm completely gone where he's concerned."

"Oh, no worries, little miss. No worries, at all."

I opened the door to my apartment and flipped on the light in the hall, kicked off my shoes and started to unbutton the jacket of my suit at the same time I hung my coat up on the tree in the hall. I'd skipped lunch and my stomach rumbled so I made my way into the kitchen. On the table, arranged so neatly, were three more vases of roses. This time bouquets of white and red with some baby pink ones mixed in. They took my breath away, they were so beautiful. A card was set up against the base of each crystal vase.

Damn him. He was so incredible and he had me in tears all over again. He was so tender and loving and I was going to break his heart. My hand moved to my chest as I walked slowly to the table and picked up the cards one by one with a trembling hand.

I love you...with everything I am.

I want you...with a desperation that consumes me.

I need you...more than air.

"Oh, Ryan," I moaned into my empty apartment, my heart expanding within my chest to the point of pain. God, I loved him and I was the luckiest woman in the world that he loved me this much in return.

What the hell am I doing even considering Paris?

It had been my plan to make his cake tonight, letting it chill overnight and giving the kirsch time to soak into the cake and the flavors of the liquor, cherries and chocolate to blend. I changed into some old sweats and a t-shirt, put my hair up on top of my head and then returned to the kitchen, glancing at the three vases of flowers on the way. I was insane to leave him for any extra time. I tried to rationalize that if everything went as planned, it would only be two months longer than our current situation. Surely, we'd survive two more months so I could have this amazing opportunity. *Keep trying to convince yourself, Abbott,* I chastised myself.

I got out my mixer and double boiler along with the ingredients and went about assembling the cake's batter. While it was baking, I made the sugar syrup and shaved the chocolate curls into a chilled bowl, putting it in the refrigerator to wait until I was ready to assemble the cake.

My thoughts played hell with my emotions as I worked. We'd been through so much sacrifice and time apart. Yes, there had been pain, but there was so much joy and love that made it well worth it. Even when we weren't together, I was completely consumed. I'd rather have a text from him than a year with someone else. Nothing had changed in the entire time I'd known him. I loved him as much, probably more, than ever. I washed the mixing bowl and put it in the freezer to chill in preparation to whip the cream that would cover the sides of the finished cake.

The buzzer went off and I pulled the layers from the oven and turned it off, leaving the cake to cool while I went to take a bath. I had an iPod dock in the bathroom and turned to the play-list of slow love songs, one Ryan and I so often played while we made love.

God...I miss him.

The water was running and I left the bathroom to get my phone in case Ryan called me while I was in the bath. *Only two more days...*I lit the candle on the vanity and peeled off my clothes, leaving them in a pile on the floor beside the tub. I sank into the scented water, letting the water soak away the tension, and the music surround me.

Singing in the bathroom was a secret indulgence. No one knew, except Ryan. He knew everything. Sometimes I would catch him listening to me through the door and other times he'd just come in and listen. I liked the acoustics in the bathroom. Cliché I know, but seriously, it sounded great in there and was easier to pick out the harmonies, a challenge that I enjoyed. Ryan used to tease me about my over-achiever tendencies. "Hmmph..." I smiled softly as the memory washed over me, "like he can talk."

Ryan was gifted at the piano and guitar and sometimes we'd sing together while he played. It started in college, hanging out in our dorms. Just one more place that we connected.

When the soft piano introduction began of one of my favor-ite songs, I started to hum and finally let the words come out. I loved the softness of the song, and it suited my mood. The lyrics spoke to me of Ryan.

Perfect timing, my phone began ringing as the song faded out and I leaned over and reached for it, knowing it would be my beautiful man.

"Hey you," I answered softly.

"Hey, yourself. What are you doing?" He sounded tired, but his velvet voice was warm and I could hear the smile behind his words.

"Mmm...taking a bath." I bit my lip, teasing and waiting for his response.

"Are you naked?"

I laughed. "No, Matthews. I usually take my baths fully clothed."

"Stop being a smart ass," he chuckled. "Mmmm...naked Julia; my favorite thing in the entire world."

"Mmmm is right."

"Were you singing in your echo chamber?"

"You think you know everything, don't you?"

"That's because I do. Deal with it." he teased.

I laughed out loud, happiness seeping through every cell of my body. "Yeah. I love you. Thank you for the flowers...again. It's too much, baby."

He let out his breath and I could almost see him running his hand through his hair. "Never enough for you," his voice dropped an octave and I could hear the love saturating his words. My heart quickened. "Are you going to bed soon?"

"Yeah, in a bit. I have a couple of things I need to finish first. I wish you were here."

"Me too. Soon. I'm bushed, honey. I spent 6 hours in class and 8 hours in clinical today."

"Okay, babe. Go to bed. Just don't forget to dream of me."

He groaned into the phone. "Always. I imagine you in that bed all alone without me. Julia...?" he hesitated.

"What?" I urged him on softly.

"Do you ever think about easing the ache?" My body reacted at his words. We'd talked about that before and he knew what I was going to say.

"I think about it. Sometimes I miss your touch so much I can hardly stand it."

"So take care of it," he suggested huskily.

"It wouldn't be the same. Your hands are the only ones I want on my body, Ryan. How many times do I have to tell you that?"

"Uhnnn...I love hearing that. You know what it does to me."

"I know, baby, me too, and it just makes me more anxious to see you. It's sort of sweet torture," I said softly.

"Now I'm going to go to bed with a huge hard-on."

I laughed softly under my breath. "You do it to yourself, honey. That's what you get for bringing it up."

"*You* do it to me. I can't wait until Friday," I could hear the sex throb through his voice and my body reacted as if he were in the room with me. "It was vindictive sending me the lingerie with your scent all over it."

"Deal with it." I threw his own words back in his face, a soft smile tugging at my lips.

"You're gonna get it, Miss Abbott."

"Mmmm...counting the minutes until I do." My heart squeezed knowing that if I went to Paris, all we'd have to sustain us for months on end, were phone conversations.

"Ugh! Baby, I'll let you go to bed. Don't forget...only my hands on your body. Only me who brings you to that."

"Uhh...Ryan..." I whispered achingly. "Yes, baby."

"God, I love you."

"Love you more."

"Baby, stop. We do this all the time."

"Okay, it's a tie then."

"That works for me. Goodnight, my love. Don't forget to ache for me."

"I can't help myself. Goodnight, sexy beast."

Ryan ~

Counting the minutes...I was counting the minutes, too. *Literally.*

I smiled a huge ass grin, my heart racing a thousand beats a minute as I hailed a cab. Still in my scrubs, I'd run to the train station straight from my rotation shift. I threw my duffle in the cab before climbing in and giving the driver Julia's address in Upper Manhattan.

I sighed and ran a hand through my hair. *Only minutes now.* She'd be surprised at the extra two nights together and I was feeling as satisfied as a cat that just ate the canary. I was so hungry for her, my mouth had gone dry and I had perpetual wood just thinking about her. *Shit.*

The cab driver glanced at me in the rearview mirror. He was an older gentleman with graying hair and a scruffy beard.

"Going to see your girl?" His smile was warm and I nodded.

"Yes. I haven't seen her in almost two months. I'm very anxious and I'm surprising her. She isn't expecting me for two more days."

"Ah. Are you sure that's wise son? Maybe she's *busy.*" I knew he was implying that she might have another boyfriend.

"Hmmph. Yes, it's fine." I rolled my eyes in disgust at any doubt over her devotion. "She'll be happy as shit to see me.

We've been together almost 8 years. Trust me, we're as tight as it gets."

"And yet you still seem excited to see her. After all this time?"

I contemplated his remark and considered how much I wanted to share. After all, I'd never see him again and he was only making polite conversation, even if the question did piss me off slightly.

"We've only been a couple for half that time, before that, best friends; inseparable from day one. Julia is an extraordinary woman, and yes, she still excites me as much as ever." I smirked and shoved my hand in the pocket of my leather jacket, fingering the red silk lingerie that she'd sent me for Valentine's Day. I was feeling mischievous and so I pulled it out, holding it up for him to see in his mirror. It was a sexy little nothing that he could clearly see my face through and his eyebrows raised and he let out a low whistle.

"Did you get her that for Valentine's Day?"

"Nope." I laughed and shoved it back into my pocket. "*She* got it for me. Getting her into and out of this sexy little thing will be my pleasure about 10 minutes from now."

She'd probably be in bed already and it was my plan to sneak in and try to catch her off guard. She could wear it tomorrow night. Tonight, I was too impatient to feel her skin on mine.

"Okay, enough said. If she's that sexy, how'd you manage to just be friends for so long?"

I shook my head as I glanced out the window and answered, more to myself. "Fuck if I know."

"I don't mean to pry. I'm just bored and my wife died five years ago. It's nice to hear some happy stories for Valentine's Day."

"Oh, I'm sorry. How long were you married?"

"38 years. She had cancer. Are you planning on marrying this girl?"

"I'm asking her this weekend." I took the ring out of the inside pocket of my jacket and flipped open the box, gazing down at the glittering stones set in platinum. My thumb brushed over the top of the solitaire. "Finally, we'll be able to be together."

"Oh? You aren't now? Why not?" he asked, his curiosity piqued.

"Well, she has a high powered job at Vogue Magazine and I'm just finishing medical school in Boston. I'm moving here in June to begin my residency at St. Vincent's."

"Wow. You two will have a great life."

"Yeah. Once it starts. It's been hell being apart, *but*...that is almost behind us now," I said, my excitement becoming more than I could bear as he pulled up beside Julia's apartment building. It was an older building, but the apartments inside were freshly remodeled and it was a very secure building in a good neighborhood.

"Good luck to you, son. You have my best wishes with your bride-to-be."

I handed him a fifty dollar bill. "Keep it. And thank you," I smiled before I slung my bag over my shoulder and bolted up the stairs and into the building. The doormen all knew me, and so I waved and rushed past him into the elevators.

"Hello there! Is it Dr. Matthews yet?"

"In a few months, David!"

I rode the elevator up to the eleventh floor, so excited that it felt like my skin was crawling around on my body. I pulled her apartment key out of my pocket and slipped it into the lock, opening the door as quietly as I could. I nudged the door open slowly and sighed in relief when only darkness met me. I caught the door and held it, letting it close carefully. I turned the deadbolt softly, set my bag down next to the door and kicked off my shoes.

I was dying of thirst so I went to the refrigerator where Julia would have bottled water en mass but was assaulted with the beautiful cake she'd made sitting on the shelf. It looked like it came from a bakery, but I knew better. She'd kill me if I cut into it until she was ready to let me, but it was hard to resist. I slammed the water and then tiptoed down the hall to Julia's room.

The apartment was shrouded in darkness and the scent of her was everywhere. My breathing sped up when I got to her room. I could hear her breathing softly, obviously deep in sleep. The comforter was slung low on her hips and she was on her back, her left arm flung above her head and her glorious dark hair flowing all over the pillow.

I knelt next to the bed and looked into her beautiful face. She was relaxed and her lips were open slightly. She licked them and turned toward me. My body tightened as the sweet warmth of her breath washed over my face. I longed to kiss her but debated about waking her. She looked so peaceful but my hand snuck out and brushed a lock of her hair back and then the back of my fingers brushed across the silky skin of cheek.

"Uhhhhh…" she sighed deeply and my name escaped with the expelled breath. "Ryan…please."

I was throbbing and twitching before, but now my cock was hard as steel and I had an overwhelming need to bury myself inside her moist heat. She would be hot and wet and so receptive. I knew it as well as I knew my own name…as certain as my love for her. She was dreaming about us making love. An immense rush of love and lust overwhelmed me. My decision was made; there was no way I wasn't giving in to the need.

I stood up and went to the foot of the bed, stripping off my clothes and watching her writhe and moan, calling to me with the siren's song of her sighs and low whimpers. Even if I'd known touching her now would mean my certain death, I wouldn't have been able to fucking stop myself.

I could see her white lace string bikini panties, dipping low on her hip bones, hinting at the treasure I craved, and her little t-shirt that came to just above her waist did little to hide the glorious roundness and hard pebble nipples from my view.

I lifted the bottom of the comforter and the sheet and crawled beneath it, moving up her body, ghosting my mouth along her supple thighs until I reached the front of her lace and silk covered mound. I rested my forehead on her tummy just above the edge of her panties so I could inhale her scent and ran my hands up the outside of her thighs. She moaned softly and arched her back. I wanted her so damn bad and she was responding to my touch even in *sleep*...responding to me in automatic recognition that I was the one touching her. I ran my tongue along the top edge of her panties and tasted the sweetness of her skin.

"Julia..." I breathed as my right hand moved up and slid below the hem of her shirt, over her firm flesh until I cupped her perfect breast. She arched into it as my left index finger hooked under the side of her panties and pulled them down.

I was already naked and I longed to feel my skin on hers, my entire body up against the heaven of her curves that fitted so perfectly to my harder frame. I moved up and placed my open mouth on the curve of her neck, sucking lightly as my knee nudged hers apart and my fingers parted the soft, hot flesh between her legs.

"Uhhhhh…" The breath ripped out of my body at the wetness I found there and her arms slid around my body pulling me to her, her fingers clawing at my flesh.

"Ryan…" my mouth found hers in a soft kiss as I urged her to wake up. I sucked her bottom lip in between mine, pulling on it again and again as I started moving my finger in small circles on her tender flesh.

Her mouth came alive under mine, as she kissed me back, sucking on my mouth like I was sucking on hers. Nothing on earth compared to being with her like this; staking my claim on her and letting her know how much she owned me as well.

Her hands slid into my hair as she pulled my mouth closer, my tongue making love to hers until we were both gasping. I couldn't help it, I was moving, grinding against her hip, unconsciously seeking a way to ease the ache.

Her lips pulled from mine and her love-soft eyes opened slowly, languidly. Luminous, she looked into mine, realizing that she wasn't dreaming, that I was indeed with her and she was on the verge of coming. Her hips arched toward my hand and she moaned.

"Am I dreaming? God, you feel so real. You smell and taste like you, too."

"Mmmm…So real, my love. Surprise. Are you surprised?" A smile tugged at the corners of my mouth, but she was beyond speaking as I continued to play with her. Her legs started trembling and I thrust three fingers inside her and continued the pressure against her clit with my thumb, making her cry out as her pleasure overtook her. "That's it, Julia. I love to see you come under my hands. You're so damn beautiful."

"Ryan. Uhnnn, God…Kiss me…I can't believe you're here."

I fell into her and took her mouth with mine as she wrapped her arms and legs around me. She was trembling and I loved that

I could bring her such intense pleasure. It filled me up. I wanted to take care of her in every way.

I dragged my mouth off of hers, and kissed her neck below her ear. "Happy Valentine's Day, my love. I couldn't bear to be away from you today. And I made it with a whole hour to spare," I said softly as I pulled back, longing to see the look on her face. We were still entwined and I throbbed in anticipation of what was coming. The blood raced so fast that it pounded in my ears and engorged my cock to the point of bursting.

"I love you." Her fingers traced my face softly. "Ryan, so much." I thought I saw sadness in her eyes and my brow fell.

"Baby, is something wrong?"

She got a little crinkle between her eyes and dropped her eyes for a split second before bringing them back to my face and smiling softly. She shook her head ever so slightly. "No…I'm so happy to see you. I've missed you, Ryan." Her voice broke slightly on my name.

"Oh, honey…it's almost over now, right? When I leave you this time, it will be for the last time. We made it through it all." I pushed her shirt up and she lifted her arms so I could slide it up and off. I wadded it up and threw it aside, hungry to get my hands on her naked breasts. "I missed you so badly," I breathed against the skin of her shoulder. I lifted her up until she was kneeling with me on the bed. My hands moved over her velvet skin, paying homage to every swell and curve.

My body was screaming for release, it had been so long since I'd touched her and I wanted her in a position that would allow my hands easy access to increase her pleasure.

"Julia, I'm wound so tight, I'm not sure how long I can make this last and I want to take care of you," I explained as I moved us both to the head of the bed and turned her around in my arms so her back was plastered up against the front of my body. She responded as only Julia would do. Her arms lifted around my neck, hands fisting in my hair as she arched into me again, grinding her ass against my erection. The friction was almost more than I could bear and I moaned into the curve of her shoulder as I dragged my mouth along it, kissing and suckling her skin. My hands roamed over her perfect breasts and taut stomach, pulling on her nipples lightly until she was gasping in response.

"Honey, is this okay?" I rasped out as I pressed into her, seeking the warmth and wetness of her body.

She nodded, not speaking and slid one hand down the side of my body to grasp at my ass and pull me toward her. She leaned forward slightly and braced herself, placing her free hand on the wall, preparing for the force of my entry.

I found her entrance and slid into her from behind. With her legs closer together, she was even tighter than usual. "Uhnnn, Julia. I love you."

"Mmmm…" she moaned as I filled her, stretching and pushing into her. My head fell to her shoulder and I held onto her with both arms around her, one hand cupping a breast and the other sliding down to touch her sensitive flesh. "Uhhhh…" She let out her breath in a rush as I moved in and out of her in long, deep strokes. It didn't take long and I had her quivering on the brink of orgasm and I was gasping, trying desperately to stop my own release until I was sure she was satisfied.

I stared down at her alabaster back, the dark silk of her hair flowing down almost to her waist. "You are so beautiful…so sexy. Julia, I'm not going to be able to stop now." My fingers slid deeper down her body to feel where my body was joining her and it was so fucking erotic I almost lost it. Here was evidence of my possession of this gorgeous woman; this glorious woman who gave of herself so freely to me in so many ways. My breathing was rough and she was panting with me. I wanted her to feel what I was feeling.

I pulled her hand down, mine over hers and guiding it down her stomach and pubic mound until she could feel me pumping into her body. "Ryan," she whispered, her head turning to nestle into my neck.

I left her hand where it was and then moved mine up to rub and pinch her clit. Almost instantly she clenched around my dick and I lost complete control and slammed into her as deeply as I could while my orgasm consumed me in waves. We were both jerking against each other as our bodies rode out the climax. I moved my hands gently up her body and ran a series of soft kisses over her shoulders as she milked me dry. My heart was swollen to the point of bursting. The passion between us never ceased to amaze me.

"Holy hell..." I breathed against her skin. "I am still so in love...I'll never get enough of you. Every time...I'm undone." I wrapped both of my arms around her pulling her back against me as I slipped out of her body, instantly feeling the loss.

She was silent as I laid her back down on the bed and pulled her close to me. She curled into me and pressed her lips to my neck. I wrapped my arms around her as her leg slipped between the two of mine. She was tired, but I was anxious to talk to her. I needed her voice and her words.

"How did you manage it?" she asked quietly as she nuzzled against me. If she didn't stop the gentle play of her lips and hands, we wouldn't be sleeping anytime soon.

"I just told my advisor that I needed a couple of days and worked my ass off to make it up in advance. He talked to my professors. I couldn't stand not touching you today." I smiled into the darkness and kissed the top of her head. "Were you surprised?"

"Mmmm huh," she mumbled. "I thought I was dreaming."

"I'm pretty sure you were dreaming when I came in here. You were calling my name. It was perfect. And then, when I started to touch you, you responded automatically."

"Yes. Because it's *you*." Her voice was quiet and she sounded sleepy.

"The way we are together...I can't live without you any-more. I'm done."

Her arms tightened around me and she sighed heavily as she pressed close to me.

"I love you..."

"I love you, too, baby girl. It's late and you have to work tomorrow, yes?"

"I'd only planned on taking half a day off on Friday, so yeah. Maybe Meredith will take pity on me if you come in and show her your pouty face. I hate to leave you alone all day." I smiled and nuzzled her forehead and used her leg between mine to pull her tighter against me. She smelled of vanilla and musk and sex and I sucked it into my lungs like it was nectar.

"Oh, that's okay. I'll sleep in, meet you for lunch and come back here and take a fork to that luscious looking confection in the refrigerator." My fingers brushed her cheek as my lids got heavy.

"I'll expect you to cut a piece, not dig into the whole thing, Matthews," she admonished and I could imagine the rolling of her eyes in the darkness as she snuggled closer to me.

"We'll see how strong my willpower is. It's bad enough that I had that nightie in my pocket all damn day. I felt like a dog with rabies! My mouth was watering, my body was shaking and I was literally going insane. If you keep that up, I'll never graduate."

She giggled softly against me, leaned up and placed a soft kiss on my lips.

"Mmm...good boy. Very, *very* good boy," she teased and I burst out laughing.

"Okay, that's it!" I said, rolling over on top of her fast enough to take her by surprise. She gasped and looked up at me. The lack of light made her eyes darker, but they were shining as she gently touched my face. "I'll show you just how good I can be," I whispered before my mouth descended on hers in hungry assault.

I almost felt guilty because I kept her up until dawn making love.

Almost.

~11~

Julia ~

I snuck out of the apartment early in the morning, leaving a
sleeping Ryan behind with a note that told him how much I
loved him and that I wanted to see his sweet ass for lunch.
Despite the heaviness of my heart concerning my possible move
to Paris, I wanted to make this weekend as special as I possibly
could. My traitorous eyes filled with tears as I made my way to
work and the reality of it hit me square in the face. I hastily
blinked them back and by the time I made it to my office I was
in control.

Meredith was still in town and had worked out the details
with John. All that was left was for me to make a decision. My
heart hurt to the point of breaking. I felt listless and I sure as hell
didn't want to work today.

I didn't bother to hang up my coat and carelessly threw it
over one of the chairs as I rounded the desk. Picking up the
phone, I quickly dialed Meredith's extension and waited for her
to pick up.

"Yeah, doll," she answered.

"Hi. Listen, Ryan came to town early and I'd really appreciate it if I could cut out of here early today and maybe take the
entire day off tomorrow. I'll get everything done. Erm...Or at
least make sure that Andrea knows what needs to be done." I
rambled on nervously.

"Julia, of course. Though, I would like to get an eye fix of him while he's in town," she chuckled suggestively.

"He'll be in around noon to take me to lunch. I was hoping I could surprise him by not coming back to work, so thank you."

"What are your plans for him?" Her voice was amused on the other end of the line.

"Well...I wasn't planning on being here tomorrow afternoon. I'm taking him to a concert in the evening and otherwise, probably just hanging out. We play it by ear a lot."

"Have you told him about Paris?" My heart dropped to my stomach at her question.

"No. I guess...I'm trying to find the right moment. Meredith, leaving him will be too hard."

Her voice hardened. "Julia, stop whining like a little baby. It's only a few months, for God's sake. You've been separated for over three years! Besides, you love this damn job. I know you, Julia. You live and breathe the magazine."

I fell into my chair as Andrea came and hovered in my doorway. I raised my right hand and waved her in. "Yes...but only because what I really live and breathe for hasn't been in the same city. Work has been a form of self-defense to keep sane."

"Look, you could have always moved to Beantown and schlepped ads at the local newspaper. You were cut out for more. We both know it," she scoffed.

Andrea raised her eyebrows at me as I sighed loudly into the phone.

"Besides," Meredith began, "Ryan will be damned proud of you."

"Um...well, if he even hears anything beyond *Hey, Ryan, guess what? I'm leaving the country, isn't that great? I know we had all these plans, but screw it,*" I retorted and put a hand to my head. I felt my voice crack and I swallowed so I could continue.

"I'm not sure if he'll be heartbroken or pissed, but it won't be pretty."

"Just tell him and see. Give him the benefit of the doubt."

"Okay, I don't want anyone spilling the beans to him when he shows up here today. I need to tell him when I feel the time is right."

"Okay. I've got to get to this pile of reports. Even from across the continent, I still have to run a magazine."

"Yeah. Life's a bitch. Talk to you later."

I leaned forward onto my desk and hung up the phone, looking up at Andrea as I did so.

"What's on the agenda today?" she asked quietly. Her expression was calm but she was gauging my mood and didn't want to upset me further by asking too many questions.

I put a hand over my eyes as I leaned back in my chair. "To be honest…I don't even give a damn, Andie. This whole Paris thing has really taken me off task."

She nodded sympathetically, her mouth turning down at the corners. "Well, does it help that you look amazing?" she smiled slightly. "I love that dress."

"It's Armani," I threw out the brand offhandedly. It was a dark blue silk wrap dress that Ryan particularly loved. "Ryan came in last night and acted out my dreams. Literally."

"What?" she said incredulously. "Where do I get one of those? Crap, he's almost too perfect."

"No *almost* about it, that's why this is so hard. I don't want to go."

"But…" Andrea hedged. "You do want this job."

"Of course. In a perfect world I could have everything, but it's not perfect, is it?" I got up and moved to the art table behind my desk. My office was a lot bigger than the one I had in Los Angeles and the view of Manhattan was amazing. I closed my eyes, remembering the first night I'd shown it to Ryan. The building was practically deserted and we shut all the lights off so we could admire the skyline. We'd made love on my desk. Blushing, I turned back to it and ran my hand along its smooth edge.

"Unfortunately, no. Will he understand?"

I brushed at the errant tear that slipped from the corner of my eye as I struggled to keep my voice from trembling. "Nope. I'm still not sure what I'm going to do. It depends on how he reacts."

"Julia, surely you have some idea of what he'll say?"

"Of course. He's going to lose it. And he has every right to."

We got down to business and before long it was lunchtime. I found myself anxiously looking at the clock every minute in anticipation of Ryan's arrival. I'd given Andrea the list of things that needed to be finished by Friday at five, straightened up my desk and then went to make some last minute adjustments on the story boards for the April issue. I rolled my eyes at the collateral list. How many different ways can you do a story on *What Your Man Really Wants in Bed? Ugh.*

I reached down to scratch the back of my thigh, lifting the edge of my skirt to gain access. I sighed and threw the boards back down on the slanted surface of the table.

"Now that is a sight for sore eyes," Ryan's perfect voice oozed like velvet around me. "I think I need to get me some of that. Get over here."

A smile spread out on my face before I even turned around. I didn't have far to go. He was right behind me and enfolded me in his arms immediately. "You're so gorgeous. I love this dress. I can feel *everything* through the material," he whispered silkily as his delicious scent enveloped me. "A thong, right? Mmm..." His fingers played with the back of it underneath the thin silk.

I heard my door close behind him and his brow shot up in question as his lips broke out in the crooked grin that I loved. "Andrea," I explained. "She's an amazing assistant. Shut up and kiss me." I slid my hands up his chest, around his neck and into the hair at his nape.

He laughed out loud at the smirk on my face. "Thought you'd never ask, my love."

His mouth swooped down on mine and my heart clenched inside my chest. I kissed him as if my life depended on it. As if it were the last time I'd ever kiss him. Ryan felt the gravity of my response and groaned into my mouth, his hands sliding over my ass to press me into his already hardening body. Our mouths fed off each other like we were starving and I forgot I was in my office, and that a hundred other people were on the other side of the door.

He dragged his mouth from mine and I whimpered in protest as he kissed the side of my jaw and then slid down the cord of my neck. His arms lifted me off of the ground and he brought my face on level with his. "Julia, you're playing with fire. What's gotten into you? Did you forget where we are?" He nuzzled my nose with his as he spoke, his breathing was shallow and his eyes were closed.

I let my hands slide out of his hair and wrapped my arms around his shoulders, resting my head on his shoulder. I nodded. "Yes." I never wanted him to let me go. "You feel so good."

"Keep it up and I'll show you just how good I feel," he growled into my neck, his lips leaving a hot trail of kisses as he moved up my jaw to my mouth.

I couldn't help a soft smile as I breathed him in. "Promises, promises," I teased.

"Don't push me. You know I'll do it," he breathed as he licked and kissed at my lips in a series of little nibbling kisses.

"I know," I laughed softly. "But Meredith knows you're here and she wants to look at you."

He pulled his head back and screwed up his features in disbelief. "Look at me?"

"Yep," I said, popping the "p" as I nodded. "You know you're beautiful, so stop with the coy bullshit."

He smiled crookedly as he set my feet down on the floor, but kept me locked tightly in his embrace. He was so gorgeous that my breath caught in my throat. He was dressed casually in jeans, boots and a long sleeved white t-shirt. His face was unshaven and his hair a wild mess.

"I look like hell today. I just rolled out of bed and ran out of the apartment in search of my girl."

He kissed me again and I sucked his lower lip into my mouth. My body was responding, the heat and wetness tangible evidence of the need he raised deep within me. His fingers were drawing circles on my lower back and he used the pressure to make sure I knew he was as aroused as I was.

"Mmmm...love you," I whispered against his mouth.

"Want you..." he responded.

"Need you..." I smiled up at him and ran a finger down his cheek to his jaw as I moved out of his arms.

"Yeah. Ugh, let's get out of here. I'm dying over here. I need a distraction and now." He plopped down in one of the chairs in front of my desk and ran a hand through his hair in agitation. "What plans do you have for me?" he asked wickedly with a big smile.

"Well, sir, if you'll remember, you weren't supposed to be here today. You're not exactly on my calendar," I pointed out as I picked up the phone and dialed Meredith's number but it went straight to voice mail.

"Hey, Mere, Ryan is here, but we're leaving in ten minutes, so if you want to bask in his glory, you need to get down here. Pronto."

Ryan burst out laughing at my words and the expression on my face as I said them. I wrinkled my nose. His hand went to his mouth as he looked at me and my heart melted. He was mine. But how would he feel after I told him about the new *opportunity*?

"Seriously, Julia? That shit is fucked up."

"What? You mean you don't have hoards of women just gazing at you in a daze wherever you go? Completely mesmerized?" My eyes widened in dramatic emphasis.

"Only one that I *want* to mesmerize. And, she has her stalkers, too."

"Mmmm, you think? Not as many as you. Speaking of stalkers, what's new with Liza?"

His brow dropped over his deep blue eyes. "Nothing new. She still tries to horn in on study groups and stuff, babe. You know I only have eyes and arms and lips and tongue and dick for you though, right?" He stopped when I gasped in shock, the corners of his mouth quirking in the start of a smile, but his tone was serious. "You've ruined me forever."

My face flushed and my body responded to his sexy words. "I can't believe you just said that," I said quietly as someone knocked on the door.

"Yes, you can. You know it's true," his eyes were sparkling at me when the door opened and Meredith poked her head in.

"Are you decent? Is it safe to come in?" she said happily before swinging the door open wide and stepping inside.

Ryan got up and hugged her lightly. "Hello, Meredith. How are you?" he said politely.

"Great. You're graduating soon, I hear. Then moving to New York, right?" I tensed at her words. The last thing I needed was having any conversations about the immediate future brought up before I'd had a chance to talk to Ryan about the Paris offer. I cocked my head at her, hoping she'd understand that I wanted her to change the subject.

"Yeah. It's soon now." He sat down on the edge of my desk facing Meredith as I moved around toward him. His hand reached for mine. "Not soon enough, though. I'm seriously done missing my girl. I can't wait to be with her every day."

Meredith shot a look between both of us. "I know she's missed you too. I mean, just look around this office? There are pictures of you everywhere."

"Oh, that's just for you when you visit, Meredith," I said sardonically.

"Yeah, right!" she mocked. "So…what are you two up to now?"

"Well, I surprised her by being here early, so after we go to lunch, I guess I'll just hit one of the museums or go down and check out the neighborhood around St. Vincent's. I'm starting my residency there in July," Ryan answered. "What are you doing in New York, Meredith? Did you transfer from Los Angeles?"

"Um…" She started but then hesitated, looking at me. "I'm here to put together a team for a special project I'm working on."

Ryan smiled and stroked my hand with his thumb, "Maybe Julia can help."

If he only knew what he was saying and what the implications were. My heart sped up as anxiety set in. All I needed was for Meredith to tell him too much.

"Yes, I'm hoping so. She's very valuable to us. I don't think I've seen anyone with this much potential since *me*."

"Yes, I'm very proud of her," Ryan stated.

"You should be, and she of you. You kids are both going places, that's for sure. Julia, why don't you take the rest of the day off?" Her eyebrow quirked at me.

"Really?" Ryan asked hopefully, his face lighting up.

"Yeah, why not? It's worth it to see that gorgeous look on your face. Get out of here, but make sure Andrea knows how to keep your ducks in line."

I laughed at her use of words and the fact that she made it sound like I'd never asked for the afternoon off. "She's been briefed and I'll have my phone on so she can call anytime. Thanks."

The minute she left Ryan looked at me knowingly. "You little brat. You left me thinking I had to suffer without you today and you'd already gotten the day off."

"Yeah, whatever. You haven't been suffering all that much at my hands, baby," I teased. "Besides, you were asleep and I didn't want to wake you up." I grabbed my coat and he helped me put it on before we left the office.

I swallowed the lump in my throat and tried to smile as his hand laced through mine. He was so happy that I dreaded telling him about the job offer, since I already knew what his reaction would be. So, for today and probably tomorrow, I just wanted to be with him and enjoy our time together. The problem was; he knew me so well that I had trouble hiding anything from him. It would take real effort not to let him see that something was bothering me.

"Okay, so what do you really want to do today?" I asked with a forced smile.

"Um, feed you and then take you home and ravish you for hours on end. Anymore questions?"

"None, except um…*what* are you hungry for?"

He threw a glance down at me as I walked by his side, his eyebrows rising and a small smile playing on his perfect lips. "Stop, Julia. I mean it. Stop teasing me or I won't be held accountable for my actions."

"What?" I widened my eyes at him innocently and bit my lip to stop from smiling. "Lunch, right?"

"Uh huh, *right.*"

*****

Ryan and I had spent the afternoon in bed. I was feeling desperate and clingy, unable to get close enough or have enough of his lovemaking. I wanted him deeper into my body and to never stop touching me. He was tender and passionate and, as always, made me feel his love with every breath. I fought back the tears the whole time, wondering what in the hell I was thinking even considering this stupid job offer.

How in the hell was I going to tell him that I was going to Paris?

We decided to stay in since we were going out tomorrow night and I smoothed the red negligee over my curves. It was completely sheer and every detail of my body was visible, the bikini panties were just as revealing and only added slightly to the coverage. I called in an order for Pad Thai and I could hear Ryan paying the delivery driver at the door to the apartment.

I had serious plans for him tonight and although I loved making love with him, I also had an ulterior motive. We usually spent hours and hours talking, but I was fragile and I wouldn't be able to keep from telling him about Paris if that happened. I wanted to make him happy, and show him how much I loved him. Truthfully, I couldn't get enough of his hands and mouth on my body. I wanted to soak it all in and commit every second to memory to sustain me, and hopefully him, through the continued months of separation.

Tomorrow night I was surprising him with the concert, but tonight I would keep him busy with love. I curled my hair and piled it on top of my head so that soft tendrils fell down around my face, and used a little heavier makeup to make my eyes smokier and applied a dark pink gloss to my lips. I left the jewelry off except for the bracelet. It never came off. I loved seeing our entwined initials on my wrist and it meant the world to me. I spritzed perfume behind my ears, wrists and over my body before shutting off the light and lighting three candles in the bedroom.

I tiptoed down the hall toward the kitchen. Ryan's back was to me and he was pulling the food out of the bag and then took plates out of the cupboard. I walked up behind him and stopped about ten feet away. I wanted him to turn around and see me.

"Hey, what are you cooking?" I said softly. He reached up and pulled two wine glasses out and set them on the counter, reaching into the drawer for a corkscrew with his other hand.

"Pfft. Do you want wine?" He glanced over his shoulder and stopped dead when he saw me, then turned and stared. His gaze roamed up and down my body slowly and he fell back against the edge of the counter. "Holy shit, Julia...you look...amazing." He licked his lips as the hand with the corkscrew in it moved up to rest on his chest.

"Don't hurt yourself with that thing," I murmured softly as I moved toward him and took it from his hand and met his burning blue eyes. My free hand moved up to cup his chin. He was speechless and I loved it. "Cat got your tongue? It isn't like you haven't seen me undressed, Ryan," I said as I walked around him to take the wine bottle and began to unwrap the covering on the cork. He watched in silence, not moving, except to turn in the direction I moved.

"I know...but it always takes my breath away. You're beautiful, but the emotion always stuns me...knowing that no one else has ever touched you...that you've only ever been mine. I'll never get used to how that makes me feel."

My heart stopped. I set the wine down so that I could wind my arms around his waist and kiss the pulse point at the base of his neck. "I love you every bit as much as you think I do...probably more."

His hands ghosted down my back and up again, sending shivers up and down my spine and goose bumps broke out on my arms and legs. "Suddenly, I'm not all that hungry..." he whispered softly as his lips opened on the curve of my shoulder. His mouth was hot and he knew how to melt me, dragging along the line to my neck and placing little sucking kisses intermittently.

"Uhhh..." I went limp in his arms, my hands unable to hold him like I wanted because of the corkscrew in my hand. "You need to eat. Baby, we've got all night and all day tomorrow..."

"What about tomorrow night and Saturday?" he whispered against my skin.

"Yeah, that too. But I have a surprise for you tomorrow night."

"Better than this? Not possible." He placed a soft kiss on my mouth and then cupped the side of my face and kissed the opposite cheekbone. His lips were soft as velvet against my skin. I closed my eyes and tried to steady my breathing. After all these years, he still had the most unbelievable effect on me. Already the throbbing was starting under his expert touch.

"Not better, just different."

"Mmmm…I'd be happy to stay here for the rest of the weekend, honey." I reached up on my tiptoes and placed a firm kiss on his mouth, trying to get him to stop his covert seduction.

I reluctantly moved out of his arms and uncorked the wine. He was watching me intently as he leaned on the counter. I poured the wine into the two glasses he'd set out, picked them up and nodded toward the living room. "Come on. I'll feed you," I said with a sly smile and his eyebrows rose in response. "Grab the food, sexy."

I preceded him into the living room as he picked up the two cartons of food and two forks. When he came toward me, I pointed toward the middle of the couch. He sat down and I bent to take one of the cartons and fork away from him. He opened one after grabbing the remote and turning on the television.

The light over the stove and one lamp in the living room was the only light. I reached over and turned it off after I set down the food in my hand.

"Julia, what are you doing? I thought you wanted to eat?" The question was clear in his tone.

The television was on low, but it was inconsequential to me as I climbed on to Ryan's lap and straddled his thighs. His eyes burning, Ryan froze with the food in one hand and his other moving high up my thigh underneath the thin silk.

I took the carton from his hand and started to fork up the noodles inside. His eyes were burning into mine as he shifted uncomfortably beneath me. I was teasing him, but neither one of us were laughing. I offered him a bite and he took it, but his hand moved further up my body to cup a breast and glide his thumb over my nipple causing my breath to leave my lungs in a rush. I bent to kiss his mouth in a soft kiss and he instantly lifted toward me to deepen it. I resisted and nuzzled his nose.

"Food," I whispered against his mouth.

His hand slid to the back of my neck and urged my mouth back toward his. "Fuck the food, Julia. I want you. You're killing me with this."

"Oh, is it fucking that's on your mind?" I teased as he removed the carton from my fingers and unceremoniously tossed it on the coffee table. The fork clattered off and fell to the floor. Undoubtedly, there would be a mess. "Hmmm...I guess *so*." I slid my hands to the front of his white shirt and began to slowly release the buttons, letting my fingers play on the firm muscles underneath. I raked my hands down his abs toward the top of his jeans. I freed the button and slid the zipper down.

He sat up and slid his arms around me as his mouth reached up for mine, but I resisted, only licking his top lip lightly. He groaned and buried his face into my neck, sucking on it with such force I thought he'd leave a mark. "Why are you playing with me? I'll make love to you all night. Don't torture me."

I turned to kiss his temple as my hands fisted in his hair and his hips moved underneath mine. "Do you want to play truth or dare?" I murmured against his skin. I sucked in his scent, so familiar and unforgettable.

He sat back, his blue eyes luminous as he licked his lips before they lifted slightly at the corners. This was our love game. We played it a lot of times when we hadn't seen each other for a while and one we came up with while I still lived in Los Angeles.

"Oh, *yeah*."

Pleased with his answer and the expectant look on his face, I bent to kiss him hard, finally opening my mouth over his and thrusting my tongue between his willing lips. He kissed me back with so much passion that it consumed me, until finally I dragged my mouth away for much needed air.

"Ok...you go first," I gasped as my forehead fell on his shoulder as my hips ground into his.

He moaned. "Ugh...Truth," he whispered against my mouth.

"What are you feeling right now?"

"So much love, I can't breathe. My body is aching. I'm so lucky...you're a miracle." His velvet voice was soft as he brushed a tendril of my hair back and pushed it behind my ear. "Your turn."

Oh God. How can I go to France? My heart hurt with the force of the love I felt for him. I was so full of pain, wanting and sadness all at once; I thought I'd burst into tears.

"Mmmm...dare," I tried to smile seductively. His features flooded with some emotion that I couldn't place, his eyes narrowed and he swallowed hard. "You love it when I take the dare." I ran my thumb across his lower lip, still wet from our kisses.

This was a game, but we were both serious; our emotions anything but playful.

He pulled on the neckline of the beautiful silk until my right breast was free. "I dare you not to make a sound for the next five minutes," he said as his mouth closed around the nipple and he started to suckle it. My head fell back and I bit my lip while his fingers found their way into the moist heat between my legs over the wisp of silk he found there. "Julia," he gasped as he released my nipple and continued to kiss my chest and along my clavicle. "You're always so ready for me; knowing you want me, too...Uhh..."

I pulled on his hair and he groaned. It was all I could do not to scream, as I fought the urge to breathe his name. I bit into his shoulder as his fingers continued to pleasure me until I wasn't sure that I could stop myself. My hand reached down to still his fingers.

"I hope it's been five minutes. I can't take anymore."

"Let yourself go, Julia." He tried to push my hand aside, but my fingers closed around his. "I want it," he protested.

"Not yet, babe. Ugh, not yet," I begged. "It's your turn."

"Okay...dare."

"I dare you not to touch me now. Not until you almost come."

"I can't do it, Julia," he said as his hands slid up my back to my shoulders and he used them to pull me down harder onto his groin as our hips moved together. "Before this weekend I haven't been able to touch you for something like seven weeks and three days."

My heart dropped in my chest and I felt the sting of tears start. My fingers brushed his jaw as I bent to place a whisper kiss on his open mouth. "Please, Ryan. I want to give you this." I got up off his lap and knelt in front of him and reached for the top of his jeans to open them. His hands reluctantly slid off me as I moved away. "No touching," I said again. I reached behind me and grabbed the remote off of the table, switching the TV off. "I want to hear every breath you take," I whispered and bent to kiss his stomach just above the open waistband of his jeans. The light trail of hair leading from his lower abs down was so sexy, like it was leading to the promised land where I would find salvation.

"Julia." The sound of my name ripping from deep within his chest was guttural, feral and causing my heart to beat faster and my body to bloom with a new wave of heat. It basically gutted me, how much I wanted him. He caused feelings within me that I never knew were possible. I never imagined a love like this could exist. Now, almost eight years later, he was more to me than I ever could have dreamed.

I pulled his jeans down and he lifted his hips to help me. His erection sprung free and I pressed my forehead into his abs above it while my hands continued to push the material down his legs. He kicked them free for me and groaned as my breath washed over him. I worked on him with my hands and my mouth, taking pleasure in the way his breathing increased and his hands fisted in the sofa cushions beside him. He moaned softly and started to pant and I knew he was close. I slowed my pace.

"Mmmmm, baby, you taste so good," I said in a moan.

He suddenly sat up and reached for me, lifting me back up to straddle his naked lap. His eyes were glazed and sparkling as he looked up at me, one hand holding my hip and the other coming up to hold the side of my neck, his thumb brushing back and forth on my jaw. He reached up to kiss me, but our mouths hovered over each other's. I wanted to taste his lips, but he hesitated.

"Truth or dare?"

I whimpered, not sure if I wanted to keep playing and longing for him to take me to the bedroom. "Uhhhh, Ryan," I whispered urgently against his lips. "Please..."

"Is this truth then?" I closed my eyes and nodded. "Okay. What do you want me to do to you right now? Anything you want, I'll give it to you." The want was dripping off his voice, leaving both of us aching.

"I want to feel you inside me forever. I want you to touch me while we make love and never stop."

"As if I could. Where?" he asked as his arms tightened around me. "The bedroom?"

I wound my arms and legs around him, pressing my heat against his hardness. The silk of my panties did little to disguise my excitement. He surged against me, one hand moving between our bodies to push the material aside and the other pulling my hip forward as he slid inside.

I pushed his shirt away frantically, my fingers hungry for the hard muscles I'd find under his smooth skin.

"Baby," he groaned as he stood up and carried me to the bedroom, our bodies still fused together. I couldn't help flexing against him in pure instinct.

I gasped and moved my hips against his, taking him in as deeply as I could. He kicked the door shut and lowered me to the bed, his elbows coming up to rest beside my head and his eyes burning into mine as he settled above me. I closed my eyes at the exquisite feeling of his body intimately entwined with mine and pulled my knees up to bring him even closer.

"Julia, look at me," he moaned softly as he nuzzled the side of my face with his nose and began the long, deep thrusts that drove me to distraction. My hips surged up to meet the familiar rhythm. I opened my eyes and took in his expression. It was pleasure and pain and pure love. I reached up to place a hand on his face. "I love you, do you hear me? I can't breathe without you."

His mouth swooped down and we kissed hungrily, our mouths locked together the entire time we made love. I couldn't get enough of my beautiful man as he brought my body to shuddering climax over and over again. By the time we lay in each other's arms exhausted, the sun was coming up and casting long shadows across the floor.

Ryan ~

Julia had been quiet all day which left me wondering if she still wasn't feeling well. I was left trying to figure out what was wrong.

The time with her had been amazing; we had two more evenings together before I had to go back to Boston. We'd spent the night making love and so slept away most of the day.

I woke up starving. Julia threw out the Pad Thai we'd left untouched and made us a simple meal of grilled cheese and tomato soup. Now we were on our way downtown. My thumb rubbed over the hand I held in mine.

"Where are we going again?" I asked anxiously.

"Uh uh. Not telling, babe. You'll see soon enough." Her eyes had a level of excitement that was lighter than I was used to seeing in her eyes. "You'll have a good time, I promise"

"Here we are, Madison Square Garden," the cab driver turned toward us. "That will be $32.50."

I handed him two twenties and followed Julia out of the car. The crowds pouring into the entrances seemed endless and I finally realized what the surprise was. "Julia, this is perfect! Thank you!" I picked her up and swung her around. I'd been working so hard that I hadn't had any time to do anything fun.

"Julia, this is how it's gonna be for us. *Finally.* We'll be together like this every day," I said into the hair by her ear. She smelled so sweet. "I love you."

"Love you, too," she kissed the side of my face and then my mouth. "Let's go! I've got really great seats."

After I set her down, I wrapped an arm around her as we pushed in with the rest of the crowd. She dug the tickets out of her pocket and handed them to the attendant. "Main box seats are to the left and up one level," he instructed and pointed toward the escalator.

We bought some beer and found our seats. The entire time, I never let go of her.

The crowd was wild, the music was loud and we sang and danced along. I loved watching Julia. The warm flush to her skin was gorgeous and her hair fell in soft waves around her face. I found myself drawing her closer and kissing her often.

The band started to play a song that had come to mean a lot to us when we were apart. Julia wrapped her arm around mine and leaned her head on my shoulder as the lyrics flooded the arena. The booms of the bass emphasized the words that held so much meaning for us. We'd made love to this song and ended up in tears in each other's arms on several occasions. It spoke of separation and wasted time and, as always, my heart tightened. She turned her face into my neck. She was getting emotional so I put my arm across her legs and kissed her forehead. Words were unnecessary. We knew each other so well.

"Hey, you...that shit is almost behind us."

She clutched at me harder and I felt her tears dripping on my skin as she nodded. I pushed her hair back but she kept her face hidden. I worried that there was something wrong, but the noise and the crowd kept me from asking.

"Julia, are you okay?"

I frowned. *Why is she so upset?* I tried to reassure her, "It's okay, sweets. Soon, forever starts for us."

She scrambled onto my lap, oblivious to the people around us, kissing me softly as the song continued. I couldn't help myself, my mouth devoured hers, deepening the kisses. We kissed again and again with a desperation that confused me. My hand slid underneath the curtain of her hair as I tilted her head so my mouth could slant across hers, kissing her deeper and sliding my tongue in to dance with hers.

I pulled my mouth from hers as the song faded out. "In just a few months, baby. I can't wait. I love you so damn much."

"Take me home, Ryan. I'm sorry, I know the concert isn't over, but I need you."

She didn't have to ask me twice.

*****

This was my last night with Julia. I was planning to ask her to marry me over dinner. The ring was in my pocket and, even though I knew that she'd accept, I was nervous. We'd talked about marriage many times and it was a given. I smiled to myself in anticipation.

She looked beautiful in a little black dress, dark hose and black heels. So elegant. Her hair was pulled up on the sides, but fell in long waves down her back and my bracelet sparkled on her wrist. She wore the diamond solitaire necklace I'd given her last Christmas and some long diamond drop earrings. Breathtaking.

Her features were calm but there was something going on behind her beautiful green eyes. She'd been so quiet today. Last night was a miracle, another amazing all night sex-a-thon that had started the minute we'd entered her apartment. We couldn't get enough of each other. No surprise, but, there was something unspoken that made her more needy and wanting than usual.

I'd pushed her up against the wall in the hall and removed her clothes slowly. From the moment our mouths touched, she was clutching at my shoulders, frantic in her efforts to get closer. The lovemaking was intense, full of emotions that swelled up inside us both. The tears on her cheeks confused me and caused me pause, but when I'd asked about it she'd shushed me, begging me not to talk and just feel. She made love to me as if she'd never see me again. Goodbye was always hard, but this time would be the last time, so I didn't really understand her desperation or her tears.

I closed my eyes as a lump rose in my throat. The way she affected me, how much I loved her...It was like my life-force. Consuming and endless.

I watched her pick at her food for twenty minutes. This was her favorite restaurant in New York and she loved coming here, but tonight she was listless, pensive…a little preoccupied.

"Julia." I reached across the table for her hand.

She looked up from her plate and set her fork aside. "Hmmmm?"

"Are you feeling alright?"

She smiled slightly. "Yes, *Doctor*. My antibiotic course only has two days left. I feel one hundred percent better."

I sighed and cocked my head to one side. "Then, when are you going to tell me?" I asked as I softly caressed her hand by rubbing my thumb in circles over the top of it.

"Tell you what?" she murmured, her eyes avoiding mine.

"Whatever it is that has been on your mind. Especially today, you've been…preoccupied and distant."

"Ryan Matthews. You didn't think I was distant when we made love in the shower not two hours ago," she said, trying to tease me but I was getting worried that something major was wrong.

She was trying to distract me, and I knew it. As wonderful as that had been, I knew her well enough to know when she was hedging. This was serious. I reached for her hand again.

"Julia, please. I'm starting to worry, so will you please just tell me what the fuck is going on? Have you…met someone else?"

Her mouth dropped open and she stared at me, stunned as she yanked her hand away from mine angrily. "Hmmph!" Her breath rushed out in a huff. "Do you think I could make love with you like I have, if there was anybody else, Ryan? Where the hell did that come from?" Her face flushed and her expression was angry.

"Sex has always been amazing between us…but it's been so desperate this weekend." My eyes bore into hers and she looked away, unable to meet the intensity of my gaze. My heart lurched. "Every touch feels like you're telling me goodbye."

"But…I've told you a hundred times in the last three days that I love you. Weren't you listening?"

"Sometimes love doesn't stop bad shit from happening. We've had so much distance between us that something could have…"

"No! Not in this lifetime, Ryan!" Her eyes were wide and wild as she spoke in angry tones. "You have to stop this. You've dealt with the same distance, so should I assume you've fucked around? I mean…If you think I could have, then…"

Heat infused the skin of my face and neck, my lungs tightened.

"No! But, think about it from where I'm sitting!" I leaned back in my chair and ran my hand, still stinging from the sudden absence of her touch, through my hair. "Here is the woman I love beyond reason, my best friend in the world, who tells me Goddamn *everything*…who I haven't seen in almost two fucking months and she's *not* talking to me! You're withdrawn and completely closed off…except in bed! Tell me what in the hell I'm supposed to think? I mean, we only have four months until I'm done with school and I want to start figuring out the logistics of being together, but it feels like you are pulling away. And it will just…" I softened my voice because my throat got tight and closed off. "Well, it will *kill me* if that's what's happening after all this time apart. I mean…*what the fuck?*"

The pain in my voice was obvious. Her eyes filled with tears as she leaned forward and reached for my hand again, finally meeting my eyes. Her grasp was hard and her voice a broken whisper.

"Listen to me! There is and *never has been* anyone else, damn you. No one else *exists* for me, and you *know* it!" she said urgently. Her chest was heaving and she looked like she was going to lose it, her free hand frantically brushed a tear off of her cheek. "I can't even believe you said that to me. I can't do this here, Ryan, okay?"

This was bad and my heart sank into the pit of my stomach. My eyes burned, stinging like they were on fire, my breathing was labored, coming in short bursts. I pulled out my wallet and threw a hundred and a twenty on the table and stood up, holding my hand out to my Julia.

My Julia. Why was I still afraid that might change? Why did I feel like I was drowning?

I put my arm around her as we walked to the car and I could hear her softly crying. After I opened the door, I caught her arm before she got in, turning her to face me.

"Just tell me you're not leaving me. I have to hear it, *now*," I begged.

Julia was hurting, too. It was evident when she closed her eyes, tears squeezed from under her lids to run down her cheeks. Her arms slid around my waist, burying her face into the front of my suit jacket and sobbed. I pulled her tightly against my chest and pressed my face into her hair, the confusion was eating me alive.

"I'll *never* leave you, Ryan. I told you the first time you made love to me that I'd be with you as long as you wanted me. So, stop with this shit, *please*. This isn't good, but it's not about us breaking up...unless that's what *you* want it to be," she cried brokenly.

I sighed in relief as the tightness in my chest lessened slightly. "That will never happen; but, it hurts that you're hiding something from me."

"Let's just go back to the apartment. I'd have told you sooner, but I wanted this weekend to be perfect."

The ride back was edged with tension and filled with silence. My knuckles whitened as I gripped the steering wheel and Julia huddled in her seat, staring out the window.

She rushed in ahead of me and I followed, aching, behind her.

I shrugged out of my jacket and pulled my tie loose, throwing both over the couch as Julia dropped her coat by the door. I unbuttoned my cuffs and started rolling the sleeves up my forearms, all the while watching her.

Waiting.

Only a few seconds passed but it felt like forever. I walked to her and took her hand gently in mine, staring into her deep green eyes. Eyes full of love and fear. My thumb brushed the top of her hand over and over as I pulled Julia with me to the end of the hall to her bedroom and closed the door behind us. I'd be glad to get her out of this apartment in a few months and hopefully move in with her, my ring firmly on her finger and wedding plans in the works. *Finally. At least...I'd thought so three hours ago.*

I sat on the bed and pulled her to stand in front of me, my hands on her hips and I lowered my head so that the top of it rested on her stomach. I made little circles on her hipbones and sighed when I felt her glorious hands thread through my hair. I could always feel the incredible love in her touch. It flowed between us like a circuit and it gave me a semblance of comfort in this shit storm.

Julia.

"Please just tell me what it is," I said in defeat, and took a deep breath, letting it out in a sigh. I thought my rigid lungs would split under the effort.

"I've been...given a promotion."

My heart leapt as I looked up quickly to her face. She didn't look happy. She was shaking, her voice full of grief. My brow fell as I frowned up at her.

"I don't understand why that makes you unhappy." I pulled her down on my lap and her forehead fell onto my shoulder. One arm cradled her back and the other came up to brush her cheek lightly. She pressed her face into my hand.

"They...they're sending me to Paris, Ryan. For at least six months," her voice cracked, "maybe a year."

The air rushed from my lungs as those words dropped like nuclear bombs around me.

"What do you mean they're *sending* you? You don't have to take it." I said harshly, fear gripping my chest like a vice.

"They want me to head up a team to work on the European issue of Vogue. It will give me experience with the workings of Paris Fashion Week and get me familiar with some of the major designers. If I ever want to be Style Editor or Creative Director here, I have to have connections over there. They think this is the best way for me to get them," she said softly.

"No," I said sternly as I tightened my arms around her in protest. "No, Julia. I'm almost done with med school! It's time to start our life together! We've waited and struggled for too damn long to screw it up now!"

Julia suddenly pushed off of my lap and walked to the window. She put one hand on her hip and brought the other up to her mouth, standing there with her back to me in silence. Finally, she shook her head and her voice trembled when she spoke.

"*No*? You're telling me *no* after I moved to New York all by myself to be near you, Ryan?" Her tone was quiet.

"Yeah! Fucking *no*!" I stood up and yelled the words, startling her. I felt like I'd been kicked in the stomach. "I can't believe you're even considering this!"

"This isn't just a job anymore! For God's sake! I could be at the top of a major pub in a year or less. I might even get *Vanity Fair* if I play my cards right. Their style editor is set to retire soon."

I knew I had to calm down if I wanted her to listen, but I was so upset my hands were shaking. I moved up behind her raising my hands to rest them on her shoulders. "Julia…" I began but she flinched away from me, whirling around to face me.

"No! You don't get to make this decision, Ryan! Not like this." She shook her head in frustration. "This is why I was scared to tell you! I knew you'd be upset, but I never in my wildest dreams expected you to dictate to me what my decision was going to be without even so much as a conversation. I mean, where in the hell do you get off!?" Her voice had elevated and her eyes wild. She was furious, but so was I.

How is this happening?

"I'm not trying to *dictate* to you, Julia! But it is un-fucking-believable that you would even consider leaving me now! What am I supposed to do? Wasn't I moving to New York for my residency? *Wasn't I?!*" She flinched as I ranted at her and threw my arms in the air. "So, now what? If I start it in Boston, I *will* finish it there. That is another four years minimum. I'm not doing this long distance shit for four more years, Julia. *I'm not!!*" Suddenly, the room felt like a shoebox as I paced back and forth. "I thought you loved me." It was a cheap shot, but damn it, I was feeling desperate.

She bit her lip to stop it from quivering as her emotions shook her. "That's not fair and you know it!" she spat miserably.

She covered her face in her hands and sobbed. I wanted to hold her, but my heart was breaking and I was angrier than I'd ever been. I was coming apart as I stood shaking in front of her. My whole world was on its way to *fucking France*.

"I don't know what to do, Ryan. I know that I love you, but I need to do this. For *me*. This time, it's about *me*." She drew in a long shaky breath.

"So, no discussion? Just *done*?" I asked flatly and raked both hands through my hair, turning away from her.

"Hmmph. What discussion? You already told me what you expect. It's just that this time, I can't do as you ask. I've been agonizing over this ever since Wednesday. Remember I wanted a coffee date? You were the first thought I had." She paused as I soaked in the meaning of her words. "I hoped you'd be happy for me. Maybe even be proud. There are 40 other people across the company who wanted this opportunity and they *asked me* to do it. I didn't even go after it, Ryan. Meredith came to *me*. That being true, how can I say no?"

I sighed. "You open your mouth and say the fucking word, Julia. That's how."

"Ryan...I never asked you to give up Harvard and stay with me. This is no different, except its only 6 months to a year. Not four."

Hell. She was right, but it didn't change how my heart was being ripped out of my body at the implications of what this meant...and half a world between us.

"Don't ask me to be happy about something that is going to ruin my whole Goddamn life, Julia." I sat down on the bed and put my head in my hands. "When?" I asked wearily. My heart didn't want to hear the answer, but my head needed to know.

"Uhhhhhh," she tried to clear the tears from her voice. "Four or five weeks, maybe? There are a few things to do first," she said so softly I wasn't even sure if she even said the words.

"Ahhhhh! I'm so pissed, Julia. It isn't fucking *fair*! It ruins everything!"

Anger? Sorrow? Unfairness or irony? Whatever it was, it was ripping me to shreds. I felt like I'd just been gutted.

Could anything be worse?

I raised my head and looked at her. She was broken too, shaking with tears running down her cheeks. In my anger and frustration, I'd failed to see that this would mean the same thing to her as it would to me…Misery at being apart.

"Julia. I'm sorry," I breathed softly. "I just…I don't want to lose you. You know that."

The sobs broke free again. "I-I-I know, R-Ryan. God, I don't want to lose you either. P-please don't l-let that h-happen because of this," she begged as she leaned up against a wall and slid down until she was sitting on the floor. She drew her knees up and buried her face in the arms she wrapped around them.

Instantly, I was beside her pulling her up and enfolding her in my arms. She wound hers around my shoulders. "I love you so m-much," she cried into my neck, her hot tears and breath raining down on me. My own eyes were stinging and my throat closing up in pain.

"I know, honey. I love you, too. If I didn't, this wouldn't even matter…but I don't want to be without you. With residency hours and shit, Julia, I won't be able to get away to Paris to see you. I can't go a year without seeing you more than a couple of times. I won't survive," I said softly as I nuzzled into the hair at her ear. It was damp from her tears and the skin underneath was hot. I kissed the side of her face and brushed her tears away with the pads of both thumbs. Her eyes were closed, her brow knitted, the rest of her face crumpled as she cried.

I lay down on the bed and then gathered her to me. She nestled easily into the nook of my shoulder as she had a thousand times before. I sighed deeply and rubbed her back, trying to calm my emotions and longing to take away her pain.

"I'm sorry I got so mad, baby." I placed a soft kiss on her open mouth as she sniffed back the tears. "I'm not happy about this, Julia, so I can't promise I won't piss and moan at the unfairness of it."

I felt her nod against me. It was a few minutes before she was calm enough to speak, though her voice still shook and I felt her hot tears continue to seep through my shirt and soak my skin.

"I don't want to be away from you either, Ryan. It's killing me, but I have to do this. I told them that I'd only do it if they flew me back to the States for a week every two or three months. I know it isn't much, but at least we'll see each other some. And, I made Meredith promise to let me come back for your graduation. I promise not to miss it."

My arms tightened around her and I closed my eyes. She was always thinking of me, even when I was being a selfish prick. I loved this woman so much, my heart swelled at the same time it was breaking. I sucked in a deep breath and pressed my lips to her forehead again. "I'll try to get over there too, if there is any way at all, Julia."

She moved so she could look into my eyes. "Ryan...would you still consider doing your residency in New York? You can have my apartment. I know I'm asking a lot because you'd be alone here for several months, but would you? When I come back to the States we can be together right away. Please?" she begged softly, her hand moving up to brush against my jaw. "Please?"

I nodded. It was the only choice. The quickest way we'd be together. "Of course, baby. I can't bear any more time apart than is absolutely necessary. Here we go again."

The ring in my pocket was burning a hole through the fabric of my pants and into my skin like acid. Eating away at me like the agony was eating away at my insides.

Tonight should have turned out differently. *So* differently, but it wasn't going to end without that ring on her finger where it belonged.

I rolled to my side and Julia moved with me, facing me, we stared into each other's eyes and I brushed her hair back off of her face. Tearstained and all, she was still the most stunning thing I'd ever seen. I was captivated...overwhelmed at how beautiful she was inside and out.

This had been killing her. The desperation I'd felt all week-end was the result of her pain at the prospect of leaving me for months. I sighed as realization washed over me; this was even more painful for her because she knew how much this would hurt me.

"Okay. I'll *let you* go to Paris," I tried to tease, despite the tremendous aching in every fiber of my being. She raised her eyebrow at me as I tried to smile. Her chin began to tremble, still so fragile. I dug in the pocket of my dress pants for the ring and pulled it out, trying to distract her from what I was doing by kissing her.

"Shh...don't cry my love." My lips gently pulled on hers and I flicked her top one with the tip of my tongue. She moaned and lifted her mouth, silently asking for more. My mouth hovered above hers, dying in the choice of whether to kiss her until we were both gasping or to put the ring on her finger.

The two carat oval solitaire was set in a delicate prong-set band, holding twenty more perfectly matched stones. The metal setting wasn't even visible with the way the stones were set. I'd spent the last four years saving up the money to pay for it. I wanted the ring to be a reflection of the woman wearing it; flawless, perfect, brilliantly beautiful and completely unique.

I whispered against her mouth, "This isn't how I wanted to do this, Julia...but yes, I'll let you go to Paris, but only with this on your finger." I held up the ring and her tear-filled eyes widened and she gasped. Her arms tightened around me as she cried even harder.

"Julia, will you marry me?" The metal and diamonds burned through my palm as I brushed the knuckles of my closed hand across her cheek. "I love you; I only want you...forever. Will you marry me, sweet?"

Julia pulled back to look into my face, her beautiful eyes liquid and she laughed through her tears. "Yes. Of course, yes, Ryan! Oh my God, yes!"

I slipped it on her hand and then kissed her mouth gently. Desperation, overwhelming love and sadness...all of it flooded around us as we clung to each other, ripping at each other's clothing in our frantic attempts to get closer together.

I understood her demeanor over the past few days, but I didn't want tonight to feel rushed or desperate. I wanted to show her with my mouth, hands and body, that I was still hers and we'd be okay. No matter what, we'd be together. I pulled my mouth from hers, needing to ease the ache in her heart and reached for her hand and pulled it to my mouth. I brushed my mouth back and forth across her knuckles slowly.

"Julia," I breathed, "I want to make love slowly tonight, baby. I love you and nothing will change that. Not even Paris. You could be going to the moon and I'd still love you. I want to remember every moment of tonight; to savor every touch."

"Ryan..." she whispered achingly.

"Shh...It's okay. It will work out, baby. I told Aaron the night I came back from that first Thanksgiving weekend that I could feel the love you have for me, how I feel it seep right into my skin. That's what I want you to feel, too. Nothing will ever come between us. I won't let it."

"I do feel it, Ryan. I know how much you love me. I don't deserve you," she whispered brokenly.

I smiled softly and nuzzled gently against her face, my hands ghosting over her breasts as she arched into me and I rolled over on top of her. I was thinking of the words we'd said to each other in the past, so I said them again.

"You deserve whatever I decide to give you and I want to give you everything. Just *don't forget to remember me*, and we'll be okay. Don't forget how much I love you..."

~12~

Julia ~

"Ellie!" I called as I folded the last load of laundry. "What are you doing in there?" She came to spend a long weekend before I headed to Paris. I sighed, full of melancholy. This was a fantastic opportunity and I kept telling myself that I'd be too busy to miss New York, to miss my friends. To miss...*Ryan.*

I glanced up as she walked down the hall holding a suit that she'd given me three years ago, clicking her tongue and shaking her head in disapproval.

"Please tell me you aren't taking this old thing to Paris, Julia."

My mouth quirked at the corners and I stood to take it from her. "I like this suit."

"You can't go to the fashion capital of the world and wear out-of-date rags," she admonished with a roll of her eyes.

"Yeah," I said quietly, preoccupied with my impending departure.

Ellie sat on the couch, watching me resume folding clothes. Her eyes followed my movements and then flashed to my face. She leaned forward and halted my movements with her hand. "Julia, it's only a few months."

I shrugged. "I keep telling myself that, but it doesn't make me feel any better. And, Ryan..." I threw the clothes back on the couch and leaned back, crossing my arms.

"He isn't taking it so well?" Ellie asked cautiously, picking up the shirt I'd tossed and finished folding it.

"Every time we talk, I can hear it in his voice. He tries to hide it, but he's miserable. I want to run to him and tell him nothing is more important to me than he is. He's my whole world."

"I know, babes, but this is an amazing opportunity. Telling Meredith no would be like a slap in her face. You'd be without him for a few more months anyway, right?"

"About three, yeah, but now it'll be at least twice that." I felt my throat tighten. "It's killing us both."

Ellie smiled weakly. "You go out there and have fun. Time will fly by."

I scowled at her. How the hell did she know what it was like?

"Imagine what it would be like if you had to be away from Harris for four years, Ellie. Then; he came to you and told you that it would be longer," I said, rising and rushing into the kitchen. "Would you feel like crap?" I suddenly felt dizzy and placed a hand out to brace myself. "Uhhh…"

Ellie followed me into the kitchen, coming up beside me as I placed a hand to my head. "Are you okay, Julia? Are you sick?"

"No. I mean, I feel fine. I just had a head rush. I got up too fast." I turned back to her. "Do you want a drink?"

"What ya got?" She plopped on one of the stools by the bar. She looked gorgeous. Her hair was longer, almost past her shoulders.

"Um…I have red wine, beer, Coke and bottled water. Which?"

"Wine, duh," she laughed.

Her easy camaraderie made me smile. "You should move here. Get Harris to move his band to New York."

"Eh…" she began, but I interrupted her.

"I mean, now that they have a contract, can't they live anywhere?" Harris's band had been struggling on the West Coast until, finally, a major record producer happened into the club they were playing, offered to help them cut a demo and then like magic, they were signed within two months.

"I don't know. My business is really out there. Why don't you move back after Ryan is finished with his residency?"

I groaned. "That will be at least four or five more years. You guys can move *now*. Aaron and Jen will still be in Boston and that's closer than we've all been in years. I miss you." I opened a bottle of water and took a big swig.

"I miss you, too."

Suddenly, I felt nauseous and my head began to swim again. I set my water down with a bang, some of the contents sloshing out. "Whoa."

Ellie was there instantly and pulling out a stool for me, her brow knit with concern. "Are you sure you're not sick?"

I sat down and put my head in my hands. "I'm fine. I mean, I was sick a few weeks ago, but I've just been tired. I've been working hard and Ryan and I have been on the phone late most nights. I think I just need sleep."

"Are you sure?"

"Yeah." I nodded.

She looked at me skeptically and then her eyes widened. "Julia, in all the years I've known you, you've only been sick that one time you had food poisoning and one little cold."

"I know. This must be my year. I think the stress is wearing me down."

She continued to eye me skeptically as she took a sip of her wine. "When was Ryan here last?"

"Um, the weekend of Valentine's Day. We tried to make time to see each other two weekends ago, but he got called into the ER, so, that pretty much scrapped it."

"Are you pregnant, Julia?"

Okay, what? My mouth gaped open for a second as I considered her question.

"*What?* No! I'm on the pill for God's sake, Ellie." I said adamantly but my mind was racing, putting two and two together. "We're getting married in a year; there is no way we'd be that careless!" My breath left my body in a rush as I looked up at Ellie in shock. It could be possible. "Oh, my God. It couldn't be." My hand went to my stomach below my navel. "Could it?"

"Well, are you guys *fucking*, Julia?" she asked innocently and scrunched her nose with a grin. "When did you last have your period?"

"I don't know, I guess…it's been…" I stopped as reality stared me squarely in the face. "Oh, God. Ellie!" She rushed to me and took me in her arms. We cried and laughed as we hugged each other. I pulled back and wiped at the sudden tears. This wasn't planned, but it would be a miracle.

Ellie smiled brightly as she held my shoulders. "Will you tell Ryan?"

"Of course, if it's true!" I was overwhelmed with joy at the prospect.

"Before or after you leave for Paris?" Ellie asked. "Ryan will freak if you're pregnant and that far away."

I tried to wrap my head around it, knowing what had to happen. "If I'm pregnant…I can't go. It's as simple as that. I'd never do that to him." I stared at her and then burst out laughing.

THE FUTURE OF OUR PAST

"Imagine how he'll be!" I said happily. "He will be so protective and want to experience every little thing." My heart swelled with love for the possibility of my unborn child and the man who was responsible for it, imagining him pressing his ear to my swollen belly.

"So...what are we gonna do?" Ellie set her glass down and shoved her feet into her boots. "You're lightheaded, so I'll run out and get a test. Stop packing those bags, Julia! Auntie Ellie will be back in a flash."

I giggled happily and grabbed both of her hands. "Oh, Ellie. I hope it's true. I *want* it to be true! I can't wait to see the look on Ryan's face when I tell him. He'll be so beautiful...I know he'll be...just speechless!"

She grabbed her coat and purse on her way to the door. "He'll spoil you rotten! I'll be back."

I walked back to the living room, still in shock, but I needed to hear Ryan's voice. I leaned over to the edge of the table, grabbed my purse, pulled out my phone and was thrilled when he answered on the first ring.

"Hey, beautiful girl! Isn't Ellie keeping you busy enough?" His perfect voice melted around me and once again my hand settled protectively over my stomach. I couldn't keep the silly grin off my face.

"Yes, she is. She went to the store, and I wanted to hear your voice," I said softly. "I love you. Can you talk for a minute?"

"For a minute, it's pretty slow right now." He sighed. "My shift ends in a couple of hours. Did you change your mind about Paris? Please say yes. Save my life."

I smiled and bit my lip. I couldn't tell him on the phone, and besides, I wasn't sure yet.

"Let's not talk about leaving now."

"Yeah, I've been trying to forget about it. I'll be a mess this weekend, just so you know. I'm such a pussy when it comes to you."

I laughed because I couldn't help myself. "Never. I think you're pretty perfect," I whispered, once again feeling the tears prick my eyes and my throat tighten.

"I already miss you," he groaned. "I'm dying to see you, but I'm not looking forward to saying goodbye."

"Then let's not say goodbye." It was out before I could stop myself.

His voice lifted a little in hope. "Julia, what are you saying?"

"Just that it isn't goodbye. I'm still yours."

"I know. That's the only thing that keeps me from going insane, but I keep hoping you'll change your mind at the last minute." I could picture the hurt look on his face…his beautiful mouth pouty and the sadness behind his eyes. My heart squeezed inside my chest as I hoped the baby would have his features.

"It isn't easy for me either. You know that," I murmured softly, forcing the words out. It was so hard not telling him in order to ease his pain. "I miss you every second we're apart. It doesn't matter where I am."

"Babe…" the longing in his voice made my throat hurt even more and I knew that if I stayed on the phone, he'd have me giving in.

"Ryan…" My heart screamed to tell him but I needed to see his face when he heard the words. "We'll talk when I get there. I have to go. Ellie will be back soon, but I love you."

"Okay, honey. I love you, too. More than anything. I can't wait to get my arms around you."

He was too wonderful for words. "Me, too. Call me tomorrow?"

"Always. Bye, my love."

"Bye."

The decision was made. I couldn't wait until the weekend to share this news. I was already in my room shoving clothes in an overnight bag when Ellie got back.

"I thought you were going to scrub Paris. I mean, if this thing is positive?" she said as she held out the paper bag to me. I just looked at it and smiled breathlessly.

"I'm going to Ryan tonight. I'm sorry, Ellie. I know you came all this way, but I have to see him. Do you want to come with me?"

"Hell, no. Don't worry about me. I'm not going to interrupt this. I'll see you in a few months." She watched as I rushed around the apartment, her eyebrow went up and her head cocked to one side. "Hey! Aren't you even gonna pee on this damn thing?"

"Oh…yeah. But I already know. I'm so happy, Ellie! Ryan is going to be the most amazing father. Just like everything else he does. I can see it all now. He'll be fucking perfect."

She raised her eyebrows at me. "You plan on kissing your baby with that mouth, mommy?"

I stopped and burst out laughing as she tossed the brown paper bag toward me.

Ryan ~

Damn, I couldn't get a break. The first time in a month I'd been able to meet the guys for three on three basketball and my pager goes off. Fourth year rotations had no hours. They called when-ever they needed a warm body, especially in ER, but I'd just finished an hour and a half ago. Plus, Julia was leaving for Paris in a week, so, I wasn't sleeping much and I hoped the exercise would help with that.

"Hey, guys, time out!" I ran to the side of the court, grabbing my towel and wiping the sweat off my face. I pulled my pager off the waistband of my shorts and threw the towel aside. It was Aaron; his number followed by 911.

Something was wrong.

"Hey Ryan, let's go man. We're winning!" Tanner called.

I put a hand up to cut him off and was already dialing Aaron's number. "There's some sort of emergency. I may need to bail."

It pissed me off that my game was interrupted. Aaron probably just wanted me to come take the end of his shift, but he answered on the first ring and his voice was frantic. "Ryan, you gotta get to the hospital."

"What? I just got off of rotation. I'm playing basketball, man. My shift is over," I said in agitation. "Work your own damn hours, Aaron."

"Ryan. Listen, to me. Were you expecting Jules in Boston tonight?"

"No." I didn't want to think about it. I was trying to push away any and all thoughts pertaining to her leaving. "Not until next weekend, before she leaves for Paris. She's flying out of Logan. Why?"

"Get to the hospital, Ryan. I think Julia is in the ER."

"What? Stop kidding around, Aaron. This isn't funny. I told you, she's not in town. Don't you think I'd know if she were?" I asked impatiently, upset that he would tease me about something so serious. I was looking forward to next weekend and dreading it at the same time. My heart felt like lead in my chest. I sat down on the bench and rubbed a towel across the back of my neck.

"I *said*; get your *ass* to the ER, *now*!! She was in an accident and it looks bad. I couldn't see her face, there was so much blood, but I know it's her." There was no mistaking the seriousness of his tone.

"What are you talking about?" I asked in disbelief but I was already running toward the parking lot, my heart pumping so fast I thought it would literally fly from my body. I dug my keys out of my pocket as my mind raced, trying to find reasons to argue with Aaron. Tanner was yelling behind me, but I ignored him.

It couldn't be Julia. She'd never travel without telling me.

"Aaron, are you sure? How do you know?" I asked, not wanting to hear the answer. "If you can't see her face then it could be anyone."

"No. It's Julia. I recognized her jewelry, Ryan. The bracelet...you know?"

Oh my God. Jesus, please. NO! My heart and my mind were screaming. I felt like I'd just been hit in the stomach with a baseball bat.

"Oh, my God! How bad is it?" I choked out. If felt as if metal bands around my chest were preventing me from breathing and my eyes were starting to blur.

"I don't know. Jen's working on her with about half a dozen others. It doesn't look good, Ryan. Just get here as fast as you can."

My car was flying down the street at breakneck speed. It would be a miracle if I didn't get pulled over, but I didn't care. The fires of hell were after me. I was frantic, but somehow the adrenaline that flowed in my veins allowed me to keep control.

"Yeah, okay. Can you call Ellie and her parents? I'll be there in three minutes. If you don't have Paul's number, call Ellie first. She'll know how to reach him."

The next thing I knew, I was bursting through the doors of the ER. I recognized several of the doctors and nurses that had relieved me only an hour earlier. The commotion, when I entered, had them all staring at me with their mouths agape.

I put both of my hands in my hair as I said loudly. "Julia Abbott. *Where is she?*"

Min Sing, another of the students, put her hands on my chest to stop me. "Ryan, they're working on her. You cannot go in there. Calm down."

I pushed her hands away impatiently and walked around her. "What are you talking about? I work here, for God's sake, so somebody please tell me which room she's in." They all stared at me like I was crazy and I wanted to fucking kill something. *"Now!" I yelled.*

Aaron came quickly out of the waiting area. "Ryan, calm down. Ellie and Julia's dad are on their way. They asked if you'd call when we knew more, but, they're both getting on planes. I couldn't reach her mother. I didn't want to leave a message, considering."

I turned toward Aaron. "Where is she? Goddamn it!" Was that strangled voice mine? I didn't recognize it. "Oh, God, Aaron! It's Julia? You're *sure*?"

Aaron's face dropped and he grabbed my wrist, pulling my hand up to place something inside it. "Yeah," he said as his eyes met mine. Sadness and resignation flooded his features.

I looked down at what he'd given me. It was the RJ bracelet she'd worn for the past three years and her engagement ring. As I stared at them in anguish, my body started to shake violently and the tears began in my eyes. "Do you know anything yet?" I asked in disbelief as I tried to blink them back. I felt like my skin was on fire as an incredible burn spread through my body. I couldn't breathe.

"They haven't been out yet. Jen is still with her and she'll keep us informed. The others wouldn't tell me anything since I wasn't related and you know the fucking HIPPA laws. Jenna brought me Julia's jewelry on the sly."

I placed the ring on my little finger, which barely went past my first knuckle and rubbed my thumb across the combined letters on the bracelet. This was the first time she'd had it off since I placed it on her wrist in the cabin in Estes Park.

"You aren't technically related either, Ryan. They probably won't let you in until Paul gets here."

"The hell I'm not related!" I ran a hand over my face and whirled around to the counter and addressed the four people standing there. "Look, all of you. We're talking about my fiancée. Somebody tell me something, or let me the hell in there!" I looked around and they all looked back with sympathy on their faces but they didn't move. "I'm *begging* you." The desperation was dripping from my voice as I dropped my head and put my hand wearily over my eyes. "*Please!*"

"Ryan, you know as well as I do that if it's bad, they need to stabilize her before you can see her. We can't distract them," Min said. The concern on her face was clear as she laid a comforting hand on my arm.

"I can help. This is what I'm trained for," I replied urgently. I couldn't stand there helpless when I was as equipped to work on Julia as any of the med students here, probably more, since trauma medicine was my focus. "Someone let me the hell in there!"

I couldn't breathe and it felt as if my heart was going to break free of my chest. My whole life was crumbling in front of me and I couldn't stop it. If Julia was dying, then I was, too.

An irresistible sneak peek into Book II of The Remembrance Trilogy as Ryan and Julia's story continues in

Don't Forget to Remember Me...

~1~

Ryan ~

I was sitting in my own personal hell. I was weeks from becoming a doctor and yet my hands were tied as Julia lay on a gurney in the next room. She was my whole world and she could be dying while I was helpless of the outcome; unable to do a Goddamn thing.

My mind raced with questions. Were they ordering blood gases? Was she in shock? How much blood had she lost and did she need a transfusion? Could she breathe on her own? When the hell were they going to do the scans that would determine the extent of her internal and head injuries? I thought my head would explode along with my lungs.

"What was she even doing in Boston?" I didn't realize I'd said the words aloud.

"What *the fuck* is happening in there?!" I yelled as panic seized my chest and made my voice unrecognizable.

Min shook her head sadly. "We don't know yet. Dr. Brighton is heading up the team. I know how much you respect him, so just let him do his job. You can't work on her, Ryan. You can't be impartial about someone you love this much. This is what's best for Julia."

Aaron put his arm around me to urge me toward the waiting room, but I shrugged him off impatiently. I felt claustrophobic; beginning to hyperventilate.

"Can you just tell me *something*? Go find out? They need to get her to radiology. When the hell are they going to order those tests?" I asked, turning back to Min. I was still trying to figure out how I was going to get in there. If I were a resident, I'd have just walked in, but not as a student. Even one who was graduating with Cum Laude honors soon.

My friend nodded and placed her hand on my shoulder before disappearing through the doors of one of the trauma rooms.

I tried to look in, but all I could see were a bunch of doctors and nurses scrambling around the room at a frantic pace. My heart stopped when I saw Julia's arm hanging off the edge of the table, still as stone. Someone was intubating her and someone else was cutting off her clothes. Jenna was hanging up an IV bag near one end of the table and then inserting some medication into a port with a syringe, while Dr. Brighton conducted an examination. My whole body felt like it would explode into a million pieces, my skin crawling so much I wanted to rip it off.

"Let's go to the waiting room," my brother said softly. "You know they can't take her anywhere until she's stabilized. Can I get you some coffee?"

I shook my head and went to gaze out the window, out at the night and the lights of downtown. "I can't, Aaron. I can't sit around in there and do nothing! My God, what am I going to do?" My voice cracked and I cleared my throat. "I have to *do* something! Tell me what you know about the accident, and don't bullshit me."

"Uh, the cops who came in with the paramedics said that the cab driver was trying to get on Starrow Drive from Leverett Circle and it was plowed broadside on the rear passenger's side. The driver is here too, but his injuries are minor. The guy driving the other car was killed; dead at the scene. The police said they found empty booze containers in his car and he was traveling at least 50 miles per hour. We're lucky Julia wasn't thrown from the car at that rate."

I closed my eyes and put my hand up to rub the back of my neck. I didn't know what I was feeling. I wanted to scream and cry at the unfairness of it all, yet I was numb, frozen. My knees were weak and I fell into a chair in the small waiting room. I dealt with this shit on a daily basis and it didn't faze me in the slightest. But this was my baby and I couldn't handle it.

There was a woman playing in the corner with a small child and I watched them build something with Legos. I stared at them, wanting something, anything, to focus on. My vision blurred and I felt a sob rise up in my chest but I struggled to keep it from bursting forth. I clasped my hands in front of me and hung my head in defeat. Aaron was sitting next to me and placed a hand on my back.

What was she doing here? I pulled her engagement ring off of my finger and rolled it around in my hand with the bracelet. *Please, God. I'll do anything. Anything!*

I drew in a shaky breath and leaned back in the chair. "Aaron, I can't just sit here."

There was a commotion and the doors opened. I jumped up and rushed toward them. Several doctors and nurses were pushing the gurney out of the room along with an IV stand, a ventilator, oxygen and EKG. I saw Dr. Brighton and Jenna with them as I strained to get a look at Julia.

"Uhhh..." A groan ripped from my chest at the site. "Dr. Brighton...please. Can I see her? Is she conscious?"

He turned sad brown eyes on me and shook his head. "I don't have time to talk right now Ryan. We need to do a chest X-ray, probably a CT scan of her head and torso. I'm fairly sure she has a pretty bad fracture on the left side of her skull. The blood is from a superficial laceration on her hairline which we've got under control, but we don't know if there is internal bleeding yet. I can't waste time talking now, son. I'm doing my best for her, I promise, but she is critical."

I started shaking again as I looked on and they wheeled her away from me. Her clothes had been cut off of her and a white blanket placed over her, leaving bare skin visible below its edge. Her hair was matted with blood and she had so many machines connected to her and over her face I couldn't recognize her. "I want to see her." I knew it would be impossible. To save her life, time was imperative.

"As soon as we get these tests and know more, Ryan. There is no time to waste." Jenna came forward and put her arms around my waist to in a quick hug.

"Here is what I know," she said as she stepped back and looked up into my face. "We intubated her, but she is still struggling to breathe. We think she has a pneumothorax on the left side, maybe some fractured ribs. Her left shoulder is dislocated; she has lacerations and contusions to her face and scalp and the left side of her body. She probably has a head injury and some internal bleeding and, as you know, that is what the scans should tell us. I have to go with her, but, I'll let you know when I know more details. I'm...so sorry, Ryan," she said before she turned and hurried down the hall after Julia and the rest of the team, disappearing behind the double doors leading to radiology.

Aaron's arms came around me, under my arms to catch me as my knees started to buckle. *This couldn't be happening.* The dislocated shoulder and broken ribs weren't life threatening, but if she had a head injury or internal bleeding, time was of the essence. Even the collapsed lung could be dealt with, but all of it together...I could lose her. I fell into Aaron's arms and began gasping for breath and clutching at his shoulders.

"Aaron," I cried brokenly. "This isn't happening. Tell me this isn't happening. Jesus...I love her so much. I can't lose her."

"We have some of the best doctors in the world here. We have to have faith, Ryan. We have to believe she'll be okay." His arms tightened around me and lifted me enough to get my feet under me. "She'll be okay. We all love Julia. We *all* love her, man." His voice broke on the last sentence as he hugged me. If Aaron was crying, then he didn't believe she'd be okay. He never fucking cried. In all the years I'd known him, I'd never seen him shed a single tear.

I pushed away from him and pulled out my phone. I dialed the familiar number, pacing back and forth in the room that Julia and the medical staff had just vacated.

"Hello?" my father answered and I felt a new wave of emotion overcome me.

"Dad..."

"Ryan? Is that you? Did something happen?" His voice was anxious and I could hear my mother's distressed voice in the background as well.

"I need you to get to Boston right away. Julia's been in a car accident. Her cab was broadsided and it looks like she has a serious head injury. Please. If she needs neurosurgery, I don't want anyone else touching her. I'm going out of my fucking mind. Just...*please come.*"

"Oh my God! Yes, we'll come, but if she does have a head injury, you have to let them treat her. Don't wait for me, do you understand? You know as well as I do that treatment must be immediate. Waiting could kill her or leave her with serious brain damage. The first hour or two are critical! Ryan!" Dad yelled when I didn't respond.

Fresh tears were forming and I couldn't get the words out so I just nodded. Aaron ripped the phone from my shaking hand.

"Hey, Dad. Yes, okay. Call me with your flight details and I'll pick you up at the airport." Aaron turned his back to me and kept talking into the phone. "No, he's not handling it well. Not at all. He's really losing it. Are you sure? Okay. Yes, I called, but her mother didn't answer. Yes, I'll call again. Love you guys. Bye."

I slid down the wall until I was sitting on the floor and rested my arms on my bent knees. Aaron closed the door and sat down on the one chair in the now empty room. The symbolism of it shook me to the core. Stark, empty space, where Julia used to be...cold and sterile.

I put my head in my arms and let the emotions I couldn't contain wash over me. My shoulders shook in silent sobs until I finally had to gasp for breath and Aaron touched my shoulder.

"Mom and Dad are on their way. Ryan, I'm so sorry. She's going to be okay."

"She has to be, Aaron. She has to, or I won't survive," I whispered brokenly. "I won't survive without her."

"You need to try to pull it together, Ryan. You have to be strong for Julia. She wouldn't want to see you like this."

"Hmmph," I let out my breath heavily. "*Julia* would want me to be honest about my feelings, and I feel like I'm falling apart...helpless; like I'm dying myself. I want to be in there and take this all away for her. I'd take her place if I could," I choked out and I fisted my hands over both eyes.

Aaron was right. Unless I wanted her parents and Ellie to freak out, I needed to get control of my emotions. Even more importantly, when they let me see Julia, I had to be calm and reassuring. *If she was conscious.*

We sat there for what seemed like an eternity. Aaron left a couple of times to get coffee, but I didn't move, praying that she would be okay and reliving so many of the wonderful times we'd shared. The day we met, the first time I kissed her or when we made love, when I put the engagement ring on her finger, the many Sunday coffee dates we were forced to spend apart, the move to New York. In all of my memories she was beautiful and smiling...whole. Not broken and bleeding. "Oh, my God," I ground out brokenly. "No, *please.*"

I ran my hand through my hair and stood up to answer my phone. It was Julia's dad.

"Hello, Paul."

"Oh, thank God. Ryan, what do you know?" His voice was panicked, the catch in his voice giving away the level of his emotion.

"Not a lot right now. They took her to radiology for some scans. She probably has a skull fracture, but we won't know the extent until after these films. She has a pneumothorax and a dislocated shoulder, contusions on her head, face and torso and probably some broken ribs." My voice had taken on a clinical tone, on autopilot, as I rattled off the list.

"You sound like a doctor, Ryan. What is a pmeumothorax?"

"Oh, sorry. Um, a collapsed lung." He gasped on the other end of the phone and my strong facade fell by the wayside when my voice thickened. I put my hand over my eyes and took a deep breath. "Paul, I'm really scared. All I want to do is get in there and help take care of her, but they won't let me. They…won't let me. I feel…so incredibly helpless."

"Jesus." Paul sighed. "Ryan, I'm sure you're doing all you can. I'm glad you're with her. I'll get there as soon as I can. I've changed planes in Chicago and I'm already onboard. Ellie called and said she was going to meet me at the hospital and Marin is on her way, too."

He was trying to comfort me when his baby girl was fighting for her life. I wished I could be that strong, but then, I'd seen her. I'd seen the blood and the machines and despite the fact I was around it all the time; but because it was Julia, it wrecked me.

"Yeah. My parents are on their way as well. If her head injury is serious, I want my father here to consult or…God forbid, operate, if it's necessary."

"I hope it's not that serious, but I'm thankful that Gabriel is coming. I've made my bargains with God already. I'll see you in a couple of hours. My little girl is lucky to have you, Ryan."

It's that serious. I closed my eyes in silent prayer.

"I'm the lucky one. She means everything to me, Paul." I could feel my chest constrict again as I hung up the phone.

"Ryan?"

I turned to a shaken Jenna re-entering the room. "They've taken her to ICU. She has a fracture to the left side of her skull. We were able to re-inflate the lung, tape up her ribs and pop her shoulder back in. There is some slight swelling to her brain but radiology didn't see any bleeding on the CT scan."

"Is she breathing on her own?" I asked, fearing the answer with everything I had. "Did you need a chest tube or did the lung re-inflate on its own?"

Jen came forward and hugged me. "We were able to suck the air out with a big syringe so we didn't need to tube her. She's on a vent and hasn't regained consciousness," she said quietly.

I hugged her back. "No doubt due to the edema. All we can do is watch her now and make sure we catch any bleeds or fluids. We're not out of the woods until she wakes up. Have they got her on blood thinners? Is the coma induced or not?" I asked wearily. I was exhausted and started rubbing the back of my neck. The next three or four days would tell the story. If she didn't wake up before that, then chances were she never would.

"Ryan, stop trying to be a doctor. You've got enough to deal with," Aaron began, but his words upset me. My jaw tightened and I bit back the words I wanted to retort.

"I want to know what is happening," I said instead.

"She's on several meds. She didn't wake up on her own, but Dr. Brighton did order barbiturates to keep her asleep so her brain can heal and to help reduce the swelling. I don't need to tell you the particulars," Jenna said. She looked as exhausted as I felt and her eyes were red and swollen.

She moved back from the embrace and took my hands. "Thank you, Jen. I appreciate all you've done. Can I see her now? Is Dr. Brighton still with her?" The array of questions fell from my lips like rain.

"I'm sure they're watching for hemorrhage. It's common with traumatic brain injury," Aaron interjected quietly and more contrite than before.

"I know that!" I shook my head and started walking out of the room, my intention to go straight up to ICU, but Jenna put a hand on my arm to stop me.

Her voice shook and she cupped my face with her palm. "Ryan," she said hesitantly, her blue eyes full of sadness. "Julia had some vaginal bleeding and it was quite excessive."

"She had internal bleeding?" I asked in panic. My heart started racing again but Jenna shook her head.

"Ryan, um..." She raised her tear-filled eyes to mine and brushed my hair back from my face.

"Jen, what is it?" I asked shortly. "What is it that you're not saying?" Fear, even more prevalent than before, engulfed me.

"Did you know that Julia was pregnant?"

Until that very moment, I thought it couldn't get any worse. I was wrong.